D.L. Law a ♻
P9-BZV-439

Cole shook his head. "And to think I actually thought I missed you."

"Yeah," she retorted, "I was just thinking the same thing."

He blew out a breath, telling himself it wouldn't do either one of them—or more importantly, the twins— any good to blow up like this right here in front of the sheriff's office. It was just that he had forgotten how easily Stacy could set him off. And half the time—like now—she did it without warning. It was like being caught in a blitzkrieg.

"Stacy," he said, growing stern, "let me take the basket in. It's heavy."

"It's not," she argued. Except that it really was. And the babies were moving. With a sigh, she relented. "It's awkward."

"All the more reason for me to take it," Cole told her.

For a few brief seconds, she debated continuing to argue the point with him.

But her arms were beginning to really ache. So, in the end, she said, "Fine, you can carry them in—but only because I'm thinking of the babies."

The Rancher's Baby Adventure

USA TODAY BESTSELLING AUTHOR

MARIE FERRARELLA
&
BRENDA HARLEN

Previously published as *Twins on the Doorstep*
and *Claiming the Cowboy's Heart*

 **HARLEQUIN**

If you purchased this book without a cover you should be aware that this book is stolen property. It was reported as "unsold and destroyed" to the publisher, and neither the author nor the publisher has received any payment for this "stripped book."

 HARLEQUIN®

PLEASE RECYCLE
THIS PRODUCT IS RECYCLABLE

Recycling programs
for this product may
not exist in your area.

ISBN-13: 978-1-335-47484-1

The Rancher's Baby Adventure
Copyright © 2020 by Harlequin Books S.A.

Twins on the Doorstep
First published in 2017. This edition published in 2020.
Copyright © 2017 by Marie Rydzynski-Ferrarella

Claiming the Cowboy's Heart
First published in 2019. This edition published in 2020.
Copyright © 2019 by Brenda Harlen

All rights reserved. No part of this book may be used or reproduced in any manner whatsoever without written permission except in the case of brief quotations embodied in critical articles and reviews.

This is a work of fiction. Names, characters, places and incidents are either the product of the author's imagination or are used fictitiously. Any resemblance to actual persons, living or dead, businesses, companies, events or locales is entirely coincidental.

This edition published by arrangement with Harlequin Books S.A.

For questions and comments about the quality of this book, please contact us at CustomerService@Harlequin.com.

Harlequin Enterprises ULC
22 Adelaide St. West, 40th Floor
Toronto, Ontario M5H 4E3, Canada
www.Harlequin.com

Printed in U.S.A.

CONTENTS

USA TODAY bestselling and RITA® Award–winning author **Marie Ferrarella** has written more than two hundred and fifty books for Harlequin, some under the name Marie Nicole. Her romances are beloved by fans worldwide. Visit her website, marieferrarella.com.

Books by Marie Ferrarella

Harlequin Special Edition

Forever, Texas

The Cowboy's Lesson in Love
The Lawman's Romance Lesson
Her Right-Hand Cowboy

Matchmaking Mamas

Coming Home for Christmas
Dr. Forget-Me-Not
Twice a Hero, Always Her Man
Meant to Be Mine
A Second Chance for the Single Dad

The Fortunes of Texas: The Secret Fortunes

Fortune's Second-Chance Cowboy

The Fortunes of Texas: Rambling Rose

Fortune's Greatest Risk

The Montana Mavericks: The Great Family Roundup

The Maverick's Return

Visit the Author Profile page at Harlequin.com for more titles.

Twins on the Doorstep

MARIE FERRARELLA

To

Nik and Melany.

Remember never to let

A day go by without saying

"I love you."

Prologue

He was getting too old for this.

A hundred years ago, at twenty-six he would not just have been married but would have had at least three, maybe four, kids. He would have been settled into his life, doing what he could to provide for his wife and children.

Instead, here he was, twenty-six years old and still trying to figure out just what his life would eventually be.

Part of the reason for his surly mood, Cole McCullough thought as he sat up and dragged his hand through his unruly, shaggy, dark blond hair, was that he was spending two nights a week with his six-foot-two body crammed into a bunk bed. Sometimes three nights. And that was because two—sometimes three—days a week, he worked at the Healing Ranch. The

Healing Ranch was a horse ranch run by Jackson and Garrett White Eagle, two of his friends. Their sole focus was to take in and help troubled boys, building up their feelings of self-worth by having them take care of and work with horses.

All in all, it was a noble calling—for the White Eagle brothers. Not that he didn't believe in it. He did. But the Healing Ranch was their calling, their mark in the world.

Just like the family ranch was really Connor's.

Oh, they had all put in their time, he and Cody and Cassidy, but the ranch, left to all of them when their father died, was really Connor's baby. The rest of them had worked on it to show their gratitude to Connor. When their father had died so suddenly, Connor gave up his dream of going to college and became their guardian so that he, Cody and Cassidy wouldn't suddenly find themselves being swallowed up by the county's social services.

He knew that going to college had meant a lot to Connor, but his big brother never hesitated to give it up. For them.

After getting dressed, Cole paused to throw some water on his face in the tiny bathroom just off the equally tiny bedroom. The area had been added onto the main bunkhouse to give him some semblance of privacy. The main bunkhouse was where the boys stayed when their families—and in some cases, social services—sent them to the ranch. The Healing Ranch was a last-ditch effort to straighten them out. Without the ranch, the next stop would have been juvie—and most likely jail.

Initially, there had been only two boys on the ranch.

And then there were four. And, as word of the ranch's success spread, there were more. A lot more. Which was why he had wound up working here part-time.

The rest of the time, he was on the ranch, helping Connor.

Always helping.

And while there was nothing wrong with helping his older brother, Cole wasn't building something of his own. Cody and Cassidy had gone on to find their places in life—not to mention that each had someone to share that life with them. Cody was a deputy sheriff and Cassidy was working at the town's only law office and taking classes at night. And Connor was running the family ranch, just the way he wanted to.

Cole sighed. He was the only one of the family at loose ends, not yet sure what ultimate course he wanted his life to take.

Damn it, he was going to be late getting back to the ranch, he upbraided himself. He wasn't going to come to any lasting, earth-shattering decisions by brooding. Besides, this life he was living was a hell of a lot easier than what he and his siblings had been faced with after their father died.

With both parents gone, they'd found themselves close to destitute. Even when their father had been alive, there were times when they had barely gotten by. Mike McCullough would hire out to neighboring ranches on occasion to make sure there was always food on the table. When he was alive, they never went hungry.

Without their father, they found that they had to scramble, doing whatever they could to scrape by.

Miss Joan, the redheaded, tough-talking firecracker of a woman who ran the diner, saw to it that they always had enough to eat. Not one who believed in handouts, she'd made a point of having them work for their supper.

"Work's hard on your hands, but good for your soul," she'd maintained more than once.

So she gave them work. Cassidy had been her youngest waitress to date, Cody did cleanup at the diner, and as for Cole, Miss Joan had him running errands.

Looking back, he was convinced that she hadn't really needed them to do any of those things, but Miss Joan felt that just handing them the money outright wouldn't have done them nearly as much good as having them earn it.

She'd been right, Cole thought now with a smile. Miss Joan had instilled a work ethic in all of them, a desire to make something of themselves.

Maybe that was why he felt so restless. He was still looking for his own niche.

"Not gonna find it here, McCullough, rehashing the same old stuff and keeping Connor waiting. Move," he ordered himself.

There'd be time enough to think about the fact that his life was stalled at the starting gate after today's chores on the family ranch were done.

With that, Cole paused to grab his hat, turned off the light in his bedroom and opened the door. He had his own separate entrance so that he could come and go as he pleased without having to pass through the bunkhouse and all its residents. Two to three days a week he worked with the boys during regular hours and sat with them in the dining hall at mealtime. But Jackson and Garrett recognized the fact that there were times when a man just needed his privacy, even when there was nothing to be private about.

He opened the door and was ready to step out and greet whatever the day held for him.

Or so he thought.

Cole caught himself a second before his foot would have made contact with the wide wicker basket, kicking it and its contents to the side.

Stunned, Cole froze in place, realizing he had come perilously close to all but drop-kicking the two infants who were nestled in the basket, looking up at him with wide, wide blue eyes.

Chapter 1

"What the…?"

At the last moment, despite his shock, Cole swallowed the expletive that was about to burst out of his mouth. Given that he had almost stepped on not one but two infants lying in a basket on the doorstep, it would have been understandable, but inappropriate—at least, to his way of thinking.

It took him a moment to come to grips with the situation, not exactly a run-of-the-mill one by a long shot.

"Okay," Cole announced, looking around in the predawn light. "This isn't funny. You just can't leave babies in a basket like this." Getting no response, he raised his voice. "You're not being responsible."

Nobody answered.

Not one to lose his temper in general, he felt himself losing it now. These were babies, not toys or props to be used in a prank.

He tried again.

"Okay, you've had your fun, come out, come out, whoever you are. I've got to get going and babies shouldn't be left outside like this in September. Or any other month of the year, either, for that matter." Again, Cole had to bite back a few choice words meant for the knucklehead who was behind this practical joke.

Cole looked around.

Nobody came out of the shadows.

One of the babies made a sound, catching his attention.

Crouching down, Cole looked at the two infants wedged together in the basket. They appeared blissfully unaware that they were completely out of their element.

"Where's your mama, guys? Or girls," Cole amended. "Sorry, your blankets don't exactly give me a clue what gender you are."

He looked around again, but there was still no one coming out to claim the babies or own up to the rather poor joke.

This didn't make any sense.

With a sigh, Cole picked the basket up and rose to his feet with it.

"Well, you can't stay out here," he said to the infants. "No telling what might come by." Just then, he heard a coyote howling in the distance. "Like that fella. He's probably hungry. Whoever left you here deserves to be taken behind the barn and given a solid thrashing," he said fiercely.

He thought about just walking into the bunkhouse with the babies to demand whose idea of a joke this was, but leaving the infants outside like that was beyond some foolish joke. It was damn dangerous. This didn't really feel like something one of the boys would do.

What if he hadn't come out when he did? Or if he'd decided, just this once, to walk through the bunkhouse to go outside instead of using his own door? There was no telling how long the babies would have remained out here, unprotected.

"Who left you out here like this?" he asked the small faces looking up at him as he made his way to the main house.

"You know, you are awfully cute," he commented to the infants. "Too bad you can't talk and tell me who your mama is, because she needs a serious talking-to. No offense," he added.

One of the infants sounded as if he—or she—was mewling in response.

Reaching the ranch house, Cole realized that he couldn't safely balance the basket and knock on the door so he used his elbow instead. When he didn't get an immediate response, he did it again, harder this time. Because he was jostling the basket and therefore the infants inside of it, he stopped and waited for someone to come to the door.

He was just about to try again when he saw the door finally being opened.

Garrett White Eagle was not usually at a loss for words but this was one of those few times when his mind seemed to go blank.

Recovering, Garrett opened the door to the main house wider and asked Cole, "Have you taken up selling babies door-to-door? Because I'm pretty sure that your brother Cody will tell you that's illegal."

Perturbed, Cole didn't bother commenting on Garrett's assessment. Instead, he told the man, "I almost tripped over these two when I was leaving this morning. Some brainless jackass left them on my doorstep."

"Cute little things," Garrett observed. "Bring them into the living room."

He gestured into the house, then led the way to where he, his brother and their wives gathered in the evening, usually with at least a few of the boys who were making progress in the program.

Cole placed the basket on the wide, scarred coffee table just as Garrett called out toward the kitchen, "Hey, Jackson, could you come in here? You've just got to see this."

A minute and a half later Jackson White Eagle, taller and slightly more muscular than his younger brother, walked into the living room.

"What's all the commotion abou—" Jackson stopped dead in his tracks. His eyes went straight to the basket on the coffee table. "Garrett, what are two babies in a basket doing on our coffee table?"

"Don't look at me," Garrett protested. "They belong to Cole."

"Cole?" Jackson asked incredulously. His eyes shifted to the cowboy he'd hired to work part-time on their ranch.

"No, they don't," Cole denied with feeling. "I just stumbled over them on the doorstep as I was leaving this morning."

"*Your* doorstep," Garrett pointed out, obviously thinking that was the key word.

Cole shook his head, trying to distance himself from any responsibility. "I'm beginning to think that was just a mistake."

"*Your* mistake?" Garrett asked, eyeing his friend closely. "Did you get some ladylove in the family way, Cole?"

Garrett sat down on the old brown-leather sofa in front of the babies. He made a few cooing noises at the infants, which seemed to entertain them sufficiently to get them to stop whimpering.

"Forever is just a little larger than a postage stamp," Cole pointed out, referring to the nearby town. "I think if something like that had happened, *everyone* in Forever would have known—if not immediately, then soon enough."

"So, these little cuties aren't yours?" Garrett asked, just to make sure.

If they had been his, Cole would have owned up to it without any hesitation and done the right thing by the babies' mother. Cole felt that his friend knew him well enough to know that.

Cole frowned at Garrett. "No."

"You're sure about that?" Jackson asked, looking at Cole closely.

"Absolutely," Cole answered, but just the slightest note of hesitation had entered his voice.

What if…?

No, no way. It wasn't possible.

The only woman he'd been intimate with in the last year had been Stacy Rowe. But Stacy had suddenly taken off not too long after that, leaving without a single word to him. Leaving as if the evening they had spent together had filled her with regrets.

Or maybe, according to the rumor he'd heard later, her Aunt Kate had insisted Stacy come with her on "the vacation of a lifetime," then whisked her off on a prolonged tour of Europe.

Having her leave like that, without warning, had really hurt him, although he'd said nothing to anyone, not even his family. He'd thought that he and Stacy had something unique going, but obviously she hadn't shared his feelings.

In time, he got over it.

Or so he told himself.

"Well," Jackson was saying, turning to look at him. "What are you going to do with them?"

Cole looked at the other man, stunned. "Me?"

"Well, yes," Jackson replied. "They were left on your doorstep."

Cole still doubted that had been the person's actual intention. He didn't always stay over the same days. He could just as likely have *not* been here. "Undoubtedly by mistake."

"Maybe not," Jackson said thoughtfully.

"What are you talking about?" Cole asked.

"Your brother Cody came to his future wife's rescue and wound up delivering a baby," Jackson reminded him. "And didn't Cassidy rescue that baby from the river not too long after that?"

"Yes," Cole answered cautiously, not sure where Jackson was going with this.

"Can't be a coincidence," Jackson told him. "Somebody probably feels that your family's good with babies. Want my suggestion?" Before Cole could say anything in response, Jackson told him, "Take the babies home with you until you can sort this whole thing out."

"Wait," Cole said, feeling as if this whole thing was just spinning out of control. "You're forgetting one important thing. You've got a ranch full of teenage boys, all of them old enough to father a child—or two," he pointed out.

Jackson studied the infants for a moment. "My guess is that these babies are about three or four weeks old. Maybe less."

"Okay," Cole said, waiting for Jackson to make a point.

"That means that if they were fathered by one of the boys on the ranch, it would have had to have happened about ten months or so ago," Jackson told him.

"Right," Cole agreed, still waiting for Jackson's point.

"Well, we've only got three boys who have been here that long," Jackson concluded. "The rest have been here for less time than that." There were several who had graduated the program and returned home in that time frame, but for now, he decided not to mention that. He still felt that the infants might be Cole's.

"Okay!" Cole was on his feet. "Let's go talk to those three hands."

The babies were making more noise. Jackson's attention shifted to them. "Well, before we do that, I think these two little people need to be fed first."

Feeling suddenly, totally, out of his depth, Cole looked around.

"Is Debi here?" Jackson's wife, Debi, was a registered nurse who worked at the town's only medical clinic.

Jackson shook his head. "She went in early today. It's her turn to open the clinic."

"What about Kim?" Cole asked hopefully, looking at Garrett.

"Sorry, out of luck there," Garrett told him. "Kim's away on assignment. She left last week. She still keeps her hand in," he explained proudly, "doing occasional stories for the magazine that brought her out here in the first place."

Obviously taking pity on Cole, Jackson volunteered, "However, Rosa's here," referring to the Healing Ranch's resident housekeeper.

Cole was immediately hopeful. "Do you think that she could…?"

"She might, if we ask her nicely," Jackson speculated.

"She's probably in the kitchen. I'll go get her," Garrett volunteered, taking off.

The babies were beginning to fuss in earnest now. Cole looked at Jackson. "You don't think that these belong to one of those boys you mentioned, do you?"

"Highly doubtful," Jackson said. Moving toward the basket, he picked up the louder of the two infants and began rocking it in an attempt to quiet the baby. "You've seen the hands. By the end of the day, they're all too tired to chew, much less try to romance some little lady. Besides, so far this is still an all-male program we have going here. To find a girl his age, our Romeo would have to ride all the way out to town or the reservation. I'd probably know about it if that happened," Jackson assured him.

"Where did these babies come from?" Rosa Sanchez asked as she walked into the living room.

"That's what we're trying to find out," Jackson told the woman.

Maternal instincts rose to the surface. Rosa picked

up the other infant from the basket and held it against her ample bosom.

"Oh, the poor little thing," she cooed. "He is hungry."

Cole stared at her, surprised. "You can tell it's a he? How?" he asked, then pointed out, "The baby's all bundled up. They both are."

Rosa merely smiled. "He is noisier. Men usually are," Rosa told him knowingly. She looked at Jackson. "Bring the other one," she instructed the man who was technically her boss. And then she turned toward Cole. "You bring the basket. There is no place to lay them down while I take turns feeding them, so the basket will do."

"Rosa, how are you going to feed them? We don't have any baby bottles," Garrett asked.

"Boil a cloth," Rosa instructed Jackson.

He looked at her in confusion. "And just how is that going to…?"

"When it is clean, we will dip a corner of the cloth into a cup of warm milk and the baby will suck on that."

"Won't that take a long time, feeding him that way?" Cole asked.

Rosa gave him what passed for a patient smile. "Just until one of you comes back from the general store in town with two baby bottles," she replied. "Now go, go," she urged them. "These babies are getting hungrier by the minute."

"I'll go to the general store," Garrett volunteered, no doubt thinking that was the safest thing for him to do.

"I'll make breakfast for the boys," Jackson told his housekeeper, handing off the baby he'd been holding to Cole. "You stay here with Cole and the babies, and do what needs to be done."

Rosa smiled at him patiently. "Yes, Mr. Jackson."

* * *

The procedure was slow and tedious, but, to Cole's surprise, feeding the infants Rosa's way seemed to satisfy them, at least for the time being.

"I think this one's going to suck in the cloth," he marveled, watching the infant in his arms going at the milk-soaked cloth he was bringing to its lips.

"Don't forget to keep soaking the cloth," Rosa prompted. "You don't want it getting dry."

"Right," Cole murmured, taking the cloth he had wrapped around his index finger away from the infant's mouth and dipping it into the milk he had standing in one of the coffee mugs.

"Mr. McCullough?" Rosa said.

Cole raised his eyes away from the infant he was attempting to feed. It was touch and go at the moment. "Yes?"

"You are sure you are not the father of these babies?" she asked in a low voice. Before he could say anything, she assured him, "It is just the two of us here right now. You can tell me." She leaned her head in toward him and said in a low voice, "I will not tell anyone."

"I'm sure, Rosa," Cole said patiently.

And, for the most part, he was. There was just this tiny little inkling of doubt left, but he knew he was needlessly torturing himself. If there had been a baby—or babies—because of that one wondrous night, Stacy would have told him.

Wouldn't she?

"Then why would someone leave them on *your* doorstep?" Rosa asked, dipping the edge of her cloth in the warm milk. "Why not with the sheriff or on the clinic's doorstep?"

"I really don't know, Rosa." The next moment, he exclaimed, "Wow! I sure am glad this baby doesn't have teeth yet. He's got really strong lips for an infant."

He carefully maneuvered his finger out of what appeared to be a steely rosebud mouth.

"She," Rosa corrected.

He looked at the housekeeper, confused. "She?"

Rosa nodded her head.

He gazed at the infant. She was all bundled up in yellow. Both of the babies were. Yellow was neutral. It didn't indicate either male or female. "How would you know that?"

Rosa smiled. "I have a gift," she told him calmly.

His eyes narrowed just a little. "You unwrapped this one, didn't you?"

The corner of Rosa's eyes crinkled just a little more as she laughed. "Perhaps I did, a bit," she admitted.

Rosa's laugh was infectious and Cole caught himself laughing, as well. Doing so made him feel just a little better—at least, for now.

Chapter 2

Stacy Rowe was amazed.

She'd been born and raised in Forever, and a little more than eight months ago she would have said that it felt as if things never changed in this tiny town. And then Aunt Kate had whisked her away on that European vacation—insisted on it, really—saying that she wanted Stacy to open her eyes and see that there was a world beyond Forever.

And, more importantly, a world beyond Cole McCullough.

The second his name flashed across her mind, Stacy clenched her fists at her sides as if that would somehow chase away any and all thoughts of the tall Texan.

She wasn't ready to think about Cole yet.

Cole was the reason that she'd left Forever eight months ago.

And he was the reason she almost hadn't come back. She didn't want to see him, not yet.

Maybe not ever.

Not after what had happened.

But she really didn't have that much choice in the matter. Aunt Kate, that unbelievably hearty, dynamo of a woman, had suddenly become ill in Venice. Never one to complain, Aunt Kate had waved away all of Stacy's voiced concerns—right up to the time she'd taken a turn for the worse and died before a flight home could be hastily arranged.

Aunt Kate's death had complicated matters far beyond the immediate emotional component. Alone in a foreign country, Stacy had felt utterly stranded. Aunt Kate had always insisted on handling everything and it was easier than arguing with the woman, so she had let Aunt Kate do it.

It had taken every fiber of her being for Stacy to rally, pull herself together and do what needed to be done.

Per her aunt's specified last wishes, she'd had her aunt's body cremated and then she'd flown back to Forever with an urn filled with Aunt Kate's ashes.

Stacy would rather have flown anywhere else, but in all honesty, she couldn't afford to travel any longer or go anywhere except the town she'd always called home. Aunt Kate had been the one with all the money.

Her aunt had left her a little money in her will, but that, too, required a trip back to Forever. Olivia Santiago, along with her partner, Cash Taylor, ran the only law firm there. As Aunt Kate's attorney and executor, Olivia had the only copy of her aunt's will.

So, with a heavy heart and more than a little reluctance, Stacy had returned. Once back, she'd presented Olivia with a copy of her aunt's death certificate.

And that was when she discovered that some things in Forever *had* changed. The house that she'd grown up in, the one that her mother had left to her when she died and where she and Aunt Kate had lived before they'd gone off to Europe, had burned down while they'd been away.

The other thing that had changed while she'd been gone was that Forever had finally gotten its first hotel up and running. What that meant was that at least she had a place to stay while she waited for Olivia to square things away for her when it came to the will.

This was her first week back and, hopefully, her last.

Getting up, Stacy got ready quickly, intending to go downstairs to get some much-needed coffee and eggs over easy. The hotel, still in its infancy, had just opened a small restaurant on its premises. She'd heard it was having some trouble with a faulty refrigerator, but supposedly that had been taken care of. She crossed her fingers.

Stacy got off the elevator and was crossing the lobby to get to the restaurant when she heard Elsie, the young woman behind the reception desk, let out a loud, blood-curdling scream.

Hurrying over, Stacy put a comforting hand on the young girl's shoulder and asked, "What's wrong, Elsie? Can I help?"

Elsie didn't appear to hear her or even be overly aware that anyone was standing next to her. Her attention was completely centered on the paper she was clutching.

"I did it!" Elsie cried, waving what looked like a

letter in her hand. "I did it! I'm going to college!" she squealed.

Scurrying out from behind the desk, she threw her arms around Stacy, and then around Rebecca Ortiz, the hotel manager who had been drawn out of her office by the noise. "I'm going to college!" Elsie repeated, obviously beside herself with joy.

"Somewhere not too far away?" Rebecca asked, obviously doing her best to share the moment with the receptionist.

Elsie stopped abruptly and then happily grinned at the manager. "I'm going to be going to the University of Texas in Austin," she told her small audience proudly.

"Oh. That means you'll be going away to school."

"Yes, it will," Elsie cried happily, her eyes all but dancing as she moved around the lobby. "And I can't wait to go."

"Well, you've still got some time," Rebecca pointed out. From her expression, she was already trying to figure out how to get a replacement for Elsie. "You just came back from an extended vacation. And next September's a long way away."

Elsie shook her head so hard it looked as if it was going to go spinning off. The young girl held the letter up higher.

"No, it says here I can start in January, just like I applied." The girl's eyes were dancing. "There are so many things I have to do! I can't wait to call my parents and tell them about this!"

"You didn't tell them when you opened the letter?" Stacy asked.

With all her heart, she wished she had parents she

could share things with. With Aunt Kate gone, she was on her own.

"I, um, didn't open the letter when I got it," Elsie confessed, sounding just a little subdued for a moment, like she was tripping over her words. "I've been carrying it around since yesterday. I was afraid that the school had rejected me. But they didn't!" she exclaimed, her voice rising again. "They said yes!"

"Yes, we know, dear." Rebecca sighed. "Looks like I'm going to have to find a new receptionist for the hotel. Quickly," she added.

Turning toward Stacy, she ventured, "You wouldn't be looking for a job, would you?"

"Well, if it'll help you out—" Stacy began, gauging her words slowly.

Rebecca's eyes widened in surprise. "Oh, it would, it definitely would," she assured Stacy. "I realize that you probably won't be staying permanently, but I'd really appreciate you taking over for Elsie when she leaves." As an afterthought, Rebecca turned toward the receptionist and asked, "When are you planning on leaving, dear?"

"This minute!" Elsie all but shouted. It was like watching champagne bubbling out of a bottle a moment after the cork had been pulled. "I've got so much to do between now and January." Moving from foot to foot, the now former receptionist gave the impression that she was about to jump out of her skin at any second. "Things are finally turning around and going my way," she cried. "I've got to get home. I've got to tell Mom and Dad I'm going to college." She paused for a split second before charging out the front door. "I'm going to college!" she cried, as if she couldn't get enough of the simple declaration.

And the next moment, she was gone.

Rebecca shook her head and laughed. "Can you re-member ever being that excited?" she marveled, glancing in Stacy's direction.

"Once, a lifetime ago."

At least, it felt like a lifetime ago. But in reality, it wasn't. She'd been that happy when she'd found herself falling hopelessly in love with Cole McCullough. In the beginning she'd been convinced that it was strictly one-sided—until he began paying attention to her.

She remembered every word of every conversation they'd ever had. Cherished all the islands of time that they'd shared together. Back then—had it really been less than a year ago?—she'd honestly believed that maybe, just maybe, they were on their way to meaning something to one another.

Oh, Cole had meant a great deal to her, he had for years now, but it wasn't until they started spending time together that she began to believe that maybe, just maybe, there was a happily-ever-after in store for her. For *them*.

She should have realized that she was too old to believe in fairy tales, Stacy admonished herself. They'd had one wonderful, magical night together, and then he'd turned around and told her that maybe things were moving too quickly. That they should slow down before it was too late.

As far as she was concerned, it was already too late. Like a lovestruck idiot, she'd thought he felt the same way about her that she did about him. She should have known better.

She'd given Cole her heart and he had stomped on the gift, offering her a bunch of meaningless rhetoric that, loosely interpreted, said *I had a great time. Don't let the door hit you on the way out.*

She'd always been the smart one in her family; at least, that was what Aunt Kate had always told her. But Aunt Kate found her crying in her room. Stacy had tried to pretend that nothing was wrong, but her aunt hadn't been fooled. Then Kate put two and two together, and just like that, the idea for the European vacation had been born.

Stacy had attempted to demur, but Aunt Kate wouldn't take no for an answer. She'd said that she always wanted to travel abroad and felt that this might be her last chance.

Little did either one of them realize that she would be right, Stacy thought sadly.

In hindsight, Stacy didn't regret taking off the way she had. Hurt, she hadn't thought that she owed Cole a single word of explanation, or even the courtesy of a goodbye since he had distanced himself from her right after their night together.

And, looking back, she was glad she'd had that time with her aunt.

What was hard was finding a place for herself now that she was back.

Well, that wouldn't be a problem for the time being. Thank heavens she'd been in the right place at the right time. Any possible future money problems, at least for now, were on hold.

"When would you like to get started?" Rebecca asked her.

Stacy shrugged. She hadn't even been thinking about this half an hour ago.

"Now would be fine," she finally told the hotel manager.

"Now?" Rebecca echoed, surprised. "You don't want a day to wind down and get used to the idea?"

Stacy saw no advantage in that. At least if she was working, she'd be doing something to occupy her mind, although she had to admit it didn't exactly look extremely busy around here.

"Why?"

The question took the hotel manager aback. "Well, when you walked into the lobby this morning, I *know* you weren't thinking about being able to get a job as a receptionist."

Stacy laughed.

"I wasn't *not* thinking about it, either."

Pleased, Rebecca put her arm around Stacy's shoulders and gave her a quick squeeze. "I do appreciate this, Stacy. It saves me the trouble of having to look for someone to take Elsie's place. You are a lifesaver. You know that, don't you?"

"It goes both ways, Rebecca." When the taller woman looked at her quizzically, Stacy decided not to tell her that she needed a job or would need one eventually. Instead, what she said was, "I need to keep busy."

"Well, we don't exactly have so much business that we have to turn people away," Rebecca told her honestly. "This *is* still Forever. But slowly we are getting outsiders passing through, especially ever since the Healing Ranch was written up in that magazine. That put us on the map, so to speak. Before then, except for the occasional lost person who found themselves in Forever by accident, looking for the right way to get back, I don't think anyone ever came to Forever on purpose.

Not unless they already lived in the general area and were just coming into town for supplies."

Rebecca was not telling Stacy anything that she didn't already know.

"All things considered," Stacy said honestly, "I'm kind of surprised that someone actually built a hotel in Forever."

Rebecca smiled. "Just between us…me, too," she told Stacy with a broad wink. "There's not much to this job, really," she went on. "I can train you in an hour. Half that time if you're as smart as I remember."

They'd attended the same high school together—everyone in Forever did—where Rebecca had been three years ahead of her. But since the classes at each grade level were rather small, it felt as if the students were more like one large family than the typical rivalry between the different grades.

Stacy blushed a little. Compliments were a rare thing in her world. Not that Aunt Kate had been belittling. She just had a way of taking everything over, silently indicating that she didn't feel that her niece was competent to do things as well as she herself could do them. For a while there, Stacy had begun to believe her.

"You're being kind," Stacy responded.

"I'm being accurate," Rebecca corrected. "Remember, I'm your boss for now. Bosses don't get anywhere by being just kind. They have to be accurate. I think you're going to be good for the hotel.

"Okay, let me go over some of the key duties, and then you can get started by going to the diner and getting some breakfast for the two of us."

Stacy looked at her, curious. "I thought the hotel

had that little restaurant on the premises." She recalled walking by it yesterday.

"It does," Rebecca told her. "But unfortunately, it's still closed for repairs."

"Repairs?"

The other woman nodded. "It seems that yesterday, just before end of day, we had a grease fire. There was some damage done. We're keeping it closed for now. Just one thing after another," she said with a sigh. "You don't mind going, do you?" she asked after seeing the slightly unhappy expression on Stacy's face.

"Oh, no, no problem."

Which was a lie. She hadn't ventured out to see anyone except for Olivia since she'd returned.

But she knew that she'd have to face people eventually and field questions. There was no such thing as "mind your own business" in Forever. But she had really thought that *eventually* wasn't going to arrive so soon.

Obviously, she'd thought wrong.

So, after a very brief review of her new duties, which, Stacy felt, anyone with an ounce of common sense could have easily figured out, she found herself walking to Miss Joan's Diner.

She knew she could have driven there, giving herself a quick avenue of escape once she'd placed and picked up her order, but that was only putting off the inevitable. She had to face the people of Forever who would have questions for her.

It was better to get it over with than to stress over the anticipation of what those questions might be.

You can do this, you can do this, Stacy told herself over and over again, like some sort of a mantra meant to give her strength as she made her way down the streets of Forever to the diner.

You can do this. You can do this.

Finally reaching the diner's front door, she pulled it open and walked inside. Several people at the counter looked up in her direction. She saw recognition ricochet back and forth on their faces.

You can't do this.

Chapter 3

The babies had both been fed and, thanks to the resourcefulness of Jackson and Garrett's housekeeper, they had been changed as well, so their whimpering, at least for now, had stopped. The twins had fallen asleep.

Cole took the opportunity to call home. It took several rings before anyone picked up on the other end.

"Hello?"

Cole could tell by the way the greeting had been barked that Connor was in less than good spirits. "Connor, it's Cole. I'm going to be late."

"You're already late," his older brother informed him.

"I know," Cole said, an apology implied in his voice. "But it can't be helped."

"*Everything* can be helped," Connor said impatiently. And then Cole heard his older brother sigh. "Okay, well, what's the problem?"

Looking at the sleeping twins, Cole moved farther away from them, afraid that if he accidentally spoke loudly he'd wind up waking them up. "You know how Cody came across Devon pulled over on the side of the road and she was about to give birth?"

"Yes?" Connor sounded perplexed.

"And then Cassidy helped save that baby out of the river?"

"I've got chores to do, Cole. For both of us, it appears. I know all this you're telling me. What I don't know is where you're going with it."

Cole took a deep breath. "Well, it seems that it happened again."

"*What* happened again?" Cole sounded as if he was coming to the end of his patience.

"I was about to leave the ranch when I found these two babies on the doorstep."

"Two babies," Connor repeated incredulously.

"Yeah. They're twins."

Connor sighed. "Of course they are. Whose are they?" he asked.

"Haven't a clue," Cole admitted. "They were just there, tucked into this huge wicker basket like laundry—breathing, moving laundry."

There was a long pause on the other end of the line and then Connor finally began to ask, "Cole, did you by any chance, um…"

Cole knew what was coming and immediately headed it off before Connor had the opportunity to finish the sentence. "No, I didn't, Connor. Those babies are not mine."

"I'm just going to ask this once, and then we'll

put this to rest," Connor promised before he pressed, "You're sure?"

"I am positive," Cole said with finality.

There was no mistaking the relief in Connor's voice. "Okay. Then you've got to find out who those babies belong to."

"I know," Cole answered. "I'm taking them into town to see if anyone there knows anything. I'm sorry about this."

Connor's voice took on his customary understanding tone. "Don't be. This isn't your fault. Give me a call when you find out who abandoned them like unwanted puppies."

"The second I find out," Cole promised just before he terminated the call.

Returning to the living room, where Rosa was sitting next to the sleeping infants, Cole began to pick up the basket.

Rosa stopped him with a look. "Where are you going?" she asked.

"I'm taking them into town to see if anyone there knows who these little guys really belong to."

"Only one of them is a little guy," Rosa reminded him.

Rosa had been right. One of the twins was a girl.

"I know," Cole answered. With that, he walked toward the front door with the basket in his hands.

Rosa was on her feet and wound up beating him to the front door. Her agility was rather impressive for a woman her age. "You cannot put them on the seat next to you in the truck," she warned.

He smiled at this protective side of the woman. "I

don't intend to, Rosa. Don't worry," he told her. "They'll be safe."

"Safe" involved some clever work with the wicker basket and a length of strong rope. Securing the latter around the former, then tying the basket to the seat, Cole was able to drive into town.

Forever had a medical clinic as well as a sheriff's office, but there was no question in Cole's mind what his first stop with the twins was going to be.

He drove straight to Miss Joan's Diner.

If anyone would have a clue as to who the twins' mother was, it would be Miss Joan. Like most of the town's other citizens, Cole was of the opinion that nothing happened in Forever and its outlying territory without Miss Joan knowing about it. Half fairy godmother, half hard-as-nails taskmaster, Miss Joan seemed to know everything about everyone.

And, if she didn't know now, she would before the end of the day. No one doubted that the woman had her finger on the pulse of the entire town.

Cole himself had an exceedingly soft spot in his heart for the woman. Miss Joan had been there for him and for his siblings when their dad died, and although she could be blustery and demanding, and had been on more than one occasion, he knew that beneath all the tough talk, Miss Joan had the proverbial heart of gold. Even though she would be the first to deny it.

However, that didn't change anything.

Cole parked his truck right in front of the diner. His vehicle was blocking the entrance to some degree, but he thought that, just this once, given the circumstances, he'd be forgiven.

Undoing the ropes that were holding the basket and

its precious cargo in place, he picked up the twins and made his way into the diner.

The moment he walked in, Cole knew he had Miss Joan's full attention, even though she was behind the counter and on the far side of the diner.

A couple of the waitresses, Eva and Rachel, reached him first, oohing and aahing over the infants in the basket.

But it was Miss Joan whose attention he was after. The moment the red-haired owner reached him, Eva and Rachel immediately, albeit reluctantly, stepped aside, giving the older woman unobstructed access to both the babies and the young man who had brought them in.

Deep hazel-green eyes swept over the scene, assessing it. "I assume that there's an explanation why you brought these babies into my diner," Miss Joan said to him.

He nodded. "I was hoping you could tell me who they belonged to."

Miss Joan's austere expression never changed, and neither did her piercing gaze. "You're the one who brought them here, not the other way around. Something you need to get off your chest, boy?" Miss Joan asked him pointedly.

He thought it best if he gave Miss Joan a quick summation of events. Beating around the bush never got anyone anywhere with Miss Joan.

"I found them on the doorstep this morning. Almost walked right on top of them," he told her, giving her all the facts he had to offer. "I've never seen them before and I thought if anyone would know who they belonged to, it would be you."

There was only the barest hint of a smile on the

woman's thin lips. "I think you're giving me a little too much credit here, Cole." She looked from one tiny face to the other. "Have they eaten yet?"

"Rosa fed them. I've got a couple of baby bottles all ready to go in the truck," he told her with a hopeful note. Garrett had returned with the bottles from the general store in record time. "So if you or one of your girls want to feed them later—"

"Back up, boy," Miss Joan ordered. "I run a diner, not a nursery." She paused, scrutinizing the expression on his face and putting her own meaning to it. "If you need help later, we can talk. But right now, you've got to find out where these babies came from."

Jeb Campbell, sitting at the counter, raised his hand. "I know where babies come from," he volunteered in all seriousness.

"Eat your eggs, Jeb," she ordered in a no-nonsense voice. "We know where they come from. What we need to know is where they belong. Anyone know of someone who recently gave birth to twins?" she asked, her gaze sweeping over all the occupants of the diner.

It was at that exact moment that the door opened and Stacy walked in.

Silence descended over the entire diner as all eyes turned in Stacy's direction.

As for Stacy, she felt as if she had just walked into one of her nightmares. It was surreal.

Her heart accelerated the second she saw Cole.

And then it all but stopped dead when she saw the babies in the basket. The basket was on the counter, but from its proximity, she assumed that the tiny inhabitants had to belong to Cole.

She'd only been gone from Forever a little over eight months. He certainly didn't waste any time, did he?

Or had he been seeing someone else the entire time he had been seeing her?

Disappointment washed over her like a giant tidal wave. She needed to get out of there, needed to get some air because she could hardly breathe.

Turning on her heel, Stacy was about to push open the door she'd just entered when Miss Joan called out to her.

"Welcome back, Stacy. I was sorry to hear about your aunt."

Stacy froze.

It wasn't her nature not to be polite, no matter how much she wanted to flee. And Miss Joan had just said something nice about Aunt Kate. Stacy couldn't just ignore the woman.

She forced herself to turn around and look at Miss Joan.

How did the woman know? she wondered. No one knew about her aunt except for Olivia, and she was certain that Olivia wouldn't have said anything. Olivia was a lawyer and prided herself on being discreet.

"Thank you," Stacy finally murmured.

"Park yourself on a stool," Miss Joan instructed. There was no room for argument. "I think Cole here might need some help getting these two little ones over to the clinic."

Cole felt all but numb, seeing Stacy walking into the diner. He'd envisioned this scene a dozen different ways in the last eight months.

More.

Envisioned seeing Stacy walking toward him, tears

in her eyes, saying she'd made a mistake leaving. And each and every time, he forgave her. Forgave her because he didn't want to dwell on what had been but rather what could be.

Forgave her because he wanted her in his life.

And now, here she was, back. Back the same day that he had found babies on his doorstep. He looked down at the infants, then up at Stacy.

This couldn't be a coincidence—could it?

Could the babies be hers? And if they were, did that mean...?

Oh, lord, he thought, that would explain so much. Explained why she'd left without a word. Guilt had made her come back, he realized. Guilt because these babies were not only hers, but his, as well.

The thought created elation and panic, and they both vied for equal space within him.

Slowly, the last thing that Miss Joan had just said penetrated the fog around his brain. She was recruiting Stacy to help him take the babies to the clinic.

"The clinic?" he repeated, looking at the woman. "You think they need to be seen by a doctor?"

"You said you found them on your doorstep, right?" Miss Joan reminded him. "It wouldn't hurt to have them checked out—just in case." Miss Joan turned toward Stacy. "Don't you think so?"

"Um, sure." Stacy felt as if she was trying to talk with a tongue that had suddenly grown two sizes. "I don't have any experience with babies and all," Stacy said, pausing uncomfortably between each word. "But that makes sense. I guess."

"Glad that you agree," Miss Joan said in a tone that indicated there was no other path open to either of them except to agree with her. "Why don't you go with Cole and help him?" Again, there was no room for argument. "He certainly can't manage those babies by himself." Before either of them could protest or even comment, Miss Joan asked Cole, "How did you get them over here?"

That he could answer, he thought, relieved. "In my truck."

Miss Joan gave him a withering look. "I realize that. How did you get them over in the truck?"

Cole thought for a second. Miss Joan's interrogation had been known to make many a person's mind go blank. "I secured the basket with ropes and looped them around the passenger seat."

Miss Joan's eyes shifted toward Stacy, the expression on her face indicating that her point had just been made. "Keep an eye on those babies for me," she instructed Stacy.

"I can help," Eva volunteered, stepping forward.

Miss Joan obviously had other ideas about the transport. "Too many cooks spoil the broth," she told the young waitress before looking at Cole and Stacy. "I'm sure these two can manage, working as a team—the way they used to," she added significantly.

Stacy took back her earlier assessment. Hotel or no hotel, nothing had changed in Forever.

The hotel, she suddenly remembered. "I can't go to the clinic."

Miss Joan's expression darkened. "And just why's that?"

"Rebecca just hired me a few minutes ago to work the reception desk," she said quickly, then blurted, "Elsie just found out she's been accepted to college."

Miss Joan looked unconvinced. "College is not for another eleven months," she pointed out.

Stacy shook her head. She could feel Miss Joan beginning to run right over her. "No, she's going in January."

Miss Joan's expression remained unchanged. "Still got time."

Determined, Stacy pushed on. "I know, but she was all excited and took off, quitting right then and there. I told Rebecca I'd take the job."

Cole looked at her in surprise. "You need a job?"

Stacy really didn't feel comfortable discussing anything personal in front of Cole. Not after the way things had gone between them. But with everyone—especially Miss Joan—looking on, she had no choice. She couldn't exactly ignore him.

"It kind of came up," she finally said. "My house burned down, so I'm staying at the hotel."

It was on the tip of his tongue to ask, "Why didn't you come to me?" but in a way he had a feeling that she had, looking at the infants. "If you need a place to stay..." he began.

"Thank you," she said stiffly, cutting him off. "But I just said I have a place to stay. The hotel," she stressed. And then she remembered that she'd only popped over for a quick bite. She needed to be getting back. "Speaking of which—"

There were those who insisted that Miss Joan was part mind reader. Stacy had a tendency to agree.

"Don't worry about it," Miss Joan said, cutting in. "I'll send Rachel over to the hotel to explain what happened. This is September," she reminded the young woman. "Not exactly the busy season for the hotel, so

Rebecca should be okay with you not being there for an hour. Or so," she added significantly.

Stacy felt as if things were snowballing out of her control.

"But—" she began to protest.

As if on cue, the babies began to fuss in earnest, each growing progressively louder than the other, as if it was some sort of a pint-sized competition.

Miss Joan nodded toward the infants. "I guess you have your marching orders," she told Cole and Stacy. "Now go. And I don't want to hear anything about you using a rope," she told Cole. "Do I make myself clear?"

"Yes, Miss Joan," he replied.

It was easier that way than getting into an argument with the diner owner. Legend had it that no one had ever won an argument with Miss Joan, and that included her husband, Cash's grandfather. But then, Henry Taylor had doted on Miss Joan, which, it turned out, was exactly the right way to get along with the woman.

"You really found these babies on your doorstep?" Stacy asked several minutes later.

She had gotten into the back seat of his truck and he had handed her the wicker basket with the babies. The infants were dozing and the silence in the truck felt overwhelming. Stacy couldn't think of anything else to say, and every other topic would set them off on a course she had no desire to travel.

"Yes, I did," he answered, getting into the driver's seat. He glanced at her over his shoulder.

As if she didn't know where he found the babies, he thought.

He was staring at her, Stacy realized, and it took

everything she had not to squirm in her seat. This was a totally bad idea, going with Cole to the clinic like this. But no one said no to Miss Joan and Stacy wasn't about to be the first. She had no desire to have her head handed to her.

"Do you have any idea who the mother might be?" Stacy asked him.

Okay, Cole thought, he'd play along. "There might be a few possibilities," he responded vaguely. "But that's why I came with them to Miss Joan. She's always on top of everything and I figure that she'd be the first to know whose babies they were."

"Miss Joan doesn't know everything," Stacy insisted.

"Maybe," he agreed. "But right now, I figured she was my best shot."

Why are we playing these games, Stacy? Tell me the truth. Are these babies mine?

For one moment, he wrestled with an overwhelming desire to ask the woman in the back seat just that. It would explain why she'd left town so abruptly. But he knew asking her was pointless. He knew her. She wouldn't answer him. In all likelihood, she'd just walk out on him the way she had the last time.

And, angry as he was about her leaving him, he didn't want that happening again. Not until he'd had a chance to talk with her—*really* talk.

Desperate for something to say, he fell back on what Miss Joan had said when she'd first greeted Stacy.

"I'm sorry to hear about your Aunt Kate," he told her. "What happened?"

"She died," Stacy said stoically.

Why are you acting as if you care? We both know

you don't. You don't care anything about me or about Aunt Kate, so stop pretending.

"I realize that," he said, doing his best to be patient. "That's why I said I was sorry to hear about her." Getting his temper under control, he asked, "Did it happen while you were in Europe?"

She looked out the window on her left. "Yes."

He felt pity stirring within him. "That must have been awful for you, having her die and having no one to turn to."

She blew out a breath. She didn't want his sympathy. She didn't want anything from him. Still looking out the side window, she said, "I managed."

"We're here," he announced, and just like that, the topic was closed.

For now.

Chapter 4

Rounding the truck's hood, Cole came to the rear passenger door and opened it before Stacy could. Bending down, he got a firm grip on the wicker basket and drew it out of the truck. The babies were just beginning to wake up again.

"I'll get the door," Stacy volunteered, sliding down off her seat as soon as he had the basket. Before she hurried to the clinic's front door, she paused to look at the babies. One of them was beginning to squirm just enough to throw the basket's weight off while Cole was carrying it. "You want help with that—um, with them?" she corrected.

Was it his imagination, or was she trying too hard to appear unaffected by the sight of the twins? For now, Cole dismissed the thought, but it continued to hover in the back of his mind.

"Just get the door," he told Stacy. "I've got the basket."

For the briefest of moments, Stacy allowed herself a fleeting smile.

"Yes, you do," she said, adding, "You surprise me." When he raised an eyebrow in silent query, she explained, "I didn't think you'd be any good with babies."

He supposed he could see her point. She hadn't been there to see him with either Devon's baby or the one Cassidy rescued. "I guess we never know what we're capable of until we're confronted with the situation."

"I guess not," she agreed.

It hurt, Cole thought, talking to Stacy like this. The only thing that would hurt more would be *not* being able to talk to her. When she'd suddenly taken off the way she had, he'd thought he would never see her again. He hadn't understood just what hell he'd been in these last eight months until just a few minutes ago, when he saw her walking into Miss Joan's.

Lord, but he'd missed her.

Cole cleared his throat. "Just get the door," he told her gruffly.

Stacy squared her shoulders as she pulled open the front door, then stepped to the side as far as she could, clearing the space for him. The basket was obviously unwieldy, despite his efforts to hold it steady, and she didn't want Cole dropping the babies.

The second they walked in, they became the center of attention.

As usual, the clinic was full. It was the only available medical facility within a fifty-mile radius, so everyone who had a complaint of some sort, or found themselves in need of a checkup, came here. These days there were two doctors on the premises, as well as two nurses. Even so, the clinic was open from around eight, sometimes earlier, until eight, sometimes later. The doors were never officially locked until every patient in the waiting room had been seen.

Initially, the din in the clinic today was a little louder than usual, with fragments of conversations crisscrossing through the air. All that came to an abrupt, startled halt when Cole walked into the reception area carrying the wicker basket with the two babies in it. The fact that Stacy, his former girlfriend, came in right behind him was missed by no one.

Jackson's wife, Debi White Eagle, was behind the desk when they walked in. She immediately rose to her feet, ready to help Cole with the infants he had in the basket.

"Cole, what have you got there?" Debi asked, even though she was actually looking at Stacy when she asked the question.

Cole appeared almost sheepish as he explained, "They were on the doorstep when I left the bunkhouse this morning. I really could have used you," he added, looking at Debi.

Debi had crossed the reception area and was beside him now, getting a closer look at the babies.

"Well, you seem to be doing all right with them," she told Cole with approval. "Whose babies are they?" she asked.

"I don't know," Cole admitted.

His response had a room full of patients murmuring to one another.

"There was no note?" Debi asked, looking from Cole to Stacy.

Cole shook his head. "Nothing," he answered.

Stacy merely shrugged. "I wasn't there."

"If you ask me, I'd say it's finders keepers." Ted Reynolds, an old ranch hand, chuckled.

"The poor darlings," Amanda Rice, the grandmother of three, cooed as she came over to join the widening circle of people admiring the babies. "Where's your mama, darlings?" She raised her eyes to look at Stacy. "And *when* did you come back into town, Stacy?" she asked warmly. "You've been missed," the older woman told her.

"Did you bring the babies in for one of the doctors to examine?" Debi asked, wanting to take control of the situation before things got out of hand.

"Well, yes," Cole confessed, "but I didn't think that there'd be this many people here already." He looked at Debi apologetically. "I've got to get back to my family's ranch—"

"Well, if it helps, you can go ahead of me," Ted Reynolds volunteered. "I've got no real plans for today. Nothing that can't wait, anyway."

"And me," Amanda said. "You can go ahead of me," she told Cole. "At my age, the best part of coming in to see the doctor is socializing with whoever's waiting on him, too."

Several other voices chimed in.

"I can wait," another patient spoke up.

"So can I."

"Me, too. This is the first break from work I've had in over a month," Jeremy Jones said to no one in particular.

Debi held up her hand before anyone else gave up their place to the babies. There were a lot of people in the waiting area and if they all spoke up one by one, this could take a while.

She looked around at the seated people. "Can I assume that it's all right with all of you if I just let Cole go on ahead and bring the babies in to see the doctor?"

A cacophony of voices rose in response to her question. The gist was that the patients in the reception area were all in agreement about letting Cole go in first.

Debi turned toward him. "All right, Cole, you heard them. The people have spoken," she told him cheerfully. "I guess that's why I love living in this town. Everyone's so bighearted.

"Let's get these little darlings checked out. Boys or girls?" she asked, leading the way into the back where the exam rooms were located.

"One of each," Cole answered. As he started to follow the nurse, he looked back over his shoulder toward Stacy. "You coming?"

She was about to beg off, saying something to the effect that it seemed as if he and Debi had the situation covered. But that wasn't strictly true. She knew that Debi had to return to the front desk and even though the other nurse, Holly, was somewhere in the clinic, that still left Cole on his own to cope with two babies. One was probably hard enough for him.

Stacy sighed. She supposed that staying a little longer wouldn't hurt, especially since Miss Joan had said she'd get word to Rebecca at the hotel, explaining about her delay. Given her present situation, the last thing she wanted was to lose her job before she actually started it.

"Yes," she answered, raising her voice, "I'm coming."

Debi opened the door to exam room three. Like the other exam rooms that had been renovated in the clinic, this room was bright and cheery, designed to put the patient in it at ease. Although, Stacy thought, in this case, it really didn't matter.

Debi took out a clipboard with two blank forms attached to it. "Since this is obviously their first visit, I'd normally ask a few routine questions about the patients so we could put the information into their charts." She looked down at the infants and then back at Cole and Stacy. "But I don't suppose you'll be able to answer any of those questions, will you?"

"What kind of questions?" Cole asked, trying to be as helpful as possible.

"The usual ones. Name, date of birth, parents' names, things like that," Debi enumerated.

Feeling a little helpless, Cole had to shake his head. "Can't help you there. You know as much about them as I do."

"That they're cute?" It was a rhetorical question on the nurse's part, asked with a wide smile. "Well," Debi decided after pausing a moment to think, "at least we can put down their weights. Get this little one undressed so I can put him—her—," she corrected once the blanket was unwrapped and Cole began to remove the diaper, "on the scale."

"Aren't they going to get cold?" Cole protested.

"They're not going to be on the scale for that long," Debi assured him.

Stacy was still trying to understand how all this was going to come about.

"How are you going to—oh." The question Stacy had about weighing an infant was answered when she saw Debi place the baby on what looked like an old-fashioned butcher's scale.

Debi smiled, obviously guessing what was going through Stacy's mind. "Might not be state-of-the-art equipment, but it gets the job done for these little ones." After jotting down the number from the scale, she lifted the naked infant and handed her to Stacy. "Definitely not undernourished," she pronounced. "That's a good sign. Why don't you put her diaper and blanket back on and I'll weigh the other one," she told Stacy, then turned her attention to the second infant. "You said this one's a boy, right?" she asked Cole.

"Right," he responded, glad to be able to contribute at least something to the process. "Rosa fed and diapered both of them before I came here. That woman's fantastic."

"That's exactly how we feel about her," Debi agreed. "Don't know where we'd be without her." Once she'd removed the second infant's blanket and diaper, she placed him on the scale. He whimpered in protest. "Guess he doesn't care for the feel of metal against his skin." She jotted down the weight she read on the scale, then glanced at Stacy. "How're we doing over there?" she asked.

It was obvious that Stacy was having more than a little difficulty in putting the diaper back on the infant.

"I don't know about *we*," Stacy said, exasperated, "but *I'm* not doing too well."

The infant seemed to be all moving arms and legs and Stacy was having trouble getting the diaper to stay on her.

Putting down the second chart she was filling in, Debi made quick work of rediapering the first infant. Stacy looked on, chagrined.

"It just takes practice," the nurse said matter-of-factly.

"How's this?" Cole asked, holding up the baby he'd attempted to diaper.

As if on cue, the diaper began a rather quick descent down the second infant's chubby little hips.

"You've almost got it, Cole," Debi told him, taking the baby from Cole and quickly refastening the diaper tabs.

After diapering the newest patients, Debi loosely swaddled each infant and placed one in Cole's arms and one in Stacy's, much to their surprise.

"There's no sense in wrapping them up in their blankets just yet," she told the duo. "The doctor will only have to unwrap them to do his exam." Debi was about to leave when she paused and turned around. "Have either of you come up with any names we could put on the charts for the time being?" She glanced over toward the charts. "Baby Boy Doe and Baby Girl Doe just sound so terribly lonely."

Cole had his doubts about doing that. "Do you think it's right, naming them?" he asked. "I mean, we're bound to find the parents."

A rather bemused smile curved Debi's mouth. She was originally from Chicago and had worked in a city hospital where a much harsher reality prevailed. Parents didn't always come back for their children. She'd had experience with babies being abandoned, left on the hospital doorstep without a backward glance and never reclaimed.

But she had come to know a kinder, gentler reality in Forever, and she really hoped that it would win out in this instance, as it had in others.

"I know," Debi said, smiling at the two people in the exam room. "This would only be temporary. I just think that it would just make things—more personal. Any ideas as to names?" she asked, looking from Cole to Stacy.

Cole debated saying anything. And then, before he knew it, he heard himself suggesting, "How about Kate for the girl?" He looked at Stacy when he offered the name.

"Kate," Stacy repeated. She could feel a warmth growing within her, as well as gratitude toward Cole for having suggested it. Very quietly, she said, "Aunt Kate would have liked that." Then, speaking up, Stacy said, "Yes, sure, why not?"

"All right, then. Kate it is," Debi pronounced. Picking up the appropriate chart, she wrote the name on top of the paper. Picking up the second chart, she asked, "And the boy?"

Stacy looked at Cole. She appreciated the fact that he had just paid her late aunt a compliment by naming the infant girl after her. Turnabout was only fair play.

"How about Mike?" she asked, looking at Debi.

Mike, Stacy knew, had been Cole's father's name. From the stories that she'd heard Cole tell, he and his siblings had all been close to the hardworking man who had raised them.

Cole pressed his lips together, getting control over his emotions. "Sounds good," Cole agreed, nodding his head.

"Okay, so now we have names for them. Temporarily," Debi added, more for Cole and Stacy's benefit than for accuracy. "I'll tell Dr. Davenport you're here," she told them. "I think he's the next one free—unless you want Dr. Cordell to see them."

"No, Dr. Davenport's fine," Cole assured her.

Daniel Davenport, a New York transplant, had been the one to reopen the clinic. Prior to that, the clinic had been closed for more than thirty years. The doctor had been the first to tell people that he didn't come halfway across the country to reopen the clinic out of any self-less devotion to his profession. He'd initially wanted to be a surgeon attached to one of the more well-known, prestigious hospitals in New York. It was his younger brother who had been the dedicated one, and he was the doctor who was supposed to come to Forever.

But the night before his brother was to leave, Dan had convinced him to go out for one last celebratory drink. On the way home, a drunk driver had plowed into their car. Dan had gotten away with a few scratches. His brother hadn't been so lucky. He'd died at the scene.

Guilt had made Dan come out to the tiny Texas town in the middle of nowhere in his brother's place, but only until he could find a suitable replacement.

That had been a number of years ago, and since then, Dan had made a life for himself here in Forever—and now he said that it was the best decision he had ever made.

A tall, robust man who seemed to thrive on the long hours he put in, Dr. Davenport came into the room less than two minutes after Debi had left.

"I hear Forever has two brand-new citizens," he said, crossing to the exam table where Stacy and Cole were watching over the two infants. The babies were lying side by side, taking in the world around them in wide-eyed wonder.

Dan nodded at Stacy. "Nice to see you back in For-ever, Stacy. You're looking a little paler than I remember. Are you feeling all right?"

"I'm fine, Doctor," she said almost defensively. "I'm just here to help with the babies."

"Well, then, I'd better get to it and make sure these babies are as healthy as they look," Dan said, turning his attention to the infant closer to him.

Stacy breathed a subtle sigh of relief, glad the focus was off her.

Chapter 5

"I'm happy to tell you that both of these little people appear to be in good health," Dan told Cole and Stacy as he put away his stethoscope and the other instruments he had used to check out the babies' state of well-being.

"Doc, about how old would you say they were?" Cole asked.

Dan laughed softly as he considered the question. "Well, unfortunately, babies aren't like trees. You can't just check their rings. There is no surefire way to ascertain just how old they are, but going by experience, I'd say that these two appear to be approximately three weeks old."

"And you don't recognize them?" Cole pressed hopefully.

Dan regarded the man next to him. "Do you mean have I seen them before because their mother or father brought them in?" He saw the hopeful expression that came into Cole's eyes, but he had to shake his head. "Sorry, these two have never been here before. I definitely would have remembered twins," he added.

Cole wasn't ready to give up just yet. "What if they were brought in one at a time?"

Dan smiled kindly at the cowboy. "Now you're really reaching, Cole—but I'm afraid my answer's still the same." He glanced at the twins, back on the exam table with Cole and Stacy positioned on either side of them again. "I've never seen them before."

Kate was wiggling and she managed to loosen the blanket that had been tucked around her after her exam was completed. Dan observed with approval as Stacy refastened the blanket around the infant.

"Have you tried bringing them to Miss Joan?" he suggested.

"Yes," Cole replied, a touch of dejection in his voice. "No luck."

Dan thought of his brother-in-law, Rick Santiago. "You could try the sheriff, I guess. If Rick doesn't recognize them, either, he might still be able to locate the mother—or the father. I would imagine that either would do in this case."

"Would they?" Stacy asked, speaking up. "I mean, if these babies were abandoned, then maybe neither one of the parents is the right person to leave them with—even if we could find them."

"You might have a point, but I think that at least to begin with, they should be given the benefit of the doubt," Dan told them.

There was a knock on the exam room door. No one came in, but Dan obviously knew who was on the other side.

"Listen, if you still have any questions for me and want to talk, why don't you drop by after hours when the clinic is closed? But right now, I've got a waiting room full of patients to see, so I'm going to have to cut this discussion short. Keep me posted," he told them, his glance sweeping over both people. "And let me know if you find their mother—or father."

Dan closed the door behind him.

The moment he did, Cole looked at the infants, who were now back in the wicker basket, nestled against each other.

"Now what?" Stacy asked.

"Well, pretty soon I'd say we're going to need a bigger basket for these two. But for now, I guess we'll do what Dr. Dan suggested and go talk to Sheriff Santiago."

"You think *he's* going to recognize them?" she asked dubiously.

Cole frowned slightly. "I take it by the skepticism in your voice, you don't think he will."

"Highly doubtful," Stacy responded. "Unless someone reported them kidnapped—at which point I think Dr. Dan probably would have known about them."

He supposed that she had a point. But Forever was growing and communication wasn't what it used to be, so there was a chance that the sheriff might be able to help.

"Still, I think the sheriff should know that they were abandoned," he told Stacy, smiling down at Mike. As he spoke, he gently slid his finger against Mike's cheek. Reaching up, the infant wrapped his tiny fingers around it. And around Cole's heart, as well.

Stacy took that a step further. "So he can arrest the

mother if he finds her? Is that really the way you want to go with this?"

Cole had been all set to pick up the basket and walk out of the exam room with the babies, but Stacy's comment stopped him. He hadn't even considered that possibility occurring.

"When did you get so pessimistic about things?" he demanded.

Stacy made no answer, she merely fixed a laser-like glare on him. He decided it was best not to pursue the matter, at least for now.

Instead, after first opening the door, he picked up the basket and made his way back to the reception area. Stacy was right behind him.

Any thoughts of a fast getaway were quickly aborted. The moment they walked out to the front of the clinic, they were engulfed in questions.

"Did Dr. Dan recognize them?"

"If he didn't, maybe Dr. Alisha knows who they are."

"Did the babies check out okay?"

"What are you going to do with them now?"

Because Cole looked as if he was a little overwhelmed with the barrage of questions, Stacy decided to run interference for both of them.

"No, Dr. Dan didn't recognize the twins," she told one woman. "Dr. Alisha didn't come in to consult, but I'm sure he would have called her in if he thought she might have recognized them. And both of the babies are the picture of health," she told the people in the waiting room with an air of finality. She'd really thought that would be sufficient enough to get them out of the clinic, or at least to the door.

But then Lyle Henderson, a big, burly rancher, spoke

up, repeating the last question. "So what are you going to do with them now?"

"We're taking them to the sheriff," Cole answered.

"A little young to be behind bars, aren't they?" Duke Crenshaw asked with a booming laugh that temporarily blocked out everything else.

It also managed to wake up the babies.

Duke's wife, who had driven her husband over to the clinic, hit his shoulder with the back of her hand. Given that she was somewhat bigger than her husband, the blow stung and Duke yelped.

"Serves you right. See what you've done? You woke them up," Mrs. Crenshaw berated him.

"No harm done," Cole tossed over his shoulder as he quickly left the clinic with the twins before any further questions threatened to keep them there longer.

"I guess nothing *has* changed," Stacy said as they walked over to his truck.

Her comment seemed to have come out of nowhere. "How so?"

She nodded toward the clinic. "It seems like everybody in Forever is still minding everybody else's business."

"They're just concerned," Cole told her.

"They're just nosy."

"Speaking of being nosy…" Cole began, setting the basket down next to him on the ground in order to open the rear passenger door. "How are you doing?"

Stacy climbed into the back seat and waited for him to hand her the basket, or at least secure it on the floor beside her feet, the way he had earlier.

"What do you mean?" she asked guardedly. She had

the uneasy feeling he was trying to make a point, but he kept skirting the issue.

"I mean how are you doing?" Cole repeated.

It didn't sound like such a hard question to answer, he thought. When Stacy continued to look at him blankly, Cole elaborated. He tried to do it carefully because he didn't want to accidentally make things worse by saying the wrong thing or by phrasing things so that they opened fresh wounds.

In the end, Cole wound up being blunt because, no matter how much he aspired to it, finesse wasn't exactly his forte.

"Your aunt died while the two of you were traveling together. That had to have been a great shock for you to deal with."

Stacy squared her shoulders, frowning. "We already covered this."

"No, we didn't," he contradicted. "Not in the way you mean. I told you I was sorry to hear about your aunt and asked what happened. You said she died and that you managed. That's not talking about it," Cole said, closing her door for her.

Rounding the back of the truck, Cole came around to his side of the vehicle. He got into the driver's seat and closed his door.

"Yes it is," Stacy insisted, struggling not to raise her voice and agitate the twins. "It's just not talking it to death."

He wasn't ready to put the subject to rest. "You were traveling in a foreign country. You must have felt awful when it happened."

"Well, I wasn't about to dance a jig. Aunt Kate was my only remaining family and she'd always been there for me. She was the one I always turned to for guidance. And suddenly she wasn't there to guide me anymore." Stacy stopped, realizing that she had said too much and that she was on the verge of tears.

She wasn't about to cry in front of anyone, least of all Cole.

This was what she got for coming back, she thought, upbraiding herself.

"That's what I mean. It must have been really awful for you," he said sympathetically, wishing he could have been there for her. "I just want you to know that I'm here if you want to talk about it."

Stacy frowned, looking down at the babies rather than at him. "I just did."

"That wasn't really talking, Stacy."

She blew out a breath, annoyed. "There were no hand puppets involved. Lips were moving. Words were said. As far as I'm concerned, that's considered talking," she informed him with finality. "Let's concentrate on finding these babies' parents and not on anything that happened in the past, all right? There's the sheriff's office." Stacy pointed out the window toward the building on the right.

"I know," he answered. "I'm familiar with it. That's where I was headed."

"Well, congratulations," she told him with a touch of sarcasm. "You've reached it."

Okay, he'd been patient enough, he thought. "Why are you mad at me?" he asked. "I'm the one who should be mad at you."

Stunned, she felt her mouth drop open before she could get control over herself.

"In what universe?" Stacy demanded.

"In this one," he retorted.

Her temper flashed and it took everything she had to rein it in.

"You know what," she said between clenched teeth, "let's just table this and bring the babies in to the sheriff before I forget I'm a lady and really say something ugly."

With that, she didn't wait for Cole to come around to open her door. She opened the opposite passenger door and got out, then quickly hurried to the other side to get the babies out before Cole could reach them.

He arrived at the same time she did. Seeing what she was up to, he glared at her. "Now you're being pig-headed," he told her.

"You always did have a silver tongue," she said sweetly.

Cole shook his head. "And to think I actually thought I missed you."

"Yeah," she retorted, "I was just thinking the same thing."

He blew out a breath, telling himself that it wouldn't do either one of them—or more importantly, the twins—any good to blow up like this right here in front of the sheriff's office. It was just that he had forgotten just how easily Stacy could set him off, and half the time—like now—she did it without warning. It was like being caught in a blitzkrieg.

She was obviously angry at him and he had no clue as to why or what was going on in her head. But then, that was nothing new, either.

"Stacy," he said, growing stern, "let me take the basket in. It's heavy."

Stacy stubbornly stood her ground and kept her fingers around the edges of the basket, refusing to release it. "I can manage."

He'd gotten some insight over the years about how to approach at least a few subjects when it came to Stacy. "Nobody's disputing that, but I think it would be better for the babies if I carried the basket."

"It's not heavy," she argued. Except that it really was. And the babies were moving. With a sigh, she relented. "It's awkward."

"All the more reason for me to take it in," Cole told her. The woman, he thought, was as stubborn as she was beautiful. That hadn't changed.

For a few brief seconds, she debated continuing to argue the point with him. There was just something about Cole; he pressed all her buttons. He always had. No matter what she tried to tell herself, that much hadn't changed.

But her arms *were* beginning to really ache. So, in the end, she said, "Fine, you can carry them in—but only because I'm thinking of the babies."

Tempted to smile, he refrained. Instead, he said, "I understand."

"Don't patronize me, Cole."

There went his temper again, snapping like an old-fashioned slingshot. "Damn it, woman, you can get my blood boiling the way nobody else ever could."

Ignoring the gist of what Cole had just said, she focused on the words he'd used. "Don't swear in front of the babies."

"They won't *remember*," he stressed. All he wanted to do was go inside the sheriff's office and make these twins someone else's problem.

"I don't want to put that theory to the test," she countered.

"Why not?" Cole demanded. "You don't seem to have any qualms about testing me."

Her eyes narrowed. "Because you're not a sweet infant."

He opened his mouth, ready to tell her off. But then he stopped.

They were here, at the sheriff's door, and any further discussion, sharp-tongued or otherwise, was going to have to be put on hold unless they wanted to have the sheriff suddenly coming out of the office and acting as a referee.

As if on cue, they both stopped bickering.

Stacy opened the door of the sheriff's office. "After you," she said sweetly, stepping to one side so that Cole could enter first, carrying the babies in the basket.

Spying only the basket that Cole was carrying, Rick Santiago called out, "I hope you brought me something from Miss Joan's Diner," from across the room as he headed toward the duo.

"I don't think this qualifies as lunch, Sheriff," Joe Lone Wolf commented. His was the first desk that Cole and Stacy passed when they entered the office and he'd gotten a good look at the contents of the basket.

"Hey, welcome back, Stacy," Cody McCullough, Cole's younger brother declared, greeting her. "It's nice seeing you again."

One look at the babies and Cody appeared to reassess the situation. Stunned, Cody's eyes darted toward Stacy, then back to his brother. "You two come here to make some kind of an announcement?"

"Yeah," Cole said, guessing at what was going

through Cody's head. "That I've got an idiot for a younger brother."

"Then these babies aren't...?" Cody looked from Cole to Stacy again and then back to the babies.

"No!" Cole said firmly, placing the basket on Joe's desk.

Cole knew he was vehemently denying parentage, but the simple truth was that he wasn't all that sure that these babies weren't his. If nothing else, the timing seemed to be right. Stacy had been gone for eight months. But she wasn't acting like she was their mother.

"Sheriff," Cole said to the tall, dark-haired man who had crossed the office to approach them. "These babies were left on my doorstep this morning and we were hoping you could help us find their mother."

He spared one quick look in Stacy's direction to see if what he was about to say was going to affect her in any manner. Her face appeared impassive.

"Otherwise, I'm going to have to bring them to social services over in Mission Ridge."

"You're going to do what?" Stacy cried, stunned. She pulled the basket protectively closer to her.

Chapter 6

Stacy noticed that her voice had gone up and she took a second to collect herself. She couldn't believe that Cole would be so dismissive of these babies, even though they did eventually need a real home.

"But you're going to wait to give the sheriff time to investigate, right?" she asked Cole, giving him a chance to redeem himself.

"Sure," he answered. "That's why we came here to see him."

Stacy had a strange expression on her face he couldn't quite fathom. He found himself going back to wondering if the babies were hers.

"One question." Rick held up his hand to get their attention.

Still wondering about Stacy's reaction, Cole glanced toward the sheriff. "Go ahead, Sheriff."

Rick indicated the babies in the basket. "What are you going to do with these two little ones while you're waiting to find out if the deputies and I can locate their mama somewhere?"

Cole wasn't following what the sheriff was asking. "What do you mean?"

"Where are they going to be staying?"

Instead of answering Rick's question, Cole turned to look at his brother. After Cody had helped a stranded Devon give birth to her baby, he'd wound up taking her in and she'd lived at the family ranch until Cody and she had gotten married.

"Um—Cody?"

Cody immediately seemed to pick up on the hopeful note in his brother's voice. "Oh, no, sorry. I'm going to have to pass. Devon's already got her hands full."

Cole turned toward Stacy next. Given how passionate she'd sounded about not taking the twins to social services, maybe she was willing to take them in for the time being.

"Stacy?"

Stacy raised her hands up, as if to physically block any arguments Cole could come up with.

"I can help out—when I'm not working," she told him. "I can't take them in. I don't even have a permanent place to stay myself. I'm staying at the hotel."

"Well, it's not like I'm not working," Cole protested. She hadn't even started her job. He had been at his for years. "Technically, I've actually got two jobs. I work part-time at the Healing Ranch and the rest of the time with Connor on our ranch, so I'm pretty much busy all the time."

"Then I'd say that these two little people have a problem," Rick concluded, cutting into the discussion. He slanted a glance at Cole and then at Stacy.

"You could take them with you to the ranch," Stacy argued, looking right at Cole. "Connor's still there, right?"

Cole frowned. He didn't like the way this was being twisted. "Well, he's kind of in charge, so yes, he's still there." He knew what was coming next. "But he's busy working the ranch, just like I am," Cole emphasized.

Joe sat up in his chair a little straighter. "You've still got that housekeeper, don't you?" Joe asked, then added her name in for good measure. "Rita."

Cody laughed. "Just when I think you're not listening to a word I say," he marveled, looking at the other deputy. "Son of a gun, you really *are* paying attention."

Joe wore the same emotionless expression he always did. "I don't have to look like I'm hanging on your every word in order to be listening, McCullough," Joe said quietly.

It was time to wrap this up before it dragged on for hours. "All right," Rick declared, directing his words toward Cole. "Then it's settled. These two," he nodded at the twins, "are going to be staying at your ranch and Rita's going to be looking after them for a bit, with help from you, your brother and Stacy."

"But—" Cole started to protest.

Rick cut him short. "If I'm going to be doing my job, trying to find these kids' mama, I don't have time to be arguing with you, Cole," the sheriff told him. "Now you take those kids on home to your place and tell Connor I'll be talking to him when I get a chance."

With that, Rick retreated into his office to make a few calls.

Cody saw the expression on his brother's face. "It's not so bad," he assured Cole. "Remember what it was like when I brought Devon and her baby to the ranch to stay with us?"

"What I remember is a lot of crying," Cole reminded his brother.

Cody grinned at him. "Yeah, but you got over it and stopped." Joe and Stacy laughed at his comment.

"Very funny," Cole retorted. He looked down at the twins, resigned. "Well, I guess I'd better bring these two to the ranch and hope that Rita's in one of her good moods."

Cody waved his hand at his brother's concern. "Rita loves babies. Remember how good she was with the one Cassidy saved from the creek when we had that big flash flood?"

Joe snorted and shook his head. "That makes a total of four babies, counting these. You McCulloughs are regular baby magnets, you know that?"

Rather than address the ribbing remark Joe had just made, Cole glanced at the senior deputy. A full-blooded Navajo, Joe Lone Wolf had been raised on the reservation that was located about fifteen miles south of the outskirts of Forever. Although he was married to the town vet, the sheriff's sister, Ramona, and lived in the town proper, Joe went back to the reservation regularly in order to visit.

"Hey, Joe," Cole began hesitantly, "do you think that you could ask around on the reservation, see if maybe these babies belong to one of the girls there?"

Rather than answering immediately, Joe scrutinized the infants that had been placed on his desk.

"I can ask around, see if anyone knows anything," he remarked.

His tone indicated that he doubted the infants belonged to anyone from the reservation.

"Thanks. I'm just covering all the bases for now," Cole told the deputy as he picked up the basket again. One of the twins made a squealing noise. "Okay, you two, time for you to meet Connor."

As he started for the door, he caught a movement out of the corner of his eye. Stacy had gone around him in order to open the door.

"Thanks," he murmured. When she continued walking beside him, he stopped for a second. "Are you coming with me?"

Did he think she was shadowing him for some ulterior motive? "Yes, I'm coming with you," she answered. "I said I'd help out, and since my first day of work was postponed until tomorrow, thanks to Miss Joan, I've got the time to help—unless you've got this covered and don't want me to come over," she added.

"No. I mean yes. I mean—" Frustrated, Cole blew out an annoyed breath. Why did he always get things so muddled up when she was around? "Oh, hell, just get in the truck. I'll drive you home when you're ready to go," he added before they could get tangled up in a discussion about how she was going to get back to town.

Stacy frowned, looking at the twins in the basket. "You're not supposed to be cursing in front of those babies," she reminded him.

"I'm not supposed to be doing a lot of things I'm doing," he told her.

Rather than just let his remark go, she challenged him.

"Just what's that supposed to mean?" Stacy wanted to know.

I'm not supposed to be letting you get to me the way you are, but it's happening anyway, even though I know you'll just wind up stomping on my heart again the way you did the first time.

The remark burned on his tongue, but he bit it back. No sense in rehashing things.

"Nothing," he answered curtly, then practically growled, "I appreciate the help." After taking a breath, he continued more calmly. "As do Mike and Kate." Opening the rear passenger door, he tucked the babies' basket in on the floor again, the way he had before.

On the opposite side, Stacy took a seat and looked down at the small, round faces. Cole made his way to the driver's side and got in.

"What do you think their real names are?" she asked Cole.

Was that just for his benefit, or didn't she really know? He kept vacillating as to whether or not she was actually their mother.

"I don't know," he replied, starting up his truck. "Maybe their mother didn't bother naming them. Maybe she figured naming them would just humanize them for her and she didn't want to get close to them."

"That's awfully cold," she commented. Especially coming from him, Stacy added silently. Cole usually saw the best in everyone. It was one of the things she'd liked best about him.

"So's leaving two infants on someone's doorstep," Cole countered.

Stacy was silent for a moment, thinking. And then she said, "I don't know, maybe their mother was desperate and she knew that you were a good person who would take care of them. That you'd make sure they were all right."

Damn it, this was going to drive him crazy. *Was it you, Stacy? Did you leave these babies on that doorstep because you knew I'd be there this morning? Are these our babies, yours and mine?*

He really wanted to ask her that.

The questions hovered on the tip of his tongue. But something told him that now wasn't the time to ask. Besides, even if he did ask her and she said no, would he believe her? He didn't know. It was better if he put off asking Stacy so he could watch her interact with Kate and Mike first.

Maybe she'd give herself away if he was patient enough.

"Why me?" he asked her out of the blue. Raising his eyes to the rearview mirror, he saw her looking at him quizzically. "Connor's the more responsible one, raising the three of us the way he did. Why not leave the babies with him?"

He saw her shrug. "I don't know. Maybe it was proximity."

He didn't follow. "What?"

"Proximity," Stacy repeated. "Maybe the babies' mother lived closer to the Healing Ranch than your family's ranch," she speculated. And then she rethought her response. "But I think the real answer's simpler than that," she told him.

"Oh? So what is the simpler answer?" Cole asked. Maybe the more he got her to talk about the twins, the more likely she'd be to admit that she was the one who'd left them on his doorstep—if she actually had.

"Their mother picked you, not Connor," Stacy stressed for a second time, "because she knew you were a good person."

He felt he had to come to his brother's defense. "Connor's a good person." All things considered, Connor was probably the best person he knew.

"I don't know, maybe she didn't know Connor. What difference does it make why?" she asked, losing patience. "The point is that she picked you to leave her babies with."

If she hadn't been the one to leave them, then there was a different way to look at the whole thing. "Maybe she just abandoned them and left them some place she figured they'd be found."

Stacy sighed. "Maybe. And maybe not. The point is that you have them, Cole."

"For now," he reminded her, thinking back to what he'd said about taking the twins to social services as a last resort.

Stacy drew back her shoulders and became rigid. "You weren't serious about what you said before." Her voice lowered to almost an ominous level. "Were you?"

He was preoccupied with what he was going to say to Connor when he took the babies in. He heard her, but her words didn't really register.

"You're going to have to be more specific than that," he told Stacy.

He knew damn well what she was referring to, she thought. Why was he playing games like this?

"That if the sheriff doesn't find their mother, you're going to bring those babies to the social services office in Mission Ridge," she said, her jaw all but clenched.

"That would be the best place for them," he pointed out matter-of-factly.

"No, it wouldn't," she argued, her voice growing louder. "How can you say something like that after the way Connor gave up his dream of going to college just to become your guardian so that you and your brother and sister didn't wind up being taken in by the system?" she demanded.

"Connor was family," he explained, then pointed out, "These kids might not have a family. Social services could find a home for them."

"They could also split them up," she retorted with passion. "There aren't that many people who are willing to take on two kids at the same time."

"How would you know?" Cole asked, dismissing her protest.

The words rushed out of her mouth before Stacy realized she was saying them. Words that gave away the secret she'd guarded so zealously for as long as she could remember. Guarded because she didn't want people looking at her differently. Above all, she didn't want people pitying her.

"Because I had a twin sister and my mother left us with social services."

"What are you talking about?" Cole demanded. "I knew your mother. She was one of the kindest women I ever met." He remembered thinking that if his mother had lived, she would have been just like Sally Rowe.

"That was my adoptive mother, not my real mother," Stacy told him.

Stunned, he raised his eyes to the rearview mirror again. "You were adopted?"

"See, you're already thinking differently of me." Even in the mirror, she could see what he was thinking.

"Only because you never told me," he said, trying to wrap his head around the revelation. "How could you not tell me?" They'd been so close, sharing dreams, sharing secrets—and all this time, she'd kept this from him. He felt as if everything he'd once thought they'd had had been built on sand. "And what's this about a twin sister?" he asked. "Where is she now?"

Stacy steeled herself off before she was able to answer his question. She'd brought this on herself. But she couldn't just ignore his question after what she'd just said.

"She died," Stacy answered stoically. "They separated us and placed us with different foster parents. Turns out that the people my sister was staying with believed in severe punishment for any minor disobedience." Her voice began to tremble and she had to take a moment to regain control. "My sister's punishment turned out to be fatally severe."

Cole pulled his truck over to the side of the road so he could turn around and really look at her. Thrown for a loop, he didn't want to risk driving into a ditch. "How old were you?"

Stacy laced her fingers together and stared at them, unable to look at Cole, afraid of what she might see in his eyes.

"I was five. Old enough to remember her. And to understand that I was never going to see her again. The memory was too painful, so I blocked it all out. My mother—the woman I called my mother," she stressed, "knew all this when she and my...my father adopted me." A sad smile curved her mouth as she went on looking down at her hands. "She did everything she could to help me adjust." Stacy's voice became a little steadier as she added, "She also saw to it that that other family was brought up on manslaughter charges. They were found guilty. I didn't know that at the time, but I found out about it later. My mother told me when she thought I was old enough to be able to understand."

He wanted to hold her. To tell her he was sorry. But he knew Stacy would only withdraw into herself. Still, he had to know. "Why didn't you tell me?"

Stacy squared her shoulders and looked up. "I just did."

"But I mean *then*," he stressed. "When we were going together."

The short laugh had no mirth to it. "Not exactly a story that's meant for sharing," she told him.

"But you told me now," he pointed out. If she told him now, she could have told him then.

"I told you now because I don't want you even *thinking* about handing these babies over to social services yet. Granted there are some very nice people out there who want to open their homes up to a child—but that's not always the case. I know that you need to find out more about them first before you take the risk."

Her eyes met his. Hers had an intensity to them he'd never seen before. "Promise me you won't take them to social services right away?"

"I promise," he told her. But he wanted her to understand the full import of what she was asking. "What if the sheriff can't find their parents?"

"I'll think of something," she told him. Exactly what, she wasn't sure, but anything was better than the kind of life that her twin had so briefly had. "Now start driving," Stacy ordered.

Cole saw tear tracks on her cheeks.

But he knew better than to point that out or say anything about them. Instead, he took out his handkerchief and passed it back to her, then started up his truck again.

He thought he heard her murmur, "Thanks," but he wasn't sure. The twins had started fussing and they were drowning Stacy out.

Cole couldn't help thinking that he was heading to the ranch—and Rita—just in time.

Chapter 7

Cole walked into the ranch house he had thought of as home for his entire life. He couldn't begin to imagine what it had to be like for children who hadn't been as lucky as his siblings and him.

Until today, he had never thought of Stacy as even remotely being in that sort of a category. He'd never had a clue that she'd known anything but security throughout her whole life.

You just never knew.

The living room was empty.

He guessed that Connor was most likely out on the range, tending to whatever problem had come up today. Just as well, he thought. He'd face his brother with the news of this latest development after the twins were taken care of.

"Rita, are you home?" Cole called out, raising his voice.

"I'm in the kitchen, Mr. Cole," Rita answered, her almost melodic, accented voice floating through the rooms. "Do you need something?"

"You could say that," Cole replied. He walked into the kitchen with the babies.

Rita's back was to the doorway. Moving between the stove and the counter, she was in the midst of preparing dinner. Because she never knew just how many people would be seated at the dinner table, the woman Cole and Connor had considered a godsend ever since she joined the household always made sure that she prepared plenty. The whole family agreed that even Rita's leftovers were beyond good. The woman clearly had a gift. Cody had once said the housekeeper could make three-day-old dirt taste delicious.

"Well, what is it?" Rita asked, chopping furiously and reducing celery stalks into tiny bits of green.

"Turn around, please," Cole requested.

Putting down the huge knife she was wielding with the expertise of a master swordsman, the housekeeper deposited the diced celery into the large pot of stew she had on the back burner and then turned away from the stove.

"Speak quickly, please. I have work to do," Rita told Cole before she fully turned around to face him.

Her dark eyes widening, Rita stared at the basket the rancher was holding. Within less than half a second, the older woman was melting.

Wiping her hands on the apron around her middle, she came forward, her eyes never leaving the infants. "What do you have there?"

"Babies," Cole answered. "Twins to be more accurate."

Rita was already beaming at the infants. "Whose?" she asked as she tickled Kate's tummy. Kate made a noise that was very close to a giggle.

"That's just it," Cole said after sparing a glance at Stacy for any last-moment intervention. Stacy said nothing so he told the housekeeper, "We don't know."

"Miss Stacy," Rita greeted the young woman beside Cole politely. She recognized her from a photograph Cole still had in his room. Asking around, the housekeeper had become aware of the backstory. "Are you here for a visit?"

"No, to stay," Stacy told her. Then, to be strictly honest, she added, "For now."

Sharp dark eyes darted from the infants toward the woman she'd just greeted. "Did you bring these babies with you?" Rita asked.

"No, she's just here to help out," Cole explained. The twins' fussing had gone up a notch, increasing in volume. "I think they're hungry. Or maybe they need changing again."

He raised his eyes, looking at the housekeeper. It was clear that he felt out of his depth and was silently asking for her help.

A knowing look came into Rita's eyes. "And you would like me to see which it is?"

He nodded, looking at her sheepishly. "Something like that."

"So, then, they will be staying here?" Rita asked. She paused to turn the burner beneath the large stew pot down to low. The stew needed to simmer for a couple of hours before it was ready.

"For the time being," Cole told her. "They don't have

anywhere else to go," he added, hoping that would win the woman over completely.

"I see. Does Mr. Connor know?" she asked.

"I told him about finding the babies, but no, I didn't say anything about having them stay here," Cole admitted.

Rita nodded. "He is a smart man, Mr. Connor. He has probably already guessed as much." Rita picked up the baby closest to her. It turned out to be Mike. Taking a deep whiff, she said, "Oh, yes, this one needs to be changed." She looked at Cole. "Did you by any chance bring any diapers with you?"

"Yes," he answered, happy that he'd at least gotten this right. "Garrett picked up diapers for them at the general store, along with a couple of baby bottles and some formula," he told her, then added, "Rosa sent him out with a list. Everything's in the truck right now. I'll just go out and get it."

"You said something about *finding* them?" Rita asked him, curious.

"They were on my doorstep." Cole tossed the words over his shoulder as he hurried out the front door to his truck.

With Cole gone, Rita turned to look at Stacy. Her expression indicated that she was waiting to be filled in on the rest of the story.

Stalling and uncomfortable, Stacy went to pick up the second twin. Kate stopped fussing the second she was in Stacy's arms and laid her small head on Stacy's shoulder.

An immense feeling of contentment and satisfaction filled Stacy. It surprised her as much as it pleased her.

"He found these babies on his doorstep?" Rita

pressed. "I don't understand. Mr. Cole's doorstep is here. He didn't find them here," she stated.

"I think he meant he found them outside the room he stays in at the Healing Ranch," Stacy explained, although she really didn't know much about that situation. From what she had pieced together, she'd learned that Cole had begun working at the Healing Ranch after she left town.

Rita shook her head, her features softening with sympathy. "Someone left these poor little lambs out in the cold? They could have gotten very sick. Who would do such a heartless thing?" she demanded, cradling Mike against her ample bosom.

"Maybe a mother who was desperate," Stacy ventured. She didn't want to sound as if she was taking sides, but there was obviously more than one side to this situation. Seeing the less than sympathetic expression on the housekeeper's face, she quickly added, "The sheriff is trying to find their mother."

Wanting to avoid Rita's condemning gaze, Stacy gazed down at Kate. As she did so, she caught herself smiling.

"You like babies." It wasn't a question on Rita's part but a judgment.

"I suppose," Stacy said, not wanting to commit herself one way or the other. "They haven't become people yet."

Rita looked as if she was considering what she'd just heard. "Then you have been hurt," Rita concluded.

She knew the other woman by sight, but Rita hadn't yet come to work for the McCulloughs when Cole and Stacy had been involved. Rita studied the young woman's face, making her own assumptions from what she was even now piecing together.

"No more than anyone else," Stacy answered vaguely. Trying to appear aloof, she deliberately put distance between herself and the other woman. She had the feeling that Rita could see right through her and she didn't want anyone in her head.

"I've got diapers, bottles and milk, and Garrett picked up a couple of pacifiers, too," Cole announced, holding two large paper bags aloft.

Walking back into the house quickly, he placed both of the bags on the kitchen table and leaned one against the other so they wouldn't accidentally spill out their contents.

"What about a change of clothes?" Rita asked him.

He looked at her, slightly bewildered. "What about it?"

Rita pressed her full lips together, searching for patience. "Do you have any in those bags that you brought in?"

"I don't think Rosa told him to get any change of clothes for the babies," he told the housekeeper.

Just to make sure, Cole rummaged through the contents of both bags, taking out everything in them and lining them up on the table. The items in the bags took up all the available space.

"Nope, no change of clothes," he announced.

"Mr. Cole," Rita began, her voice trailing off along with her patience.

Cole did his best not to sigh. "You want me to go to the general store and buy some clothes for the twins," he guessed.

"Very good," Rita replied, smiling at him.

"What size do you want me to get for them?" he asked.

"Why don't you get the outfits to fit a three-month-old, just to be on the safe side?" Stacy said, speaking up.

He'd almost forgotten she was there. "Okay," he said gamely. "How many outfits do you want me to buy?" he asked Stacy.

The housekeeper took over. "Three for each should do," Rita told him, adding, "As long as you don't mind doing a lot of washing."

Cole frowned slightly. The idea of having to wash clothes—even tiny ones—didn't warm his heart. "I'll get five," he told Rita.

Rita turned before he could see the smile on her face. "Whatever you say, Mr. Cole," the housekeeper replied.

"Yeah, right." Cole laughed under his breath. "Be back as soon as I can. We should have thought of this earlier, when we were in town," he said to Stacy as he walked out.

"Yes, we should have," Stacy answered, addressing his back.

From Stacy's tone, he didn't know if she was agreeing with him or mocking him. He decided that he was better off not knowing.

"Come," Rita said to her as she cradled Mike in the crook of her arm while picking up a package of disposable diapers with her other hand. "We can change these two in the guest bedroom." She led the way to the other room.

"What are you doing back in town?" Miss Joan asked sharply when she saw Cole walking through the diner's door.

Accustomed to her prickly manner, Cole came up to the counter. "That's no way to make a customer feel wanted, Miss Joan."

"You're not wanted," Miss Joan informed him. "In case it slipped your mind, you're supposed to be with those babies." Her hazel eyes pinned him with a look. "Where are they?"

"I left them with Rita and Stacy at the ranch," Cole told her. He thought that would please her. He quickly discovered that he was wrong.

"And you ran off?" Miss Joan accused. "Responsibility getting to be too much for you already, boy?" Cole wasn't sure if that was disappointment in her eyes, or if she was just trying to goad him. "Lucky for you your brother didn't feel that way or you, Cody and Cassidy would have been scattered to the four corners of Texas."

"I'm not shirking my responsibility, Miss Joan," Cole assured her. "I just came back to town to get them a change of clothes at the general store. Rita insisted that they were going to need them."

Rather than saying anything about making a mistake, or even that she'd known, in her heart, that he would come through, Miss Joan focused on what his housekeeper had said.

"Of course they will," Miss Joan agreed with feeling. "You can't have those babies in the same clothes day in, day out."

Day in, day out. That sounded much too long a stretch of time to him. He just couldn't think about that now. Instead, he defended his reasoning.

"They're babies, Miss Joan. They just need blankets tucked around them and they've already got those."

Miss Joan just shook her head. "You are going to

need a lot of work, boy," she commented with feeling. Her eyes narrowed as she pinned him with a look. "If you came into town for extra clothes, what are you doing here?" she asked. "In case you hadn't noticed, I don't sell baby clothes."

"I just wanted a cup of your hot, bracing coffee before I went back to the ranch," he told her.

"You just wanted to stall before you went back," Miss Joan corrected. "Don't forget, I've known you since you were no taller than the heel on that boot you're wearing. I know how you think. Babies are nothing to be afraid of, Cole," she said, pouring him a tall container to go. "And neither is Stacy," she added in a low voice.

"I'm not afraid," he said defensively. "She made the decision to go her own way eight months ago," he added, lowering his voice so that no one else but Miss Joan could hear.

Miss Joan made no comment. Instead, she placed a lid on the coffee she had just poured and pushed the container toward him.

"Just take your coffee and get back to the ranch—and your responsibilities."

"They're not my responsibilities, Miss Joan," he reminded her.

"Haven't you heard?" Miss Joan asked. "Possession is nine tenths of the law and they're on your property. That makes them yours."

Cole sighed, digging into his pocket. Arguing with Miss Joan about *anything* was futile. "So, what do I owe you?"

Her eyes met his. "Prove me right and we'll call it even," Miss Joan told him. "Now get your tail out of here. Those kids are waiting."

Again, he couldn't argue with her, even if he wanted to. Because somewhere in his heart, he felt that she was right.

He drank the coffee on the trip back.

When he walked into the ranch house with the extra baby clothes that Rita had sent him out to get, he found his housekeeper and his former girlfriend sitting on the living room sofa, feeding the twins and laughing. Obviously, in the time it had taken him to go to town and back, a lot of bonding had taken place.

"There you are," Rita announced when she saw him come in. "I was beginning to think you decided not to come back."

"I haven't been gone that long," Cole protested. He handed her the bag of clothes he'd bought. "Still don't see why I had to buy these. All they need are their diapers, their undershirts and those blankets they were wrapped up in when I found them in that basket on the doorstep."

"And you are an expert on babies?" Rita asked.

Maybe he wasn't an expert, but he did have some experience. "We've had two here."

Rita frowned at him. "And how much attention did you pay?" she asked.

"Enough," Cole answered defensively.

Rita shook her head and he got the feeling that she was pitying him. Standing up, she handed over Mike to him. "Here, you hold him. I have dinner to finish preparing. See that you do not drop him," she ordered, walking back into the kitchen.

"I like her," Stacy told him as Cole sat down beside her with Mike.

"You would," he answered. And then his curiosity got the better of him. "What were you two laughing about when I walked in?"

"Oh, were we laughing?" Stacy asked innocently. "I hadn't realized."

"Even the twins realized it," he pointed out, still waiting for her to answer his question.

"Just girl talk," she finally answered. "Nothing important."

She wasn't about to say anything more, he thought. For now, he let it go—but he promised himself that he would find out eventually.

Chapter 8

After parking his truck near the front of the ranch house, Connor remained seated behind the steering wheel for a couple of minutes, gathering his strength together just to make it to the front door.

He felt really drained. He was going to have to get some part-time help, he told himself. Even with Cole's help—which he hadn't had today—there was just too much work on the ranch.

Uttering a deep sigh he opened the driver's side door and got out. Connor recalled that his father had an expression that rather aptly described the way he was feeling as he all but dragged himself up to his front door: he felt as if he had been ridden hard and put away wet.

Of course, the expression more accurately applied to a horse, but Connor felt that, in this case, it also could have just as easily described him.

Walking into the house, the first thing he saw was Cole, pacing the floor with what looked like a doll wrapped up in a blanket in his arms. Connor blinked and realized he was looking at an infant, not a doll.

At least, he assumed it was an infant. He'd heard that these days they had realistic-looking dolls that did everything except chop wood and herd cattle, so it could still be a doll.

He took a closer look.

It wasn't a doll.

"You know, I could have used a hand today," Connor said, shrugging out of his jacket and letting it fall over the back of the easy chair as he walked past it.

"I'm really sorry about that," Cole said. "But something came up." He nodded at the infant in his arms, then raised his eyes to look at his brother again. "Or maybe I should say *two* somethings came up."

That was when Connor noticed that Cole wasn't alone in the living room. There was a young woman sitting on the sofa.

Stacy Rowe.

She was back—and she was holding another infant in her arms.

Stacy turned around just then to look at him and she smiled in acknowledgment.

"Stacy." Remembering that he was still wearing his hat, Connor took it off as a sign of respect. "I didn't know that you were back in town," he told her. "How are you?"

Rather than answer Connor's question with the all-encompassing word *fine*, because she wasn't really fine, Stacy told Cole's older brother, "I'm well, thank you for asking, Connor."

Connor recalled his brother's phone call earlier today, saying something about finding babies on his doorstep. Because he always took the simpler route if it was opened to him, Connor put two and two together and asked, "Are they yours?" nodding toward the infant she was holding.

Again, rather than give Connor a direct yes or no answer, Stacy replied, "Cole found them on his doorstep today."

Suppressing a weary sigh, he turned his attention back to his brother. "So you still don't know who the mother is," Connor concluded, remembering what his brother had said earlier when he'd called.

Cole shook his head. "No one's come forward to claim them," he said. "The sheriff's going to see what he can find out, and Joe Lone Wolf's going to do a little poking around on the reservation just in case they belong to one of the women there."

Connor filled in the blanks. A desperate young girl finding herself pregnant and alone, taking the only avenue she felt was open to her. It wasn't that unusual a scenario. Still, he hoped that wasn't the case.

"You told Miss Joan about the babies, right?" Connor asked, thinking, the way everyone else in the area did, that if anyone would know who the babies' mother was, it was Miss Joan.

"Right," Cole answered. "She told me that she'd let me know if she heard any talk about someone having recently given birth to twins."

Connor paused beside Stacy, his mind going a mile a minute as he looked at the infant in her arms.

"I think we still have Cassidy's old crib in the attic," he said. "We took it down while Devon and the baby were here, but I took it apart and put it back up in the attic. Looks like we need to bring it back down again."

Stacy knew that Connor was nothing if not kind-hearted. All the McCulloughs were. But taking in two extra children—infants at that—was an imposition. She was surprised that he didn't balk at the idea. "So it's okay if they stay here?" she asked.

"They got anyplace else to go?" Connor asked her matter-of-factly.

"No."

"Then I guess that settles that question. They can stay here until their parents turn up or something else can be arranged." Connor turned toward his brother. "Cole, I'm dead tired. Help me bring that crib down. We'll put it together so these kids can have something softer to sleep in than that basket you've got over there." He nodded at the wicker basket that was on the floor near the oversize coffee table.

For a second, Cole looked as if he was at a loss as to what to do with the infant in his arms. Spying the basket his brother had just referred to, he placed Mike in it. He brought it back around and put the basket next to Stacy's feet.

"Okay," he told Connor. "Let's do this."

They found the crib more or less where Connor had put it. It was in four pieces, not counting the springs and the mattress that would eventually rest on the springs once the four sides of the crib were joined together.

It took them three trips each to bring down all the pieces.

Working together, with some slight supervision coming from Rita, who had decided to check on the babies,

Connor and Cole put the crib together rather quickly, considering that some of the hardware was missing.

Cole didn't believe in just throwing things together and he wasn't satisfied until he'd tested the crib for sturdiness.

"That looks really strong," Stacy told them once Cole and his brother were finished and had stepped back from their project.

"It would have to be," Cole said. "Cassidy was the last one to use it on a long-term basis and she was always hard on her things—furniture, clothes, you name it."

"She'd shake those bars until she finally found a way to climb out," Connor said, smiling and remembering. "And then she'd make a break for it whenever she could. Dad talked about tying her up for the night. The rest of us knew he was kidding, but that made her even more determined to climb out."

"I'm surprised the crib wasn't in pieces," Stacy commented. "I guess they made things to last twenty-three years ago."

"Our dad made this crib," Connor told her. "Our mother told me that he made it just before I was born and all four of us slept in it until we outgrew it—which, in Cassidy's case, was pretty quick."

He looked at the infant she was still holding. It had fallen asleep in her arms. "I think because these babies are on the small side, they can both fit in the crib together," he remarked.

"Are you going to leave it right here in the middle of the living room?" Stacy asked skeptically. "Wouldn't everyone, including the twins, be better off if the crib was in that back bedroom that's down here?"

Connor thought the matter over for a moment. "You might have a point. But the other two times we've made use of it this last year, there was always someone to sleep in the same room as the baby. First Devon, and then Cassidy slept in the room with the baby she rescued."

"Well, how about Cole?" Stacy suggested, a smile curving the corners of her mouth for the first time that day as she turned to look at him. "After all, he was the one who found them."

Cole was far from sold on the idea. "Well, I—" he began to demur.

"Are you going to tell me that a man can't do something a woman can do?" Stacy asked. She was clearly challenging him and he knew it.

"Not *can't*," Cole stressed. "But in this case, a woman could do it better." A way out occurred to him. "Stacy, didn't you say you had nowhere to stay?"

"No, I said I was staying at the hotel," Stacy corrected.

"*Because* you had no place to stay," Cole reminded her. He brought up an obvious point. "Your house burned down while you were away so when you came back, you didn't have a place to live."

"I know all that," she said impatiently. She didn't need him to bring up the obvious. She was still having a hard time dealing with that loss as well as the loss of her aunt.

"Instead of staying at the hotel, why don't you stay here?" Connor asked.

She didn't want to stay here because she didn't want to set herself up for any more pain than she'd already gone through. The memory of the way she'd felt over eight months ago, when she'd left Forever, was still fresh enough to not just make her wary, but make her want to keep away from Cole as much as she possibly could.

And how's that working out for you? Stacy mocked herself.

Out loud, she said, "I appreciate the offer, Connor, but I have a job at the hotel. I just got hired today to take over the reception desk."

"We could really use your help here," Connor told her. "And I'd take it as a personal favor if you pitched in," he added.

She felt herself wavering and struggled to remain steadfast. "But I can't just leave Rebecca high and dry like that. I've already postponed starting my job for one day because of the babies—well, I didn't exactly postpone it, Miss Joan told me that she would do it for me." Coming from Miss Joan, it had sounded more like an order than an offer.

"You seem to have a knack for these babies," Connor said, playing on her sympathies. "And in the grand scheme of things, taking care of infants is a lot more important than working a reception desk at a hotel that only has a moderate amount of business most of the months of the year.

"Of course, I can't tell you what to do, but since Cole seems to have brought these lost little souls here, and I have the ranch to run while Cole works both here and at the Healing Ranch, I would *really* take it as a personal favor if you could help out at least part of the time," he stressed. "In exchange, you can stay here for as long as you'd like. You can have your own bedroom and Rita will help with the—they *are* twins, aren't they?" he asked.

"Dr. Dan seemed to think so when we had them checked out at the clinic," Cole told his brother.

That was good enough for Connor. "Twins it is. And Rita can help you take care of them until we get home at night."

Stacy felt as if she was being hemmed in. "I would love to help," she began, "but—"

"You already made plans and your mind is made up," Connor guessed. Resigned, he nodded. "I understand. I have no intentions of forcing you to do something you don't want to do." He took a breath. "I didn't see another car out front besides Cole's when I came home so I'm assuming you came over here with him. He'll take you back," Connor told her.

She rolled it over in her mind. "Yes, he will," Stacy said as she stood up. "He'll take me back so I can explain to Rebecca in person why I won't be able to take the job after all, and so I can pack my things," she added. "I'm going to need a few changes of clothing myself if I'm going to be staying here—for a while."

Connor beamed and took both of her hands in his. "I can't thank you enough," he told Stacy.

Looking up at him, Stacy smiled. "Maybe I should be the one thanking you," she said. "I'd forgotten what it's like here in Forever—with people going the extra mile for each other, even when they don't have to."

"I can't pay you much, but—" Connor began.

She stopped him before he got any further. "No, it's all right. I'm sure this is just going to be temporary— and Aunt Kate did leave me a little in her will, so I'm not exactly hurting for money yet." She could see he was about to protest and she knew what he was going to say. "I took the job at the hotel mainly to keep busy, not because I was destitute."

Connor seemed to hardly hear the second half of her statement.

"My lord, I forgot all about your aunt's passing." Sympathy flashed through his eyes. "I am really sorry to hear about that. Your aunt was a fine lady."

Stacy nodded. "Aunt Kate had a good life. And she got to see Europe the way she always wanted to," she pointed out.

The import of her own words hit her for the first time. Until just now, she had thought of the last eight months as her aunt rescuing her and taking her away from her source of pain, but now she realized that she had actually rendered a service to her aunt, as well. For as long as she could remember, Aunt Kate had always talked about traveling someday. By giving her aunt a reason to take her away, she had inadvertently provided that "someday" for Aunt Kate to finally see Europe.

Everything happened for a reason, Stacy remembered her mother used to say. She supposed that, in this case, she had ultimately done good for her aunt by letting the woman whisk her away from Forever.

"All right then," Connor was saying. "Cole, why don't you take Stacy back to the hotel so she can collect her things and make her peace with Rebecca? Meanwhile," he went on, turning toward the twins, who were now comfortably nestled in the crib he and Cole had put together, "I'll wash the dust off and roll up my sleeves so I can take care of these two until you get back."

"Dinner will be ready in another hour, hour and a half," Rita called out to Cole and Stacy, as if on cue, despite the fact that she wasn't in the room. "Make sure you are back from the town by then, Mr. Cole. Miss Stacy," she added pointedly.

From the housekeeper's tone of voice, Stacy got the impression that it wasn't a suggestion on the woman's part—it was an order.

Taking her arm, Cole guided Stacy out the door and then to his truck.

Seated, she eyed him quizzically as Cole got in on the driver's side.

"I think we'd better get a move on if we're going to be back in time," he told her, starting up his truck.

She buckled up. "You make it sound like Rita rules the roost around here."

Cole laughed under his breath. "Let's just say I've learned not to make her unhappy. Connor's her boss, but as for the rest of us, I think, given her age, she kind of sees us like her kids. Trust me, staying on the right side of that lady has its advantages," he told her with feeling.

"The rest of you," Stacy repeated. Aware that things might have changed while she'd been gone, she was trying to get a handle on the way things were. "Then Cody and Cassidy still live on the ranch?"

"Not anymore," he told her. "But they come by often enough, along with their spouses and the kids."

"Spouses," she echoed as if she was having trouble absorbing the word and what it meant, at least in one case. "You mean that Cassidy got married?"

He saw the stunned expression on her face. He'd felt the same way at the time.

"That's right. You weren't here for that." Cole grinned broadly, relishing being able to reveal the details to her. "And you're never going to guess who she married."

Stacy had no idea who her friend had married. But she was fairly certain about one thing. "Well, I know she didn't marry Will Laredo," Stacy began.

The grin on Cole's face widened, stopped her dead. "Wrong."

Stacy's eyes widened. She looked at him, stunned. "You're kidding."

Enjoying this, Cole shook his head.

"Cassidy married Will? Really? But those two couldn't be in the same room without verbally slicing each other to ribbons," Stacy recalled.

Cole laughed. "I think they got over that."

Stacy looked at him, allowing herself to *really* look. She'd forgotten how much she'd missed seeing that grin and hearing that laugh.

These last months, Stacy had tried with all her heart to put that behind her. But she'd been in town less than two days and it was flooding back with a vengeance.

If she had a lick of sense, she'd run for the hills the first opportunity she had, Stacy told herself.

Somehow, she had a feeling that wasn't going to happen.

Chapter 9

Cole pulled his truck into the near-empty parking lot and turned off his engine. "I can wait in the truck if you'd rather talk to Rebecca alone," he offered.

Was he saying he didn't want to go in with her, afraid that people might get the idea that they were back together again? Or was there something else going on? Stacy decided to treat the matter lightly for the time being.

"Is that your way of getting out of carrying down my suitcases?" she asked.

"No, I can still bring those down to the truck. I just thought you'd feel less awkward talking to Rebecca if I wasn't standing right there."

Cole appeared slightly insulted, she thought. If she was going to cast any sort of aspersions in him, she wouldn't waste her breath doing it about something so trivial. Everyone knew the man was the total opposite of lazy.

"I was only kidding about the suitcases," she said. "And as for feeling awkward with you there, talking to Rebecca has nothing to do with it."

Cole cut through the rhetoric and got to the heart of her meaning. "In other words, you'd feel awkward with me around no matter what."

Stacy was *not* in the mood for an argument and waved away his words. "I'll work it out," she said.

They were in the parking lot behind the hotel—Cole had driven more quickly than she'd anticipated—and rather than go round and round about this latest point with him, Stacy just got out of the truck. Without the twins to focus on or having anyone else to serve as a buffer between them, the feeling of awkwardness when they were near each other had returned—in spades.

Closing her door, Stacy told him, "Come inside or stay in the truck. It's all the same to me."

He didn't even have to think about it. "Then I'll come in," Cole responded. He got out and closed the door behind him.

They found Rebecca behind the reception desk, typing on the computer's keyboard. Looking up, the moment she saw Stacy, Rebecca's face dissolved into a wreath of smiles. "I didn't think I'd see you until tomorrow morning," the woman said. She started to come around the desk.

"About that—" Stacy began.

Rebecca stopped where she was. "Wait, I know that tone of voice. You've changed your mind." It wasn't a question.

Stacy wished she didn't feel guilty. Taking the job

had been a spur-of-the-moment thing, at best, but that didn't make letting the older woman down any easier.

"Something's come up," Stacy began, trying to edge her way into the explanation.

Rebecca's brown eyes washed over Cole. "Yes, I see that."

For a split second, Rebecca's comment caught her off guard. "What?" The next moment, she realized what the hotel manager was thinking. Stacy quickly tried to set the woman straight. "Oh, no, it's not what you think. I just agreed to help take care of a couple of twins."

Rebecca looked at her in surprise. "You don't strike me as the nanny type."

"That's because I'm not," Stacy answered. "I'm just helping out a friend for a few days—maybe a week or so," Stacy amended. "In any case, I need to check out. If you could have my bill ready when I come back downstairs, that would be great," Stacy requested.

"Certainly," Rebecca agreed. "Sorry to see you go, Stacy—on both counts."

"Thank you. I hope you find somebody to take over the front desk," Stacy told her as she walked toward the elevator.

"Not as quickly as I found you," Rebecca called after her.

"I feel guilty," Stacy murmured, getting on the elevator.

The comment hit Cole the wrong way. He bit back the response that rose to his lips. Stacy felt guilty about telling the hotel manager she wasn't taking the job she'd been hired for, but she hadn't given any indication that she felt guilty about just taking off without a word to him the way she had eight months ago.

Cole told himself there was no point in getting angry, but her comment still felt like having salt poured on his wound.

He decided it was best if he didn't say anything to her—about *anything*—for now.

At least, not until he cooled off.

Following her into her hotel room, he waited for Stacy to pack her things. When she was finished and had snapped the locks into place, he took the two suitcases off the bed. Heading toward the door, Cole stood waiting until she exited, then followed her out.

He continued to maintain his silence as he rode down the elevator with her. When they got out to the main floor, he walked out the entrance and took the suitcases to his truck. After loading them into the back, he got in on the driver's side and waited until Stacy took care of her bill at the front desk.

It took her longer than he anticipated, but he said nothing when she finally came out to his truck.

He was giving her the silent treatment, Stacy thought when she finally got into the passenger seat and buckled her seat belt. For the life of her, she had no idea why, or what had changed in the last hour.

If anything, he should be telling her how grateful he was that she had agreed to help out. After all, these babies had been left on his doorstep, not Connor's, and that made them his responsibility. Which actually meant that she was going out of her way to help *him* with them, not Connor.

But then, she didn't know Cole the way she thought she did. There was a time when she would have sworn she knew every thought that entered his head. That was before he'd ridden roughshod over her heart the way he had, completely abandoning her without a second thought.

She supposed that it was lucky for these babies that he'd grown up a bit.

Three minutes into the trip back, the silence was really getting to her.

Because she was not about to ask Cole what was wrong—since that would have given him the impression that she cared—Stacey reached over and turned on the radio.

A popular country singer had only managed to utter the first three words of his song before Cole reached for the dial and, with one quick movement of his wrist, shut the radio off.

"I was listening to that," Stacy protested indignantly.

Cole kept his hand over the dial, stopping her from turning the radio back on. The whole situation had started him thinking. He could come up with only one reason she'd left town and why she was back now, volunteering to help care for the infants he'd "found" on the doorstep.

"Are they yours?"

"What?" she cried sharply, staring at Cole. He couldn't be asking her what she thought he was asking.

"The twins," he specified. "Are they yours? Did you leave them on my doorstep—on the bunkhouse doorstep?" he clarified.

Her eyes flashed as she looked at him. "We've already had this discussion. I don't know how bad your memory is, but I answered that question for you and the answer was—and still *is*—no, they are *not* mine," she underscored.

Blowing out a breath, struggling to rein in her temper, she glared at him. Like it or not, she was still able to read him.

"You don't believe me, do you?" Cole didn't answer her. It was getting harder for her to hold on to her temper. "Do you think that little of me that you believe I'd just leave two helpless infants crammed in a basket on a doorstep?" she demanded heatedly.

"My doorstep."

That did it. "I didn't know you even *had* a damn doorstep other than at the ranch until this happened so, no, it wasn't me. They're not mine—get over yourself, Cole."

"I can get over myself with no trouble at all," Cole assured her. And then, in what he realized was a moment of weakness, he told her, "What I can't seem to get over is you."

Did he honestly think she was going to believe that? Maybe she never really knew him at all, she thought sadly. "I stopped believing in Santa Claus a long time ago, Cole. So please stop trying to snow me."

"You don't believe me." Served him right for saying anything to her, he upbraided himself.

"No," she told him flatly. "I don't."

He spared her one piercing glance, then looked straight ahead at the flat terrain. "Yeah, well, I don't believe me, either, but there it is." And then he couldn't help throwing in, "Even though you left without a single word of explanation—"

Was he delusional? Or was he just trying to make her doubt herself? "I didn't think I needed to explain anything, considering that *you* were the one who decided to bail out."

"I didn't bail out," he insisted. "I just needed time to think."

"Yeah, think about how to bail out," she retorted angrily. They'd made love and after what she'd thought was the most wonderful night of her life, he'd vanished on her. "Face it, you got what you wanted, so the bloom was off the rose and you wanted to explore other fields."

The more he talked to her, the more confused he became.

"What the hell are you talking about?" Cole demanded. "This is Forever, population *small*. There *are* no other fields."

He was almost convincing, she thought. But she'd lived through it, lived through the humiliation of having him take off the way he had, without a backward glance. Well, two could play that game, and thanks to Aunt Kate, she had.

"Denial is only a good weapon when you're on a diet and find yourself stranded in a bakery. In your case, denial is definitely not good—especially for your soul."

"Let's stop right here," Cole warned her, "before one of us says something we can't take back. It's best for everyone all around if we just focus on those two babies back at the ranch who need to be reunited with their mother."

She didn't want to argue, and if she remained around him, they were bound to argue. "Maybe I can be more useful if I volunteer to help the sheriff look for her."

"Maybe," Cole allowed. "It's an option you can look into in the morning. Right now, if I don't bring you back in time for dinner, neither one of us might live to see morning."

He almost succeeded in making her laugh. "Rita can't be *that* fierce."

"Let's put it this way. In our house, nobody has ever tried to call her bluff. Besides, she cooks like an angel," he told her. "And I don't know about you, but I'm really getting kind of hungry."

She didn't want to admit it, but now that Cole had mentioned it, she was rather hungry herself. "Just drive," she told him, waving her hand toward the road in front of them, and let it go at that.

Connor appeared genuinely relieved when he saw Stacy walk in with his brother.

"I was afraid you might have changed your mind," he told her. "I don't mind admitting that I think I'm out of my depth here." He nodded at the infants currently in the crib. "Feeding two of these is a lot harder than just feeding one," he told his new houseguest. "When Devon was here with her newborn, we all took turns helping out, but she did most of the heavy lifting, so to speak. And then when Cassidy rescued that baby and brought her here, Rita had started to work for us. And there was also Will to pitch in."

"Will," Stacy echoed. "Laredo?" She said the rancher's last name just to be sure they were talking about the same man. "I don't think I can picture him helping with a baby."

Cole laughed. "He kind of felt it was his duty because—Cassidy didn't like letting anyone know this at the time—Will actually rescued Cassidy rescuing the baby."

"They were in the middle of a flash flood and the current got pretty strong pretty fast, according to the locals. If it hadn't been for Will, Cassidy and the baby might have both been swept away," Connor told her. "My point is that there was always just one baby to a whole bunch of us. Now there're two babies, and our numbers have decreased considerably."

When she'd walked in, Stacy had been having serious second thoughts about what she was signing on for—even if it turned out to be only for a short while. But listening to Connor just now, she'd had another change of heart. As annoyed as she kept getting with Cole, she couldn't, in all good conscience, bring herself to just leave Connor high and dry.

"Well, if it helps any," she told Connor, "consider those numbers to have increased by one. I officially terminated my job at the hotel and I'm here to help until the sheriff locates their mother."

"Dinner is ready," Rita announced, walking into the living room. "Eat," she ordered, waving the three people into the dining room. "I will take care of the babies. That means you, too," she told Stacy when the latter made no move to leave the room.

And, just like that, Stacy found herself an unofficial member of the family—at least for the time being.

The first couple of days on the ranch seemed to run together for Stacy, turning into an endless stream of feedings and diaperings with occasional fitful snatches of sleep. The twins seemed to take turns being awake, never sleeping at the same time.

Initially, trying to keep up with them felt like an exercise in futility to Stacy until the housekeeper took over, ordering her to her room.

"You sleep, I will take care of the babies," she told her.

"No, that's all right, Rita," Stacy protested, sounding a little exhausted around the edges. "You have work to do."

"Yes," the woman agreed, leveling a penetrating gaze directly at Stacy. "And you are making it hard for me to do it." With one baby tucked into the crook of her arm, Rita pointed to the ground floor bedroom, next to the twins' room, that had been set aside to act as Stacy's. "Now go lie down and get some rest before Mr. Cole accuses me of letting you run yourself into the ground."

It wasn't in her to argue for longer than half a moment, but she couldn't leave without correcting Rita's obvious mistake. "You mean Mr. Connor."

"No," Rita countered, "I mean Mr. Cole. Mr. Cole wanted me to keep an eye on you and make sure you get your rest," the housekeeper told her. "He said that if I didn't watch you, you would try to do too much and forget about taking care of yourself. Nobody wants to see you getting sick."

Stacy frowned. That didn't make any sense. She and Cole weren't exactly on the best of terms after that ride back from the hotel. "Are you sure you're not talking about Mr. Connor?"

"I am sure," Rita told her. "They do not look alike. And besides, Mr. Connor is a good man, but he is not the one who is in love with you."

The housekeeper had to be imagining things. "Well, I have news for you, Rita. Neither is Mr. Cole," Stacy assured her. "And whatever he might have told you—" she began, positive that the woman had misunderstood something or taken it out of its context, but she never got the chance.

"He did not tell me anything, Miss Stacy," the housekeeper said with finality. "He did not have to. I can see it in his eyes."

There was no arguing with the woman, Stacy thought, giving up. Rita was just like Miss Joan, stubborn to the very end.

Stacy sighed. "I think I'll take that nap now," she told the woman, surrendering.

Rita smiled. "That is a very good idea. And don't worry about the little ones, they will be in good hands."

It must be nice, Stacy thought as she went into the small bedroom, to be so confident. The only time she had been that confident about something, she turned out to be wrong.

Even if Rita was determined to argue that point.

But Rita was wrong even if she didn't know it.

Stacy put her head down on the pillow and was sound asleep before she could complete her thought.

Chapter 10

It was dark when she woke up.

And there was a blanket draped over her.

Stacy didn't remember pulling a blanket over herself. She barely remembered lying down. What she did remember was that she'd intended to sleep for no more than twenty minutes—if that much.

The sun had been coming into her room when she lay down. It was gone now. This had to be way past twenty minutes.

Sitting up, she pulled the blanket off and placed it on the edge of the bed. She became aware of people talking to each other. And laughing.

Stacy got off the bed and walked to the door. Opening it allowed not just the living room light and the laughter to enter, but the feeling of warmth, as well. Both Connor and Cole were home and each of them was holding one of the twins. She couldn't help thinking how totally natural that looked.

"I'm sorry," Connor said the moment he saw her coming into the living room. "We were making too much noise and woke you up."

"Don't apologize," she told him. "I wasn't supposed to sleep this long." She looked around for a clock. "What time is it?"

"Just a little after six," Cole answered.

"Six?" Stacy echoed incredulously. "It was just one o'clock when I lay down. I was only supposed to nap for a few minutes," she said, totally distressed.

"You were supposed to nap for as long as you needed to," Cole told her. You've been up for practically the last forty-eight hours. It was bound to catch up with you," he pointed out.

Rita was in the room, as well, and she turned her attention toward the housekeeper. "I'm sorry, Rita," she apologized. "I didn't mean to leave you with all this work."

"You did not leave me with anything," the older woman informed her. "I was the one who told you to get some sleep," she reminded Stacy. "You were more tired than you knew. Mr. Connor and Mr. Cole each took turns dropping by during the day so I was not alone the whole time. And they have both been here since five o'clock. The babies have been angels," the housekeeper added, then told her, "You are up just in time for dinner."

"Dinner? Didn't you already serve dinner?" she asked. Dinner was on the table like clockwork at five every night. Why had the woman postponed serving it?

"Tonight, Rita decided to wait," Cole told her.

She couldn't help wondering if it was Rita who'd made the decision or if Connor and Cole had told the housekeeper to hold the meal until she woke up. She slanted a glance at Rita. The housekeeper was beginning to seem more like a benevolent dictator than a tyrant to her.

"Did you come in and cover me when I was asleep?" Stacy asked the woman as she followed Rita to the dining room.

Rita paused for a moment to turn and look at her. "You are a grown woman. You can cover yourself if you feel the need. Besides, I was busy taking care of the babies. Sit," she ordered, then went into the kitchen to bring in the meal she had prepared.

Connor and Cole placed the drowsy twins back in the crib and came to the dining room behind her.

Stacy looked over at the McCullough brothers who were taking their seats at the table, Connor at its head and Cole across from her.

Connor smiled as he observed, "You look better now, Stacy. I don't mind admitting that I was getting worried about you."

Cole avoided making eye contact with her. She suspected she knew why.

"It was you, wasn't it?" she asked him. "You came in and covered me. Why didn't you wake me up?"

"Because you looked so peaceful." Not to mention beautiful, he thought, looking at the fiery redhead. And then Cole stopped abruptly. "That was a trick, wasn't it?"

"I don't know what you mean," Stacy answered innocently.

He would have denied being the one who covered her

if Stacy hadn't distracted him by asking why he hadn't woken her up. Blue eyes met blue. "I don't remember you being devious."

Stacy smiled, tossing her head and sending waves of red swinging about her face. "I prefer to think of it as resourceful—and that's something I've had to become. Resourceful, not devious," she clarified.

The strong aroma of fried chicken preceded Rita as she came in carrying a large heaping platter of legs and breasts. The housekeeper placed it in the middle of the table.

"That smells heavenly," Stacy told the woman with deep appreciation.

Rita beamed. "I know. Mashed potatoes and green beans are coming," she announced.

Stacy began to get up. "Let me help you with that."

Rita pushed the chair back in under her. For a small lady, the housekeeper was surprisingly strong.

"You sit," she ordered. Turning to Cole, she instructed, "You, come with me."

"Yes, ma'am," he replied with a grin.

Watching Cole get up and follow Rita, Stacy felt her heart being tugged. His grin had the same effect on her now that it always used to have—before things went so wrong.

If she wasn't careful, Stacy silently warned herself, she was going to fall into the same trap she had all those months ago. She was supposed to learn from her mistakes, not make them all over again.

Coming back into the dining room, Cole placed the large bowl of warm mashed potatoes right next to her.

"I remember you were partial to mashed potatoes," he told her.

Stacy had no idea why that should have touched her. But it did. He had remembered a small, inconsequential detail about her that made no difference in the grand scheme of things—but it did to her. And he had remembered.

"There is gravy," Rita said, putting the gravy bowl right next to the potatoes. Retreating, she went to bring in the green beans. When she returned, the housekeeper placed the vegetables beside the fried chicken. "Now eat," she dictated, declaring, "Everything is already getting cold."

A small wail was heard from the living room. Reacting in unison, Connor and Cole both began to rise.

"I said eat," Rita reminded them in a firmer voice. "I will take care of the babies." Her eyes swept over the threesome seated at the table. "I expect to see clean plates when I come back."

Stacy smiled to herself. "Definitely a benevolent dictator," she said after the woman had left the dining room.

"I'm beginning to think that she's actually Miss Joan, wearing a wig," Cole said.

"No, she's too short," Connor pointed out. "But somewhere, way back a couple of generations ago, those two had to have shared the same forebearers."

No sooner had they finished discussing the similarities of the two women's approaches to the people around them than Rita walked back into the room with one twin in her arms.

"I need to get a bottle," she told them matter-of-factly. On her way to the kitchen, the housekeeper still paused to see if the people she technically worked for were eating as she had told them to. "How is everything?" she asked.

From her tone it was clear that she expected only to hear good things.

Stacy spoke up first. There was no hesitation in her voice when she said, "Perfect."

"You've outdone yourself, Rita," Connor said, adding his voice to Stacy's.

"Fried chicken's a little dry," Cole deadpanned. And then he couldn't keep it back any longer and laughed. "Just kidding."

Rita's dark eyes narrowed as she gave Cole a piercing stare.

"You are lucky that my hands are busy with this baby right now, or you would learn that there is nothing funny about saying something insulting about my cooking that is not true."

Cole backed off immediately. "Everyone knows you couldn't ruin anything you made if you tried, Rita," Cole told her, turning his charm up full volume. He gave her a soulful look. "Am I forgiven?"

Stacy fully expected the woman to relent, succumb to Cole's charm and say yes.

Instead, she heard Rita tell him, "I do not forgive so easily. I will be keeping my eye on you, Mr. Cole," she warned.

"Then I'll just have to do something special," Cole teased.

In response, Rita's expression only grew darker. Stacy couldn't tell if the woman was only pretending to be annoyed, or if her humor was on a completely different wavelength than Cole's.

Cole appealed to his older brother. "You're her favorite. Tell her I was only kidding."

"Don't look at me," Connor said, pretending to want nothing to do with the joke that had fallen so completely flat on its face. "I was busy eating and enjoying this wonderful meal that Rita made for us. And by the way, the chicken, Rita," he said, looking at the housekeeper, "is fantastic."

"Fantastic," Cole echoed with enthusiasm.

"You had your chance," was all Rita said to Cole as she walked into the kitchen with the baby.

"Maybe you shouldn't tease her like that," Stacy told Cole.

Now that the housekeeper was in the other room, Cole appeared totally unfazed. "Rita knows that I don't mean anything by it. It's a way for everybody to blow off some steam. We'd all go through fire for that lady and she would readily do the same for all of us. It's a given," he told Stacy.

Stacy wasn't a hundred percent convinced. "I don't know. Rita looked pretty annoyed to me just now."

Stacy fell silent as Rita returned to the dining room. Mike was tucked into the crook of her arm and she fed him with the warmed bottle. She tossed an icy glance in Cole's direction.

"Only one piece of pie for you tonight," she decreed as she continued walking to the living room.

Rita was kidding, Stacy thought. The slight smile at the corners of the woman's thin mouth right before she walked out gave her away.

"I guess she does realize that you're kidding," Stacy said. "This is going to take some getting used to."

It was only after she'd said it that she understood

what that sounded like—like she intended to stay longer than just a few days or, at most, another week looking after the babies until their mother could be tracked down or came forward on her own.

From the smile she saw on Connor's lips, that was exactly what he was thinking. If she said anything in protest, that would only make things worse, so she decided to let the whole thing go.

Instead, she asked, "Anyone hear anything from the sheriff about the babies' mother? Has he got any leads yet?"

Cole laughed at the way she'd worded her question. "This isn't exactly a detective novel, Stacy. And I think if the sheriff had any *leads*, he would have either sent Cody to the ranch to tell us or come himself. Looks like the kids' mother is going to remain a mystery for at least a while longer."

"You don't think that anything happened to her, do you?" Stacy asked as she suddenly thought of that possibility.

"Exactly what do you mean by 'happened'?" Cole asked.

She resisted saying more, but she supposed that there was no getting away from the possibility of that being one of the scenarios.

Even so, the words were hard for her to utter. "You know, like, she died."

"You mean right after leaving them on my doorstep?" Cole asked.

This was gruesome, but she was the one who had brought it up, so she continued advancing the theory. "I know that sounds like a coincidence, but coincidences *do* happen sometimes."

"This is a very small town, Stacy," Connor gently reminded her. "Unless the twins' mother was buried in a rock slide without a trace, if someone dies in or near Forever, Rick would know about it."

"All right, let's look at this whole thing from a different angle," Stacy suggested.

"Such as?" Cole asked, unclear as to where she wanted to go with this.

"Such as the twins' mother deliberately *picked* you to leave her babies with," Stacy told him.

He still didn't understand. "What are you saying?" Cole asked.

"I'm saying that the easiest thing for the twins' mother to do might have been to leave the babies on the clinic doorstep. Or on Miss Joan's doorstep, for that matter. But, instead, their mother left them on *your* doorstep. She *picked* you, not anyone else," Stacy stressed.

Cole was definitely not ready to go with that theory. "Maybe she just picked the first doorstep she came to."

Stacy shook her head. "The Healing Ranch is out of the way. And the bunkhouse is even *more* out of the way than that. No, I think she picked you on purpose." The more she considered the matter, the more Stacy was sure that she was on to something. "I'm not saying the twins are yours. I'm just asking if you know anyone who was, well, in the family way recently? Someone you were nice to?"

The look he gave Stacy said she had to be kidding. "I spend most of the week here, working with Connor, and usually a couple of days and nights at the Healing Ranch, which is dedicated to helping troubled boys, so, no, I haven't noticed anyone in the *family way* in the last few weeks—or before then, either," Cole told her.

Stacy sighed. So much for that idea. "So then you haven't noticed anybody who looked as if they were expecting a baby?"

"No, *nobody*," Cole answered, just in case there was any room for doubt.

"Why don't we just leave this up to the professionals?" Connor suggested, specifying, "Rick, Cody and Joe."

Stacy sighed. "I guess we don't have any other choice."

"Don't sound so depressed about it, Stacy," Connor told her. "Forever might be a small town, but Rick's not a hayseed and he's been at this for some time now.

"And you're forgetting about the reservation. If their mother is still out there, they'll find her. Now let's do justice to Rita's dinner or she just might decide not to let *any* of us have dessert."

That sounded a little over the top, considering that the woman did work for him. "You're kidding, right?" Stacy asked.

"When it comes to Rita," Connor answered, "I've learned not to kid."

Stacy couldn't tell if he was serious or not. She decided not to question him. They had bigger concerns right now.

"You know," Cole said, thinking, "what you said isn't half bad."

Stacy looked at him a little uncertainly. "You mean about someone deliberately leaving the babies so that you'd be the one to find them?"

"Yeah. It doesn't have to be someone I know, just someone who knows me."

"Because you're so wonderful?" Had he gotten a swelled head after all? It occurred to her that he might have changed a lot in the last eight months.

"No, because whoever their mother is, she knows I wouldn't let anything happen to those babies and I'd make sure they were safe."

Much as she hated to admit it, Stacy knew he had hit the nail on the head. And, if she was being honest, she was rather relieved that the babies weren't Cole's—even though she told herself that wasn't supposed to matter to her.

But it did.

Chapter 11

Stacy frowned slightly to herself as she was feeding Mikey. Mikey was more restless than his twin, but that wasn't why she was frowning.

Almost two weeks had gone by and there was still no sign of the twins' mother. Stacy found that rather disturbing and upsetting. Primarily for the twins, because abandonment like that brought issues with it down the line.

However, on a personal level, she found herself hoping that their mother would take a little longer coming forward. She was really beginning to enjoy taking care of the infants, who seemed to be growing daily right in front of her eyes.

Maybe she felt this way because she told herself that this was just temporary, that she'd have to give them up to their mother soon. Not only was she enjoying every minute she was spending with Kate and Mike, but she kept finding new things to enjoy about them.

Like bath time.

Initially, Stacy had been afraid to attempt to bathe either twin and had just used a washcloth to clean them. It was Cole, not Connor or Rita, who showed her how to properly bathe the twins. He'd helped her get over her fear of somehow inadvertently allowing one of the twins to slip beneath the water and drown.

"There's really nothing to it," Cole told her. "You just make sure you support the baby's head by resting it in the crook of your arm and you use your other hand to wash the baby. You take a washcloth that you've soaped up, rub it along that little body and then you rinse the baby off with the water in the little tub."

"Little tub?" Stacy repeated.

"Yes. I brought it down from the attic last night," Cole told her, then added, "Cassidy left it behind when she married Will and moved to his ranch."

"Why not just use the kitchen sink?" Stacy asked. She knew that Connor and Cole had done some renovations to the house, including replacing the old sink that had been there for decades. "It certainly seems big enough, at least when the twins are this size."

"The tub's softer," Cole told her. "It's easier on their little bottoms. Miss Joan took up a collection for the baby that Cassidy rescued the same way she did when Devon had hers. Being Miss Joan, she'll probably do the same for these two if their mother doesn't show up," he said, nodding at the twins, who were both in the crib they shared. "The woman's got a heart of gold even if at times it seems like she has a tongue that can cut a person in half at ten paces."

Stacy laughed. "That's a pretty accurate description of Miss Joan. I guess that's what makes her so interesting."

"She is that," he agreed. "No doubt about it." And then he looked at Stacy. "All right, enough talking. Are you ready to do this?"

"You mean give the twins a bath with you?" She actually felt butterflies fluttering in her stomach, but she did her best to ignore that.

"More like you give the bath and I'll be there if you need me," Cole corrected. "Too many arms in the tub might get in the way," he explained.

She supposed he had a point, although she wished it was his arms in the tub, not hers—at least, this time around.

"Sure, I can do this," Stacy said, only because saying she couldn't, or would rather that he do it, made her sound like she was afraid, and she refused to come off that way—even if it was true.

"Yes, you can," he agreed quietly, his eyes meeting hers.

He was just encouraging her, Cole told himself. It had nothing to do with the growing feelings he was trying to deny.

Cole fetched the tub and placed it on the spacious kitchen counter. "Okay," he told Stacy, stepping back. "It's all yours."

She filled the small rubber tub halfway with lukewarm water, making sure she had soap and washcloths handy. "It's ready."

Cole nodded and went to her room, where they'd moved the crib a few days ago. "Looks like you're up first, Mikey," he said. He swiftly took off the baby's shirt and unfastened the diaper's tabs for easy removal, then holding him, quickly brought the infant into the kitchen. "He's all yours," he told Stacy.

Taking Mikey, she positioned him in the crook of her arm, just the way Cole had told her. Then, before immersing Mikey in the tub, she looked at Cole and asked, "You're not leaving, are you?"

Cole smiled reassuringly at her. "I'm going to be right here. Because bath time's fun, isn't it, Mikey?" he asked the baby.

He splashed the little boy ever so lightly, just enough to get a response, but not enough to frighten him or make the woman who was trying to bathe him nervous.

Stacy felt as if time had stood still as she gently lathered the infant's body then rinsed away the soap film on it.

"I guess I'm finished," Stacy said several minutes later, glancing at Cole to see if he thought she'd missed anything.

"Let's see, lather, wash, rinse—yes, you're done," he agreed. "Why don't you take this big boy out of the tub and I'll wrap a towel around him, and then you can dry him off?"

"Sounds good."

Within moments, Cole had a large, fluffy towel wrapped loosely around the baby and she was patting him dry.

"We did it," she declared with a note of triumph a few minutes later. This was just a minor thing, but she still felt really good about the accomplishment. "I guess we make a pretty good team," she told Cole happily.

Their eyes met over the infant's head and Cole felt an all-too-familiar pull. One he hadn't felt since Stacy had left his life. He'd almost forgotten the swirling warmth that accompanied that feeling.

"I guess we do," Cole answered.

For a split second, he struggled with the strong urge to kiss Stacy. Just to kiss her, to reconnect with this woman he had once felt so strongly about.

But just then, Rita walked in, scattering the moment as she surveyed the kitchen.

"Are you going to be finished soon?" she asked, looking from Cole to the woman holding the baby. "I need my kitchen."

"One twin down," Cole told her, "one to go."

"All right," Rita said. "But don't take all day."

"You heard the lady," Stacy said, handing over Mike to him. "Bring me Katie."

"I'll just get him dressed and be right back with twin number two," Cole told her, hurrying out of the room.

It went faster this time. Stacy didn't know if it was because she felt a little more confident about what she was doing after having bathed Mikey, or if it was because she knew Rita wanted to take the kitchen over and she didn't want to keep the housekeeper waiting indefinitely.

"You're getting really good at this," Cole told her as he wrapped a dripping Katie up in another soft white towel.

His praise pleased her and Stacy smiled in response. "Piece of cake," she said, trying to sound blasé. But in her heart, she was really grateful for his kind words.

Careful, Stace, you don't want to risk going down that path again. He just gave you an offhanded compliment. It wasn't a declaration of love. Besides, you know where a declaration of love leads you—nowhere.

She had to remember that this was first and foremost a favor to Connor. She was also doing this to make sure that the twins didn't wind up getting shipped off to social services. There was no other reason for her to be here, Stacy told herself. She *had* to remember that and focus all her attention on the twins, not on a man who had disappointed her and broken her heart.

Not unless she wanted to endure a repeat performance—which she didn't.

But it was hard to look at Cole in such a negative light. Especially when every time they interacted, she was seeing him at his best. Seeing him being so good with the twins.

The solution to that was not to interact with him, Stacy knew that. However, that was much easier said than done because, although Cole worked hard and was away from the house a good part of each day, somehow it felt to her that he was there a great deal more than he was.

Another week passed and Stacy found that life had arranged itself into an amicable routine for her. Most important of all, although it somehow seemed to happen without her realizing it, she really had become part of a family unit.

Not since her parents died had she been with a family. Feeling so close to the McCulloughs didn't mean that she loved her Aunt Kate any less. Aunt Kate had been a vital part of her life both before her parents had died and after.

But Kate had been only one person. What Stacy found with the McCulloughs was the same thing that she'd found when she'd first been adopted. People to depend on—who also depended on her. People who cared and whom she was slowly but surely finding herself caring about.

Try as she might to resist and talk herself out of it, it was happening. Happening because she knew that part of her needed this, needed to feel as if she was part of a thriving unit.

During that third week, Connor and Cole had moved the twins' crib upstairs to Cassidy's old room. Meanwhile, Stacy had been moved into Cody's old bedroom, which was next to the twins' new room. That way, she could get some much-needed rest at night but still be able to hear the twins if one of them cried.

The move to the new quarters did something else, as well. It made the situation begin to feel permanent, and she knew she couldn't allow herself to get used to that, because despite appearances to the contrary, this *wasn't* permanent. These babies had a mother out there somewhere. A mother who, once she came back to her senses, would rush to reclaim the twins.

And, Stacy told herself, *she* had a life out there, as well. A life that had nothing to do with the McCullough family.

Or with Cole.

She kept reminding herself of that, but she found that it took more and more effort on her part to hang on to that thought.

Feeling restless one evening, Stacy went outside after dinner and after the twins had been put down for—she hoped—longer naps than they'd been taking up to this point.

After checking with Rita to see if the housekeeper

needed any help with the dishes—and being summarily turned down—Stacy slipped out the front door to get a little air. She had gone out alone, but it wasn't long before she had company.

She'd expected that Connor would come out to make sure she was all right—he was like that. She was beginning to think of him as her own big brother, and since she was an only child, it was a nice feeling.

But instead, when she turned around, she found herself looking up at Cole.

Suddenly, she felt her blood rushing through her veins at a speed that would have made a flash flood envious.

Damn it, what's wrong with you? Stacy scolded herself for being so juvenile. *He's just coming out for some air, same as you.*

"Are you all right out here?" Cole asked.

Was it her imagination, or was he standing too close? It was a cold night, but she was far from that at the moment. She felt warm.

"I'm fine," Stacy told him. "Why?"

Cole shrugged. Maybe he shouldn't have followed her out here. He thought about turning around and going back in. But it was as if his feet were glued to the ground. He wasn't going anywhere.

"Well," he answered, "it's kind of cold tonight and you went out without a jacket or anything. I thought you might have forgotten to take it with you."

She struggled to work up some resentment over the fact that he was treating her like a child—but she couldn't quite do it.

Still, she had to say something. She didn't want him thinking of her as some hapless adolescent. "I think you've been taking care of the twins too long. I don't need looking after."

"Humor me," he told her. Saying that, he produced a shawl. "It was the first thing I could find. I think it's Rita's," he added.

She glanced at it. It looked silver in the moonlight. "She's not going to be happy that you took this."

He had a different take on Rita's reaction. Her first concern was the health and well-being of everyone in her household.

"Don't let that gruff exterior fool you," he told Stacy. "She'd be the first one to tell me to get you to wrap this around your shoulders." He continued holding it out to her.

With a sigh, she took it and threw it over her shoulders. "Okay. I put it on. Happy?" she asked, looking anything but that herself.

His mouth quirked in a grin. "Delirious," he responded.

She thought it best if she changed the subject to something neutral, rather than go on looking up into his eyes, because she'd wind up drowning here. So she turned to look at the land stretching out to infinity beyond the ranch house.

"You know, traveling around with Aunt Kate and going to all those cities that she wanted to see, I forgot how peaceful and quiet it is out here."

He couldn't quite make out if she thought that was a good thing—or a bad one. "Some people would say that translates into *deadly dull*. A lot of people who grow up in Forever can't wait to spread their wings and do exactly what you did—see the world."

She hadn't left because she wanted to see the world;

she'd left because she needed to get away from him, away from the pain of being here. But she wasn't about to get into that again. She struggled to focus her thoughts and not get caught up in Cole and the way things had once been.

Going back to what he'd just said, Stacy asked him, "Didn't you ever want to do that?"

He looked at her for a long moment, as if weighing whether or not to answer her. Trying very hard not to get lost in eyes that had always been his undoing. Finally, he asked, "Honestly?"

"Of course."

"No," he told her. "I like it here. I like knowing everyone who lives near and around Forever. Like the feeling of accomplishment when I can help someone— not some anonymous stranger, but a neighbor, someone I *know.* And everyone's a neighbor around here." He smiled to himself, thinking of how that had to sound to her after her extended European vacation. "I guess that someone as sophisticated as you probably finds that kind of simplistic."

"No," Stacy answered. "Since we're being honest—" She took a breath, then said, "I find that kind of heart-warming."

"No you don't."

His response made her temper flare. Before she could tamp it down, she heard herself saying, "Don't tell me what I think or don't think. You don't know me as well as you think you do."

That brought up old wounds. "I found that out eight months ago."

The moment was ruined. She wasn't about to rehash

their past. There was no point to that and it wouldn't change anything that happened.

"I think you're right," she said, her voice taking a distant, formal tone. "It is cold out here. I should be getting back inside." She grasped at the first excuse she could think of. "It's probably time to feed or change one of the twins."

"Connor said he'd watch them."

"That doesn't make it any warmer out here," she told him, turning on her heel to go inside.

"Maybe not," Cole agreed.

But instead of following her inside, Cole moved and blocked her path. When she looked at him in confusion, he made no verbal response, tendered no excuse. Instead, he took hold of her shoulders and did what she'd been aching for him to do from the first moment she'd seen him in Miss Joan's diner.

He kissed her.

And she knew instantly that she wasn't over him.

Damn it, Stacy thought as she laced her arms around his neck, she really wasn't over him.

After all the hurt feelings, all the promises she'd made to herself about never opening up her heart to Cole again, she wasn't over him. Because if she were over him, she'd be pushing Cole away from her as hard as she could. And just as he would have looked at her, startled by her display of combined anger and strength, she would have told him what he could do with himself and those lips of his.

Those lethal, lethal lips.

But instead, Stacy found herself melting against him, kissing Cole back as hard as he was kissing her. Holding on to him when she should have been doubling up her fists and punching him, instead.

But she couldn't.

And didn't.

Because for the first time in more than eight very long months, she felt alive again. Eight months filled with going to museums and cafés, of seeing sights that others only read about, of touring places where history had once been made. She'd done all this and *none* of it made her pulse rush and her head spin the way both were doing right at this moment.

Where was her strength? Her self-respect?

Where the hell was *she*? Stacy silently demanded of herself.

She was absolutely lost in a kiss that not only took her breath away, but blotted out her mind, whisking her off to a place that only Cole could create for her.

This wasn't right. And yet she couldn't make herself pull free—and a part of her was praying that what was happening right now would never end.

Chapter 12

Cole could feel his heart slamming against his chest, making it hard for him to breathe. His pulse was racing, just the way it used to whenever he and Stacy were together like this.

Right at this moment, all he really wanted to do was pick her up in his arms and take her to his bed so they could make love. But even in his growing ardor, he knew that wasn't really possible. He'd left Connor upstairs with the twins in their room. His brother could come out at any moment.

And heaven only knew where Rita was. The woman had an uncanny knack of popping up at the most inopportune times, not to mention that in all likelihood Connor would hear them once they were upstairs in his room.

Much as he hated to admit it, this couldn't go any further.

Not tonight.

And he knew that if he continued kissing Stacy like this, despite his common sense, it definitely would go further. He was only human and had just so much self-control before he cracked. Every single fiber of his being wanted to make love with her.

What makes you think she wants to make love with you? the voice in his head mocked.

It was the voice of logic, but right now logic had very little to do with the way he was feeling.

Still, at least for now, he had to back off. Better to wait than to be shot down.

So, with the greatest reluctance, Cole ended the kiss and drew back his head. He had a feeling that an apology was due her, but it wouldn't come. All he could say was, "Lord, but I've missed you."

Stacy desperately tried to steel herself. A little more than eight months ago, Cole had pushed her away. Not physically but verbally. Even so, she was the one who had disappeared, not Cole.

And she'd left with just reason, but still, the act of actually leaving Forever—and him—had been hers. So, maybe, on some level, she should be explaining why— or at least telling him she was sorry.

But all that came out of her mouth now was, "I guess maybe I missed you, too."

Not exactly the greatest words of love to go down in the annals of history, Cole thought, but he knew that for someone like Stacy, who had a great deal of pride and trouble accepting fault, this was nothing if not a huge step forward.

Bending slightly toward her, Cole inclined his head and leaned his forehead against hers.

"I guess maybe we should go in before Rita comes out to find out what happened to us."

Stacy didn't really want to go inside. She wanted to stay out here, with him. But she'd be far safer going into the house.

Safer, not from Cole, but from herself.

Because she could feel herself succumbing to him, just the way she had the first time. But as glorious as that felt then, there would be consequences in the aftermath. And this time, she felt she had obligations. She couldn't just run off. Not until the twins' mother turned up.

"What if she doesn't turn up?" Stacy asked suddenly as they walked into the house.

"Rita?" he asked, slightly confused. Was she talking about the housekeeper coming out to look for them?

"No." Stacy's tone was impatient. "The twins' mother," she clarified. "What if the twins' mother doesn't turn up and the sheriff can't find her? What then?"

"It's been less than a month."

"What if she doesn't turn up?" Stacy repeated more insistently. "What are you going to do with the twins?"

Cole paused. He knew how Stacy felt about going to social services so soon, and now that he'd had time to think about it himself, he had to admit that he agreed with her on that score. That didn't exactly leave many options open to him.

Still, he shrugged away Stacy's concern. "I'll think of something. Something'll come up." Cole knew that sounded vague and nebulous, but it was the best he could do for now.

"And if it doesn't?" Stacy pressed.

"It will," Cole countered. Right now, he couldn't promise any more than that.

Coming up to them, her hands on her hips, Rita regarded both of them critically. "If you two are going to argue like this, go back outside."

Remembering that Cole had given her the housekeeper's shawl, Stacy quickly removed it from her shoulders and held it out to Rita.

"I think this is yours," she told the woman. "Thank you for letting me use it."

Rita's expression temporarily softened long enough for her to murmur, "Don't mention it."

Time for her to make her retreat, Stacy thought. "Well, I'd better go check on the twins," she said, one hand on the banister as she was about to go upstairs.

Rita's words stopped her in midstep. "They are asleep."

Stacy looked at the housekeeper, curious. "How can you tell?"

"When they are awake and need something, they cry. You can hear them through the floor," Rita told them, pointing toward the ceiling above her. "Do you hear anything through the floor?"

Stacy listened for a moment, then shook her head. "No."

"Then they are asleep," Rita concluded. A warning look came into her eyes. "Don't you go in now and wake them up, you hear me?" she told Stacy. "Not after all of Mr. Connor's hard work," the woman added as Connor came downstairs at the tail end of her words.

"I didn't work that hard," Connor assured the two women.

Rather than accept the man's protest, Rita gave him a withering look. "Do not contradict me."

"Wouldn't dream of it," Connor assured her.

He flashed the housekeeper a smile, the same one that always professed to the woman that they were on the same page and that he would never go against anything that she said.

"Good," Rita declared. "Then we understand each other—as we always do," she added, a slight twinkle coming into her eye. "If none of you require anything, I think I will go to bed. It has been a long day—and there is a book that I would like to finish."

"A book?" Stacy echoed, curious. She couldn't picture the woman immersing herself in anything other than the day-to-day realities of life at the ranch. "What kind of a book?"

"The old-fashioned kind. One with pages in it," Rita replied, her tone signaling that the conversation was going no further.

With that, the housekeeper turned on her heel and went to her quarters, which were at the rear of the house behind the kitchen.

"I didn't know Rita liked to read," Cole commented, turning toward his brother. "Did you?"

"No, but I suspect that there's a lot about Rita that we don't know," Connor told him.

"Aren't you the least bit curious what she reads?" Cole asked.

"Sure," Connor freely admitted, "but Rita deserves to have her privacy. She'll tell us if she wants us to know something," he added. And then he turned toward Stacy. "The twins are both sleeping at the same time for a change. I suggest that maybe you should turn in, too, and take advantage of that rare situation while you can."

"Maybe I will, at that," Stacy decided.

She was careful to avoid looking in Cole's direction, afraid that he might think she was talking about something other than just going to sleep.

Stacy had to admit that she'd been tempted—sorely tempted—earlier, but once she came back into the house and the full impact of what she'd been thinking of doing hit her, she knew that she couldn't give in to Cole—or herself, for that matter.

As much as he stirred her blood, there was no reason to think that this wouldn't all blow up on her again. A little more than eight months wasn't exactly a huge amount of time. There was no reason to think that Cole had actually changed his thinking when it came to what might be their future together.

He'd told her that he needed his space then. He probably still did. The fact that they were both under the same roof now only gave him the opportunity to give that classic old saying a try: having his cake and eating it, too.

Well, she wasn't a piece of cake and she wasn't about to let him sample anything more than he just had out on the front porch. If she did, she was convinced that she'd be the one to regret it.

Saying good-night to Connor and then, in a more reserved voice, to Cole, Stacy made her way upstairs to her room.

Closing the door, she locked it for good measure— just in case Cole was tempted to come in while she was sleeping.

Or is that wishful thinking on your part? a little voice in her head asked, taunting her.

She was too tired for this.

Damn that man, anyway. Cole's kiss had stirred up things he had no business stirring up. And the sooner she got to sleep, Stacy told herself, putting on her nightgown, the better off she'd be.

Except that she couldn't get to sleep.

Not for a long, long time.

Instead, Stacy tossed and turned, fervently hoping that somewhere along the line, sleep would somehow sneak up on her.

But the only thing that did sneak up on her were memories that she'd thought she'd successfully managed to bury. Obviously, she was wrong. Those memories weren't buried. They were very, very fresh.

This was all Cole's fault. If he hadn't kissed her, she'd be well on her way to getting over him.

Who are you kidding? Your pulse starts to rise any time he gets close to you. If you really wanted to get over him, you wouldn't be here, *you'd be at the hotel, clerking for Rebecca.*

With a deep, weary sigh, Stacy attempted to punch her pillow into a more comfortable, more accommodating shape. She failed.

It took her a long time to finally drift off. Just before she fell asleep, she promised herself that she was never letting Cole get close enough to kiss her again.

Never!

She woke up feeling more tired than when she'd gone to bed.

It took her a few moments to realize that one reason could be that she'd been dreaming about Cole. It seemed like even her subconscious mind was ganging up against her.

So then she tried to remember what she'd dreamed about. But the more she tried, the more elusive and out of reach her dreams became. All she could recall was that the dreams were about Cole and that when she'd finally woken up, she was smiling from ear to ear.

Sitting up in bed, Stacy dragged her hand through her hair, struggling to come to and pull herself together.

It was after she'd finished washing her face and while she was still brushing her teeth that she noticed almost seven hours had passed by since Connor had said he'd put the twins to bed.

They'd slept through the night!

That seemed almost impossible, given their age. Stacy remembered hearing that, on the average, babies usually slept through the night only by the time they reached about four months—if their parents were lucky.

"I guess the twins are really exceptional," she said aloud, feeling a tinge of pride for a second.

However, that was followed, for some reason, by a sense of urgency. It swept over her, starting in the pit of her stomach and quickly progressing on to the rest of her.

Something was wrong.

She could feel it.

Stacy quickly threw on her clothes, all the while telling herself that she was overreacting and letting her imagination run away with her. After all, she had no real experience when it came to dealing with babies and she really had no reason to suspect that something might be wrong.

She just did.

Even so, Stacy forced herself to calm down before she left her bedroom. The last thing she wanted was to have Connor or Cole thinking she was some crazy person, given to flights of fantasy and anticipating the very worst for no reason.

After putting on her shoes, she took a deep breath and left her bedroom, then immediately went into the twins' room.

They were both in their crib. Drawing closer, she saw their little chests were subtly moving up and down.

See, they're breathing. You're just being paranoid.

Calm now, Stacy turned away and was about to tip-toe out again.

She had no idea what made her turn back again, or what made her lean over the crib railing and kiss first Katie's forehead and then Mikey's, but she did.

The twins were both burning up.

Chapter 13

Stacy's heart instantly felt as if it had constricted and was now lodged in her throat. Rushing out of the twins' room, she knocked urgently on Cole's door.

"Cole, wake up!" she cried through the door. "They're sick, the twins are really sick!"

As if in unison, the door she was knocking on as well as the one next to it, Connor's door, flew open. The oldest McCullough was wide awake, wearing a pair of old jeans and shrugging into his shirt.

"Sick how?" he asked.

"What's wrong with them?" Cole asked, his voice blending with his brother's. "Give me details." Shirtless, he was the first one into the twins' room.

"They're burning up," Stacy told them. She was doing her best to stay calm, but it wasn't working. All sorts of soul-draining scenarios were flooding her head.

"Have you taken their temperature?" Connor asked.

She looked at him blankly for a second before she felt her brain kicking in. "Do you have a baby thermometer?"

Connor shook his head as he followed her into the twins' room. Cole, already there, was passing his hand over first one small forehead, then the other. He was frowning.

"If we had one," Connor told her, "either Devon or Cassidy took it with them when they left. There wasn't any need to have a baby thermometer—until now."

"All you have to do is touch them to know that they're running a fever," Stacy told Connor. "Their foreheads and little bodies are really hot."

"She's right," Cole told his brother. "They are."

Wanting to see for himself, Connor went the old-fashioned route. He pressed his lips against each of the twins' foreheads the way he remembered his mother doing whenever Cody or Cole were sick.

Straightening up again, he nodded grimly. "You're right," he told Stacy. "They are hot."

"I hate being right," she retorted. "Shouldn't we be trying to lower their temperatures by immersing them in a tub of cold water or something?" For some reason, she recalled reading an article once describing lowering a baby's temperature using that method.

Cole thought he had a better idea. "Why don't we get them to the clinic?" he said, looking from Stacy to Connor. "They probably need medicine and one of the doctors at the clinic would know the best one to prescribe."

Stacy glanced at the watch that was hardly ever off her wrist. "Isn't it too early for the clinic to be open yet?"

"I'll call Dr. Dan at his house," Connor told Stacy, adding as he walked out of the room, "You two get them ready to drive into town."

Stacy's hands were shaking as she tried to slip a pull-over shirt and a pair of pants over Katie's sleepwear. She didn't want to risk the baby getting chilled when she was being taken out to the truck.

Cole noticed the way her hands shook. "They're going to be all right," he assured her, his voice low, comforting. "Babies run fevers all the time. It's just the first time it happens that's the scariest."

He sounded so calm, Stacy thought. How did he do it? "You're not worried?" she asked Cole, slipping a hat on the baby.

Katie was fussing, resisting being dressed. It was obvious that she was miserable and cranky. Lying next to her, Mikey was whimpering.

"I didn't say that," Cole answered. "I am," he admitted. "I just know that this is not unusual."

"It is to me," Stacy told him, fervently wishing that she was the one with the fever, not either one of the twins.

Connor came back into the bedroom. "Okay, I called Dr. Dan. He said he'd meet us at the clinic."

"You've got work to do here," Cole reminded his older brother. "No sense in all three of us going to the clinic with the twins."

"But—" Connor began to protest.

"That's okay, I've got this," Cole assured him. "Stacy can sit in the back, holding one of the twins, the other can make the trip in the basket I found them in. They can't both fit in there anymore, but if I put one of them in it, he'll still fit. I'll strap the basket in with a seat belt." Cole could see what his brother was thinking.

"Way ahead of you, Connor," he said. "The second we get back from the clinic and bring the twins home, I'm heading back into town to buy a couple of car seats at the emporium so that we can transport the babies safely."

Connor still appeared a little dubious. "Sure you don't want me to drive?"

"I've got this," Cole repeated, taking out the keys to his truck.

"Maybe you should put a shirt on?" Connor tactfully suggested.

Cole glanced down at his chest. "Oh. Right. One second," he told them, hurrying back into his bedroom.

"And boots," Connor called after him.

"Right!"

Less than a minute later, Cole was back in the twins' bedroom, pulling on a work shirt. Closing a few buttons, he tucked his shirt into his jeans and looked at Stacy. "You ready?"

She barely nodded. "Let's go," she urged, holding Katie against her. She could feel the heat from the baby's little body permeating her own skin. If anything, it felt as if Katie's temperature had gone up.

They all hurried outside to Cole's truck. Stacy handed Katie off to Connor so she could get into the back seat.

He gave the twin back to her, then helped secure the seat belt around both of them. Meanwhile, Cole had placed Mikey in the wicker basket, then pulled the seat belt tightly around it before pushing the metal tongue into the slot.

Without a word, Cole rounded the rear of the truck to get to the driver's side.

"Last offer," Connor said as Cole climbed in behind the steering wheel.

Cole flashed him a heartfelt smile. He was grateful for the offer, but at the same time, he knew how the work on the ranch was beginning to pile up. He'd cut back on his time at the Healing Ranch in order to juggle helping out with the twins with working on the family ranch alongside of Connor.

"Thanks, but we'll be okay," Cole told him. "All of us. Tell Rita I'm going to be hungry when we get back so she should set a big breakfast aside for me and one for Stacy."

"Yeah, I'll be sure to tell her," Connor told him. "Call me when you know anything." He closed both doors, but the windows were each cracked open so they could hear him.

"In Cole's case, that might not be for a long time," Stacy quipped. It was her way of trying to stave off another attack of nerves.

"Call anyway," Connor said with a smile.

He stepped back as his brother started the truck.

Within a few moments they had pulled away from the main house and were on the road that led straight into Forever.

There was only the sound of the twins, fussing and whimpering for several miles. Cole could almost *feel* Stacy's tension as it continued to grow in the truck.

This couldn't be good for her.

"At least we don't have to worry about running into traffic here," Cole said in an attempt to distract Stacy and draw her into a conversation.

"Just the occasional stray mountain lion," Stacy commented. She didn't even bother looking up. Her attention was entirely focused on the two babies in the back seat.

"It's a big truck," Cole answered. "I can outrun a mountain lion if it comes to that." He glanced up into the rearview mirror to catch a glimpse of her face, "How are you holding up?"

"I'm not the one running a high fever."

"No," he replied, "you're the one who looks as pale as a ghost."

She didn't want any attention focused on her. She was too worried about the twins. "I didn't get a chance to put my makeup on."

This time when he looked up into the rearview mirror, his eyes met hers for a split second. "You don't wear any makeup."

She felt herself growing defensive. "Done right, it's not supposed to look like there's any makeup on at all."

"Then what's the point?"

"A question for the ages," she answered. And definitely one she didn't think merited discussion. "Can this thing go any faster?" she asked.

"Yes," he answered patiently. "But I don't want to shake the twins up."

She just wanted to get them to the doctor as quickly as possible. "Their fevers are practically sky high. I don't think they'll notice."

"Okay, faster it is," he told her, giving in and throwing the truck into fifth gear.

The truck responded instantly.

They made it to Forever in record time and drove right past Miss Joan's diner and several other establishments, coming to a screeching halt right in front of the clinic.

Dan was standing there, obviously waiting for them. He moved toward the truck the moment he saw them approaching.

"Bring them inside to the first exam room," he told them, waving the two adults into the clinic.

By now the twins were both crying, very vocal in registering their mutual distress.

Cole carried Mikey while Stacy brought in Katie.

Holding the baby to herself, she was murmuring to the little girl, saying anything and everything that came into her head in an effort to soothe the infant a little—and maybe herself in the process.

Because it was too early for either of the nurses to have come in yet, Dan had Stacy provide the extra set of hands he needed during each exam. When he finished with Katie, he handed the infant over to Cole and had Stacy help him with Mikey.

The entire time he conducted his examination, Stacy never took her eyes off Dan. She was watching the doctor's every move, gauging his every expression so that she could determine whether or not Dr. Davenport was telling her the truth about the babies' condition, or if he was just handing her a bunch of platitudes to keep her from overreacting.

She'd liked the doctor ever since he first came to Forever, but this was different. This involved two tiny human beings who had managed, without any effort at all, to wrap her heart around their tiny little fingers. She cared deeply about their welfare.

She didn't realize she was holding her breath until Cole leaned over and whispered, "Breathe," into her ear.

She shivered, shrugged off his words and moved a few inches away from him. Any farther and her view of the twins would have been obstructed.

She made an elaborate display of drawing in a big breath.

"Better," Cole mouthed.

She pretended she hadn't seen him do it.

Finally finished with his exam, Dan prepared two syringes, each filled with acetaminophen. He proceeded to inject a dose into the upper portion of first Katie's and then Mikey's chubby little upper thigh.

Stacy winced each time the needle went in. The babies didn't seem to even feel it. There was no change in their whimpering.

"Why did you just give them shots?" she asked.

"That was to lower their temperatures. A shot works faster than oral medication." The doctor carefully threw the syringes he'd used into a self-sealing hazardous waste container. "Their temperatures should be going down by the time you get them back to your ranch," Dan estimated.

That was best-case scenario. She wanted to be prepared for what happened if it wasn't.

"And if not?" Stacy challenged. "What if their temperatures remain high?"

Dan glanced in her direction for half a second, saying, "You give it a little longer."

She needed more than something so vague to go on. "How much longer?" Stacy asked, taking in a jagged breath.

Dan paused, as if to weigh a few factors, then answered, "An hour, at most. If their fevers still don't go down—which would be highly unusual—bring them back."

"And then what?" she asked.

"I'll keep them here for observation," Dan answered her calmly. He put a comforting hand on her shoulder. "One way or another, we're going to lick this thing, so don't worry."

She let out a shaky breath. "I hope you're right, Doctor."

"So do I, Stacy. So do I," he told her with a warm smile. "Wait here," he said, stepping out of the exam room. "I'll be right back."

"What do you think he's doing?" Stacy asked, gazing after the doctor. Picking up Katie, she cradled the baby against her and began rocking her.

"Possibly getting tranquilizers for you," Cole told her, picking up the other twin.

She turned to look at him. "Me?"

He pinned her with a look. "You're about to go off like a Roman candle. I think he's worried about you."

"*He's* worried about me?" she questioned, knowing that Cole was actually referring to himself.

"Maybe we're all worried about you. But you're not going to do these babies—or yourself—any good if you don't get a grip on yourself, Stacy."

She'd just about had it with his advice. "You told me that I wasn't going to be of any use to them if I didn't get some sleep. So I got some sleep and look what happened," she cried, looking down at Katie. "They're sick."

"Stace, your sleeping had nothing to do with them getting sick," Cole insisted.

"But if I wasn't asleep, I would have realized they

were coming down with fevers and I could have called the doctor *before* it got to be this bad."

"And if you had wings and a propeller, you could be a plane."

She stared at him. "That doesn't make any sense."

"And neither are you," Cole told her. He could see that she didn't understand. "Take a deep breath. Calm down," he ordered. "The doc's the best there is. You've got to have a little faith, Stacy."

Stacy felt tears forming in her eyes. She tried to blink them back, but they only slipped out.

"They're so little. And so helpless," she told him, her voice cracking.

Cole put his arm around her. "And they're going to grow up nice and healthy and bigger than you are," he told her. "Trust me."

Stacy let out a very shaky breath. "It's not up to you."

"No," Cole agreed. "But the faith part comes in when you have it about the one who it *is* up to."

She found herself wishing she could be like Cole: easygoing and trusting. "It's not as easy for me as it is for you," she told him.

He smiled at Stacy. "It's not easy for me."

Dan walked in just then with a box of small packets in his hands. "I want you to dissolve one of these in each of their bottles twice a day until the packets are all gone. That should take care of any remaining fever as well as the infection they seemed to have gotten. It's not as uncommon as you think," he assured Stacy and Cole. "Call me anytime if you have any questions or concerns, but if all goes well, these two are going to be back to their normal, healthy, noisy little selves within twenty-four hours," Dan promised.

"That fast?" Stacy questioned uncertainly.

Dan nodded. "Kids can have a high fever in the morning, be fine in the afternoon and suffer a slight relapse in the evening only to be a hundred percent well the next morning. They're resilient that way. The bad news is that this sort of thing goes on until they're about seven, so brace yourselves, you're in for a bumpy ride," he told them with a laugh. "Between you and me, as a proud father of three, I wouldn't have it any other way."

She felt just the slightest bit better. "I can't thank you enough," Stacy told the doctor.

"You already have. Now, I've got to excuse myself," he told them, crossing the threshold. "I've got a clinic to open up."

Turning away from them, he went to do just that.

Chapter 14

The babies' fevers broke before noon, first Mikey's, then Katie's. By one o'clock, both babies' foreheads were cool.

Even so, Stacy refused to let either one of the twins out of her sight. She held them, rocked them and sang to them, separately and together.

Clucking her tongue at Stacy, Rita brought her lunch to the twins' bedroom. When she came to clear away the tray an hour later, the housekeeper obviously saw that nothing had been touched.

Rather than picking it up, Rita just looked down at the tray, frowning.

"You don't like my cooking?" she questioned. However, instead of taking offense, the way Stacy expected her to, the woman actually made her an offer. "I can bring you something else."

Stacy gave the older woman a contrite smile. "I'm really not hungry right now, Rita. Why don't you just leave that?" she suggested. Sitting in the rocking chair, she was rocking Mikey to sleep. Katie had already drifted off and was in the crib, asleep. "I'll eat it later."

Rita's frown deepened just a tad. "Later it won't be warm."

"I'm sure it's good cold, too," Stacy told the housekeeper. "Everything you make is delicious."

Rita leveled a look at her, as if to tell her that flattery wasn't going to get her off the hook. "Mr. Cole and Mr. Connor won't be happy when they come back and find out that you are not eating."

It had been hard enough convincing Cole that he could leave and help Connor with the horses when they got back to the house with the twins this morning. She didn't need him clucking over her the way Rita was doing.

Stacy offered the woman her widest, albeit weariest smile. "Then we won't tell him, will we?"

Rita passed her hand over Mikey's forehead, no doubt to reassure herself that the baby's fever was gone.

"Maybe *you* won't," Rita began.

Stacy went all out in her appeal. "Rita, please. I just had the scare of my life with these two little ones. They're getting better, but my appetite's going to need some time to recover. The last thing I want—or need—is a lecture from Cole."

Rita pressed her lips together, a sure sign that she was suppressing some well-chosen words.

Sighing dramatically, Rita said, "It is against my better judgment, but have it your way." She paused, lingering over the crib and the other twin. She touched

Katie's forehead so lightly the baby didn't wake up. "Thank heavens their fevers are gone." Still looking down at Katie, she glanced over toward the other infant in Stacy's arms. "They are getting bigger. Soon they are going to need to be in separate cribs."

Stacy thought of the money her aunt had left her. There wasn't enough for a lavish lifestyle, but that sort of thing had never interested her. She just needed enough to get by until she eventually found work. But for now, since she was still staying here, she could afford to buy a second crib.

"That won't be a problem," Stacy told the house-keeper.

Rita said something under her breath in Spanish. Stacy couldn't tell from the woman's tone if she was saying something antagonistic, merely critical or just neutral. For now, Stacy thought it was more prudent to just let it go. She felt too tired and dull to engage in any sort of a lengthy verbal exchange.

After Rita left, Stacy rose from the rocking chair, and moving very slowly, she laid the sleeping infant in the crib near his twin. She held her breath, waiting, but Mikey continued sleeping, as did Katie.

Stacy returned to her rocking chair. Wanting to be there the minute one or both of the twins woke up, she sat, waiting.

It wasn't too long before Stacy found herself dozing off. She knew that she could just go to her own room right next door, but for now proximity meant everything to her. She needed to reassure herself that the twins were all right the minute she opened her eyes.

A sudden, unexpected thunderstorm delayed Cole and Connor's return to the house. Not because any road was washed out—there wasn't enough rain for that—but because the thunder wound up spooking a couple of the horses. They broke out of the corral and took off for open country.

Cole and Connor were forced to go after the two stallions, wanting to find them before it got dark and the horses ran the risk of falling prey to one or more of the hungry wolves that had been sighted in the area.

It wasn't easy, but they kept at it until they managed to find both horses.

It was well after seven by the time they brought the horses back to the stable and finally walked into the house.

As if they had phoned ahead to tell her they were returning, Rita was right there when they opened the front door.

"I have seen drowned rats that have looked better," Rita told them emotionlessly, greeting the two men at the door with towels.

"You're a saint, Rita," Connor said, taking one of the towels from her and drying off his face and hair.

"Albeit a sharp-tongued one," Cole couldn't help commenting, taking the other towel and vigorously rubbing it over his head. He felt as if he was wet clear down to the bone. "What about the twins?" he asked. He hadn't seen the babies in the last eight hours and he had found himself worrying about them. "How are they doing?"

"Much better. Their appetites are back and they finished their bottles. Twice," Rita happily reported. "Which is more than I can say for Miss Stacy."

Cole stopped toweling his hair and looked at the woman. "What do you mean?" he asked.

"I mean that she has not been out of their room except to get their bottles," Rita answered, disapproval dripping from each word.

Connor placed the towel down on the coffee table. "Has she eaten?" he asked Rita.

"No. I have brought her two trays, one with her lunch, one with her dinner when you did not return at the usual time." She paused for effect, then said, "I left the second tray next to the first one. I am willing to bet that they are both still exactly where I put them, untouched."

That was all he needed. Cole hurried over to the stairs.

"You need to eat, too," Rita called after him. "And to get out of those wet clothes."

"Later," he tossed over his shoulder, taking the stairs two at a time to the second floor.

Stacy stifled a startled squeal when the door to the twins' room flew open and Cole walked in, leaving drops of rainwater on the floor to mark his passage.

"You get caught in the rain?"

He saw the trays butted up against each other. As Rita had predicted, there was nothing touched on either one of them. Didn't Stacy realize that she needed to keep up her strength? Sometimes, she could really exasperate him—or was that just frustration because he wanted her so much? Wanted what he knew he couldn't have. She'd made that clear by leaving Forever with her aunt.

"No," he answered Stacy sarcastically. "I swam back home."

Stacy didn't even react to his sarcasm. She blinked, trying to focus and wishing he wouldn't look at her like that, making her feel vulnerable. Taking a breath, she asked Cole, "What time is it, anyway?"

"Late," he answered. Taking a breath and telling himself that upbraiding her for not taking care of herself would just have the opposite effect on her—she had always been as contrary as hell—he tried talking to her as if they were nothing more than friends. "The thunder spooked a couple of the horses. It took us this long to find them."

She nodded, as if this was an everyday occurrence. "You should change," she told him, looking down at the puddle forming at his feet. "And eat."

He found her suggestion ironic. "I could say the same thing to you."

"Why?" Too tired to get out of the rocking chair, Stacy remained sitting and gazed up at Cole. "I haven't been out in the rain."

"According to Rita, you've hardly been out of the room. And you haven't eaten," he said, gesturing toward the two trays the housekeeper had prepared and left on top of the bureau.

"The twins' fever is gone, just like Dr. Dan told us it would be."

As far as Cole was concerned, it only reinforced the point he was trying to get across to her. "Then why haven't you eaten?"

Stacy lifted her shoulders in a half shrug. "I'm not really hungry. I could stand to lose a few pounds," she interjected, hoping he'd accept that not eating was a choice on her part.

His eyes washed over her. "Only if you want to fill in as some farmer's scarecrow," he replied. "If you lose a few pounds, Stacy, you're going to be nothing but skin and bones."

Stacy laughed drily. "Words every woman wants to hear."

"You want words every woman wants to hear?" His hands on either side of the rocking chair's arms, he leaned in and with his face less than five inches from hers, he told her, "Go to bed."

Stacy raised her chin defensively. "You're not in charge of me."

"I am if you collapse in my house," Cole countered. Taking her by the wrist, he was about to raise her out of the chair and take her over to the neglected trays of food.

Annoyed, Stacey yanked her wrist free. Didn't he think she could take care of herself? That she knew if she needed to eat or not?

"I'm fine," she snapped at him. "Now go take care of yourself. Eat. And for heaven's sake, change your clothes." She wrinkled her nose. "You smell of rain and sweat."

He sighed, knowing it would do no good to argue with Stacy when she was like this. Turning on his heel, he walked out.

She was right, he needed to get out of his wet clothes. More than that, he needed to cool off. She'd managed, in the space of a few minutes, to press all his buttons, and right now he didn't trust himself not to say things to her that he couldn't take back once he calmed down.

"How is she?" Connor asked when Cole finally came downstairs again, this time in dry clothes.

"Peppery," Cole answered, sitting down at the dining room table.

"Well, I think you've come to expect that," Connor commented. He had already helped himself to the pot roast as well as an assortment of vegetables that Rita had made for dinner. "Still, I always liked Stacy. If you ask my opinion—"

Cole took a serving of pot roast. He was choosier with the vegetables, taking only the potatoes and carrots. "I'm going to get it if I ask for it or not, aren't I?" he asked stoically.

Connor went on as if his brother hadn't said anything. "She's the nicest girl out of all the ones you ever went out with. I actually thought the two of you were getting close to a commitment." He paused before asking, "What happened?"

Cole avoided his brother's eyes. "She took off," he said matter-of-factly, stating something that they were both aware of.

"And you didn't have anything to do with that?" Connor asked his brother.

Cole put his fork down and sighed as he looked at his brother. "Why all the questions? You really need a life, Connor," he concluded.

"I have a life." Connor finished the piece of roast beef he was eating. "The ranch and my family are my life, and right now, one of my family is in danger of having the best thing that ever happened to him slip through his fingers."

Cole looked at him, confused. "Just how did we go from my saying she's peppery to this?"

"When you're my age, you get pretty good at filling in the blanks," Connor answered.

Ignoring his dinner, Cole just stared at his brother.

"What do you mean, *your age*? You're only two years older than I am," he pointed out.

"And a hell of a lot smarter, apparently," Connor said. "All I'm saying is that Stacy left once. She's back now so you've got another chance. Make sure you don't wind up blowing it."

He wanted to tell Connor that he was wrong, that his big brother was sticking his nose into something that didn't concern him. But in both cases, Cole couldn't say that. Because having Stacy back *did* feel like a second chance and, just as importantly, because they were McCulloughs and family business *was* their business— even if it drove him crazy to be the recipient of all this so-called wise advice from Connor.

"I won't blow it," Cole finally said. "As long as you promise to back off a little." He finished his vegetables first. He'd always liked ending his meal with meat. "You know I'm not at my best with you looking over my shoulder, watching my every move."

"Well, somebody's got to keep you from going over the cliff—but I'll back off," Connor said to placate Cole for the time being. "Are the twins doing okay?"

Relieved to change the subject, Cole nodded. "The worst of it seems to be over. You know—" he reached for the apple pie and cut himself a slice now that he'd finished with dinner "—I don't know how Mom and Dad did it, Mom with the three of us and Dad with all four." Suddenly, all the sacrifices that his older brother had made for them came to mind. "For that matter, I really don't know how you did it."

Connor smiled. "Well, for one thing, I didn't have much of a choice."

That was a crock and Connor knew it, Cole thought.

"Yes, you did. You could have just gone off to college like you were planning to before Dad died."

Finished, Connor pushed his dinner plate aside. "And what kind of a person would that have made me?" he asked. "Leaving the three of you to be split up and placed with who knows what kind of people? I might be selfish, but I'm not *that* selfish."

Cole looked at his brother as if Connor had taken leave of his senses. "You don't have a selfish bone in your body. You never had. And I guess I never said this to you," he said, feeling a tinge of guilt, "but I really appreciate the sacrifice you made for Cody and Cassidy and me. And I know that they do."

Obviously embarrassed, Connor shrugged off his brother's gratitude. "We were all in this together. No need to thank me."

"Yeah, there is," Cole insisted. "I never really thought much about it until now, but there's a *huge* need to thank you. If you hadn't stepped up the way that you did, there's no telling how any of our lives would have turned out."

"You still would have been you, just as Cody and Cassidy would have still been who they are. Everything would have worked itself out. It usually does."

"Damn it, Connor," Cole said, frustrated, "I'm trying to thank you. Just accept it and stop telling me I don't need to."

"Okay, gratitude accepted," Connor told him. "Now, why don't you go back upstairs and see if you can coax Stacy out with some of Rita's fantastic apple pie?" he suggested, waving his hand at the pie that Rita had baked less than an hour ago. It was going fast. "I just had a piece myself and my mouth is still smiling. If this doesn't get Stacy to eat, nothing will. But get her down here fast before I'm tempted to eat the rest of it."

"I've got a better idea," Cole told him. "I'm going to bodily carry Stacy out of the room and bring her down to the table."

"You're going to strong-arm her?" Connor asked. "I'd do it carefully if I were you. That little lady is a lot tougher than she looks."

"That's okay," Cole told Connor. "I'll just toss her over my shoulder, fireman style."

Connor didn't bother hiding his amused smile as he helped himself to more pie. "If you say so."

Taking the piece he had cut for Stacy, Cole didn't bother answering as he left the room.

A little extra ammunition never hurt.

Chapter 15

Opening the door to the twins' room slowly so he wouldn't wake them up—if they *were* asleep—Cole held the plate with Rita's pie out in front of him like a peace offering.

"I come bearing apple pie."

When he received no response, Cole pushed the door farther open. And then he saw why Stacy hadn't said anything.

She was slumped in the rocking chair, her head to one side, sound asleep.

Looking at the scene, Cole smiled to himself. "Looks like it all caught with you, didn't it, Stacy? These little guys can really wipe you out if you're not careful."

Once he'd set the pie down on the tray closest to him, he turned his attention back to Stacy. He couldn't just leave her sitting there like that. If nothing else, she was going to wake up with an awfully stiff neck.

Very gently, he slipped one arm under Stacy's legs, the other around her back, and exercising extreme care, he lifted her up off the rocking chair. Watching her face, he half expected her to wake up at any second and demand to be let go.

What he *didn't* expect was to have Stacy curl up against his chest like a pet kitten. The old pull that had once been so much a part of their relationship was back. In spades.

"Good thing for you, you're asleep," he whispered under his breath. Moving carefully, he managed to close the door to the twins' room, then carried Stacy into her bedroom.

He crossed to her bed and gently laid her down. For a second, he just stood there, watching her. And then he sighed. "You tie me up in knots, Stacy. You know that, don't you? I'm not sure how much longer I can stay on my good behavior."

Cole was just pulling the covers over her when, still appearing to be asleep, Stacy caught his arm. The sudden move threw him completely off balance and he fell on her before he could stop himself.

Stacy woke up with a start, pushing him off her and to the floor before she was even fully conscious. Scrambling into a sitting position, she looked down at Cole, glaring at him.

"What the hell do you think you're doing?" she demanded.

Cole laughed drily. He would have thought that the answer would have been self-evident to her. "I'm trying to put you to bed."

"Yes, I can see that."

"No, really," he insisted. "Just you, just bed. You

were the one who caught my arm and pulled me down on you. I was just about to tiptoe out again."

Stacy rolled her eyes. "Oh, please, you can't come up with a better story than that?"

"I don't have to," he informed her. "It's the truth." He got up off the floor and dusted off his jeans. She was on her knees on the bed and he towered over her. "You've been here for over three weeks, Stacy. Given our history, don't you think that if I wanted to go to bed with you, I would have been a little more subtle about it than to leap on you while you were asleep?"

Stacy took a deep breath. It made sense, but she still wasn't all that sure. She felt her stomach tightening.

"I don't know. Would you have?" Her heart was pounding in her chest as she asked the question. The next moment, a surge of guilt made her relent. "I'm sorry, that wasn't fair. But you startled me." Still on her knees, she looked around the room blankly. "Where are the twins?"

"In their room. Sleeping peacefully," he added before she could ask. "I just thought that since they were sleeping, maybe you'd like to do the same." He frowned slightly. "I don't want to be rushing off with you to see Dr. Dan in the middle of the night."

She sniffed. "Don't worry. You won't have to. I don't get sick."

"Ah, I had no idea I was in the presence of a superwoman." His tone was slightly mocking. He blew out a breath. "Well, I'd better let you get your rest." He turned to leave, but this time she caught his hand in hers instead of his arm.

Turning back, he looked at Stacy, puzzled, waiting for an explanation.

"Don't go," she requested in a subdued voice. "Stay with me for a while."

That totally disarmed him.

"Okay," Cole responded cautiously.

He sat down on the bed beside her, not knowing what to expect. He tried to focus on the fact that she'd asked him to stay and not on the fact that she looked so desirable or on how much he wanted her. It wasn't easy because all he could think of was that last night they had spent together and how warm, pliant and giving she'd felt in his arms. If he took her into his arms now, would she feel that way again?

Get a grip on yourself, not her, Cole upbraided himself.

"I'm sorry I've been so surly and difficult," she said.

That surprised him. In the face of an apology, he relented and forgave her. "You were worried about the twins. We all were."

"No, I was surly and difficult even before they got sick." She flushed. This was hard for her, but she had to say it for her own peace of mind. "You've been nothing but nice to me since I got here and I've been taking things out on you."

"It's okay," Cole began, not wanting to dig up old wounds. It served no purpose, in his opinion. It could only hurt.

"No, it's *not* okay," Stacy insisted.

He sighed. "Stacy, I'm trying to move forward." He could see by the look on her face that *forward* wasn't a destination they would be reaching, at least not soon. Feeling as if his back was against the wall, he tried another, albeit blunt, approach. "What do you want from me, Stacy?"

Her eyes held his. "I want you to tell me what happened."

That didn't make any sense to him. "You know what happened. You were there."

"Yes," she acknowledged, "I was. And one minute it was the most wonderful night of my life and the next, you were putting enough distance between us to build another continent."

"You're the one who left."

She squared her shoulders. "Only after you did."

What was she talking about? He'd stayed right here in Forever. She was the one who had taken off. "I didn't leave."

"Yes, you did," Stacy insisted. "You left emotionally."

"You scared me."

Her eyes narrowed. Now he was just making things up. "I'm five foot two. You're over six feet, how could I have possibly scared you?"

"Because of the way I felt about you," he told her. "I thought we were just having a good time, but then suddenly it turned into something so much more. Something really intense." His eyes held hers. "Something, I felt, that was going to change the rest of my life."

"So you disappeared," she concluded.

"I backed off," Cole corrected. "I just needed a little time to get my head together, to deal with what I was feeling. By the time I did," he told her, "you were gone. Gone without a single word." And it had ripped out his heart. "I had no idea where you went or what had happened to you." The mere memory of it frustrated him even now. "Your aunt was gone, too, so I didn't even have anyone to ask."

She shook her head, confused. "I thought you wanted it that way."

"No. I didn't know what I wanted." Cole shifted so that they were only inches apart. "But I do now."

He looked at Stacy, knowing that he was taking a big risk, putting his feelings into words. But if he didn't take a chance, then he would probably lose the one thing that people strove so hard to find. "I want you."

She felt her heart leap up. With effort, she struggled to put it all into perspective. "Don't toy with me, Cole."

"I'm not." He took her hand in his. "I don't expect you to forgive me, or even to believe me. But if you could find it in your heart to—"

Cole never got the chance to finish his sentence. His mother and then his father had drummed it into his head not to talk with his mouth full, and right now, his mouth was completely engaged in something he'd only been dreaming and reminiscing about.

Stacy had sealed her lips to his in a passionate kiss, and all he could think of was that he needed to kiss her back or he'd lose her.

His heart rate accelerated to the point that he doubted any sort of a medical instrument could accurately register it. It was pounding hard against his chest and if he died now, he didn't care—as long as it was in this moment, a moment he'd been yearning for, praying for, for the last nine months.

Slipping his arms around Stacy, Cole pulled her urgently to him.

The kiss heated and deepened until it completely consumed him. With his pulse racing so fast it made a lightning bolt seem slow, he moved his lips to her throat, to her face, to her eyes, then back to her mouth.

The sound of Stacy's heavy breathing echoed in his soul, inciting him.

He wasn't sure just how they wound up lying on her bed, sealed against each other's bodies as passion flared to yet a higher level. Everything seemed blurry to him, happening both quickly and, somehow, also in slow motion.

He began to undress Stacy, eager to feel her, to have her, the way he had that night an eternity ago.

And then he froze.

What the hell are you doing? he silently demanded of himself as he pulled back.

Startled, Stacy looked at him in utter confusion.

"Why did you stop?" she cried. Was he doing it again? Was he pulling away from her? She didn't understand what was going on.

"You're vulnerable and I don't want to take advantage of you," Cole confessed, even though stopping like this was killing him by inches.

Stacy blinked. "I was the one who started kissing you. How does that make *me* vulnerable?"

"Because you're tired—" he began to explain.

"I'm tired," she agreed. "I'm not in a coma. There's a difference," she insisted. "Now, if you're having second thoughts because you don't want me—"

This time, she was the one who didn't get to finish her sentence because this time, struck by the absurdity of what she was about to say, his lips were covering hers. Silencing her.

And this time there was no hesitation on the part of either of them.

It was as if they had suddenly been freed of all impediments, all emotional baggage, and were able to finally act on what they were feeling right at this very moment.

Fire ignited within Stacy.

All the emotions she had struggled so hard to push away and bury, denying what she'd felt for Cole, what she had been feeling for Cole all along, surfaced and burst forward, consuming her and taking her prisoner.

She slid her hands all along Cole's body, touching him, needing to reassure herself that he was real, that he was here. She wasn't just dreaming this the way she had during all those long months touring the European cities that her aunt had always longed to see.

European cities that meant nothing to her because Cole wasn't there to see them with her.

Stacy's breathing was growing faster by the moment, as if she was racing to some invisible finish line. And yet, she was loath to do so, because once she did reach it this exquisite moment in time would be over.

And maybe permanently.

She didn't want it to be over, didn't want him to leave her bed, her room, her life, the way he had the last time. She knew if that happened, she wouldn't be able to survive it again.

This time, there would be no Aunt Kate to rescue her from the deep pit. There would be no hope, no salvation for her, only a vast feeling of emptiness.

Cole couldn't get enough of her.

She was just the way she had been before—but, oh, so much more.

It was as if he had a wildcat on his hands, an untamed spirit that aroused so many desires, so many emotions within him that he couldn't begin to count them. They swarmed around him like the funnel of a twister. He had no choice but to let it take him wherever it was going.

He didn't want this moment to end.

Cole kissed her over and over again, his lips trailing along her body, reacquainting himself with what he had gone over so many times before in his mind. Everything was both familiar and brand new—just the way she was.

And when he could no longer hold himself in check, when he felt that he was about to explode if he held back for even a single moment longer, Cole worked his way up along her body, nipping her tender skin, branding it with his lips and his tongue. Rejoicing in the way she squirmed beneath him, doing her best not to cry out so that she wouldn't be heard and possibly bring the moment to an end.

Cole could tell by the way she moved that he'd created several small climaxes for her, working his way up her body and up to the final moment.

And then he was over her, his eyes holding hers as his body aligned with hers.

Just a little pressure from him and she parted her legs in a silent invitation.

His heart racing, he entered her, sealing his body to hers.

Then it began, the dance that would take them to the one place that they both wanted to reach, the summit that loomed above them, calling to them.

As he moved, Stacy echoed his movements, going faster and faster.

The pace stole away their breaths until it became so fast that they all but set her bed on fire.

She clung to him when the final moment overtook them. The fireworks surrounded them, blotting out everything except for the two of them and the mind-numbing sensation that had been created.

Stacy dug her fingers into his back, as if desperately trying to anchor herself to the moment, to him. Not wanting it to end, not wanting to revert to the world that existed just beyond them, waiting to receive them back into its embrace.

He felt her heart pounding wildly against his chest, felt his own matching it, beat for beat.

Whatever might happen from this moment forward, he would have this. Have it and treasure it.

Embracing Stacy, he held her against him and pressed a single tender kiss to her forehead.

"I love you."

Chapter 16

Stacy froze.

Raising her eyes, she looked at him. Her imagination had to be playing tricks on her, taking a glorious experience and making it into something even more. Something that she knew wasn't true.

He must have felt Stacy suddenly stiffening in his arms.

"I'm sorry," he said quietly.

Well, that was one mystery cleared up. It wasn't her imagination. "So you did say it."

"It just slipped out."

She put her own interpretation to his words. "But you didn't mean it."

He raised his eyes to hers, unable to gauge what she was thinking from her tone of voice. So he had to ask. "Would you want me to?"

Oh, no, he wasn't going to get her to tell him how

she felt if he was apologizing for saying the words that she had longed to hear. "I didn't want you to say anything you didn't want to say."

"Oh, the hell with it," he muttered, giving up and pulling her to him.

"What are you doing?" she cried, startled.

Cole grinned wickedly. "If you have to ask, either I didn't do it right the first time, or you are seriously in need of a refresher course. In either case—"

He ended his statement with a kiss—which happily began everything all over again.

She was gone from her bed when he woke up.

Dawn was just beginning to paint lighter shades along the darkness on the horizon.

Cole sat up, shaking off the last remnants of sleep. He should have gone to his own room long before now, he upbraided himself. But they'd made love two more times, and after that, he'd been too exhausted to move. He didn't remember falling asleep.

Cole quickly pulled on his jeans and shrugged into his shirt before stepping out into the hallway. He assumed that Stacy was in the twins' room and debated knocking on their door. But if they were, by some chance, asleep again, he didn't want to take a chance on waking them up. So he finally just twisted the doorknob and eased the door opened.

When he walked in, Stacy was already looking in his direction, having anticipated his entrance when she saw the doorknob move.

"Morning," he said, smiling broadly at her.

"It certainly is," Stacy agreed. When she'd slipped

out of bed, he'd been sound asleep. "Did I wear you out?" There was a note of pleasure in her voice.

"In the best possible way," he admitted.

For now, Cole felt it was for the best not to bring up last night. She still hadn't really let him know, one way or another, how she felt about his having said the three most important words one human being could say to another. He didn't know if he had frightened her, or if his loving her was just something she had to get used to.

In any event, she hadn't given him any idea how she felt and certainly hadn't indicated that she felt that way about him, too. If she didn't love him, it wasn't something that he wanted to face right now.

He nodded at the twins, both of whom were awake and kicking their little legs. "How are they?"

"Hungry," she answered. "I changed them and was just about to go downstairs to get their bottles."

"You stay here," he told her. "I'll go get the bottles." He left the room before she could argue the point.

Connor was seated at the table, enjoying his first cup of inky black coffee of the day. Seeing Cole walk into the kitchen, he commented, "Well, you certainly look happy."

"Why shouldn't I be?" Cole asked. "The twins are better, we found the runaway horses, the rain is gone and it's the beginning of a brand-new, beautiful day."

Connor smiled to himself as he took another long sip of his coffee. "Uh-huh."

"I'm going to ignore that," Cole told his brother, taking two bottles filled with formula out of the refrigerator. He warmed them individually.

"Ignore what?" Connor asked innocently. "I'm agreeing with you."

"I know that *uh-huh*. That's the sound you make when you're humoring me."

Connor finished off his coffee. "You're letting your imagination get the better of you." He cocked his head, studying his brother. "Or is that just a guilty conscience?"

Cole's eyes darted toward his brother. Did he know? Had Connor somehow guessed that he had spent the night with Stacy?

Since Connor wasn't saying anything specific, Cole decided to go with denial. "I don't have anything to be guilty about."

"Good to hear. Glad we're on the same page," Connor said, clapping his brother on the shoulder as he put his empty coffee cup in the sink. "It should be a pretty light workday today. You can check in at the Healing Ranch to see if they need you, or—" a whimsical smile playing along his lips "—you can stay here to spell Stacy and take over taking care of the twins. Sounded like she wore herself out yesterday."

Cole avoided making eye contact with his brother. "I think she got some sleep when the twins fell asleep," he said evasively.

The bottles were warm enough and he picked them up to take to Stacy.

"Did she, now?" Connor asked, turning to walk out the front door.

Was he that transparent? Cole wondered. Could Connor guess at and predict his every move even before he made it, at least, when it came to Stacy? Or was Connor just reading things into everything he said, again, because of Stacy?

Cole decided that was a riddle for another time. He had things to do.

Walking back into the twins' bedroom, Cole announced, "Breakfast is served. Why don't you go downstairs and get yourself some while I take care of these guys?"

"My breakfast will keep," she told him. "I want to make sure these little people stay on some sort of a regular schedule, and right now, it's time to feed them."

Cole handed her one of the bottles and held on to the other one himself. "Might as well help you out," he told Stacy.

She tried to take the second bottle from him, but he continued to hold it. Stacy gave up. Nevertheless, she asked, "Don't you have something to do?"

Cole feigned being hurt. "Are you trying to get rid of me?"

She shrugged as she picked up one of the twins and sat down in the rocking chair.

"I just don't want to take you away from what you normally do."

"Stop being so noble," he chided. "You're confusing me."

"Meaning I'm not normally noble?" Stacy asked, a slight edge in her voice.

Cole grinned the moment he heard her tone. "There's that fire I know so well," he told her with a laugh.

Stacy sighed and shook her head. In her arms, Mike greedily went at the bottle she held to his lips. "You're crazy, you know that?"

"Highly possible," Cole agreed. He turned toward the remaining twin in the crib. "Okay, Mikey, time for one of your many feedings," he said, picking the baby up in his arms.

Amused, Stacy corrected him. "That's Katie you just picked up."

He was certain he could tell them apart. "No, it's not."

Stacy merely smiled. "I just changed them before you came in. That's Katie. Trust me."

Well, he couldn't very well argue with anatomy. "Okay, Katie," he began again amicably, "time for one of your many feedings."

Stacy laughed softly, shaking her head. She liked the way that Cole rolled with the punches. He was a lot more adaptable than she was, she'd give him that.

Sitting down on the edge of the nightstand to feed Katie, Cole glanced in Stacy's direction. "Something funny?" he asked.

"No, not really." She didn't really want to tell him she was giving him marks for his amicable behavior.

Stacy fell silent for a few minutes as they both sat there, feeding the twins. Despite the fact that Cole was actually perched on the edge of the nightstand, it struck her as an incredibly tranquil moment. The kind that every parent looked forward to and relished in the midst of a day filled with small and large chores, surrounded by chaos and organized disorder.

She could get used to this.

"Why do you think she did it?" she asked suddenly, turning toward Cole.

The question came out of the blue and caught him totally off guard. "Who?"

"Their mother." Stacy nodded at the twin in her arms. "Why do you think she abandoned them?" She just couldn't wrap her head around the concept, not after being with them, holding them, taking care of them. "What would make a mother just walk away from her child? Especially *two* of them?"

Cole shrugged. Although he felt the same way, he tried to put himself in the twins' mother's shoes. "Maybe she felt that she couldn't provide for them. It is possible, you know. Or maybe she felt she was too young to be a mother. One night of passion and suddenly, she's faced with this huge responsibility for the next eighteen years. It was too much for her."

He looked at Stacy. "At least she had the presence of mind to leave them on someone's doorstep, in this case, mine. If she'd been completely self-centered, she could have just left them out in the desert."

Stacy shivered, refusing to even go there in her mind. "Don't even say that."

"What I'm saying is that at least she wanted to give the twins a fighting chance. A chance at a decent life."

Stacy pressed her lips together, thinking.

"I'm going to adopt them," Stacy said after a very long pause.

"You're going to *what*?"

"I'm going to adopt them," Stacy repeated very deliberately. "If their mother doesn't turn up—and it's beginning to look like that's highly likely—I'm going to adopt these twins."

That was just her emotions talking, Cole thought. Stacy couldn't possibly know what she was thinking of taking on.

"Stacy…"

She pretended that he wasn't trying to interrupt. He

was undoubtedly going to try to shoot her down with logic and she was in no mood to hear it.

Instead, she laid out the plan she'd just come up with. "I have some money that my aunt left me and I can get a job at Olivia's law firm before that runs out. I can be an administrative assistant. And if that doesn't work out, Miss Joan would give me a job. So would Rebecca," she recalled.

His jaw all but dropped open. "You want to be a waitress or a desk clerk?"

It was important to her that she make Cole understand she was serious about this.

"I want to do and be whatever it takes to take care of these little people. They deserve a chance at a life," she insisted. "They deserve to grow up feeling loved, and I do love them."

She looked at Katie and she could feel her heart swelling. This was her purpose. This was what she was meant to do and why she had come home.

"Stacy, you'd be taking on a really huge responsibility." He didn't want to shoot Stacy down, but at the same time, he wanted her to think about what she was getting into.

"I can do it," she assured him without any hesitation.

There was one more point that she was overlooking. "You also need to have a judge approve you adopting the twins," he reminded her. "You're a twenty-five-year-old single woman."

Stacey raised her chin defiantly. The more he argued against it, the more determined she became. "So? Twenty-five-year-old single women have twins," she insisted.

"That they gave birth to. There's a difference if

you're trying to adopt them," Cole pointed out. Didn't she see that?

"I'll just have to convince the judge, then." She said that as if it was just a small bump in the road she was going to have to negotiate.

He could see that talking her out of it was out of the question. She had her heart set on this, so he needed to help her.

And himself.

"You'd stand a better chance of adopting them if you were married."

"Yeah, well, I'm not," she said with a toss of her head. "So I'll just have to work harder at convincing the judge—"

"What if you were?"

"What if I were what?" she asked, distracted.

Putting down Mikey's bottle, she placed him against her shoulder and slowly began patting his back, trying to coax a burp out of him so that he would be comfortable.

"What if you were married," he said, wondering if Stacy was paying attention to him at all, or if she was preoccupied trying to find a way to con a judge into letting her adopt the twins.

"Well, I'm *not* married," she reminded him, irritated that he was harping on that point.

Crossing over to her, with Katie against his shoulder, he stood in front of Stacy and asked again, "But what if you could be?"

She stopped patting Mikey's back and looked up at Cole. Confusion gave way to utter surprise as his question sank in.

"Are you asking me to marry you?" she asked in a disbelieving whisper.

"Yes," he said simply, "I am."

"So I can adopt the twins?"

"Well, that would be part of it," Cole admitted, "but—"

"No," Stacy answered firmly. "I can't have you making that sort of a sacrifice. It wouldn't be—"

Damn, but she made it hard to get a word in edgewise. "For once in your life, will you stop talking and let me finish what I have to say?"

Stunned, Stacy stared at him. And then, when she found her voice, she said, "Go ahead."

"I said that you adopting the twins was only part of the reason I'm asking you to marry me. The main reason is because I *want* to marry you. Now that you're finally back and we've cleared up that ridiculous misunderstanding about why you left—which was totally my fault," he quickly interjected lest she went off on another tangent again, "I want to spend the rest of my life with you. I love you, I'm pretty sure you love me and I can't think of any better way to add meaning to my life than to help you raise these twins."

Having said everything that he wanted to say, he paused, waiting for Stacy to answer him.

The pause stretched out, making him feel progressively more uncertain with each second that passed by.

Was she going to turn him down?

Finally, when the silence was close to deafening, Stacy asked, "Are you finished?"

He drew in a breath, bracing himself. She was going to say no. He could see by the expression on her face. But if that was the case, if she was going to turn him down, then he had to face up to it. Better sooner than later.

"Yes," he told her.

"And I can talk now?"

"Yes," he said a little more forcefully.

"Okay, then my answer is—"

Just then, a loud, urgent knock coming from downstairs disrupted everything.

Someone was at the front door.

Chapter 17

The next moment, they could hear Rita responding to whoever was knocking on the door.

"I am coming. I am coming. Have a little patience!" It was more of an order than a request.

Cole exchanged looks with Stacy. Much as he wanted to hear her answer to his question, he could see that her attention had temporarily refocused on the commotion downstairs.

"I'd better go see what's going on," he told Stacy. "I'll be right back."

Stacy felt that she was part of the family now, at least for the time being, and there was no way she was about to just hang back and ignore whoever was knocking on the door so hard.

Maybe she was being paranoid, but she had an uneasy feeling that this wasn't some rancher looking for advice from one of the McCullough brothers.

The knocking had had an ominous sound.

"I'm going with you," she informed Cole before he could leave the room. "Grab a twin," she said, picking up Katie.

Cole frowned. He had not intended to go downstairs to discover what all this noise was about with a baby in his arms. However, since Stacy was obviously coming with him and taking one of the twins, he couldn't very well just leave the other one behind. It didn't seem right.

Scooping Mikey up from the crib, he wound up following Stacy to the stairs.

Apparently, having opened the door and seen who was on the doorstep, Rita had simmered down. Stepping back, she opened the door even wider, allowing Sheriff Rick Santiago to walk into the house.

"Is there something wrong, Sheriff?" Rita asked the man just as Cole and Stacy reached the bottom of the stairs with the twins.

Instead of answering her one way or another, Rick made a request. "I'd like to see Cole or Connor if they're home. Ms. Rowe, too, if she's still staying here."

"Oh, yes, she is still here," Rita assured him as she closed the door again. "She is helping to take care of the babies, you know."

Rick removed his hat. "No, I didn't know. To be honest, I thought she was just helping Cole out with the infants when he stopped at my office."

Rita was not one to waste time with unnecessary dialogue. "You have news?" she asked pointedly.

That was when he saw Stacy and Cole walking into the living room. Each of them was holding an infant.

"I have news," Rick answered, addressing his words

to the two younger people rather than to the woman who had let him in.

"What kind of news?" Stacy asked, her voice strained and hollow. She could feel her fingertips instantly turn icy. Her heart racing, she held on to Katie a little tighter. Katie whimpered. Realizing she was gripping the baby too tightly, Stacy loosened her hold a little. She could control that, control her hold. But she couldn't control the way her heart was pounding. If it hammered any harder, it was going to start breaking ribs.

"Is it bad?" Stacy asked, her eyes holding the sheriff's.

Again, he didn't answer the question. Instead, he told them, "Joe Lone Wolf found out who the twins' mother is."

Stacy stopped breathing. She looked at Cole, mutely asking him for help. She couldn't make herself ask the question.

Cole got the message. "Who *is* their mother?" he asked.

Rick gave them the background information first. "For the last six months, the girl was staying with her best friend, Ann Fox Fire. Ann lives with her older sister on the reservation. No one really noticed that the girl was expecting," Rick explained delicately. "I gather that she didn't put on much weight, even though she was carrying twins.

"According to everyone Joe talked to, on the reservation and in town, she really didn't show." Rick paused and then added, "And she worked right here in town."

"Who is it?" Stacy asked impatiently, her nerves getting the better of her. She could just envision the twins' mother being seized with regret and tearfully coming forward, saying it was all a huge mistake and that she wanted her babies back.

"It's Elsie," Rick said.

Stacy stared at the sheriff. "You mean the receptionist from the hotel? The one who was so excited about getting accepted into college that she quit right on the spot?" Stacy asked incredulously.

He had to have made a mistake. It couldn't have been her. Elsie couldn't be the twins' mother. She was practically a baby herself.

"That's the one," Rick told her.

Stacy shook her head. "There has to be some mistake," Stacy told the sheriff. "I was there when she opened her acceptance letter."

"Turns out that was for everyone else's benefit."

Stacy wasn't sure that she understood what he was telling her. "Then she was lying? Elsie wasn't accepted to college?"

"Oh, she was. But she knew about it before she came to work. A full day before, according to Ann." There was no judgment in Rick's voice as he went on to give them the details. "Elsie agonized over the letter and what she was going to do. According to Ann, Elsie felt that finding a really good home for the twins was the best thing she could do for them. And college was the best thing she could do for herself."

Rick looked at Cole. "Your family's getting quite a reputation as being a haven for babies." To drive his point home, Rick elaborated. "Cody wound up taking in not just the baby he helped birth, but the baby's mama, as well. And Cassidy took in that baby she and Will saved from the river."

"So this Elsie decided that it was my turn to get a baby?" Cole asked in disbelief.

"Babies," Rick corrected, nodding at the infants Cole and Stacy were holding. "Yeah, that's about the size of it."

So now she knew who the twins' mother was, Stacy thought, but that still left a lot of questions unanswered—and she was far from at ease.

"Where is Elsie now?" Stacy asked.

"She took off," Rick told her. "Most likely for college. At least, that's what Ann hopes."

That still didn't eliminate possible complications. "What about the twins' father?" Stacy asked. "Doesn't he want them?"

She could just envision giving up her heart to the twins, thinking that they could form a family, only to have their father step out of the shadows and demand custody of the children.

"I really don't think so," Rick said. "According to what Ann said, he was a guest of the hotel for a couple of nights about ten months ago." It was an old, all-too-familiar story. "You know the type, good-looking, sweet-talking. Elsie never stood a chance," Rick concluded, shaking his head. "They spent the night together and then he was gone.

"When she found out she was pregnant, Elsie didn't even know how to get in touch with him. Turns out, the address and phone number that he gave at the hotel when he registered were both fake."

Rita had been standing by quietly all this time, but now broke her silence and shook her head. "That does not surprise me."

Well, they had the parentage straightened out, such as it was, Cole thought.

"So, now what?" he asked the sheriff.

"Now I can get in touch with social services," Rick told them. "It might take a few days, but they'll send someone out to take the twins—"

"No," Stacy cried.

Rick looked at her, surprised by the fierceness of her reaction.

"That's the next logical step," he told her, "since their mother obviously has given up all claim to them and no one knows where their father is."

"No," Stacy insisted. "The next logical step is to make sure that they get a good home."

"That's what I just said," Rick began.

"With me," Stacy stressed.

Rick looked as if he was trying to understand what she was saying. "Let me get this straight. Are you saying you want to be their foster mother?"

"No, Sheriff. What I'm saying is that I want to *adopt* them."

Rick might have been surprised by her declaration, but Rita appeared to take it in stride, as if she had expected this all along.

"They don't need a foster home or to be passed around from one home to another," Stacy continued. "Or to be separated. What they need is a stable home. They need *me*," she insisted. "And I'll do whatever it takes to keep them."

"And I will help her," Rita said, speaking up authoritatively.

"Stacy," Rick began, "I understand how you feel, but it's not up to me—"

"Elsie obviously wanted to leave them with me," Cole interjected. "She had her pick of places to leave the twins—a lot more accessible places than the side of the bunkhouse at the Healing Ranch," he pointed out to the sheriff. "The fact that she sought me out and left them on what amounted to my doorstep means that she wanted me to look after her twins."

"Go on," Rick said gamely, listening.

"So, in essence," he told the sheriff, "she was asking me to adopt them."

Rick seemed to mull over what Cole had just said. "You have a point."

"And I have the twins," Cole told him. "Possession is still nine-tenths of the law, right?"

"We're not talking about property," Rick pointed out. "We're talking about children—"

"Who are in real danger of getting swallowed up by the system if we turn them over to social services," Stacy insisted. She looked plaintively at Rick and made her appeal. "These kids need a break."

"And you're it?" Rick asked her. Did she realize what she was asking to take on?

"*We're* it," Stacy corrected him, stepping closer to Cole.

"So, you're each going to take one?" Rick questioned uncertainly.

"No," Stacy told him. "I'm going to answer the question that Cole was asking me when you knocked on the door earlier." Turning toward Cole, she smiled up at him and said one word. "Yes."

"You're sure about this?" Cole asked, almost afraid to jump to the conclusion that was shimmering right in front of him.

"Very sure," Stacy answered.

He needed to be sure himself. "You're not just saying yes because—"

She wouldn't let him finish. "I'm saying yes because it's been yes for a long time. And if you hadn't gotten cold feet, you would have known that, you big idiot—"

Cole turned toward the sheriff and said, "Hold on to Mikey for me."

Before he could say anything to Cole, Rick found his arms filled with baby.

Taking Katie from Stacy, Cole turned toward his family housekeeper and told her, "Hold Katie for a minute."

"What are you doing?" Stacy cried.

"A man doesn't just propose to a woman and then go on as if it's business as usual," he told her. "At least, not without sealing the bargain."

"And just how do you intend to do that?" Stacy asked.

"Like this," Cole answered, pulling her to him and kissing her soundly.

"I guess that means that Olivia and I are invited to the wedding?" Rick asked.

Neither party answered, being far too occupied to talk at the moment.

Rick smiled and looked at the baby in his arms. "Looks like you and your sister have got yourselves a brand new mommy and daddy, Mikey," he told the baby.

"Sheriff," Rita said, addressing Rick. "Come with me, please. I have just finished making a pie that you have to try." She began to leave the room, then glanced over her shoulder to make sure the sheriff was following her. "You should know this could go on for a bit. You might as well eat something."

"I like the way you think, Rita," Rick said with a laugh.

Carrying Mikey, he followed the housekeeper out of the room.

Epilogue

The moment she heard that Cole had proposed to Stacy, after announcing a self-satisfied "I knew it!" Miss Joan insisted on throwing the wedding.

"Don't worry, I'm not trying to live out some fantasy," she assured Cole when he protested that it would be too much trouble for her. "I got the wedding of my dreams when Henry came to his senses and finally married me."

Everyone in Forever knew it was actually the other way around and that it was Henry who had finally managed to wear Miss Joan down so that she accepted his proposal, but Cole was not about to be the one to point that out to her.

However, he felt that he did have to make an attempt to protest. "Stacy doesn't want a fuss," he told the woman who had been like a surrogate mother to him.

"Everyone wants a fuss," Miss Joan contradicted him. "But it'll be a small fuss," she promised, patting him on the cheek. "Just right for the occasion. Leave everything up to me. Just give me a date."

"As soon as possible," Cole answered.

He thought that would dissuade her, but he should have known better.

"Perfect," the whiskey-voiced woman said. "I'll call you with the details once I have them. Now shoo." She gestured him out of the diner.

"Careful what you wish for," one of the waitresses murmured to Cole as he walked to the door.

But Cole could only smile. He already had what he wished for. He had Stacy. The fact that he was also going to be the instant father of twins only seemed to make the entire thing that much better.

As far as he was concerned, the wedding ceremony was just an afterthought.

"It's beautiful," Stacy told Miss Joan as she looked at her reflection in the mirror in the tiny room right off the church vestibule. She was wearing an empire-waisted wedding gown she could have never afforded to buy on her own.

Pleased, Miss Joan smiled. "Just because I wear that old uniform at the diner every day doesn't mean I don't have taste, girl," she told Stacy.

Stacy was afraid she might have insulted Miss Joan. "I didn't mean to imply—"

Miss Joan was quick to assuage her guilt. No harm had been done. "I know, I know. Just get yourself out there and marry that young man. Cole'll be good to you—and to those babies," she told Stacy with unshakable certainty. Miss Joan allowed herself just a hint of a smile as she added, "You all deserve each other."

She looked up as the strains of Mendelssohn's "Wedding March" came floating through the air, reaching the tiny back room of the church. "That's your cue, girl. Time to go out and meet your future."

Stacy turned toward the woman. "Not without you, Miss Joan."

"Excuse me?"

"Walk out with me," Stacy requested. "You can give me away," she told the for-once-speechless older woman. "You put this together for us. That makes you the closest thing I have to family." She paused and then added, "Please?"

Miss Joan sighed. "We'd better go before that old woman gets tired of playing," she mumbled, referring to the church organist.

Stacy threaded her arm through Miss Joan's, and together they came out of the back room and to the back of the church.

Everyone in the church rose in unison. If some were surprised to see Miss Joan leading the bride to the altar, they gave no indication. Everyone had come to expect the unexpected when it came to Miss Joan.

Besides, they were more taken with how beautiful the bride, someone who was, ultimately, one of their own, looked in her bridal gown.

Certainly Cole couldn't take his eyes off her. He could hardly breathe as he watched Stacy slowly walk toward him.

Each of his brothers were holding one of the twins, Mikey, who was dressed in a miniature tux, and Katie, who had on a tiny bridesmaid's dress. As if aware of the special celebration they were part of, both babies were quiet and taking in their surroundings with wide-eyed wonder.

Finally, Stacy reached the front of the church and the man she had been heading toward all of her life.

"Ready?" Cole whispered to her as Miss Joan handed Stacy over.

"More than you could ever possibly know," Stacy answered.

"Then let's get married."

They turned as one to face the minister, ready to say the words that would unite them today and for all eternity.

* * * * *

Brenda Harlen is a former attorney who once had the privilege of appearing before the Supreme Court of Canada. The practice of law taught her a lot about the world and reinforced her determination to become a writer—because in fiction, she could promise a happy ending! Now she is an award-winning, RITA® Award–nominated national bestselling author of more than thirty titles for Harlequin. You can keep up-to-date with Brenda on Facebook and Twitter, or through her website, brendaharlen.com.

Books by Brenda Harlen

Harlequin Special Edition

Match Made in Haven

The Sheriff's Nine-Month Surprise
Her Seven-Day Fiancé
Six Weeks to Catch a Cowboy
Claiming the Cowboy's Heart
Double Duty for the Cowboy
One Night with the Cowboy

Those Engaging Garretts!

The Single Dad's Second Chance
A Wife for One Year
The Daddy Wish
A Forever Kind of Family
The Bachelor Takes a Bride
Two Doctors & a Baby

Visit the Author Profile page at
Harlequin.com for more titles.

Claiming the Cowboy's Heart

BRENDA HARLEN

For Neill—with love and gratitude. xo

Chapter 1

"Oh, no," Liam Gilmore said, shaking his head for emphasis when he saw his sister Katelyn walk through the front doors of the inn with her briefcase in one hand and a rectangular object that he knew to be her daughter's portable playpen in the other. The baby was strapped against Katelyn's body and an overstuffed diaper bag was draped over one of her shoulders. Loaded down with the kid's stuff, she looked like a Sherpa ready to embark on a mountain trek.

"I've got an emergency hearing at the courthouse in half an hour," she explained, as she dropped the diaper bag next to his makeshift desk and set her briefcase beside it.

"And I've got interviews scheduled for this afternoon," he told her.

"You've got a manager, a weekend housekeeper and a

breakfast chef—what more does a boutique hotel need?" she asked, as she unzipped the carrying case of the playpen.

Because he couldn't sit there and watch his sister struggle, he took the portable enclosure from her and opened it up, then clicked to lock each of the sides, pushed down the center support and slid the mattress pad into place. "Andrew decided to take a job in Los Angeles, so I no longer have a manager," Liam admitted.

"I'm sorry," Kate said sincerely, as she unbuckled the baby carrier and carefully extracted the sleeping baby.

He shrugged. "Not your problem," he said. "Just as your requirement for a last-minute babysitter—*again*—isn't my problem."

"And yet I'm willing to help you out, because that's what siblings do," she told him.

"Tell me how you're going to help me," he suggested.

She pressed her lips to Tessa's forehead, then carefully laid the sleeping baby down in the playpen.

And maybe his heart did soften a bit as he watched his sister with her little girl, and maybe that same heart had been known to turn to mush when his adorable niece smiled at him, but he had no intention of admitting any of that to Kate, who already took advantage of him at every opportunity.

"By giving you the name of your new manager," she said.

"Please do. Then I can cancel the interviews I've scheduled."

"Your sarcasm is unnecessary and unappreciated, and if I didn't have to be in court in—" Kate glanced at the slim silver bangle on her wrist "—sixteen minutes, I'd make you not just apologize but grovel. Since I do have to be in court, I'll just say *Macy Clayton*."

Liam recognized the name. In fact, Macy was scheduled for an interview at two thirty, but he didn't share that information with his sister, either. "And why should I hire her?" he prompted.

"Because she's perfect for the job," Kate said. "She's been working in the hotel industry in Las Vegas for the past eight years, including several as a desk clerk and concierge before she was promoted to assistant to the manager at the Courtland Hotel & Casino."

"If she had such a great career in Las Vegas, what is she doing in Haven?" he wondered aloud.

"That's something you'll have to ask her," she told him.

He hated when his sister was right.

And as he looked through the applications on his desk after Kate had gone, Liam couldn't deny that she was right about the woman she'd recommended for the managerial position.

Macy Clayton was, at least on paper, perfect for the job. Then again, he'd thought Andrew would be perfect, too—and so had the Beverly Hills Vista. Not surprisingly, Andrew had chosen the possibility of celebrity sighting on the West Coast over the probability of boredom in northern Nevada.

Most of the locals had expressed skepticism about his plan; opening a boutique hotel in a sleepy town off the beaten path was a risky venture. David Gilmore had been less kind in his assessment, referring to his oldest son as both a disappointment and a fool.

"Gilmores are ranchers" had been his refrain every

time Liam tried to talk to him about the inn. And while it was true that the family had been raising cattle on the Circle G for more than a hundred and fifty years, Liam had been chafing to get away from the ranch for more than fifteen years.

Not that he'd had any specific plans. Not until he'd seen JJ Green affixing a New Price sticker to the faded For Sale sign stuck in the untended front yard of the Stagecoach Inn.

The old, abandoned hotel had been falling apart when Hershel Livingston bought it for a song nearly a decade earlier. The Nevada native had made his fortune in casinos and brothels, but he'd planned to make his home in Haven, one of only a few places in the state where those vices were illegal.

Hershel had spent millions of dollars on the rehab, then abandoned the project just as it was nearing completion. No one knew why, although the rumors were plenty. One of the more credible stories was that his wife had visited Haven during the renovation process and immediately hated the small town. A different version of the story suggested that his wife had caught the billionaire dallying with a local girl.

There were as many variations of this claim as there were single women in town. The only indisputable truth was that Hershel had abruptly ordered his construction crew to vacate the premises, and then he called Jack Green to put a For Sale sign on the narrow patch of grass in front of the wide porch.

The real estate agent got a lot of calls about the property in the first few weeks, but they were mostly local people who wanted to walk through and take a gander at the work that had been done. None of them was seriously interested in buying the inn, because they didn't believe a fancy hotel could survive in Haven. As a result, interest had faded more quickly than the paint on the sign.

Then, nearly two years ago, JJ Green—now working in the real estate business with his father—slapped that New Price sticker across the weathered sign. More out of curiosity than anything else, Liam had called the agent to inquire and learned that the price had been drastically reduced.

Without any prompting, JJ confided that the elusive Mrs. Livingston had filed for divorce from her cheating husband and was going after half of everything. To retaliate, Hershel was selling off his assets at a loss to decrease the amount of the settlement he would have to pay to her.

Kate had pointed out that the wife could argue fraud and claim half of the fair market value rather than half of the sale price. On the other hand, the property was only worth what someone was willing to pay, and the fact that the old hotel had been on the market for years without anyone making an offer might support Hershel's decision to slash the price. Either way, Liam wasn't going to protest the lower number. In fact, after securing the necessary financing, he managed to negotiate an even further reduction before he signed on the dotted line.

Now he was only weeks away from opening, still waiting on deliveries and attempting to schedule the final inspections—and trying to fill unexpected vacancies in his staff.

If Macy Clayton had responded to the original posting, he might have hired her rather than Andrew and not been feeling so panicked right now. Of course, he was making this assumption on the basis of her résumé and his sister's recommendation without even having met the woman. So while he agreed that she seemed to have all the necessary qualifications for the job, he was going to reserve judgment.

Then she walked in—and his body stirred with a purely sexual awareness he hadn't experienced in a long while. And in that first moment, even before the introductions, he knew there was no way he could hire her. He also knew that he had to at least go through the motions of the interview.

When she accepted his proffered hand, he felt a jolt straight through his middle as their palms joined. Her skin was soft but her grasp was firm, and he caught a flicker of something that might have been a mixture of surprise and awareness in her espresso-colored eyes when they met his. Her hair was also dark, with highlights of gold and copper, and tied away from her face in the messy-bun style made famous by the Duchess of Sussex before she was royalty.

He guessed Macy's height at around five feet five inches, though her heeled boots added a couple of inches to that number, and her build was on the slender side, but with distinctly feminine curves. The long coat she wore in deference to the season had been unbuttoned to reveal a slim-fitting black skirt that fell just below her knees and a matching single-breasted jacket over a bright blue shell.

"It's a pleasure to meet you, Ms. Clayton." He resisted the temptation to brush his thumb over the pulse point at her wrist to see if it was racing; instead, he let his hand drop away.

"Likewise," she said.

"Can I take your coat for you?"

"No need." She shrugged it off her shoulders and draped it over the back of the chair before perching on the edge of the seat. "I have to tell you, I was skeptical when I'd heard that the old Stagecoach Hotel was being renovated and reopened, but based on what I've seen so far, you've really done a wonderful job with this place."

"Most of the major renovations were done by the previous owner—I just hired the right people to pick up where he left off," Liam admitted.

"Well, the actual coach at the back of the lobby is a nice touch," she noted.

"I thought so, too," he said. A simple idea that had been a lot more complicated to execute, as the antique carriage had to be taken apart to get it through the doorway and then reassembled inside.

"You're planning to open in three weeks?" she prompted.

He nodded. "Valentine's Day."

Her smile was warm and natural. Friendly. He imagined she'd make the guests feel welcome—which was, of course, what he wanted, but didn't alleviate his other concerns.

Sexual harassment in the workplace was a serious issue, and Liam had been raised to be respectful of all women. Still, he suspected it would be a mistake to hire a woman who, upon their first meeting, made him think all kinds of inappropriately tempting thoughts.

"Your résumé shows that you spent the last four years working at the Courtland Hotel in Las Vegas," he noted, forcing himself to refocus on the matter at hand.

"That's correct."

"So why did you leave Las Vegas and move to Haven?"

"I moved *back* to Haven," she clarified. "I grew up in this town and my parents still live here and—" Her words stopped abruptly, as if she'd caught herself saying more than she wanted to.

"And?" he prompted.

She offered another easy smile and a quick shrug. "And I was ready to come home."

It seemed like a reasonable response, but he doubted it was what she'd initially intended to say.

He looked at her résumé again, skimming through the pages that attested to a wealth and breadth of experience. She'd worked a lot of different jobs on her way up to her most recent position as assistant to the manager of the Courtland Hotel & Casino in Las Vegas: she'd served drinks in a hotel casino, worked as a hostess in the restaurant and even done a stint cleaning rooms.

"Your experience is impressive," he told her.

"Thank you."

"But why do you want to work here?"

"Because there are no openings at the Dusty Boots Motel."

His brows lifted. "Is that a joke?"

The corners of her mouth tipped up at the corners. "Yes, Mr. Gilmore."

"Liam," he said.

"I'm not sure it's appropriate to call my boss by his given name."

"I'm not your boss," he pointed out.

"Yet," she clarified, and smiled again.

Before he could reply to that, he heard a rustling

sound in the playpen behind him, followed by a tiny, plaintive voice asking for, "Ma-ma?"

Macy leaned forward in her seat, looking past him to the little girl who'd pulled herself up into a standing position, holding onto the top rail.

"Mama's going to be back soon," Liam promised. *Hoped.*

"You have a beautiful daughter," Macy said.

"What? *No*," he responded quickly. Firmly. "She's not my daughter—she's my niece."

"Then you have a beautiful niece," she amended.

He looked at the child in question and felt a familiar tug in the vicinity of his heart. "Yeah, she is kinda cute."

Tessa lifted her arms, a wordless request.

Liam glanced at his watch and tried to remember if Kate had told him when she expected to be finished in court. Out of the corner of his eye, he saw Tessa's arms drop back down and her lower lip thrust forward in a pout.

He sighed and reached for her. "I'm conducting an interview here," he said, as he settled his niece on his hip. "So let's try to keep things professional, okay?"

She responded by leaning forward and pressing her puckered lips to his cheek.

"Not really a good start," he noted dryly.

But his potential innkeeper smiled, clearly charmed by the little girl.

"And if your diaper needs changing, that's going to have to wait until your mom gets back," he warned his niece.

"You don't do diapers?" Macy guessed.

"Not if I can help it. And Kate promised she'd be

back from court before Tessa woke up so that I wouldn't have to."

"Either Kate was delayed or Tessa woke up early—maybe because she was wet," she suggested. "Did your sister leave a diaper bag?"

"If you can call something that would likely be tagged 'oversized' by an airport luggage handler a *bag*," he remarked, gesturing to the multipocketed behemoth.

Macy reached for the bag and, after rifling through its contents, pulled out a change pad, clean diaper and package of wipes, which she set on the table in front of him.

Still, Liam hesitated. "I'm sure she can wait until we've finished our interview."

"Maybe she can, but she shouldn't have to be uncomfortable," Macy said. "I can step out of the room, if you want privacy."

"Do you have much experience with babies and diapers?"

The corners of her mouth tipped up again. "Some."

He unfolded the changing pad and laid his niece on top of it. "Then you should probably stay, because I might need some pointers—or an extra set of hands," he said, as Tessa started to roll away from him.

While Macy seemed willing and able to help, he managed to unsnap his niece's corduroy overalls with one hand and hold her in place with the other.

"Give me some specific examples of guest complaints you've heard and tell me how you dealt with them," he suggested, as he pulled a wipe from the dispenser.

Macy shared anecdotes from her work experience while also jiggling a plastic ring of colorful keys she'd found in the diaper bag to hold the little girl's attention while he focused on changing the diaper.

Her stories proved that she was creative and clever, and by the time he'd slid the clean diaper under his niece's bottom, he didn't doubt that the Courtland Hotel had been sorry to lose her when she left Las Vegas.

"Usually I fasten the diaper tabs before I do up the pants," she remarked, as he began to pinch the snaps that lined the inseam of Tessa's overalls together.

"What?"

"You didn't secure the diaper."

"Of course I did." He finished his task and let Tessa roll over. She immediately pushed herself to her feet and clapped her hands. Since she'd learned to stand and, more recently, walk, she'd become accustomed to her every effort being applauded.

His own efforts were hardly cause for celebration, because the awkward bulging in her pants confirmed that Macy was right. He sighed. "Apparently I didn't."

So he scooped up Tessa again. "Uncle Liam messed up," he said. "And now we need to fix it."

But Tessa didn't want to be reasoned with—she wanted to be free. And she kicked and screamed in protest.

"What's this?" Macy said, offering the little girl a sippy cup filled with juice that she'd found in the bag.

Tessa stopped kicking and reached out with both hands. "Joosh!"

"Do you want your juice?"

The little girl nodded.

Macy gave her the cup and Liam unsnapped her overalls again—only to realize that the diaper tabs were stuck to her pants. He tried to peel them away from the fabric, determined to salvage the diaper—but his fingers felt too big and clumsy for the task.

"I think I need some help," he admitted.

Macy didn't hesitate to brush his hands aside, unstick the tabs from the little girl's pants, reposition the diaper and deftly fasten it in place. Though the woman kept her gaze focused on the child, she spoke to Liam as she completed the task. "I trust you know that a good employee is one who steps up to do a job that needs doing, even if it falls outside of her job description."

"You can't expect me to hire you just because you helped change my niece's diaper," he remarked—*after* the task was completed.

"Of course not," she agreed, passing the clean and happy little girl to him. "I expect you to hire me because I'm the best person for the job."

Chapter 2

In retrospect, Macy acknowledged that she should have taken a change of clothes when she left home for her interview. Whenever she headed out with Ava, Max and Sam, she triple-checked to ensure she was prepared for every possible contingency. But when it came to making plans for herself, she couldn't seem to think two steps ahead.

Her friend Stacia called it "pregnancy brain" and confessed that she'd experienced similar bouts of absentmindedness during both of her pregnancies. But that title suggested to Macy a temporary condition that would correct itself after she'd given birth. Instead, it had transitioned to "momnesia."

Apparently there was scientific proof that the hormonal changes designed to help a new mother bond with her baby could interfere with the brain's ability to process other information. This explained why Macy could jolt from a deep sleep to wide awake when any of her babies stirred in the night but the cook at Diggers' had to repeat her name three times before she realized that an order was up. And even though the triplets were close to eight months old now, her brain apparently hadn't gotten the memo that she'd bonded with them and could, perhaps, start to focus on other things again.

So she was feeling a little bit guilty about boasting to Liam Gilmore that she was the best person for the manager's job—because what if she wasn't? What if she'd forgotten everything she'd ever learned about the hospitality industry? Maybe her only real talent now was being able to diaper three squirming babies in less than a minute.

But she wanted the job. She'd been excited about the possibility as soon as she'd learned that the new owner of the Stagecoach Inn was looking for a manager, and even more so when she'd walked through the front door and breathed in the history and grandeur of the old building.

Her only hesitation derived from the frisson of *something* she'd experienced when Liam Gilmore clasped her hand in his. It had been so long since she'd felt *anything* in response to a man's touch that she hadn't been sure how to respond. Thankfully, her brain had kicked back into gear and reminded her that the handsome cowboy was her potential boss and not a man she should ever contemplate seeing naked. Which was a shame, because the breadth of his shoulders—

No, she wasn't going there.

The admonishment from her brain had helped refocus her attention on the interview. She could only hope he hadn't sensed her distraction, because she really wanted the job.

Macy had started working at Diggers' Bar & Grill because she'd wanted—needed—to do something to help support her family. But she missed the hospitality business more than she'd anticipated. Working at the inn wouldn't just be a job, it would be a pleasure. For now, though, she was still a waitress—and if she didn't hurry up, she was going to be late for her shift.

She took a few minutes to play with Ava, Max and Sam, though, because they weren't just the reason for everything she did but the center of her world. Yes, she'd been stunned—and terrified—when she'd discovered that she was pregnant with triplets, but after only eight months, she couldn't imagine her life without her three precious and unique babies.

Ava, perhaps because she was the only girl, was already accustomed to being the center of attention. Of course, it helped that she had a sweet disposition and was usually quicker to smiles than tears. She also had big blue eyes with long dark lashes and silky dark hair that had finally grown enough that Macy no longer felt the need to put decorative bands on her head to broadcast that she was a girl.

Max was her introspective child—usually content to sit back and watch the world around him. His eyes were green, his hair dark, and his happy place was in his mother's arms.

Sam looked so much like his brother that it was often assumed they were identical twins, though the doctor had assured Macy they were not. Sam was the last born and smallest of her babies. He was also the fussiest, and

Macy felt a special bond with the little guy who seemed to need her more than either his brother or sister did.

When she could delay her departure no longer, Macy headed out again, entrusting her precious babies to the care of their doting grandparents.

Bev and Norm had been shocked to learn of their unmarried daughter's pregnancy—and even more so when she confided the how and why it had happened. To say that they disapproved would be a gross understatement, but they'd put aside their concerns about the circumstances of conception to focus on helping their daughter prepare for the life-changing event.

And having triplets *was* life changing. Macy's apartment in Vegas had been far too small for three babies, but she couldn't afford anything bigger. And she'd budgeted for the expense of daycare for one baby, but triplets meant that cost would be multiplied threefold. So when she was five months pregnant and already waddling like a penguin—another perk of carrying three babies—she did the only thing she could do: resigned her position at the Courtland Hotel, packed up everything she owned and moved herself and all of her not-so-worldly possessions to her parents' house in Haven, Nevada.

At least she hadn't had to move back into her childhood bedroom, instead taking up residence in the in-law suite downstairs. The apartment was originally designed for her maternal grandmother, so that Shirley Haskell could live independently but close to family, and she'd occupied the space for almost six years before her dementia advanced to a stage where she needed round-the-clock nursing care. After that, Bev and Norm had occasionally offered the apartment for rent, most recently to Reid Davidson, who'd come to town to finish out Jed Traynor's term when the former sheriff retired. Almost two years later, most people still referred to Reid as the new sheriff—and would likely do so until he was ready to retire.

The apartment had remained vacant for a long time after the sheriff moved out, and Macy suspected it was because the rooms were in dire need of redecorating. The sofa and chairs in the living room were covered in bold floral fabrics that attested to their outdatedness, and the coffee table, end tables and lamps all bore witness to the tole painting class Bev had taken while her mother was in residence.

When Macy moved in, the first thing she did was buy covers for the furniture and strip away all evidence of cabbage roses and daisies and tulips. If Beverly was disappointed that her art wasn't appreciated by her daughter, she never said so. Instead, she focused her energy on getting ready for the arrival of three new grandbabies.

For the first few months after Ava, Max and Sam were born, Macy had done nothing but learn how to be a mother. It was a bigger adjustment than she'd anticipated. With three babies, she felt as if she was constantly feeding, burping, changing, bathing or rocking one or more of them. Bev helped as much as she could, and Macy knew there was no way she would have made it through those early days without her mother.

Norm had done his part, too. Although he occasionally made excuses to avoid diaper duty—not unlike Liam Gilmore had attempted to do earlier that afternoon—Macy's dad was the first to volunteer to take the babies for a walk in their stroller or rock a restless infant to sleep. And he never once complained about the fact that the presence of his only daughter and her three children had completely upended his life—as she knew they had done.

Life was busy but good, so Macy had been a little surprised when, shortly before the triplets' six-month birthday, Beverly suggested that her daughter think about getting a job. Macy had assured her mom that she had savings and could increase the amount of rent she paid—because she'd refused to move into their home without contributing at least something to the cost of the roof over her head.

Of course, they'd argued about that, with her parents recommending that her savings should remain that, as there was no way to know what unexpected expenses might arise in the future. But Macy had insisted, and her parents had finally relented—then promptly started education savings plans for Ava, Max and Sam with the money Macy paid to them.

"We don't need you to pay more rent," Bev had assured her. "But you need a reason to get out of the house and interact with other people."

"I do get out of the house."

"Taking Ava, Max and Sam to the pediatrician doesn't count."

"But...if I got a job—who would look after the kids?"

"Oh, well." Bev tapped a finger against her chin, as if searching for an answer to a particularly difficult question. "Hmm...that *is* a tough one."

"I can't ask you to do it," Macy explained. "You already do so much for us."

"You don't have to ask, I'm offering. In fact, I'm insisting."

And that was how Macy found herself replying to the Help Wanted ad in the window at Diggers' Bar & Grill.

At first she'd only worked the lunch shift two days a week. But after a couple of weeks on the job, Duke had added dinner shifts to her schedule—and dinner occasionally extended to late night. Usually she worked the restaurant side, but she was sometimes tagged to help out in the bar when it was particularly busy.

Tonight she was scheduled to work 6 p.m. to midnight in the bar. It was six-oh-seven when she parked her car and six-oh-eight when Duke found her in the staff lounge—really not much more than a closet where employees hung their coats and stashed their personal belongings—tying her apron around her waist.

Her boss folded his beefy arms over his chest and pinned her with his gaze. "You're late."

"I'm sorry." Macy's apology was automatic but sincere. "Max was fussing and I wanted to help settle him down before I left."

"I've got kids," Duke said. "Of course, mine are grown now, but I remember the early days and can empathize with your situation. However, your customers don't care if Sam's cutting teeth or Ava's got a fever— they just want to order food and drink from a waitress who's on time."

"You're right. I'm sorry," she said again.

"You were bussing tables here while you were still in high school. We both know you're overqualified for this job, but as long as you're working here, I need you to do the job you were hired to do."

She nodded.

"Of course, if you were to get another job more suited

to your interests, then I could hire someone who is more interested in waiting tables," he remarked.

"I had an interview with Liam Gilmore today," she told him.

"Good. Because I interviewed Courtney Morgan for your job here."

"Hey," she said, because she felt compelled to make at least a token protest. Though it wasn't her lifelong dream to wait tables, she usually enjoyed working at Diggers'—the hub of most social activity in Haven. Of course, the town only boasted two other restaurants: the Sunnyside Diner and Jo's Pizzeria, so if residents wanted anything other than all-day breakfast or pizza, they inevitably headed to Diggers'.

Early in the week, business wasn't nearly as brisk as it was on weekends, but Macy didn't mind the slower pace because it meant that she had more time to chat with the customers she served.

"Somebody was hungry," she commented, as she picked up the now-empty plate that had contained a six-ounce bison burger on a pretzel bun, a scoop of creamy coleslaw and a mountain of curly fries when she'd delivered it to Connor Neal.

"Yeah, me and the sheriff got caught up with a case and worked right through lunch," the deputy told her.

Macy hadn't really known Connor while she was growing up in Haven. He was a few years younger than she was and, even as a kid, he'd been known around town as "that no-good Neal boy."

She'd never been sure if he'd earned his bad-boy reputation or simply had the misfortune of living on the wrong side of the tracks with his unwed mother and younger half brother, but notwithstanding this difficult start, he'd managed to turn his life around. Not only was he a deputy in the sheriff's office now, he'd recently married Regan Channing, whose family had made their substantial fortune in mining.

"Do you want dessert?" Macy asked him now.

"No, thanks. But I do need an order to go." He scrolled through the messages in his phone, then read aloud: "Buffalo chicken wrap with extra hot sauce, fries and onion rings, and one of those big pickles."

"It sounds like your wife might have worked through lunch, too," she noted. "Or it might just be that she's eating for two."

"Three actually," Connor confided.

"Three?" Macy echoed.

The deputy nodded. "She's having twins. *We're* having twins," he hastily amended.

"I hadn't heard," she said. "That's wonderful news—congratulations."

He smiled weakly. "Two babies are twice the fun, right?"

"For sure," she agreed. And twice the diapers and midnight feedings, but she kept *that* to herself. The reality would hit him quickly enough when the babies were born. "Do you know if you're going to have two sons or daughters or one of each?"

"Daughters. They're both girls. Although I've been told that sometimes the techs make mistakes," he added.

She couldn't help but laugh at the obvious hopefulness in his tone. "Sometimes they do," she agreed. "And sometimes expectant mothers get cranky when they have to wait too long for their food, so I'll get this order in for you right away."

"Thanks," Connor said.

Aside from being freaked out by the idea of two girls, it was obvious to Macy that the deputy was looking forward to the family he was going to have with his wife. And as she made her way to the kitchen, Macy found herself envying Regan that.

It was what she'd always wanted—not just a child, but a husband who was her partner in every aspect of life and a father for her children.

She'd given up on that dream and opted to go it alone. And though she wouldn't give up her babies for anything in the world, there were moments when she regretted that she hadn't been able to give them more.

A family.

It was almost eight o'clock when Liam left the inn. His booted feet pounded on the recently stained wooden slats of the porch that wrapped around three sides of the building. In the spring, there would be an assortment of benches and chairs to entice guests to rest and relax, interspersed with enormous pots of flowers to provide both privacy and color. But now there was only a light dusting of snow on the steps and the rail.

It had been snowing when Kate came back after court to pick up her daughter, he recalled. He'd noted the flakes melting in his sister's hair and on the shoulders of her coat when she walked into his office—while he was meeting with another applicant for the manager's job. He'd pretended to be annoyed by the interruption, but the truth was, he'd been grateful for an excuse to cut the interview short.

Having left his gloves in the truck earlier, he shoved his hands deep into the pockets of his jacket now and hunched his shoulders against the bitter wind as he considered his next move. He had an apartment on the third level, so that he'd be onsite overnight if his guests needed anything. But since there were no guests to worry about just yet, he'd postponed his move to continue helping with morning chores at the Circle G. If he was smart, he'd head back to the ranch, grab a bite to eat and hit the hay for a few hours before he had to be up again to help with those chores. Apparently he wasn't very smart, because he turned toward Diggers' instead.

The double doors opened into an enclosed foyer and two other doorways—one clearly marked Bar and the other designated Grill. Once inside, patrons could easily move from one side to the other as there was only a partial wall dividing the two sections, but the division ensured a more family-friendly entrance to the restaurant side. The interior was rustic: the floors were unpainted, weathered wood slats, scuffed and scarred from the pounding of countless pairs of boots; framed newspaper headlines trumpeting the discovery of gold and silver hung on the walls alongside tools of the mining trade—coils of rope, shovels, pickaxes, hammers and chisels.

"You look like you've had a long day," Skylar remarked when he straddled a stool at the bar. The regular bartender at the town's favorite watering hole was also a master's candidate in psychology—and Liam's younger sister.

"You have no idea."

"So tell me about it," she suggested, already tipping a glass beneath the tap bearing the label of his favorite brew.

"You heard that Andrew took a job in California?"

"I did," she confirmed.

"Well, that leaves me without a manager three weeks before opening," he told her.

"Macy Clayton," she said without hesitation, and set the pint glass on a paper coaster in front of him.

He shook his head. "Not you, too."

Sky's brows disappeared beneath her bangs. "Too?"

"Kate mentioned her name earlier," he explained.

"Maybe because Macy's the only person in Haven who has the kind of experience you need."

"How does everyone seem to know so much about her?" he wondered aloud.

"It's Haven," his sister pointed out unnecessarily. "Everyone knows everything about everyone in this town—unless they've been living under a rock...or buried in the details of a property renovation."

"Well, I interviewed her today," he admitted, and lifted his glass to his mouth.

"And?" she prompted.

"And...she's got the kind of experience I need," he agreed.

Sky set a bowl of mixed nuts on the bar beside his glass. "So why haven't you hired her?"

He nibbled on a cashew. "I don't know."

"You're attracted to her," Sky guessed.

He scowled, not because it was untrue but because he was uncomfortable with the accuracy of his sister's insights. "Where is that coming from?"

"The fact that I know you. And the fact that she's an attractive woman, *but* not at all your type," she cautioned.

"You've always said I don't have a type," he reminded her.

"You might not show any preference between

blondes, brunettes and redheads, but since your one failed attempt at a grown-up relationship—"

"I've had several grown-up relationships," he interjected.

"I'm not talking about sex," she said dryly. "I'm talking about meaningful interactions that happen with your clothes on."

"Now you've lost me."

She sighed. "And that's Isabella's fault. When you were with her, you actually seemed to be growing into a mature and responsible human being. But since she broke your heart—"

"She didn't break my heart," he denied.

"—you've been all about having a good time," she continued, ignoring his interruption. "And Macy is all about responsibility."

"I can't remember the last time I had a good time," he lamented.

"At Carrie and Matt's wedding—with Heather," she surmised.

"Oh, yeah." He smiled. "That was a good time." Until Heather decided that one night meant they were back together again. "It was also seven months ago."

"Working for a living really sucks, huh?" she teased.

"You know I'm not just putting in a few hours at the hotel every day. I'm helping out at the ranch every morning, too."

"Why is that?" she prompted, because she got her kicks out of digging into other people's psyches and prying into their motivations. "You've made no secret of the fact that you want a life away from the ranch, but you keep going back."

"Because there are chores that need to be done."

"You don't think there are enough hands to manage without you?" she asked.

He shrugged. "Okay, so maybe I don't want the old man to forget that he's got two sons."

"He's not going to forget you," Sky assured him. "He's also not going to get over being pissed off any quicker just because you're mucking out stalls every morning."

"I know. But at least when I'm there, he has to talk to me."

His sister's sigh was filled with exasperation. "He's reverted to the silent treatment again?"

"He's barely spoken a dozen words to me since January 2," Liam confided. Because the holidays had officially ended then and, with them, the détente Katelyn had imposed on her family. During the period of eight days between Christmas Eve and New Year's Day, she'd forced her father and brother to play nice, threatening to celebrate Tessa's first Christmas without them if they couldn't get along. But now the holidays were over and so, too, was the father-son ceasefire.

"I'm sorry," Sky said. "Obviously Dad's going to need some time to accept that the hotel is more than a whim to you...assuming it is more than a whim."

He scowled at the implication. "You think I'd invest all my money—and a fair amount of our grandparents'—on a whim?"

"Maybe not," she allowed.

"Not to mention that the whole town will benefit from the reopening of the hotel," he assured her.

"Everyone except the owner of the Dusty Boots," she remarked dryly.

"No doubt there's a specific type of clientele that will still opt to pay the hourly rate at the budget motel."

Sky chuckled at that. "No doubt," she agreed. "And in addition to being an opportunity for the community, the hotel is an opportunity for you to finally escape the ranch you've hated since—"

"I've been thinking the hotel should have a bar," Liam said, deliberately cutting his sister off. "It would be nice to have a place to grab a beer without being psychoanalyzed by the bartender."

"A bar isn't a bad idea," she said. "A restaurant would be even better."

"Have you been talking to Grams?"

"Occasionally, since she happens to be my grandmother, too. But yes, she told me about The Home Station."

He shook his head. "We don't have a restaurant, only a solarium where we're going to serve breakfast. I don't know where she got it in her head that we should offer an upscale dining option, but you shouldn't encourage her."

"It's not a bad idea," Sky mused.

"It's not happening," he assured her.

Then a movement in the corner of his eye snagged his attention and he turned his head for a better view of the waitress delivering a tray of drinks to a nearby table. His gaze skimmed slowly up her long, slender legs to a nicely rounded bottom, trim waist and—

Sky interrupted his perusal by reaching across the bar to dab at the corner of his mouth with a cocktail napkin, as if he was drooling. He swatted her hand away and resumed his perusal.

Between the ranch and the inn, he'd had little time

for anything else since the wedding his sister had referred to—and even less interest. But somehow, after months had passed without anyone snagging his attention, he'd felt his body unexpectedly stir in response to two different women in the same day. Obviously it was a sign that he needed to readjust his priorities and find the time—and a willing woman—to help him end this unintended period of celibacy.

Then the waitress turned from the table, and his jaw nearly dropped. Because the female he'd been eyeing wasn't different at all—she was Macy Clayton.

Chapter 3

"You didn't know she worked here?" Sky guessed, her tone tinged with amusement.

Liam shook his head. "This job wasn't on her résumé."

"She's only been here a couple weeks. Or maybe I should say *back* here, because apparently she worked for Duke when she was in high school."

"Is she a good waitress?"

"Why? Do you want to hire her to work in your restaurant?" his sister teased.

"There is no restaurant," he said firmly. "And I'm asking you because you have an opinion about everything."

"Then I'll tell you that she's got great people skills. She's friendly without being flirty, and she knows when and how to placate an unhappy customer but she's not a pushover. Definite management material."

"I'll keep that in mind," he said dryly.

"And I'll go put in your food order."

"I haven't told you what I want."

"Steak sandwich with mushrooms, onions and pepper jack cheese with fries."

"Yeah, that sounds good," he admitted.

With a smug smile, she turned toward the kitchen.

And he shifted his attention back to the waitress who'd caught his eye. "Macy."

She pivoted, her eyes widening with surprise and recognition. "Mr. Gilmore."

"Liam," he reminded her.

"Liam," she echoed dutifully.

"You didn't mention that you had a job here."

"It's a temporary gig," she said, then smiled. "Just until I start my job at the Stagecoach Inn."

He couldn't help but smile back. "Confident, aren't you?"

"Qualified," she clarified.

"So why is a former assistant to the manager of a Las Vegas hotel working at a bar and grill in Haven?"

"I needed a job and Duke needed a waitress."

It sounded like a simple enough explanation, but he couldn't shake the feeling that he was missing a major piece of the puzzle that was Macy Clayton. And though he knew he was treading dangerously close to a line that should not be crossed, he was intrigued enough by the woman to want to know more.

"I didn't give you a tour of the hotel today," he noted.

"And I was so hoping for one," she confessed.

"Stop by tomorrow, if you want," he said. "As long as I haven't had a kid dropped in my lap, I should be free to show you around."

"I want," she immediately agreed. "Anytime in particular?"

"Whenever it's convenient for you."

"Okay. I'll see you tomorrow."

He watched her move away, making her way toward a table of six that had just sat down. Regulars, he guessed, as they didn't seem to need to look at the menus that were tucked beneath the tray of condiments on the table.

"It's my fault," Sky lamented, as she set a plate of food and his cutlery on the bar in front of him.

"What's your fault?" he asked.

"I should have realized that saying Macy wasn't your type would compel you to prove otherwise."

"Maybe you should tell me why you're so sure she's not my type," he suggested, lifting his sandwich from the plate.

"And maybe you should trust me for once," his sister countered.

His gaze shifted to Macy again. "Yeah, I'm having a little trouble with that."

"Then keep in mind that she's going to be working for you."

He wanted to argue that point, but after interviewing three other candidates for the job, he'd been forced to acknowledge that none of them was even remotely qualified.

Darren, currently a bouncer at a honky-tonk bar in Elko, was looking for a day job so he could go to night school. When Liam, simply out of curiosity, asked him why he wasn't choosing to study during the day and continuing to work nights, it was immediately apparent that Darren hadn't considered the possibility—an oversight that didn't bode well for success in his future studies.

Felix's résumé indicated that he was already college educated and had a master's degree in English literature. Unfortunately, he had absolutely no experience in the hospitality business and even less interest. During the interview, he confided that service industries were tedious and boring and acknowledged that he'd only applied for the job because employment opportunities in the town were limited.

And then there was Lissa, a college dropout who claimed that her life experience made her uniquely qualified for the job. When Liam asked her to give him an example, she explained that she'd lived with her in-laws for eighteen months without killing either of them—though she confessed that she'd given the idea more than a passing thought on a few occasions.

Which meant that, for the sake of the business, there really was only one choice for Liam to make.

He was going to have to hire Macy Clayton.

As he chewed on his sandwich, he accepted that whether she was or wasn't his type, hiring Macy Clayton would definitely put her off-limits for any romantic overtures.

And that was a damn shame.

Macy showed up just as the delivery truck was pulling away from the inn the following afternoon. Liam had kept himself busy directing the unloading and placement of the furniture so that he could pretend he wasn't watching and waiting for her to arrive for the promised tour of the property. At the same time, he reassured himself that his response to her couldn't possibly have been as powerful as he remembered.

Then he saw her, and the awareness hit him again, like a sucker punch in the gut.

It wasn't just that she was beautiful, though she was undoubtedly that. Even dressed casually, as she was today, in slim-fitting jeans and a cowl-neck sweater beneath a charcoal-grey wool coat belted at her waist, she was stunning. But he'd crossed paths with plenty of attractive women in his twenty-nine years without ever experiencing such an immediate and intense reaction, and he couldn't deny that it worried him a little.

"Good timing," he said, in lieu of a greeting as she walked up the steps.

"Was that the delivery truck just leaving?" she asked.

He nodded.

"I recognized the logo," she said. "You're obviously a man of exquisite taste."

"Garrett Furniture has a great collection of pieces that coordinate without being exactly the same," he told her. "The idea is that every room will offer the same level of luxury but in a distinctly individual setting, so that guests who enjoyed their stay in the Doc Holliday Suite might want to come back to experience the Charles Goodnight Suite—or upgrade to the Wild Bill Getaway Suite."

"Are all of the rooms named after famous people?"

"They are," he confirmed. "It was my grandmother's idea, and she did the research, from Annie Oakley to Wild Bill. Interesting details about their lives are engraved on plaques in each room—but instead of telling you about them, why don't I show you?"

"Sounds good to me." She reached toward the door

before he could, but instead of grasping the handle, her fingers traced the outline of the raised panel on which was carved an intricate and detailed image of a horse-drawn stagecoach. "This is amazing."

"The previous owner wanted to acknowledge the building's origins," Liam told her. "There's a series of paintings in the library—original oils by local artists—that also pay tribute to the town's history."

Since the door opened into the lobby on the main level, that's where they started the tour.

Macy had come in the same way when she'd arrived for her interview the day before, but the folding table and cheap plastic chairs that had created an ad hoc interview space had been replaced by an elegant double pedestal executive desk with dentil molding and antique brass hardware. The high-back chair behind the desk was covered in butter-soft leather that coordinated with the sofa and oversized chairs that faced the stone fireplace.

"You should have a lamp for that table," she suggested, pointing. "And a focal point for the coffee table. Maybe a copper bowl—wide and shallow. Have you ever been to the antique and craft market out by the highway?"

"I don't think so."

"You should go," she told him. "There's a local artist who sells his pieces there. I bet you could find all kinds of unique things to add not just visual interest but local flavor."

"I'll keep that in mind," he said, as he directed her toward the library.

The room had the potential to live up to its name, with two walls of built-in floor-to-ceiling bookcases—

currently completely empty of books. She thought about the fun she could have stocking those shelves to provide guests with a variety of reading materials. Maybe she'd even throw in some board games, lay out a chess set on the square table between the two silk-upholstered wing chairs.

She took a moment to study and admire the paintings he'd told her about, appreciating not just the talent but the subjects represented in every brush stroke and color.

"Basque linens," she said, as they moved down the hall to the main floor guest rooms.

"What?"

She chuckled. "Sorry—I'm sure that seemed to come out of nowhere, but I was just thinking about other ways to highlight the history of not just this building but the local area."

"I know about the Basques but nothing about their linen."

"It was originally made from flax grown in the fields and woven with colorful stripes, traditionally seven, which was the number of Basque provinces in France and Spain. The source of the fabric and the process has evolved over the years, but the colorful stripes remain a defining feature."

"How do you know this?"

"In high school, I did a research paper on how the Basque people and culture have influenced our local community, which is just one more reason—" she offered a hopeful smile "—I'd be an asset at your front desk."

"I'll keep that in mind," he promised, leading her down the hall to the Annie Oakley Room.

She wondered if he'd chosen the color palette and

furnishings, or if his grandmother had taken the lead in that, too. Either way, the overall impression of the room was warmth and comfort, and she could imagine herself contentedly curling up in the middle of the half-tester and dreaming sweet dreams. That tempting fantasy was followed closely by one of sinking into the claw-footed tub filled with scented bubbles when she peeked into the bath.

Appropriately, Bonnie & Clyde were adjoining rooms—the former with a single queen-size sleigh bed, the latter with two double beds of the same style.

"A, B, C," she realized. "I assume you did that on purpose?"

"Yeah, although it kind of fell apart upstairs where we jump from D to F."

"What's beyond those doors?" she asked.

"Serenity Spa."

She sighed, a little wistfully. "When I heard you were looking for a manager, I knew I wanted the job," Macy told him. "Because it's what I've trained to do— and what I'm good at. But that was before I'd seen what you've done here, and now that I have, I want it even more."

"You haven't seen half of what we've done here," he said, leading the way to the second floor.

He was right. And with every door she walked through, she fell more and more in love. The rooms were all spacious and inviting, with natural light pouring through the windows, spilling across the glossy floors. She'd often thought hardwood was cold, but the rugs that had been added provided warmth, color and texture. There were crown moldings in one room, window seats in another, elaborate wardrobes and antique dressing screens, padded benches and hope chests. The en suite baths boasted natural stone tiles and heated towel bars, waterfall showerheads inside glass enclosures and freestanding soaker tubs.

Each room was unique in its style and substance, and Macy honestly couldn't have said which one was her favorite—until they reached the third floor and Liam opened the door to Wild Bill's Getaway Suite.

Everything about the space screamed luxury, from the intricate mosaic pattern in the floor tile to the elegant chesterfield sofa and forty-two-inch flat-screen TV mounted above the white marble fireplace. Beyond the parlor was the bath, with more white marble, lots of glass and even an enormous crystal chandelier. There was a second fireplace in the bedroom, along with a king-size pediment poster bed flanked by matching end tables, a wide wardrobe and even a makeup vanity set.

"Well, it's not the Dusty Boots Motel," she remarked dryly when they'd made their way back down to the main level—and the solarium where he told her breakfast would be served.

Liam chuckled. "The idea was to give visitors to Haven another option."

"I'd say you succeeded."

The solarium had two sets of French doors that opened onto the deck, where additional bistro tables and chairs would be set up for guests to enjoy their breakfast in the warm weather.

"Did you have another space in mind for more formal, evening dining?"

He shook his head. "We're limiting our service to breakfast-slash-brunch, with an afternoon wine and cheese in the library on Fridays and Saturdays."

"I like the wine and cheese idea," she said. "But if you're not offering an evening meal, you're missing out on the opportunity for guests to spend more of their money right here."

"There are other places people can go for dinner," he pointed out.

"There's no place in town that offers an upscale dining experience. When my parents celebrated their fortieth anniversary last year, they drove all the way to Reno because they wanted candlelight and a wine list that wasn't printed on the bottom of a laminated page below the kids' menu."

He smiled at that. "I can see your point, but I know nothing about the restaurant business."

"Which is why you hire people who do," she said.

"Like you?" he guessed.

She immediately shook her head. "No. That's not my area of expertise. But Kyle Landry studied at the School of Artisan Food in England."

"I'm sure his mother could have taught him everything he needed to know about making pizza."

"Except that Kyle doesn't want to make pizza. He wants to run his own kitchen in a real restaurant."

Liam winced. "Don't let Jo hear you say that."

"His words, not mine," Macy explained.

"Maybe that's why he's not working in her kitchen right now," he suggested.

"Yeah, she's not happy that Duke gave him a job. But Kyle's not really happy, either, because Duke won't even contemplate any changes to the menu. Kyle added chili-dusted pumpkin seeds to the coleslaw to give it a little bit of crunch and zing, and three customers sent it back. They grudgingly acknowledged that it was good but complained that it 'didn't taste right.'"

"People want what they want, and local people don't want fancy food."

But Macy disagreed. "They might not want fancy food in a familiar setting," she allowed. "But a new restaurant would open up a world of new possibilities. Not to mention that a restaurant would create another revenue stream for your business."

"Have you been talking to my grandmother?"

She laughed. "No, but I'm guessing she said the same thing."

"Yeah," he admitted. "And maybe it is something to think about."

"You might think about talking to Kyle, too" Macy suggested.

"I might," he agreed.

She didn't ask him about the job.

Macy figured there was a fine line between eager and pushy and she didn't want to cross it. Besides, Liam had promised to make a decision by the end of the week, so she would hold on to her patience a while longer.

But by Friday afternoon, with another long and late shift at Diggers' looming ahead, her patience was running out. She was grateful that she had a job, but it was hard to keep a smile on her face when she was working on less than five hours of frequently interrupted sleep.

Her babies, now eight months old, had started sleeping a lot better, more consistently and—maybe even more important—concurrently, which allowed Macy to get more sleep. But the past couple of weeks had been rough as two of the three were cutting teeth. Two tiny buds had poked through Ava's bottom gum almost a week earlier with minimal fuss, but her brothers were struggling and miserable.

And despite Macy's optimism after she'd completed her tour of the Stagecoach Inn—and Liam Gilmore's promise to be in touch by the end of the week—she still hadn't heard anything from him about the job. So she left a little early for her shift at Diggers' and stopped by the hotel on her way. There was no one in the main lobby when she arrived, so she peeked inside the library, but that was empty, too. She wandered a little further and finally found Liam in the kitchen, muttering to himself as he opened and inspected a stack of boxes on the island.

"Is this a bad time?" she asked.

He held up a dinner plate. "Does this look like white to you?"

"Only if tangerines are white," she noted.

He set the plate on the counter and selected a bowl from another box. "How about this? Is this—" he glanced at the notation on what she guessed was an itemized list of his order "—dove?"

"Um, no. I'd say that's lemon," she said.

"And this?" He showed her a salad plate.

"Lime."

"Great," he said dryly. "I ordered tableware and they sent me fruit salad." He held up a mug.

"I'm tempted to say blueberry." She fought a smile. "But it's actually closer to turquoise."

He shook his head, obviously not amused.

"I'm guessing you got someone else's order."

He scrubbed his hands over his face. "An order that I've been waiting on for three months."

She moved to the island and set the salad plate on top of the dinner plate, then the bowl in the center of the salad plate and the mug beside it. "I like it," she decided.

He lifted a brow. "You're kidding."

She shook her head. "White and grey are basic, boring. This tableware makes a statement that's more reflective of what you're doing with the distinctive décor in each of the guestrooms—providing your visitors with a unique experience."

"I wanted basic and boring," he said stubbornly.

"So you can send this back and find basic and boring tableware somewhere else, or you can keep this and negotiate a price reduction from the supplier."

He looked dubious. "You really think I should keep it?"

"I do, but it's not my decision to make. Unless that kind of thing falls under managerial duties," she added hopefully.

"Someone once told me that a good employee is someone who steps up to do what needs to be done, even if it isn't in her job description."

"Touché."

"And I'm guessing that's why you're here," he realized.

"Well, you did say you'd make a decision by the end of the week, and it's the end of the week."

"So it is," he agreed. "And there's no doubt you're the most qualified of the applicants I've interviewed."

"Why do I get the feeling there's a *but*?" she asked warily.

"But I have some reservations about hiring you," he admitted.

"What kind of reservations? Did Duke complain

about me being late? Because that was once. Okay, maybe twice, but—"

"Duke gave you a glowing recommendation," he interjected to assure her.

She frowned. "Then why don't you want to hire me?"

"Because you're an incredibly attractive woman and… I find myself incredibly attracted to you."

His reply wasn't at all what she'd expected, and it took Macy a moment to wrap her head around it and decide how to respond to it—and him.

She was undeniably flattered. Liam Gilmore wasn't at all hard to look at, and he was built like the rancher she knew he'd been before he bought the old Stagecoach Inn. And she admittedly felt a stir of something unexpected whenever she was near him, but she hadn't let that dissuade her from going after the job she wanted, because she knew that a man like Liam Gilmore would never be interested in a woman whose first, second and third priorities were her children.

"I fail to see how that's relevant to my ability to do the job you need done," she finally said.

"You don't think the attraction might make our working relationship a little…uncomfortable?"

"Not at all," she assured him. "Because I have no doubt that you want this venture to succeed, and that requires hiring the right person for the right job. Aside from that, an initial feeling of attraction is always based on superficial criteria, and once you get to know me, you'll realize I'm not your type."

He scowled. "Why does everyone keep saying that?"

"While I must admit to some curiosity about the 'everyone' else who might have said the same thing, the reason is simple," she said. "Because I'd guess that someone known around town as 'Love 'em and Leave 'em Liam' is only looking for a good time and—"

"That nickname isn't just ridiculous, it's completely inaccurate," he interjected.

She ignored his interruption to finish making her point: "And, as a single mom, I don't have time for extracurricular activities of any kind right now."

Liam took an actual physical step backward, a subconscious retreat.

"You have a kid?"

Macy's lips curved in a wry smile. "Yeah, I figured my revelation would have that effect."

"I'm sorry," he said. "I just... I didn't know."

"Like I said—not your type," she reminded him.

And she was right.

Everyone was right.

Because as much as he adored his niece—and he did—he wasn't willing to play father to some other guy's kid.

Not again.

He looked at Macy, dressed for another shift at Diggers' in a different short skirt and low-cut top, and couldn't help but remark, "You sure as heck don't look like anyone's mother."

She smiled at that. "Thanks, I think. But I don't want platitudes—I want a job. I want the manager's job," she clarified. "I don't mind waiting tables at Diggers', but the late hours mean that I miss the bedtime routine with my kids almost every night."

"Kid*s*?" he echoed, surprised to learn that she had more than one.

She nodded.

"How many?"

"Three," she admitted. "They're eight months old."

He waited for her to provide the ages of her other two children, then comprehension dawned. *"Triplets?"*

She nodded again.

"Wow."

"Yeah, that was pretty much my reaction when the doctor told me—although I might have added a few NSFW adjectives."

"And the dad?" he wondered. "I imagine he was shocked, too."

"I'm not sure it's appropriate to ask a prospective employee about her personal relationships," she noted. "But since there are no secrets in this town, I'll tell you that he's not in the picture."

"You're right—it was an inappropriate question," he acknowledged.

Also, Macy's relationship with the father of her babies was irrelevant. She might be the sexiest single mom he'd ever met, but he had less than zero interest in being the "dad" who transformed the equation of "mom plus three kids" into "family."

"I guess the only question left to ask is—when can you start?"

Chapter 4

The smile that curved Macy's lips illuminated her whole face. "I've got the job?"

Liam nodded, though he worried that his heart seemed to fill with joy just to know that she was happy. Clearly the wayward organ hadn't received the message from his brain that his new manager was a single mom or it would be erecting impenetrable shields.

"I'd have to be a fool to hire anyone else," he said.

And from a business perspective, it was absolutely true.

From a personal perspective, it might turn out that he was just as big a fool to hire her.

During their tour of the inn a few days earlier, he'd been driven to distraction by her nearness. And he'd wanted to move nearer, so that he was close enough to touch her—or even kiss her. Would her skin feel as soft as it looked? Would her lips taste as sweet as he imagined?

"A lot of people think you're foolish to reopen the hotel," she noted.

Her comment dragged him out of his fantasy and back to the present.

"I guess it's lucky for you that I didn't listen to those people."

"I guess it is," she agreed. "But in response to your earlier question, I can start whenever you need me."

"Two weeks ago?"

She chuckled softly. "Are you running behind schedule on a few things?"

"A few," he acknowledged.

"Since I have to go so I'm not running behind schedule for my shift at Diggers' tonight, why don't you fill me in on Monday morning?"

He nodded. "That works for me."

After a late Friday night at Diggers', Macy usually struggled to drag herself out of bed on Saturday mornings. But knowing that this was her last such morning after her last late night, she was able to greet the day with a little more enthusiasm.

"What are you doing up so early?" Bev asked, when Macy tracked down the triplets—and her mother—in the upstairs kitchen.

Ava, Max and Sam were in their high chairs, set up side-by-side at the table where their grandmother could keep a close eye on them while she fried bacon on the stove.

Sam spotted his mama first, and he gleefully banged his sippy cup on the tray of his high chair. Ava, not to be outdone by her brother, stretched her arms out and called "Ma!" Max just smiled—a sweet, toothless grin that never failed to melt her heart.

"I wanted to get breakfast for Ava, Max and Sam today." And though caffeine was required to ensure that she could function, she paused on her way to the coffee pot to kiss each of her precious babies.

"Because you don't think I can handle it?" her mother queried, transferring the cooked bacon onto paper towels to drain the grease.

"Because you handle it all the time," Macy clarified, reaching into the cupboard for a mug that she filled from the carafe.

After a couple of sips, she found the box of baby oatmeal cereal in the pantry. She spooned the dry mix into each of three bowls, then stirred in the requisite amount of formula. Ava, Max and Sam avidly watched her every move.

"You guys look like you're hungry," Macy noted, as she peeled a ripe banana and cut it into thirds. She dropped a piece of fruit into each of the bowls and mashed it into the cereal.

"Ma!" Ava said again, because it wasn't just her first but also her only word.

She chuckled softly as she continued to mash and stir.

"While you're taking care of that, I'll make pancakes for us," Bev said, as she gathered the necessary ingredients together.

Macy had given up asking her mother not to cook for her, because the protests had fallen on deaf ears—and because it was a nice treat to have a hot breakfast prepared for her on a Saturday morning. Especially pancakes.

"You always made pancakes as part of a celebration," she noted, with a smile. "Whether it was a birthday or a clean room or an 'A' on a spelling test."

"Which is why you got them more often than your brothers," her mother remarked, as she cracked eggs into a glass bowl.

It wasn't true, of course. If Bev made pancakes, the whole family got to eat pancakes, but she always acknowledged when one of her kids did something special to warrant a breakfast celebration.

"Well, we've got something to celebrate today, too," Macy said.

Her mother looked up from the batter she was whisking. "You got the job?"

Macy grinned and nodded. "You are looking at the new manager-slash-concierge of the Stagecoach Inn."

Bev set down the whisk to hug her daughter. "Oh, honey, I'm so proud of you."

"I'll work Monday through Friday for the next few weeks, and then, when the hotel is open, Wednesday through Sunday, eight a.m. until two p.m."

"That's perfect," her mom said. "You'll have more time with your kids and be able to work at a job you enjoy."

Macy carried the bowls of oatmeal to the table. "I'm already looking forward to getting started," she confided. "This is exactly what I've always wanted."

Her mother sprinkled a few drops of water on the griddle, testing its readiness. "Except that it's in Haven," she pointed out.

Macy scooped up some oatmeal and moved the

spoon toward Max's open mouth. "You don't want me to stay in Haven?"

"Of course, *I* want you here," Bev said, ladling batter onto the hot pan. "But I know that was never your first choice."

"Where are you getting that from?" Macy shifted her attention to the next bowl, but she was sincerely baffled by the statement.

"Maybe the fact that you were on your way out of town practically before the ink was dry on your high school diploma."

Macy used the spoon to catch the cereal that Sam pushed out of his mouth with his tongue. "I graduated in June and I moved in August—three days before the start of classes at UNLV."

"Well, you've hardly been home since," her mom remarked.

"I came home every chance I got, which wasn't a lot because I was juggling two part-time jobs along with my studies." Ava swallowed her first mouthful of cereal, and Macy gave her a second before making her way backwards down the line again.

"We could have helped you a little more," Bev said.

"You offered," Macy assured her. "But the experience of those jobs was even more valuable than the paycheck."

"I know you've always wanted to work in the hospitality industry—ever since we visited your aunt at The Gatestone in Washington when you were a little girl," her mother noted, as she began to turn the pancakes. "And, of course, the best career opportunities are probably in Las Vegas."

"There were *zero* career opportunities for me in

Haven when I left," Macy pointed out, as she continued to feed her babies. "The only place around that offered any kind of temporary accommodations was the Dusty Boots Motel, and they weren't hiring.

"I came back to Haven because I knew I couldn't handle—or afford to raise—three kids on my own in Vegas. Maybe I was a little disappointed to give up my career, but I was happy to be home and happier still to know that my babies would grow up close to their extended family.

"I might not have envisioned an arrangement quite this close," she said. "But it works. And if I haven't mentioned it lately, I'm incredibly grateful to you and Dad for everything you've done for all of us."

"You tell us every day," Bev said. "And we're happy to help."

"Still, I should probably look into making other arrangements for part-time childcare, don't you think?"

"What?" Her mom turned around so fast, the pancake on her spatula dropped to the floor. "Why?"

Macy got up to retrieve the broken cake and toss it into the sink. "Because I feel as if I'm taking advantage of you and Dad."

"That's ridiculous," Bev said. "Your father and I aren't doing anything that we don't want to do."

"You're also not doing things that you *would* like to do," Macy pointed out. "Like last Saturday, when Dad had to cancel his fishing trip with Oscar Weston because I was working a double shift and you were in bed with a migraine."

"Well, he's fishing with Oscar today."

"And you gave up your pottery classes because I worked almost every Wednesday night."

"I was happy to have an excuse to quit—I couldn't ever make a lump of clay look like anything else."

"I don't believe it." Macy scraped the last of the cereal from the bottom of Ava's bowl. "But I appreciate you saying so."

"And since you won't be working nights anymore, I can join Frieda's book club."

She wiped Ava's mouth with her bib, then offered the little girl her sippy cup of juice. "Mrs. Zimmerman has a book club?"

Her mother nodded. "She started it last summer, after she saw the movie."

"*The* movie?" Macy echoed, because she was pretty sure that the local movie theater would have shown more than one movie the previous summer.

"*Book Club*."

"Ahh, that makes sense," she said, helping Max finish his breakfast.

Bev stacked three pancakes on a plate, added four strips of bacon, then set it on the table. "Eat while it's hot," she instructed her daughter.

Macy picked up a slice of crisp bacon, nipped off the end. "I'm glad the pediatrician finally approved the introduction of solid foods for Ava, Max and Sam," she said, pouring maple syrup over her pancakes. "They're definitely sleeping for longer stretches now and waking up happier."

"You're grumpy, too, when you're hungry," her mom noted, bringing her own plate and mug to the table to eat with her daughter.

"Is that why you always have breakfast ready for me when I get up on a Saturday morning?"

"One of the reasons," Bev acknowledged. "Another is that I really do enjoy having someone to cook for."

"You cook for Dad," she pointed out.

"Bacon and eggs. That's what it's been every Saturday morning for forty years."

"That doesn't mean *you* have to eat bacon and eggs."

Her mother shrugged. "It seems like too much bother to make something different just for myself, but it's a pleasure to make it for you."

"Maybe I'll make breakfast for you tomorrow," Macy offered impulsively.

"You've got enough to do with three babies without worrying about cooking for anyone else," Bev protested. "Plus, you've got to get ready for your first day at your new job on Monday."

"There's nothing to get ready for. And you managed to raise three kids and put meals on the table while also working outside the home."

"My kids weren't all in diapers at the same time."

"On the plus side, they'll hopefully all be out of diapers around the same time," she said.

"There is that," her mom agreed.

Macy glanced over at Sam, who'd started banging his cup on his tray again to get her attention. When he had her attention, he smiled.

"What's that in your mouth, Sam?" She pulled his high chair closer to the table for a better look. "Have you got a tooth in there?"

He grinned again, giving her another glimpse of a tiny white bud barely poking through a red and swollen gum.

Macy felt her eyes sting. "My youngest baby has his first tooth."

"It had to come sooner or later," her mother pointed out with unerring logic.

"I know," she agreed, as she lifted a hand to ruffle his wispy curls. "But he's been miserable for so long, I was starting to wonder."

She turned her attention to his brother, gnawing on the spout of his cup, drool dripping down his chin. "What about you, Max? Do you have a smile for Mommy?"

He did, of course, but he had no new teeth—or any teeth at all—to show off to her.

"Yours will come," she promised. "Probably just another day or two."

"Don't be in a hurry for them to grow up," Bev cautioned her daughter. "I know it seems like they're making slow progress now, but before you know it, your babies will have babies of their own."

Macy was up early Monday morning, because today she had something to look forward to besides feeding her babies their breakfast.

She was excited about starting her new job at the Stagecoach Inn. Although the boutique hotel wasn't scheduled to open for another two weeks, she knew there would be a lot of last-minute details to take care of in advance of the big event, and she was happy to help. Liam had agreed that 8 a.m. was an acceptable time for her to start, but she was there by 7:30. In fact, she pulled into the parking lot beside the inn at the same time as her boss.

"You're early," he noted, as he fell into step beside her.

"I've got three babies who are up by five every morning," she confided. "Plus I'm eager to hear all about your plans for this place."

"Compared to Las Vegas, they're not very grand," he warned.

"Since this isn't Vegas, it would be silly to make such a comparison. And while Haven isn't ever likely to be a tourist mecca, there are people who visit Nevada for reasons other than gambling and quickie weddings," she noted.

"And weddings are really just a different kind of gambling, aren't they?" he remarked.

Her brows lifted. "Spoken like a man who has some experience in the matter."

"Just one close call," he said, as he slid his key into the lock of the front door.

Not wanting to pursue what she sensed was a touchy subject, she instead shifted the direction of their conversation. "When I was growing up in Haven, no one locked their doors."

"A lot of people still don't," he told her. "And with this property being centrally located, I'm not really worried about theft or vandalism, but I don't want people sneaking in after hours to nose around.

"There will be pictures on the website, of course, but I'm hoping that residents who are curious enough to want an up close and personal look at the rooms will book a stay."

"You'll get some of those," she assured him. "And when they tell their friends what an amazing job you've done with the renovations, you'll get more."

"Fingers crossed."

She grinned. "You don't need luck when you've got a fabulous property and a savvy manager."

* * *

Macy threw herself into assisting with the preparations for the opening, willing to tackle any task Liam assigned to her. She also seemed determined to make him buy more stuff.

When he'd given her the tour, he'd thought the rooms were ready for the arrival of guests. But while Macy approved of the furnishings and linens, she thought there should be a ladder shelf in the corner of one room, perhaps a quilt rack in another room, a fabric bench at the foot of this bed, more pillows on those window seats.

He balked at her suggestions, reluctant to spend more money on a property that wasn't yet generating any income.

"Let me show you," she urged, and dragged him out to the antique and craft market.

Her first find was a wooden wash-basin stand with ceramic pitcher and bowl and a swivel vanity mirror.

"This will fit perfectly in that empty corner in the Charles Goodnight Suite," she told him.

Aside from the fact that he didn't believe every corner needed to be filled, he had to ask, "Isn't one of the benefits of having running water the ability to turn on the tap to access that running water?"

"Your point?" she challenged.

"In the era of indoor plumbing, an antique wash-basin set has no practical purpose."

"In the beginning, you're going to draw guests for one primary reason," she explained, in the same patient tone he imagined she'd use to reason with a stubborn child. "Either they're visiting Haven or just passing through town and looking for a place to sleep that has a little more ambience than the Dusty Boots Motel.

Sure, you'll get some locals booking a room or suite for a night, to celebrate a special occasion or score points with a special someone. But for the most part, your early guests will show up more by accident than design."

"So far this explanation is doing nothing to convince me that I need to fork over—" he looked at the tag affixed to the back of the mirror and winced "—a lot of money that is unlikely to give me any kind of return on my investment."

"But it will," she insisted. "Because it's part of your brand. And I know you know what I'm talking about—it's why you invested in quality furniture and pillow-top mattresses over cheap laminate and economy sleep sets."

He did know what she was talking about. In his business courses at college, they'd discussed image and branding as a way of making a company or product stand out from the rest. And as she'd noted, he'd already distinguished his property from the Dusty Boots Motel, which represented the total sum of the rest of the overnight accommodations available in town.

"So why do you think this other stuff is necessary?" he asked her.

"Because there aren't enough people just passing through town to keep you in business. You need to make the Stagecoach Inn a destination—not just a place for guests to lay their heads on their way to somewhere else, but a place they want to come to and stay at."

"And a wash basin and pitcher are going to do that?" he asked dubiously.

"It's the details that make a lasting impression. It's the reason guests post online reviews to share their experiences with other potential guests. Almost better than reviews are the pictures. And people don't take pictures of empty corners—they take pictures of antique wash stands and Arts and Crafts andirons."

"Andirons?" he echoed.

"We'll get to those next," she promised. "The point is, you don't want to give your guests a room, you want to provide them with an experience. One that they'll want to enjoy again and again and tell their friends and family about, enticing those friends and family to book a room—no, an experience," she immediately corrected herself. "To see for themselves what all the fuss is about.

"Which leads me to another idea I wanted to discuss with you."

"How much is it going to cost me?" he wondered aloud.

She ignored his question. "Spa packages."

"The spa isn't really part of the hotel."

"I know. I was talking to Andria yesterday," she said, naming the woman who owned and operated Serenity Spa. "And I won't tell you that you missed out on a terrific opportunity there, but I will suggest that you could partner with her to offer special rates and packages for guests of the hotel.

"There could be a separate page on the website," she said. "The word *indulge* in a flowy script at the top of a page, maybe with an image of a woman wrapped in a plush robe, her feet in a warm bath. Or a man facedown on a massage table with a woman's hands sliding over his strongly muscled back. Or both. And the copy could read something like—pamper your body and your soul, from head to toe, with a unique package of exclusive services offered by Serenity Spa at the Stagecoach Inn."

He could picture it, exactly as she described, and he

couldn't deny the appeal. "You really are good at this," he acknowledged.

"Told you." Her smile was more than a little enticing.

And if she'd been anyone else—not an employee and not a single mom—he might have lowered his head to taste those sweetly curved lips.

But she wasn't anyone else. She was the manager of the inn, and he had to respect that professional relationship and keep his hands off.

She also had three babies at home, a fact that should have destroyed the last vestiges of temptation. But when he was with Macy, it was an effort to remember all the reasons he shouldn't be attracted to her. Because he couldn't deny that he was.

She, however, gave absolutely no indication that she felt the same way, and he knew that was probably for the best. His unrequited attraction might be the cause of physical frustration, but at least it wasn't going to lead to a broken heart.

While he was mulling over these thoughts, she was chatting with the vendor. Haggling over the price on the tag, he realized, but in such a way that the seller looked pleased to be able to negotiate a sale with her. She waved as she walked away, with a smile on her face and his business card in hand, and Liam following with the much more cumbersome wash-basin stand.

"And now the andirons," she said.

He just sighed. "Can I put this in the truck first?"

She nodded. "That's probably a good idea."

Liam had never been a fan of shopping, but he couldn't deny that he had fun exploring the market with

Macy. And the happiness that lit up her face whenever she spotted what she referred to as a hidden gem was almost worth the price of the trio of brass oil lamps she talked him into buying.

And when they got back to the inn and she'd arranged his purchases as she'd envisioned them, he couldn't deny that she had a good eye.

Actually, she had gorgeous eyes. Deep and clear and dark.

And a temptingly shaped mouth with a sexy dip at the center.

And he really needed to stop focusing on all the parts that appealed to him and remember that she was off-limits.

On Wednesday morning during her second week on the job, he got a pointed reminder when he found her in the kitchen, arranging spices and seasonings. She moved with her usual brisk efficiency, but he noticed that she was wearing something a little different than her usual business casual attire.

"Is that part of the uniform in Vegas?" he asked, gesturing to the baby carrier strapped to her body.

"So much for thinking you wouldn't notice," she remarked. "But a stylish accessory, don't you agree?"

He eyed the contraption dubiously as he took a few steps closer to peek at the baby snuggled up against her mother's chest. "Cute kid," he noted.

She smiled. "This is Ava."

"Eight months?" He seemed to recall that was a number she'd mentioned.

"Eight months, two weeks and four days now," she clarified. "I hope you don't mind that I brought her with me, but my mom had an appointment this afternoon and my dad would struggle on his own with three babies."

"I don't mind," he said.

In fact, he was kind of glad she'd brought Ava with her today, because the more time he'd spent with Macy over the past several days, the harder it had been to remember all the reasons she wasn't his type. Now one of those three reasons was strapped to her chest, and he refused to acknowledge that he found the sight of his new manager and her infant daughter at all appealing.

But the baby really was a cutie, with her adorably chubby cheeks, little button nose and big blue eyes fringed with ridiculously long lashes. She was also surprisingly content to be hauled around in the carrier, those big eyes taking in every detail of her surroundings.

When she shoved her fist into her mouth and began sucking on her knuckles, Macy took a bottle out of the fridge. She didn't miss a beat in her telephone conversation but switched the phone to speaker mode and set it on the counter so that her hands were free to unhook the carrier and lift out the baby.

She expertly cradled her child in the crook of one arm, and Ava's little hands helped hold the bottle as her mouth worked the nipple. Liam was so preoccupied watching the baby that he didn't realize Macy was wrapping up the call until she pressed a button to terminate the connection.

"Fifteen percent," she said.

"What?"

"That was your dinnerware supplier. He'll be emailing you a revised invoice with the amount due reduced by fifteen percent."

"I'm impressed."

She smiled. "Impressed enough to add a fifteen percent bonus to my paycheck?"

"Not this week," he said. "But we'll discuss your salary at your performance review after six months."

"You're going to give me a raise," she said confidently.

He didn't doubt it was true. If he'd learned nothing else during their trip to the antique and craft market, he'd learned that his new manager knew how to get what she wanted.

She gently pried the nipple of the now-empty bottle from her daughter's mouth, then lifted her to her shoulder and rubbed her back. The baby emitted a shockingly loud burp for such a little thing, then yawned hugely and closed her eyes.

"She'll sleep now for at least an hour," Macy told him. "Is it okay if I put her down in the library for her nap while I meet with the wine merchant?"

She'd set up the baby's playpen in that room earlier, so he knew she was informing him as a courtesy more than asking permission, but he nodded anyway.

While she was in her meeting, he signed for a delivery and carted the boxes from the bookstore into the library. Four boxes of books—and each one weighed as much as a sack of grain.

He'd just torn open the flaps on the first box when Ava woke up.

She didn't make any sound at first. It was the movement he noticed, as she rolled herself over from her back to her belly. She lifted her head, a happy smile on her face as she looked up, no doubt expecting to see her mama—and finding a strange man instead.

The smile disappeared, and her big blue eyes filled with distress.

Chapter 5

Macy lost track of time while she was with the local wine merchant, selecting options for the daily wine and cheese hour Liam had proposed and negotiating quantities and prices. When she finally signed the order and glanced at her watch, she hurried to the library and her daughter.

Any concerns she'd harbored about momnesia interfering with her job performance had, so far, proven to be unfounded. In fact, with each day that passed, she felt more and more confident in her role.

And increasingly unnerved by the unexpected—and unwanted—attraction to her boss.

The revelation that she had three infants seemed to have effectively killed any romantic interest on his part, for which she knew she should be grateful. Instead, being in close proximity to the sexy cowboy-turned-innkeeper only made her feel churned up.

And that was before she stopped in the doorway of the library and saw him cuddling her baby girl in his arms.

"You really are just a little bitty thing, aren't you?" he mused aloud. "Of course, you're a few months younger than Tessa, but I don't think my niece was ever such a lightweight."

Ava's gaze was focused on his face, as if trying to decide if he was a friend or foe. She didn't have a lot of experience with strangers, and the furrow in her tiny brow along with the quiver of her lower lip warned Macy that the little girl was close to tears.

She started to take another step forward but paused when Liam spoke again, obviously reading the same signals and wanting to soothe the baby's distress.

"I know I'm not your mama," he said. "But your mama's busy right now, so we're just going to hang together until she finishes her meeting. She shouldn't be too much longer, and if you give me a chance, you might discover that I'm not such a bad guy, really.

"And when I say 'give me a chance,' I mean no crying, okay? Because I'm at a complete loss when it comes to tears."

What was it about a strong man showing his gentle side that arrowed directly to her heart? Macy wondered.

Or was it specifically this man?

Or maybe the fact that her baby was the beneficiary of the tender demonstration?

Regardless of the rationale, she suddenly realized that she was in trouble.

Prior to this exact moment, she'd been so focused on

her excitement over the job that she hadn't let herself worry that working in close proximity to a sexy man would be a problem.

Obviously she'd been wrong.

"Some people might say I'm clueless about a lot of things when it comes to women," Liam continued his confession. "And they'd be right, but tears are probably my biggest weakness. Thankfully you're too young to understand what I'm saying—so this will be our little secret, okay?"

"My lips are sealed," Macy promised.

Liam started and turned toward the doorway, then spoke to Ava again, "See? I said your mama wouldn't be too long."

The baby squirmed in his arms, stretching her own out toward her mother.

"Your books were delivered," Liam said, as Macy took Ava from him. "And when I came in to unpack the shipment, I discovered that she was awake. I hope you don't mind that I picked her up. She seemed to be looking for you, and getting distressed when she couldn't find you, so I tried to distract her."

"Of course I don't mind," she said. "I'm grateful you were here." She patted Ava's bottom, then reached for the tote bag beside the playpen. "But I do wonder—if my meeting had gone five minutes longer, would she be wearing a clean diaper?"

"Not likely," he said.

She laughed softly. "At least you're honest."

"I've found that's the best way to eliminate misunderstandings."

"In which case—" she unfolded the portable change

pad and laid Ava on top of it "—there's something I should tell you."

"What's that?" he asked, wariness evident in his tone.

"This probably won't be the last time I have to bring one or more of my kids to work with me."

"You don't have an unsuspecting brother you could leave them with?" he asked dryly.

She smiled as she unsnapped Ava's pants. "Actually, I have two brothers, but neither of them lives in town."

"I was only joking, anyway," he assured her. "I've grown to appreciate the juggling act that is required of a working mom, and I don't have a problem with you bringing your kids to work on occasion. But if I have a choice, I don't do diapers."

"I'll keep that in mind," she promised, sliding a dry one under her daughter's bottom.

"And since you're busy with that…do you want me to shelve these books? Or will you just rearrange everything when I'm done?"

"Can you group them by genre then alphabetize them by author?"

"I can take them out of the box and put them on the shelves."

She shook her head as she refastened the snaps on Ava's pants. "I'll do it."

And she'd be grateful for a task that required her focus and attention, keeping her mind busy so it wouldn't spin any romantic fairy tales about handsome cowboys and single moms and sweet babies.

"Okay," Liam agreed readily. "I was planning to head out to the Circle G after the staff meeting to show my grandparents the new brochures this afternoon, anyway."

While they were at the antique and craft market, he'd confided that his grandparents had helped him with the down payment on the property, allowing him to move ahead with his plan to purchase the Stagecoach Inn.

But it was the first part of his statement that snagged her attention. "Staff meeting?"

"'Meeting' sounds more official than 'greeting,'" he explained. "But it really is just a chance for the employees to get acquainted with one another."

The total number of employees was six—including Liam and Macy. Rose was a part-time desk clerk who would be called upon to fill any gaps in the schedule, Camille would help out with the housekeeping on weekends, Emily would cook breakfast for the inn's guests and her grandson Nathan would serve it. Macy was pleased that Liam had thought to bring them together to make the introductions and, after that was done, she was looking forward to working with all of them.

"How was work today?" Beverly asked, when Macy sat down for dinner with her parents later that day. "Did you manage okay with Ava?"

"Ava wasn't a problem at all," she said. "And work was good. Of course, the inn isn't officially open yet, but I've loved helping with all the little details. Folding sheets and fluffing pillows, cutting flower stems and arranging decorative soaps. With every task, I feel more invested in the inn and its success."

"You always did love playing house as a kid," Norm recalled. "You would push that pretend vacuum around with one hand, carrying a doll in the other."

"Multitasking," she said.

"Fake multitasking," her mother pointed out. "You were never as eager to push around a real vacuum."

"I learned, though," Macy said. "I vacuumed more guest rooms than I could count when I worked in housekeeping."

"And now you're the manager of Haven's own upscale hotel," Bev said proudly.

"Which sounds good but doesn't get me out of folding sheets and fluffing pillows."

"I've thought about stopping by, to sneak a peek into one of those fancy guest rooms," her mother confided.

"You should do more than sneak a peek," Macy said. "You and Dad should spend a couple of nights."

"Why would I pay to sleep in a hotel less than five miles away from the perfectly good bed I have here?" Norm wanted to know.

"You wouldn't have to pay—it would be my treat," Macy said, knowing it was the least she could do to thank her parents for everything they'd done for her. "As for the why…it might add a little romance to your marriage."

Her father scoffed at the notion. "I don't think we need to be taking romantic advice from our unmarried daughter."

He was teasing, of course, but it still stung when the barb struck home.

Because her dad was right—compared to her parents, who had been married for almost forty-one years, Macy knew less than nothing about romance. And when she'd become disillusioned with the whole dating scene, she'd given up hope of ever finding love.

Except that wasn't really true. Even while she'd

moved forward with her plan to have a baby, she hadn't completely written off the possibility that she might someday meet a special someone. A man whose eyes would meet hers across a crowded room and be drawn to close that distance by the instant sparks he felt. Then they'd meet and they'd talk, they'd kiss and fall in love, and he'd love her baby, too, and want nothing more than to marry her so they could be together forever— a family.

It was, admittedly, a romantic dream.

When she'd realized she was going to have three babies, that romantic dream shot straight into the realm of fantasy.

Because only in the pages of a novel could she imagine a man wanting to take on the responsibility of three kids who weren't his own.

"This was not a good idea," Macy muttered, as she juggled the baby while rifling through the diaper bag for the tube of homeopathic teething gel she was certain she'd tucked inside—to no avail.

Sam continued to cry, deep, wracking sobs that shook his whole body. She offered a teething ring, which he immediately threw to the ground.

"I'm sorry," she said. "But I can't give you what's not here."

He wailed louder.

"Shh." She jiggled him gently, swaying and swirling, trying to take his mind off his obvious distress. "It's going to be okay, I promise. But you need to pipe down a little so that Mama's boss doesn't fire her."

"Do you really think your boss would be that callous?" Liam asked.

"No," she said, turning to face him. "But I think he'd be justified in feeling irritated that there's a screaming baby in the lobby of his fancy hotel."

"A fancy hotel that is, at the moment, empty of guests who might complain about the screaming baby." He took a few steps closer to peer at the infant in her arms. "Who's this big guy?"

Sam looked back at Liam through tear-drenched eyes, then he drew in a deep, shuddery breath and stretched his arms out.

"Benedict Arnold," Macy muttered.

Liam chuckled. "Do you want me to hold him while you pack all that stuff back up?"

"Please," she said, and willingly passed him the baby.

Sam sniffled…then offered his new friend a droolly smile as Macy began to shove diapers and toys and various paraphernalia into the bag.

"I didn't think there existed, anywhere in the world, a diaper bag bigger than the one my sister hauls around," he noted. "But I think hers would fit inside of yours."

"I have three babies," she reminded him, then shook her head as she looked at the one currently snuggled contentedly in her boss's arms. "And that one was crying for forty minutes before you showed up. Nothing I said or did would make him stop. Now suddenly he's all smiles and cuddles."

"Kate says that babies sense when their mothers are stressed," he said. "And that mothers with babies are almost always stressed."

"I won't argue with that," Macy told him. "And I promise, this won't be a regular occurrence, but my mom was going to Battle Mountain with Frieda Zimmerman today and, as great as my dad is with his grandbabies, I couldn't leave all three of them with him for the whole day."

"Is Frieda having her surgery today?"

She shouldn't have been surprised by the question. After all, this was Haven, where everyone knew everyone else's business, and her mother's best friend hadn't been shy about telling people that she was having a double mastectomy—a preventative measure after two of her sisters were diagnosed with breast cancer in the past year.

Macy nodded.

"Well, there's nothing urgent happening here today, if you want to take Ben home."

"Sam," she corrected automatically, then smiled when she realized that he'd derived the name from her comment about her traitorous son—whose gaze was riveted on the face of the man who was holding him. "And it might not be urgent, but I'm meeting with Emily to go over the breakfast menus."

"Breakfast menus?" Liam echoed blankly.

"We talked about this yesterday."

"When?"

"First thing in the morning. You did seem a little distracted," she noted. "But when I suggested that cook-to-order breakfasts had more appeal than a buffet—and would result in less waste—you said you'd defer to my expertise."

"I was distracted," he acknowledged. "My dad refuses to listen to anything I say about the ranch, because obviously I don't care enough about the ranch to stick around and help run it."

"And yet, you're there every morning," she remarked.

"Ranching isn't a part-time job," he said, in what

she suspected was an echo of words his father had spoken to him.

"Neither is owning and operating a hotel," she pointed out.

"Or parenthood," he commented, as Sam dropped his head down on Liam's shoulder.

Macy felt her heart swell inside her chest as she watched her baby curl his hand into a fist and lift his thumb to his mouth, totally content and secure in the cowboy's arms. "You know, you're much better with kids than you think you are."

"So it would seem," he agreed.

"Sam doesn't usually take to strangers."

"Well, maybe I'm not as strange as you think I am."

She smiled at that. "Actually, I think you're pretty great. If you could keep an eye on Sam while I meet with Emily, I'd bump 'pretty great' up to 'awesome.'"

For the first few months after her babies were born, Macy stuck close to home. Worried about their premature immune systems, she'd tried to shield them—as much as possible—from the potentially hazardous germs carried by those who might want to pinch their cheeks or tickle their toes.

Maybe she was a little paranoid, but she'd seen how people gravitated toward babies. Twins drew twice as much attention, and triplets—adorable times three—were an even bigger draw.

She got a little braver after Ava, Max and Sam had had their six-month immunizations. She'd even taken them to the mall in Battle Mountain to see Santa before Christmas, though she'd questioned the wisdom of that decision the whole time they'd waited in line with countless runny-nosed kids and likely would have bolted if her mother hadn't been there to stop her.

Now she was more willing to venture out with them, but their outings were restricted to venues that could be navigated with the triple tandem stroller. The Trading Post was one of those places—if she was picking up a limited number of items that would fit in the basket beneath the stroller. For a major shopping excursion, she usually took only one of her babies.

This week, it was Max's turn to go, but her sweet baby boy had woken up with a bit of a fever, so she let him stay home under the watchful eyes of his grandparents and took Ava instead. Her little girl already thought herself a princess and accepted it as her due when strangers oohed and ahhed over her.

On her way to the grocery store, Macy popped in to Diggers' to say "hi" to her former boss. After a brief visit that included lots of fussing over Ava, she headed out—just as Liam and an older woman were on their way in.

He introduced his companion as his grandmother, Evelyn Gilmore, and Macy and Ava as his innkeeper and her adorable baby girl.

"I've been meaning to stop by the inn to meet you," Evelyn said, shaking Macy's hand warmly.

"Now you don't have to," Liam told her.

"My grandson doesn't like me poking around in his business," Evelyn confided to Macy.

"Because my grandmother has trouble with the *silent* part of our silent partnership," he said.

The older woman waved a hand, dismissing his comment. "Have you had your lunch already?" she asked Macy.

"No, we just stopped in to see Duke for a minute on our way to the Trading Post."

"Then you can join us," Evelyn decided.

"Thanks, but we really need to get to the store—"

"The store will still be there after you've had a bite to eat," Evelyn said reasonably. "Besides, I want to talk to you about The Home Station."

Macy sent a quizzical glance in Liam's direction.

"That's the name Grams has chosen for the restaurant we don't have," he explained.

"Yet," Evelyn clarified.

And that was how Macy ended up having lunch with her boss and his grandmother—and Ava ended up wrapping another new acquaintance around her tiny finger.

As opening day drew nearer, Liam had to admit that hiring Macy Clayton was the smartest decision he could have made for the business—even when she brought one or more of her kids in to work with her. Truthfully, he didn't mind having the babies around and was sometimes disappointed when she showed up alone.

He'd thought the little ones would act as a buffer between them, but the more time he spent with her, the more his attraction continued to grow. However, she gave him no reason to suspect that his feelings might be reciprocated—until the day before Valentine's Day, when they were doing a final check in preparation of the grand opening.

"Tomorrow's the big day," she said, practically bubbling with enthusiasm.

"So it is," he agreed, unwilling to admit that he was probably more apprehensive than he was excited. The family and friends who'd stopped by over the past few weeks had raved about everything, so he had no concerns about the adequacy of the accommodations. And he'd taken Macy's suggestion and partnered with the spa to offer special weekend packages, but he still worried that no one would show up.

"Another two reservations came in today," Macy said, and that information eased a little of his worry.

"How many is that now?" He asked her because he knew she'd be able to answer the question more quickly than he could look it up in the reservation system.

"Five," she immediately replied. "Two rooms are booked for single nights, but three more are occupied through the weekend."

"Out-of-towners?" he guessed.

She nodded.

"I can't imagine how they're going to keep busy for three days and two nights."

"They're in town for a company retreat, participating in team-building exercises at Adventure Village," she told him, naming the local family-friendly activity center that was primarily responsible for the modest rise of tourism in the northern Nevada town.

"Team building exercises?" he echoed dubiously. "Is that really a thing?"

"A very popular thing," she assured him.

"Who would've guessed?"

"Anyone who picked up one of the brochures in the rack by the front desk," she told him.

"You were right," he admitted. "The rack was a good idea. Partnering with local businesses was a good idea."

"The partnerships were a *great* idea," she amended.

But it had been an uphill battle to convince Liam of the benefits of working with Jason Channing, the owner and operator of Adventure Village. Because Jason's mother was a Blake, and the Gilmore–Blake Feud was deeply entrenched in Haven's history, dating back to the settlement of the area more than a hundred and fifty years earlier. Both Everett Gilmore and Samuel Blake had been sold deeds for the same parcel of land and, unwilling to admit that they'd been duped, they decided to split the property down the middle.

As Everett Gilmore had arrived first and already started to build his homestead on the west side of the river, he got the prime grazing land for his cattle, leaving Samuel Blake with the less hospitable terrain on the east side. While the Circle G grew into one of the most prosperous cattle ranches in the whole state, the Crooked Creek Ranch struggled for a lot of years—until gold and silver were discovered in the hills. But the change in their fortunes did not change the bad blood between the families.

"And don't you think it's long past time the Blake–Gilmore Feud was put to rest?" she asked him.

"It's hardly up to me," Liam said.

"Well, I'm glad you and Jason were able to overlook the history between your families for the benefit of both of your businesses."

"Did I have a choice?" he asked.

His dry tone made her smile. "You made your choice when you hired me."

"Probably the smartest decision I've made since buying this building," he said.

Grateful for his comment—and the job she already loved—she impulsively hugged him. "Thank you."

The gesture was intended as a simple and sincere expression of appreciation. The heat generated by the contact between their bodies was *un*intended and *un*-expected. And undeniably arousing.

His arms went around her, as if to prevent her retreat. And though she knew she should draw away, she didn't want to. She didn't want to continue pretending she was unaware of the chemistry that hummed between them. She didn't want to ignore her growing feelings for him.

So instead of drawing away, she pressed closer and lifted her mouth to his.

Chapter 6

It was a casual kiss—a whisper from her lips to his, tentative, testing.

Liam's response wasn't at all tentative.

He didn't just kiss her back, he took control of the kiss. One hand traced its way up Macy's spine to cup the back of her head, tipping it back a little more so that he could deepen the kiss. His tongue slid between her lips, stroked the roof of her mouth, making her shiver and yearn.

His scent, clean and masculine, teased her senses. His hands, strong and skilled, tempted her body. His mouth, clever and talented, clouded her mind.

Had her brain not completely clicked off, she might have realized that she was treading on very dangerous ground. But she was no longer capable of rational thought. She could only feel and wish and want.

And she wanted more.

So much more.

He gave her more, kissing her deeply and oh-so-very thoroughly. Only when they were both desperate for breath did he ease his mouth from hers so they could fill their lungs with air. But even then, he continued to hold her close, his forehead tipped against hers.

"This is why I didn't want to hire you," he reminded her. "I knew it would be a struggle to keep my hands off you."

"This was my fault," she said, because it was true. And though she knew she should be ashamed of her actions, she didn't regret kissing him. She only regretted that it was over, because she knew it couldn't happen again. "*I* kissed *you*."

"I wasn't looking to assign blame," he said, sounding amused. "If anything, I'd like to express my appreciation."

"That's what I was trying to do," she admitted.

"And then the chemistry took over."

That chemistry continued to spark and sizzle between them, but she ignored it. Or tried to. She finally pulled out of his arms, putting some much-needed space between them. "It won't happen again."

"Do you really believe that?" he challenged.

The heat in his gaze warmed her all over. "I'm not your type."

"You sure felt like my type when you were in my arms."

"Single mom," she reminded him, gesturing to herself with her thumb. "Three kids. *Babies*."

And that quickly, the heat in his gaze cooled. "Yeah, I guess I shouldn't forget about them, should I?" he asked. "A guy would have to be crazy to get caught up with all that."

His response dashed any tentative hope she might have harbored about a romance developing between them. But it was his blatant disregard of her children—the center of her world—that made her angry.

"And a woman with all that would have to be crazy to get caught up with a guy like you," she retorted.

He held up his hands, a gesture of surrender. "I didn't mean to upset you. It's just that…kids aren't really my thing."

"Yeah, you've made that point quite clear."

And yet, she couldn't help but note that his words were in marked contrast to his actions.

The man who claimed kids weren't his thing was the same man his sister trusted with her little girl when she needed a babysitter on short notice. Of course, family usually stepped up to help family in a pinch.

But he'd stepped up for Ava, too. The day Macy had run late dealing with the wine merchant, he'd been there for her daughter when she'd awakened from her nap. He'd also been there for Sam, when her little guy was distressed by his sore gums. And he hadn't appeared to be the least bit reluctant or uncomfortable in either of those situations. But Macy wasn't going to waste her time trying to figure him out. The whole point of taking this job was to spend more time with her children, who were waiting at home for her right now.

"Good night, Mr. Gilmore," she said, and made a hasty retreat before she said something that might jeopardize her employment.

But her lips tingled all the way home, because the

kiss she'd shared with Liam was, without a doubt, the most amazingly incredible first kiss of her life.

If she'd ever known another man who'd made her feel half as much with a single kiss, she might not have been so eager to mate her eggs with the sperm of Donor 6243. But she hadn't and so she did, and now she had three beautiful babies as a result—and no business kissing a man who wasn't just her boss but who had made it clear that he was absolutely not interested in a relationship with a single mother.

"You better not be here with some kind of lame excuse about why you can't be at the party," Kate said, when Liam stepped into her office a short while later.

He halted in midstride. "Party?" he echoed, as if he had no idea what she might be talking about.

His sister's gaze narrowed. "You better be joking."

He grinned. "I have not forgotten my favorite niece's first birthday party," he assured her. "I even have a present for her."

"Is it wrapped?"

"With a big pink bow on top."

"You had it done at the store, didn't you?"

"Of course," he agreed unapologetically.

Apparently satisfied now that he wasn't trying to get out of attending her daughter's party, Kate turned her attention to other matters. "So why are you here?"

"Because I'm an idiot," he said.

"That's hardly a news bulletin," she remarked.

"But this is," he began. Then, realizing her office door was still open, he pushed it closed before continuing. He trusted that Kate's legal assistant-slash-receptionist understood the concept of client confidentiality, but he still didn't want anyone else to know what he was about to confide to his sister. "I kissed Macy."

"Yep. Idiot," Kate agreed, shaking her head despairingly. "Do you listen to *nothing* I tell you?"

"I always listen," he assured her.

"You just don't heed my advice," she surmised.

"Actually, the truth is that *she* kissed *me*," he told her.

"So you're here to file a sexual harassment suit?"

He scowled at that. "Of course not."

"Then you want me to tell you all the reasons that it was a bad idea to kiss a woman who works for you?" she suggested as an alternative. "In which case, you should have a seat, because I promise you, the list is long."

"I know all the reasons it was a bad idea," he admitted. "Except that it sure seemed like a good idea at the time."

"You are the boss. She is the employee." She spelled out the facts, clearly and concisely. "That's a lawsuit waiting to happen."

"*She* kissed *me*," he said again.

"It doesn't matter."

"You're right," he acknowledged. "I know you're right. But… I think I really like her, Kate."

"No, you don't," she denied. "You want to have sex with her."

"Well, yeah," he agreed.

"Well, you can't," she said. "There are lots of other women in this town who don't work for you. Go have sex with one of them."

"I don't want one of them. I want Macy."

"Lawsuit. Waiting. To. Happen."

"You're so cynical," he chided.

"I'm a lawyer," she reminded him. "That's part of

my job description." Then both her expression and her voice softened. "But I'm also your sister, and I don't want to see you hurt again."

"I don't think you need to worry about that. Macy was none too happy with me when she left."

"Hmm…maybe your technique needs some work?"

"It had nothing to do with the kiss," he assured her. "It was after the kiss—when I told her that I didn't want to get involved with a woman with kids."

"Maybe you're not such an idiot, after all."

"Except that what I feel for Macy, even after only knowing her a few weeks, isn't like anything I've ever felt before," he confided.

She shook her head. "Why can't you fall for a woman who isn't carrying child-sized baggage?"

"Everyone's got baggage," he pointed out.

"It's like kids are your kryptonite."

"You're mixing your metaphors."

"I'm trying to knock some sense into your thick head," she told him. "Do you not remember Isabella?"

"Of course I remember Isabella." And he remembered Simon, the little boy who'd asked Liam to be his dad. But that was before Izzy decided to reconcile with Simon's real father.

"You were devastated when she cut you out of her son's life."

"That was four years ago," he pointed out. "And yeah, it sucked for me, but—"

"It sucked for you?" she echoed in a disbelieving tone. "You were gutted."

She was right. In the years that had passed since, he'd managed to put most of the heartache behind him. But when memories of Simon occasionally surfaced, they were always bittersweet.

Isabella's son had been three years old when she started dating Liam, about six months after separating from her husband. It hadn't taken him long to become attached to the little guy who enjoyed building blocks and piggyback rides. Then Izzy had decided to give her husband—and her marriage—another chance.

Liam had been devasted. He hadn't been in love with Izzy, but he'd fallen hook, line and sinker for her kid. With a little time and distance, he'd come to accept that she'd done the right thing for her child. Nevertheless, he'd vowed that he wouldn't ever set himself up for that kind of heartache again.

So yeah, Macy Clayton, mom of eight-month-old triplets, was definitely not his type.

Because if he let down his guard and fell head over heels for Macy and her three children and then she got back together with their father, it would be three times as devastating.

And that was a chance he wasn't willing to take.

He should have stayed in town.

With the grand opening scheduled for the following day, Liam had any number of reasons not to make the trek out to the Circle G when he left Katelyn's office. He made the trek, anyway.

Three hours later, his extremities were so numb he had to look to be sure they were still attached. After parking the ATV in the garage, he stomped his feet on the hard ground to restore circulation and headed to the barn to feed the horses.

He found them already chowing down, proof that

someone else had taken care of the chore, so Liam moved to the office for the pot of coffee that was always on the warmer. At this time of day, it would undoubtedly be stale, but right now, he only cared that it was hot.

"Where've you been?" Caleb demanded, when Liam walked through the door of the enclosed space.

David was there, too, inputting some data into the computer, but he said nothing to acknowledge the appearance of his eldest son.

Liam shoved his gloves into the pockets of his jacket and reached for a mug. "Up in the northeast pasture, retrieving a lost steer."

That got his father's attention—and earned a frown. "One of ours?"

"According to the brand on his flank," Liam said.

"How the hell did one of ours get away from the herd and all the way out to the northeast pasture?" Caleb wondered aloud.

Liam shrugged, because the how didn't matter as much as the fact that the steer had got away—and been brought back home again.

David shook his head. "Some things will do anything to escape a life they don't want."

Caleb snorted. "I doubt the stupid steer was—oh." His gaze shifted between his dad and his brother. "You weren't really talking about the cow," he realized. "And now that the horses have been fed, I'm going to head up to the house to see if our dinner's ready."

When his brother had gone, Liam turned to his father. "Do you have something you want to say to me?"

"It seems that I do," David acknowledged.

Liam folded his arms over his chest. "Go ahead and say it then."

"You should know better than to ride that far out on your own and without telling anyone where you're going."

And for just a second, Liam thought his dad was worried about him.

David's follow-up remark quickly disabused him of that notion. "The last thing I need is to send out more men and horses on a rescue mission because you did something foolish."

"I took an ATV and Wade knew where I was," Liam said, naming the ranch's foreman. "He was going to ride out himself, but I said I'd go because his wife's just getting over the flu and he wanted to get home to check on her."

"Well, alright, then," David said.

"That's it?"

His father shrugged his broad shoulders. "What more do you want me to say?"

"I don't know—maybe thanks for showing the initiative and retrieving valuable stock."

"A rancher doesn't do his job for thanks—he does it because ranching is in his blood."

"And that brings us full circle now, doesn't it?"

"I guess it does," David agreed. "And I guess, since you're supposedly a hotelier now, I should say 'thanks.'"

Liam sipped the hot, bitter coffee. "As you've pointed out on numerous occasions, you don't need me around here. So why are you so opposed to me having a life and a career away from the ranch?"

"Because you're running away."

"If I was running away, I would have gone farther than town," he pointed out.

"Are the snow drifts deep in Horseshoe Valley?"

Liam puzzled over the abrupt shift in topic as he lifted his mug to his lips again. "I didn't go through the valley," he admitted. "I followed the western boundary."

"Would've been quicker to go through the valley."

"Maybe," he allowed.

"No maybe about it," David said. "But you ride around the valley rather than through it whenever you can, don't you?"

It was true, though Liam hadn't realized it himself until just now. Because the valley was where his mother had been riding the day she was thrown from her horse. She'd broken her neck as a result of the fall and died a few hours later. "I got where I needed to be to bring back the damn steer, didn't I?"

His father nodded. "But until you deal with your grief, you're always going to be running."

"Thanks for your concern, but it's seventeen years too late."

"You're right. I didn't do anything to help you and your brother and sisters at the time, because I was grieving, too."

"I know," Liam said, not unsympathetically.

"And it took me a long time to realize it, but I understand now that that's when and why you started to hate the ranch."

"I don't hate the ranch," he denied.

"That's good," David said. "Because your mother loved it. And she loved to ride. And though she would never have chosen to leave her kids without a mother,

I've found some solace in the fact that she died doing something that she loved."

"That's great for you," Liam said.

David shut down the computer and pushed his chair away from the desk. "We should head up to the house. Martina will be eager to get dinner on the table."

"Actually, I'm going to go back into town tonight," Liam decided.

His father frowned. "Why?"

"The grand opening's tomorrow, and I need to do a final check to ensure everything's in place."

"You should have something to eat first."

Liam knew the words were the verbal equivalent of an olive branch, but there were too many emotions churning inside him right now to allow him to take it. "I've got food at the inn."

David shrugged. "Your call."

"You could stop by tomorrow," he suggested. "See what all the fuss is about."

"I've got enough fuss here to worry about."

As Liam headed back to town, he understood what it meant to be caught between a rock—his father's stubborn refusal to see any viewpoint but his own—and a hard place, which was the inn, where every room held the echo of Macy's laughter.

Macy knew that kissing her boss had been impulsive—and completely unprofessional—but since that one very steamy lip-lock, she tried to convince herself that at least her curiosity had been satisfied. Now she needed to forget about her sexy boss and his toe-curling kisses and focus on the job he'd hired her to do.

But that was easier said than done, because even if

she could pretend that her curiosity had been satisfied by the kiss, all her female parts remained dissatisfied. Thankfully, she had plenty to do to keep herself busy on Valentine's Day—the day Liam had chosen for the grand opening of the Stagecoach Inn.

To her mind, February 14 was no more or less significant than any other day of the year, but that opinion hadn't prevented her from capitalizing on the date to push Sweetheart Deals at the inn. The upgraded room packages included bubbly wine and chocolate-covered strawberries from Sweet Caroline's Sweets and/or bouquets of roses from Blossom's Flower Shop, and they'd proved to be popular options with several of the guests who'd booked rooms for that night.

Although Blossom's offered delivery, the florist had warned that she couldn't guarantee the arrangements would arrive by a specific time—especially on Valentine's Day. So Macy texted Liam—a completely legitimate and totally casual message—asking him to pick up the order so they could ensure they were in the appropriate rooms prior to the arrival of their guests. There would be red roses in each of Doc Holliday, Charles Goodnight and Wild Bill (three dozen! Of course, she figured anyone who could afford the luxury suite could afford three dozen roses—and the champagne and chocolates, too), pink in Annie Oakley and Clark Foss.

When she returned to the lobby after delivering the flowers and double-checking that everything else was as it should be for their expected guests, she found Liam sitting in the chair behind her desk with a single long-stemmed red rose in hand.

"Where did that come from?" she asked, when he offered it to her. "Did it fall out of one of the vases?" And since she hadn't thought to count when she'd tweaked the arrangements of the flowers, she would have to go back now and—

"No, it didn't fall out of one of the arrangements," he assured her. "It's for you."

"But...why?"

"Because it's Valentine's Day," he said simply.

She couldn't remember the last time anyone had given her flowers on February 14—or any other day of the year—and she was absurdly touched by the gesture. And maybe a little wary.

"Thank you," she said, taking the stem he offered.

"And before you start wondering and worrying, it's not an overture—it's just a flower...and maybe an apology."

"It's beautiful," she said, gently tracing the velvety edge of a deep red petal with her fingertip. "And you're forgiven."

"I meant what I said yesterday, but I didn't mean it the way I said it," he explained.

"No need to say anything more," she assured him.

And then there was no time to say anything more, because the inn's first guests had arrived.

Clint and Dawna MacDowell were long-time Haven residents celebrating not only Valentine's Day but their thirty-fifth wedding anniversary. They'd been encouraged by their daughter, Hayley, to splurge on a night at the inn, and they walked slowly through the reception area after Macy gave them their key, marveling at all the little details.

Liam led the way, carrying their luggage. And Macy knew exactly when they spotted the antique stagecoach by the doors leading to the courtyard, because she heard

Dawna gasp, and Liam patiently answered some questions about the age and origins of the conveyance before nudging them on toward their suite.

There was a steady flow of people in and out throughout the afternoon. Though there were only seven rooms in the hotel—and they were all booked—a lot of locals stopped in to congratulate Liam on his endeavor and wish him success. Having anticipated exactly this, Macy had arranged for complimentary refreshments to be set up in the solarium—coffee, tea and lemonade, along with a variety of cookies and pastries from The Daily Grind. Among the well-wishers were other business owners, friends and family, including Liam's grandparents and both his sisters—Sky on her way into work at Diggers', and Kate on her way home from the office.

Liam mingled with the visitors while Macy covered the front desk, checking in guests, taking reservations for future bookings and answering inquiries.

"I know it's short notice," Kate said, stopping by the desk on her way out again. "But we're having a party at the Circle G to celebrate Tessa's first birthday on Sunday afternoon."

"That sounds like fun," Macy said.

"I'm glad you think so, because I'd like you to come."

"Me?"

"And Ava, Max and Sam, of course," Kate clarified.

"That's very kind of you," Macy said. "But the triplets can be a real handful…are you sure you want them at your daughter's party?"

The other woman laughed. "Of course, I'm sure. I know first birthday parties are usually more about the parents, but I really want Tessa to meet and make friends with other little ones. Reid has been encouraging me to get her into daycare so we're not constantly juggling our professional responsibilities along with our daughter, but since I haven't done that yet, I'm relying on playdates and parties to develop her social skills."

Macy didn't really have to worry about that, because Ava, Max and Sam were always together. In addition, her mom had recently conscripted her neighbor and friend, Frieda Zimmerman, to accompany them to a story-time group at the library. Beverly had said it was a good opportunity to get them out of the house so they could interact with other babies; Macy suspected it was also an opportunity for her mother to get out of the house and interact with the parents of other babies—to which, of course, she had absolutely zero objection.

"And there will be cake," Kate said, adding further incentive for Macy to accept the invitation.

"Who could say no to cake?" Macy wondered.

The other woman grinned. "Great. I'll see you at the Circle G around two. Best wishes only."

As Kate made her way out the door, Macy told herself it would be a good experience for the kids—and a chance for her to maybe get some ideas for the triplets' first birthday, which was now only a few months away. She refused to admit, even to herself, that her boss's guaranteed presence at the party had been a factor in her decision, even if she was curious to know more about the man who'd hired her to help manage his hotel.

Of course, aside from the curiosity, there was the attraction. And what was wrong with her that she could want a man who'd made it clear that he considered her children a burden rather than a bonus? Obviously the attraction was purely physical. And maybe that wasn't so surprising, considering the sheltered life she'd led through her pregnancy and the first six months that followed the triplets' birth. When she'd finally ventured away from home to work the occasional shift at Diggers', she'd still been preoccupied and sleep-deprived. It was only in the past few weeks, since her babies had started eating cereal and sleeping through the night, that she'd started to feel human again.

So it was reasonable, she decided, that an increased awareness of the outside world might also allow her to experience sexual awareness, too. Of course, she had no intention of abandoning her self-respect and indulging her hormones, and giving in to her attraction to a man who'd made it clear he had no interest in a relationship with a single mother would be doing exactly that.

But as her gaze shifted to the single red rose on her desk, she acknowledged that her resolve didn't prevent her body from continuing to yearn whenever he was near.

Chapter 7

At the end of the day, she took the rose home with her.

Liam had said that it was just a flower—and maybe an apology. She appreciated both.

Not that saying "I'm sorry" changed anything, but it did clear the air between them. And although his harsh words had stung, they'd also opened her eyes—forcing her to accept that the attraction between them wasn't ever going to develop into anything more.

So she put the flower on the little table beside her bed, then went upstairs to get her babies.

Macy wasn't surprised to see the cut-crystal vase in the middle of the dining room table filled with a dozen long-stemmed red roses. It was her dad's traditional Valentine's Day gift to his wife. He would have grumbled as he placed the order and paid the florist, lamenting—as he always did—that the cost of flowers skyrocketed on the fourteenth of February "every single goddamned year." But he always ordered them anyway, and his wife's eyes always got a little misty when she read the card that was simply signed *Love, Norm*. Because after forty years, those words weren't just a complimentary closing but a testament to the deep and abiding love they continued to share.

Macy knew she was fortunate to have grown up in a home with two parents who loved one another. Bev and Norm weren't overtly demonstrative and they occasionally argued, but she'd never had cause to doubt that they were committed to each other, their marriage and their family.

And she'd taken for granted that, when she was ready to get married and have a family, she'd find the right person and fall in love, just as her parents had done. She'd thrown herself into the task of meeting that future husband and father of her children. She'd accepted every invitation to dinner, every set-up arranged by her friends and colleagues, even when she was skeptical. And when none of those dates had led to anything further, she'd tried online dating.

She'd dated so many guys she'd lost track of the number, ever hopeful that one of them would be The One. After four years, she'd met some interesting men, but none with whom she wanted to establish a relationship. Obviously this was a major snag in her plan for a husband and a family, but she refused to let it get in the way of her determination to have a baby.

It had never occurred to her that she would end up with more than one. As far as she knew, there was no history of multiples on either side of her family. Apparently she was just lucky.

And she knew that she was. She had the children she'd always wanted, but she hadn't considered—couldn't have imagined—how much of a struggle it would be to raise them on her own. Thankfully, she didn't have to. She had her parents to help. But it wasn't the same as having a partner to share not just all the milestones in the lives of their children but all the moments of their own. "For better, for worse, for richer, for poorer..."

Not that she needed a man to complete her life, but she was admittedly a little worried that the choices she'd made might not have been the best choices for her children. She'd decided to have a baby because it was what *she* wanted and, in retrospect, she had to acknowledge that it might have been a selfish decision. She hadn't given a lot of thought to what was best for her babies, or what it would be like for them to grow up without a father. She'd been so determined to prove that she could do it on her own she hadn't considered that maybe she shouldn't.

She knew a lot of women who weren't just single moms but proof that a woman could do it all. But none of those single moms had triplets. Of course, it was far too late to make a different choice now. And when she entered her parents' living room and saw them with her babies, she was reminded once again that although she was technically a single parent, she wasn't doing it alone. Ava, Max and Sam might not have a father, but they had amazing grandparents who would—and did—do anything for them.

"Look who's home," Bev announced.

Three little heads turned, three smiles beamed and Macy's heart filled to overflowing, assuring her again that she didn't need a man to make her life complete. She had everything she needed right here.

But when she went to sleep that night, she dreamed of being snuggled in Liam's embrace.

Macy could understand why Tessa's parents had planned a big bash for her first birthday, and even why Katelyn had invited her and Ava, Max and Sam. But when she'd accepted the invitation, Macy obviously hadn't been thinking about the logistics of taking three babies out on her own, in the middle of winter, when she would have to haul not just the kids but all their essential paraphernalia through snow, up the long drive—already packed with vehicles—to the house.

"Why did I agree to this?" She muttered the question to herself as she unbuckled Sam from his car seat.

"Because there will be cake."

Macy jolted at the unexpected response and turned, her cheeks flushing, to face the amused birthday girl's mom.

"I was talking to myself," she confessed.

"I do that all the time," Katelyn told her.

"She does," her husband—the sheriff—confirmed.

"Because my husband doesn't listen," his wife said pointedly. "But he does have two strong arms, which is why we came out to give you a hand."

"I appreciate it," Macy said, as Reid took the baby from her. "I don't often venture out on my own with all three of them, so I sometimes forget how much stuff they need."

"Liam claims that I look like a Sherpa when I'm hauling Tessa's gear—and she's only one kid," Kate noted, reaching into the vehicle to unbuckle Ava from the middle baby seat.

After she transferred the little girl to her husband's other arm, she moved around the vehicle to get Max while Macy opened the back of her SUV.

"You won't need your playpen," Reid told her. "We've got an enclosure set up inside that's big enough for all the little ones."

"That simplifies things," Macy agreed, sliding the diaper bag onto her shoulder.

"And what is that?" Katelyn demanded, when Macy reached for the gift bag stuffed with pink tissue.

"Just a little something for the birthday girl."

"Did I forget to say *best wishes only*?"

"You didn't," Macy admitted. "But Ava, Max and Sam wanted to bring a little something."

"So they're responsible, are they?" the hostess asked, clearly skeptical of this claim.

"You're not going to scold my babies, are you?"

Kate shook her head. "I might, but they're just too cute." She looked at the little boy in her arms. "I guess the boys get their green eyes from their dad?"

Macy was used to fielding questions about her babies' paternity—and often much less subtle ones—so she responded easily, "Well, there's no green on my side of the family."

"And since we don't want them turning blue from the cold, we should get them inside," Reid interjected.

As they moved toward the house, Macy thanked them again for their help with Ava, Max and Sam. Once inside, it was fairly quick work—with Kate and Reid's assistance—to get the triplets out of their snowsuits and into the secure enclosure with the other little ones in attendance. Macy recognized Tessa, of course, but the little boy with her didn't look familiar.

Before she could ask, the parents of the birthday girl went off in different directions, but a moment later another woman approached, a baby girl in her arms.

Noting the arrival of three new babies, she said, "You must be Macy," and shifted her baby to offer a hand.

"I guess being the mom of triplets has made me infamous."

"Katelyn described you as Wonder Woman without the sword and shield."

Macy laughed. "A flattering—if completely inaccurate—description."

"I'm Emerson," the other woman said. "Kate's oldest and best friend, and mom to Keegan—" she gestured to the boy with Tessa "—almost two-and-a-half, and Karlee, eight months."

"Mine are eight months, too," Macy told her.

"I know," Emerson said. "They're in the same story-time group as Karlee at the library."

"I didn't know that. I don't make it to story-time with them."

"You shouldn't feel guilty. Your mom and Frieda seem to enjoy it as much as the kids. And Kate says you've been a godsend to Liam and the inn."

"I know it's early days yet, but I love working there."

"I've been bugging Mark to book a room for our anniversary," Emerson confided. "Usually we go out of town, but with Karlee being so young, I don't want to be too far away. Not to mention that I've been dying to see the place."

"You don't have to book a room to get a tour," Macy said. "Stop by anytime that I'm there and I'd be happy to show you around. Although I promise, you'll be even more eager to stay there after the tour."

"Then I'm definitely going to come for the tour—and to book the room," Emerson promised.

Another mom came over to talk to Emerson then, and Macy excused herself to get a drink. The non-alcoholic punch was pink—no doubt to coordinate with the other decorations in the oversized family room that had been designated as the party spot. There were bouquets of balloons and streamers and banners and paper lanterns and floral centerpieces. Macy made mental notes of what she liked (everything!) and the variations she might consider for her triplets (2:1 ratio of blue and pink decorations).

She sipped her punch and smiled to see Tessa plucked out of the enclosure by a man she recognized as Caleb Gilmore. Liam's younger brother was as tall—and nearly as handsome—with light brown hair, hazel eyes and the powerful build of a rancher, which Macy knew him to be. Skylar was there, too, of course, as were Tessa's great-grandparents. Jack and Evelyn Gilmore were still involved with the daily operation of the ranch as well as contributing to the larger community.

"Me-um! Me-um!" Tessa called, toddling across the floor toward her uncle when Liam finally arrived.

"There's the birthday girl." He scooped her into his arms and planted a noisy kiss on her cheek.

Tessa giggled.

The interaction made Macy smile—and marvel again at the man's inherent contradictions. How could he claim that he didn't really like kids when it was obvious he adored his niece—and that she adored him right back?

Regardless of the answer to that question, Macy wasn't going to let herself adore the man. She had other priorities right now—and Ava, Max and Sam were at the top of the list—so she turned back to the punch bowl to refill her cup and found David Gilmore with the ladle in his hand.

"Can I top you up?" he offered.

"Yes, please." She held her cup toward him.

"You're Bev and Norm's daughter Macy, aren't you?" he asked her.

"I am," she confirmed. It wasn't uncommon in Haven for people who hadn't been introduced to at least share acquaintances. As a result, she was accustomed to being referred to in connection with her parents—or as the sister of her brothers. Since returning to Haven, she'd frequently been referred to as "the triplets' mother," but now she was also known as "the manager of the inn"— a title she wore proudly.

"How are your folks doing?" David wondered.

"They should be enjoying their retirement," she acknowledged. "Instead, they've taken on new careers as daycare providers to those three." Macy gestured to the enclosure where the triplets—and a few other little ones—were confined.

"Being a grandparent is the best job in the world," he said, and sounded as if he meant it. "I know Tessa's just a year old, but I almost can't wait for Katelyn and Reid to give her a little brother or sister."

"Well, you're going to have to," Kate said, obviously having overheard her father's remark. "Because I'd like to get my first kid out of diapers before I have a second one."

"Macy seems to manage well enough and she's got

three in diapers," David pointed out, with a conspiratorial wink in her direction.

"I only manage well enough because I've got so much help at home," she was quick to clarify.

"And if you're so eager for another grandchild, you've got three other kids who could help you out," Kate suggested.

"Caleb isn't ready to settle down, Sky would rather poke into a man's brain than win his heart, and Liam's too busy playing at being an innkeeper to make any effort to find a suitable wife."

Macy sipped her punch and wished she was anywhere but in the middle of what she sensed was a family argument brewing—especially when Liam drew nearer. Maybe she could slip away on the pretext of checking on her babies, but they were currently being fussed over by Liam's grandparents and basking in the attention.

"And what kind of woman do you think would make a suitable wife?" Liam wondered, joining the conversation. "No, wait. Let me guess—a woman who would convince me to sell the inn and come back to live and work on the ranch?"

"Gilmores are ranchers," David said, his tone growing steely.

Kate exhaled a weary sigh. "Can we please not do this at my daughter's birthday party?"

"We're just having a conversation," her father said.

"A conversation that's quickly going to turn into an argument," she predicted.

"No, it's not," Liam promised.

And then, to be sure, he set his glass on the table and walked out of the room.

* * *

Macy didn't want to interfere in something that was clearly none of her business. But during the brief exchange between her boss and his father, she couldn't help but notice that Liam had been gripping his glass so tight his knuckles had gone white. So when he set that glass down and slipped away from the gathering, she double-checked that Ava, Max and Sam were in capable hands and then followed.

She saw him disappear through the back door, and quickly grabbed her coat and shoved her feet into her boots. He was already halfway to the barn while she was still pushing her arms into her sleeves.

When she muscled open the door of the barn, her senses were immediately assailed by the scents of fresh hay, oiled leather and horses. She hadn't grown up on a ranch, but she'd always loved horses and had learned to ride at a young age. Of course, it had been years since she'd been on the back of a horse, but the familiar setting brought the memories—and an unexpected longing to climb into the saddle—rushing back.

She closed the door again and took a moment to allow her eyes to adjust to the dim light. As she made her way down the concrete aisle, she noted the shiny nameplates on the stall doors and the glossy coats of the equines within. The Gilmores obviously took pride in and care of their animals—of course, they could afford to do so as the Circle G was one of the most prosperous cattle ranches in northern Nevada.

She found Liam inside a birthing stall at the far end of the barn.

"What are you doing out here?" he asked.

"I was going to ask you the same question," she said.

"I just needed some air," he told her.

"You must have needed that air pretty desperately," she remarked. "You rushed out of the house without even grabbing a jacket."

He shrugged. "I knew I wasn't going very far."

"Who's this?" she asked, stroking the long nose of an obviously pregnant dappled mare who'd come over to greet her visitor.

"That's Mystery."

"You don't know her name?"

He managed a half smile. "Her name is Mystery," he clarified. "While we were growing up, all the kids took turns naming the foals that were born. This one came when it was Sky's turn, and she demanded to know if it was a boy or a girl. At that point, only her head and forelegs were out, so Grandad said it was a mystery, and Sky decided that was a good name."

"And when is Mystery going to have her own mystery foal?" Macy asked.

"Any day now," he said, stroking his hands over the mare's swollen flank. "But probably not today."

"That's too bad," she remarked. "I'm sure birthing a foal would be a welcome diversion—although checking on a pregnant horse serves the same purpose."

He didn't respond to that but gave the horse a last affectionate pat before he unlatched the gate and exited the stall.

Macy tried again. "Families are complicated, huh?"

"Yeah," he finally agreed.

"Anything you want to talk about?" she prompted.

"Nope."

She sighed. "It's obvious that there's some tension between you and your dad."

"And, like I said, it's not anything I want to talk about," he told her.

"I've been told that I'm a pretty good listener."

"You're also a really good kisser," he noted, tugging on the belt of her jacket to draw her toward him. "And I prefer kissing over conversation."

"Now you're trying to distract me," she accused, but even knowing it was true, she couldn't resist the temptation of his embrace.

"Is it working?"

Before she could respond to his question, his mouth was on hers.

And, yeah, it was working.

Very effectively.

And just like the first time he'd kissed her—or she'd kissed him—her mind went blank and her body came alive.

She lifted her hands to his shoulders, holding on to him as the world tilted and swayed beneath her feet. She'd almost managed to convince herself that the kiss they'd shared couldn't possibly have been as amazing as she remembered. That her body, long deprived of any adult male attention, had conspired with her over-active imagination to turn the memory of that kiss into more than it had been.

But his second kiss proved otherwise. If anything, her memory had not done the first one justice.

Was it Liam? Was this incredible chemistry specific to him? Or were her hormones overactive because of all the changes her body had been through, carrying and birthing three babies? She wanted to believe it was just hormones, and yet she suspected otherwise. She'd had plenty of male customers flirt with her at Diggers', and she'd received a few interesting propositions—but not one that had tempted her. No man she'd met had made her remember that she was a woman, with a woman's wants and needs. No one before Liam. Before now.

He banded an arm around her waist, gently drawing her closer. Even through her puffy coat, she could feel the heat emanating from his body—a heat that warmed the blood flowing through her veins. He skimmed his tongue over her lips, and they parted willingly for him. She wanted this—wanted *him*—with a desperation she couldn't remember experiencing in a very long time. Or maybe ever.

"Let's sneak up to the hayloft and pretend the rest of the world doesn't exist for an hour," he suggested against her lips.

Yes. Oh, please, yes.

But while her hormones were running rampant through her system, her brain was still in charge of her mouth, and she managed to hold that desperately needy response inside her head. She drew in a slow, steadying breath before responding lightly, "I've never had a literal roll in the hay."

"We could change that right now," he offered.

She laughed, a little weakly, and took a step back. A not-so-subtle retreat from the temptation he represented. "You're a dangerous man, Liam Gilmore."

His lips curved, but his gaze was serious. "I wouldn't hurt you, Macy."

She knew that wasn't a promise he could make. Oh, she trusted that he wouldn't want to hurt her, but she suspected that getting involved with "Love 'em and Leave 'em Liam" would inevitably result in a bruised heart.

Under other circumstances, she might have decided

that the risk was worth it. Though she'd never had much success with relationships, she wasn't opposed to putting herself out there. But while she might be willing to risk her own heart, she had Ava, Max and Sam to think about now. She had to think not just about what she wanted, but what was best for her children.

And Liam had made it clear that he wasn't interested in a relationship with a single mom. If she gave in to the attraction between them, it wouldn't be anything more than a physical release. Of course, she was wound so tight right now she was almost ready to consider the benefits of a quick, no-strings affair to alleviate the sexual tension that simmered between them. But she'd never been the type to engage in casual sex, and she wasn't sure it was a habit she wanted to start now.

"I need to get back to—"

"Knock, knock," Skylar called out, as she pushed open the door, bringing a blast of cold air into the barn with her.

"Go away," Liam told his sister, his gaze never shifting from Macy's.

"I will," Sky promised. "But Kate wanted me to tell you that they're getting ready to bring out the cake, and she didn't want you to miss it."

"Well, you can tell Kate that her timing sucks," he said, because now that he had Macy in his arms, he didn't want to let her go. Then he sighed. "And that we'll be right in," he added, because he didn't want to miss Tessa's celebration, either.

"Will do," Sky said.

"Do I owe you another apology?" he asked when his sister had gone.

"Are you sorry?" Macy wondered.

His gaze dropped to her mouth and he shook his head. "Not for kissing you. But I didn't give you a lot of choice in the matter."

"I wasn't an unwilling participant," she assured him.

"But that doesn't change the fact that this—" he gestured between them "—is a bad idea, does it?"

"A very bad idea," she confirmed.

He sighed and dropped his arms, letting her out of his embrace. "In that case, let's go get cake."

Chapter 8

So they went back to the house, where Reid carried out a stunning three-tiered cake. The bottom layer was decorated with pale pink fondant icing with polka dots of darker pink, lilac, purple and white; the middle layer was covered in lilac fondant with stripes of light and dark pink, purple and white; and the top was decorated to look like a crown. After the birthday song had been sung, the crown layer was removed and set on a plate for the birthday girl, who immediately dug into the confection with both hands.

Gifts followed the cake—because Macy wasn't the only one who had ignored the "best wishes only" instruction—and then the party guests began to make their way to the door. Macy started bundling up her kids at the same time that everyone else was putting on their coats and boots, and after calling the barn to enlist Wade's help with another matter, Liam gave her a hand.

It was harder work than he'd anticipated, because Sam stiffened up and refused to cooperate and Max kept trying to wriggle away, but eventually the triplets were bundled up against the cold.

He picked up either Max or Sam—he couldn't remember which one had been wrestled into the blue snowsuit with matching knit hat and gloves—and then his brother, who was clad in a similar green snowsuit with hat and gloves of the same color, leaving Macy to carry her daughter, in red outerwear, and the enormous diaper bag.

She halted at the edge of the porch, having finally noticed the vehicle he'd asked the foreman to ready and park near the house.

"It's a double seat cutter sleigh," he said, before she could ask. "I thought we could take a little ride, so you could see more of the ranch."

She nibbled on her bottom lip. "You can't really expect me to put my babies in that."

"Look in the back seat," he suggested, as he guided her down the steps.

"You just happened to have three extra car seats hanging around?"

"Four, actually," he said. "They belong to our foreman and his wife, for when their grandkids visit. Wade even installed proper child seat anchors, so you can rest assured that your babies will be snug and safe."

Still, she hesitated.

"It's a perfect day for a ride," he cajoled. "And Barney and Betty are already harnessed and ready show you around."

"Barney and Betty, huh?" Her lips twitched as she

fought a smile. "Well, the sleigh doesn't look like rub-ble, so let's give it a go."

He helped her buckle Ava, Max and Sam into the car seats, then Macy settled onto the velvet-tufted seat in front and he took his seat beside her and the reins in hand.

"It's so beautiful out here," she commented, as they glided over the snow-covered fields. "So peaceful."

"It is, isn't it?" he acknowledged.

She shifted a little in her seat, so that she could look at Ava, Max and Sam. He glanced over his shoulder to do the same, noting their wide eyes and happy smiles. Their cheeks were pink from the cold, but they were obviously having fun—as evidenced by the occasional giggles that punctuated the silence when the sleigh dipped or rose as the horses navigated the rolling hills.

But the motion must have simulated rocking—or maybe the triplets were just tired out from the party—because it didn't take long before their eyes grew heavy. The one in green drifted off first, he noted, but his brother and sister weren't far behind.

"Napping this late is going to wreak havoc on their bedtime," Macy noted.

"Did you want to head back?"

She shook her head. "There's no point now. And truthfully, as much as I like schedules and routines, having triplets has taught me that ideals don't always mesh with reality."

"It must be challenging, raising three babies on your own."

"It would be even more challenging if I was really on my own," she said. "Thankfully, my parents help out a lot."

"But not their dad?" he wondered.

"No."

The abrupt response didn't invite further questions, so Liam let the subject drop, though his curiosity remained unsatisfied.

"So why did you leave all this to become an innkeeper?" Macy asked, after several minutes had passed.

And now he was the one facing the question without a simple or straightforward answer.

"Growing up out here… I loved the ranch and everything about ranching," he confided. "I used to follow my dad around, wanting to do everything that he did. Wanting to be just like him when I grew up.

"Then my mom died…and everything changed."

Macy reached over and laid a mitten-clad hand on top of his, offering a gentle squeeze of encouragement.

"And after that, I hated the ranch," he admitted.

"Did it happen…did she die…on the ranch?"

He nodded.

"How old were you?" she asked.

"Not quite eleven."

She was silent for a minute, considering. "Loss is never easy," she finally said. "But for a young child to lose a parent… I can't imagine how difficult that must have been for you. It's understandable that you'd want to get away from where it happened, and you shouldn't be made to feel guilty about choosing your own path."

"But is it my own path?" he wondered aloud.

"What do you mean?"

"I'm not sure if I really wanted to go into the hospitality business or if I saw the For Sale sign and decided that reopening the old Stagecoach Inn would give me an opportunity to finally get away from the ranch.

"I'd always been fascinated by the old building and

its history," he confided. "But I don't know that I would have taken the initiative to turn that interest into anything more if the pieces hadn't all fallen into place."

"Whatever your reasons, you've made something out of nothing," she told him. "You've created jobs for local people and, over the next few months, you'll get to watch the inn's success generate renewed interest in local tourism."

"And it only cost me all my savings and my relationship with my father."

"I noticed that he didn't show up for the grand opening," she said.

"He had more important things to do." Then he quoted his father: "Ranch business doesn't take vacations, you know."

"Your grandparents made the trip into town, though. Obviously they don't subscribe to the theory that Gilmores are ranchers."

"They want me to do whatever makes me happy, and they believe the inn is an investment in the community."

"They're right," she agreed.

"Right or wrong, my father isn't giving any indication that he'll ever forgive me for leaving the ranch."

"He'll come around," she said, speaking the words with such confidence that he almost believed they were true.

Or maybe it was simply that being with Macy made him want to believe in second chances.

Liam was in the barn at the Circle G, checking on Mystery and her newborn foal when Kate tracked him down Wednesday morning.

"What are you doing so far out of town so early on a weekday morning?"

"I've got a full-day trial in Winnemucca, so Martina's going to look after Tessa for me."

"You ever think about putting the kid in daycare instead of dropping her in the laps of friends and relatives?"

"Martina offered," she said, just a little defensively. "As if that would matter."

"Be nice to me," his sister cautioned. "Or I might invite Caleb to dinner Friday night instead of you."

"Why are you inviting me to dinner Friday night?" he asked, a little warily. Because while he never turned down a free meal, he'd learned that nothing in life was ever really free. "What's the catch?"

"There's no catch," she denied.

"Okay, so maybe you don't think it's a catch, but there's something you're not telling me. What is it? Are you and Reid going to walk out the door as soon as I walk in?"

She sniffed indignantly. "If I wanted you to babysit, I'd ask you to babysit."

He waited.

"We're having a little dinner party and I need one more to round out the table," she finally told him.

"How big is this little dinner party?"

"Not very."

"You're being evasive."

"It's just me and Reid, Emerson and Mark, Em's cousin and you. And Tessa, Keegan and Karlee, of course," she said, adding her daughter and her friend's two little ones to the tally.

"Is this cousin of Emerson's female?" he asked suspiciously.

"As a matter of fact, she is," his sister admitted.

"It's not a dinner party—it's a setup," he accused.

"It's not a setup."

"Then invite Caleb."

"I was hoping to round out the table with someone actually interested in making conversation," she said, because they both knew their brother could be rather taciturn at times.

Liam shook his head. "Do you really think I'm incapable of finding my own dates?"

"You've been so busy with the hotel, you haven't had much time to go out, so I thought this would be fun. And Jenna is really sweet."

"It's a setup," he said again.

"It's an introduction." She tried another tack. "With two kids—and one of them still a baby, Emerson doesn't have much time to show Jenna around, so she asked if you might be willing to play tour guide."

"Is that all I'm supposed to play?" he challenged.

"Well, that would be for you and Jenna to figure out."

"While I appreciate your efforts, I don't need you to find me a date," he said firmly.

"Maybe not, but you do need to stop thinking that anything's going to happen with Macy."

He frowned. "I thought you liked Macy."

"I do like Macy, but I don't like to see you chasing after a woman you can't have."

"I'm not chasing anyone," he denied. And the truth was, he'd never had to chase a woman before—or maybe he'd never known another woman who was worth the effort. Macy was definitely worth the effort, but her children were a complication and he liked to keep his relationships simple.

"I'll admit that there seems to be some chemistry between you," Kate continued, ignoring his denial. "But you can't ever act on it."

"I know you're worried about a sexual harassment lawsuit—"

"As you should be," she interjected.

"But I would never take advantage of a woman," he assured his sister. "Whether she worked for me or not."

"I know," she acknowledged. "But your working relationship ensures an inherent power imbalance."

He frowned at that.

"You can scowl all you want, but that's not going to change the fact."

"You told me to hire her," he reminded his sister.

"Because she's the best person for the job."

"And now I have to fire her."

"You are *not* going to fire her," Katelyn told him. "That's pretty much the definition of unlawful dismissal."

"You haven't left me with any other choice," he said.

"You have all kinds of other choices, but sleeping with Macy isn't one of them." And apparently that was the end of that topic, because then she said, "Dinner's at seven. You can bring dessert."

"What am I bringing for dessert?" he asked. Because his sister had clearly mapped out every other detail of the evening, he had no doubt that she'd also decided what she wanted him to bring.

"Caramel fudge brownie cheesecake from Sweet Caroline's."

Her immediate reply confirmed his suspicion—and aroused another one. His gaze narrowed. "Are you pregnant again?"

"No." She laughed. "Definitely no. We've got more than we can handle with Tessa right now."

"As I recall, you didn't exactly plan to get pregnant with her."

Her only reply to that was "Cheesecake. Seven o'clock."

"I'll be there," he promised.

Because although she hadn't told him what she'd be cooking, Sweet Caroline's made the best cheesecake in Haven.

A promise was a promise, but when Friday rolled around, Liam found himself wishing that he'd never agreed to attend the so-called dinner party at his sister's. But he picked up the cheesecake and pulled up in front of his sister and brother-in-law's at precisely 6:55 p.m., because Kate was a stickler for punctuality and he tried not to irritate her without good reason.

But he nearly turned around again when he walked up the steps to the door, through which he could hear a baby crying.

Right—the plan for the so-called dinner party was two couples, two singles and three kids.

"I should have brought alcohol instead of chocolate," he muttered.

"Don't worry," a female voice said from behind him. "I've got the alcohol covered."

He turned to discover a young woman standing on the edge of the step, a paper bag from The Trading Post tucked in the crook of one arm. She was tall—probably close to five-ten, he guessed—with the long, lean body of a dancer. She had pale blond hair, cool blue eyes, slashing cheekbones and full lips that a cover model would envy.

As a man who appreciated beautiful women, Liam had no trouble acknowledging that she was that. She was also young—*much* younger than he'd expected.

"Two bottles of red and two white," she said.

"That's a good start," he decided, then felt compelled to ask, "But are you old enough to drink it?"

She smiled, revealing even white teeth. "Unless the legal drinking age is twenty-five in Nevada, there's no danger of me breaking any laws."

"You must be Jenna," he said, shifting the bakery box to his left hand so that he could offer the right.

"And you must be Liam." She smiled. "You're every bit as cute as Emerson promised."

"Cute?" he echoed dubiously.

She laughed. "I meant it as a compliment—as did my cousin, who has no idea that I've been dating a security analyst for almost three months, so I apologize if anyone gave you the impression that I was looking for a setup or a hookup while I'm in town."

"No apology necessary," he told her. "As I wasn't looking for either but was encouraged to show you some of the sights while you're in town."

"I've already walked the whole length of Main Street," she noted.

"Then you've seen the sights," he said.

Jenna laughed and took a step toward the door. She hesitated, her hand poised to knock, as another wail sounded from within. "Maybe we should take the wine and dessert and have our own dinner party somewhere else."

"A tempting offer," he admitted. Especially since he

knew now that she had no illusions about a potential romance developing between them. "But Katelyn would hunt us down—or at least the caramel fudge brownie cheesecake."

"Cheesecake?" She laughed again. "Dinner is sounding a lot better already," she said, and rapped her knuckles against the wood.

Macy knew that Liam had hired her so that he didn't have to be on-site at the inn 24/7. Notwithstanding that fact, for the first few weeks, he'd rarely ventured any farther away than Jo's to pick up pizza. So she was understandably surprised when, on only the second weekend after opening, she didn't see him at all.

He did call to check in a few times, but their conversations were brief and to the point. He didn't offer any information about where he was, and she didn't ask. But she suspected she knew the reason for his sudden disappearing act when a woman stepped up to the desk around 10:00 a.m. Wednesday morning and said, "I'm looking for Liam."

She was young—early twenties, Macy guessed—blonde, built and stunningly beautiful.

"Liam?" Macy echoed, wondering why it bothered her that his name rolled so easily off the girl's tongue. As if she'd had plenty of practice saying it—and maybe had done so in a sleepy voice when she rolled over in bed that morning and saw him beside her in bed.

And how ridiculous—and inappropriate—a thought was that? It shouldn't—*didn't*—matter to Macy who Liam spent the night with or even if it was a different woman every night.

"Liam Gilmore," the girl clarified. "This is his hotel, isn't it?"

"I'll see if he's avail—"

"No need," the girl interrupted, a wide smile curving her glossy pink lips. "I've found him."

And she sashayed across the tile floor to greet the man who'd just exited his office.

Macy had never seen anyone sashay before. She hadn't been sure that type of movement ever happened outside of historical novels and romantic movies—until she saw Liam's visitor sashay toward him, her short skirt twirling around her thighs with every gliding step. The blonde gave him a quick hug and a peck on the cheek. He said something close to her ear, and she responded with a tinkle of laughter like a melodic wind chime dancing in the breeze.

Macy heard the murmur of their voices pitched low, but she couldn't make out any words of their conversation. Not that she was trying to eavesdrop, because that would be inexcusably rude. But she couldn't deny that she was curious about the woman—who she was, where Liam had met her, if he was sleeping with her.

He had a private suite of rooms on the third floor with a separate entrance, so it was entirely possible that he'd been curled up with his blonde bombshell all weekend while Macy had been greeting guests, setting up their activities and making their dining arrangements.

And so what if he had been?

That was his prerogative and absolutely none of her business.

But she couldn't tear her gaze away from them as they made their way toward the front door. They really did make a beautiful couple: Liam so dark and muscular; his female companion so slender and fair.

Macy wasn't jealous, she was just…surprised to realize that he was seeing someone. Especially when he'd been kissing her in the barn at the Circle G barely a week earlier. And even if those kisses had made her head spin and her toes curl, they'd agreed a relationship between them would not be a good idea. So there was absolutely no reason for him not to go out with other women. In fact, she should be relieved that he was dating, because now she could stop weaving inappropriate fantasies about any kind of romance developing with her boss.

But did he have to hook up with someone who was so young and so pretty? Face-to-face with the beautiful girl, Macy couldn't help but feel old and worn. Of course, she was a thirty-three-year-old mother of almost nine-month-old triplets, so if she looked tired it was because she *was* tired.

And wasn't this exactly why she'd decided to go ahead and have a baby without waiting to meet a man she might want to marry and have a baby with? Because men were fickle and untrustworthy. But being in Liam's arms had reminded her of all the reasons that a woman wanted a man, anyway.

She forced herself to watch them walk out together, and to acknowledge that whatever brief moment she'd shared with her boss had obviously passed. Now maybe she could focus on what was truly important: her family and her career. She didn't want or need a sexy cowboy messing with her head or her heart.

Not half an hour after Liam had gone, his sister came in with Tessa in her arms, looking frantic and stressed.

"Please tell me he's in his office," Katelyn implored.

Macy shook her head. "Sorry. He stepped out a little while ago."

"Where'd he go? When's he going to be back?"

"I don't know," she said. "He didn't share any of those details with me."

Katelyn muttered an expletive under her breath.

"Do you need someone to keep an eye on Tessa?" Macy asked her.

"Desperately," the other woman admitted. "I drew Judge Longo for a bail hearing, and he's generally pretty good about me bringing her into court when I have to, but she's a little out of sorts today. She's been fussing and squawking all morning, and I know that will not go over well."

"You can leave her with me."

"I'd feel too guilty asking," Kate protested. "I'm sure you come to work to get away from fussy babies."

"I come to work because I love my job," Macy said. "And you didn't ask—I offered. Plus, the Stagecoach Inn prides itself on being a full-service hotel."

"The best thing my brother ever did was hire you," Kate said. "You truly are a gem."

"Can you tell him that before my six-month performance review? And suggesting that I deserve a raise wouldn't hurt, either," she added.

"I will," Kate promised, already halfway out the door.

Chapter 9

Macy really didn't mind keeping an eye on Tessa while the little girl's mother was in court. In fact, she was happy to have her company. While there were always innumerable details to take care of at the inn, there were also quiet times, and right now was one of them.

She took Tessa into the library and let the little girl choose a book from the shelf. Although most of the rooms were designed for couples rather than families, they occasionally had younger guests, so Macy had ensured there was a modest selection of books for them in the library, too. They sat together on the sofa and Macy read the story aloud to Tessa.

As the little girl studied the colorful illustrations, Macy studied the child, noting that Tessa's delicate features favored her mother, but there were obvious hints of her father in the shape of her eyes, the color of her hair, the stubborn tilt of her chin. Tessa was obviously a mix of both her parents, as Macy suspected her own babies were. Everyone commented on the similarities between Ava and her mama but suggested that the boys favored their father.

Macy wasn't sure that "father" was an appropriate title for the man who had contributed to the triplets' DNA. Truthfully, Donor 6243 had done nothing more than deposit his specimen in a cup. She didn't even know if he knew that his donation had succeeded in mating with an egg and creating a child—or three.

Ava, Max and Sam weren't his babies—they were her own.

Tessa turned the page, drawing Macy's attention back to the book in her hands. When the story was done, the little girl decided that her mama had been gone long enough and called out for her. Of course, Macy's patient explanations about Katelyn's whereabouts and responsibilities did nothing to appease the child, who grew distressed when her increasingly insistent demands failed to result in her mother's appearance.

Thankfully, Macy had read a lot of parenting books, so she put on some music and began to dance, encouraging Tessa to move her body, too, hopeful that the activity would work to both distract the little girl and burn off some of her excessive energy. Since there were only a handful of guests staying at the inn and they'd all departed for their chosen activities, she cranked the volume a little and got into the groove. And when one of her all-time favorite songs came on, she added vocals to the dance routine.

She picked Tessa up and twirled her around, making

the little girl grin and giggle. So she twirled again, still singing, until the music abruptly shut off.

"Ma-ma!" Tessa announced.

Sure enough, the little girl's mother had returned and was standing in the doorway of the library, amusement in her eyes, her briefcase and a large take-out bag from Diggers' in her hands.

Macy was admittedly a little embarrassed to have been caught belting out tunes and shaking her booty— and relieved that it was Katelyn rather than Liam who had come in during the impromptu song-and-dance routine.

"How do you do it?" Kate wondered aloud.

"Are you referring to my complete and total lack of rhythm or my ability to sing so boldly off-key?" Macy asked her.

Tessa's mom laughed. "I was referring to your ability to effortlessly roll with the punches. I have honestly never seen you flustered by anything."

"Believe me, I get flustered," Macy said. "I just try not to show it when I'm at work."

"As a mom, you're always working," Kate said. "You're just not always getting paid."

"But there are other perks."

Kate's lips curved as she looked at her little girl. "You're right about that," she agreed. "And thank you, again, for watching Tessa for me."

"We had a good time, didn't we, Tessa?"

When the little girl nodded and leaned forward to plant a sloppy kiss on Macy's cheek, her heart melted just a little.

"Trade you," Kate said, offering the take-out bag in exchange for her daughter.

Macy handed over the child, who squealed as she reached for her mother. "How was the hearing?"

"My client was remanded in custody," Kate told her. "I figured she would be, but I wouldn't be doing my job if I didn't at least try to get her released. And since her fate was sealed before noon, I decided to pick up lunch for us."

"You didn't have to do that," Macy said, but she took the bag and followed the other woman into the kitchen.

"Are you kidding?" Kate set her briefcase on the floor and settled on a stool at the island with her daughter in her lap. "It's the very least I could do to thank you for bailing me out today."

"It's not easy, balancing a career and parenting, is it?" Macy remarked.

"It's not at all," the lawyer agreed. Then, as Macy began to unpack the bag: "There's a chicken Caesar wrap and fries for you." Because, of course, all the staff at Diggers' knew the usual orders of their regular patrons. "Cheeseburger and fries for me."

Macy distributed the food and Tessa immediately stretched her arms out, reaching for the fries.

"You have to wait a minute," her mother cautioned. "They're still hot."

The little girl pursed her lips and blew out puffs of air.

"That's right." Kate selected a fry and, following her daughter's example, blew on the hot potato to cool it.

"Reid keeps nudging me to register her for daycare," she confided, picking up the thread of her conversation with Macy. "But that seems too much like handing her over to someone else to raise. And Tessa is still so young—and vulnerable—that the idea of leaving her with strangers makes me shudder."

"Believe me, I know how fortunate I am that my parents stepped up to help out with the triplets," Macy acknowledged.

"You are lucky," the other woman said. "I lost my mom when I was twelve, and you'd think that seventeen years should be enough time to come to terms with her death, but it seems like I miss her even more now that I'm a mom myself."

"I can imagine. I'm constantly asking my mom for advice and reassurance. I don't always follow her advice," she admitted. "But it's nice to have somebody to talk to."

Kate nodded and chewed. "My grandmother stepped in to fill the void as much as she could, but as I'm the oldest sibling, my brothers more often confide in me—if they confide in anyone."

Macy smiled as she watched Tessa sneak another fry and carefully blow on it.

"As a result, I sometimes fall into the trap of thinking I know what's best for them when I don't," the other woman continued.

"Why do I get the feeling this is leading to some sort of confession?" Macy wondered aloud.

"Because you're both smart and astute—and because I saw Liam having lunch at Diggers'."

"There aren't many other places to eat in this town," she remarked, her tone deliberately casual.

"When I stopped by earlier, you didn't mention that he was with Jenna."

"I didn't know her name."

"She's Emerson's cousin, visiting from out of town,"

Kate said. "I asked Liam to show her around, as a favor to me."

"I'm sure he'll be a great tour guide," Macy said.

"But there's nothing else going on." Kate nibbled on the end of a fry. "Though, if I'm being perfectly honest, I'd hoped there might be."

"It's really no concern of mine," Macy told her.

"Are you sure about that?" the other woman asked. "Because I don't usually butt into things that aren't any of my business—at least, I try really hard not to," she allowed. "But when it comes to family, it's not always easy to know where to draw the line."

"I can understand that," Macy agreed cautiously.

"And I've been worried about Liam for a while now."

"I don't think there's any cause for concern—when he and Jenna walked out of here, they looked as if they were completely wrapped up in each other."

"She's a nice girl—and totally his type," Kate confided. "Or what I thought was his type."

"So what's the problem?" Macy wondered.

Tessa's mom pretended not to notice as the little girl stole another french fry. "The problem is that I tried to set him up with Jenna because I wanted him to forget about you."

"Me?" Macy echoed, stunned.

Kate seemed amused by her reaction. "You can't tell that my brother's completely smitten with you?"

She shook her head. "He's not. I mean, there was a moment...a kiss," she said, and that acknowledgment was enough to bring the memories of that first kiss rushing to the forefront of her mind—and heat rushing through her veins. And a few days after that first kiss, there'd been a second. "But then...nothing."

"Because I told him that if he pursued a relationship with you, he'd be opening himself up to a sexual harassment lawsuit," her boss's sister confided.

Macy was aghast. "You think I'd sue him?"

"My concern wasn't specifically about you," Kate explained. "I just think anyone in a position of power should be hypervigilant to ensure they don't abuse that power. And I wasn't just looking out for him—I was also looking out for you."

"Thank you," she said dubiously. "But I don't think you need to worry about your brother harboring any romantic feelings toward me—when I reminded him that I was a single mom, he was eager enough to back off. And even if that hadn't dissuaded him, my children are my priority, which means I'm not in any position to be thinking about a romantic relationship right now."

"That makes perfect sense," Kate decided. "But logic aside…how do you feel about him?"

Macy sighed. "Confused."

Kate's smile didn't completely erase the worry in her eyes. "Reid confused the hell out of me when I first met him. Four hours later, we were naked."

"Well, that's something I didn't know," she noted.

The other woman chuckled. "Yeah, it's not something many people do know, but since that's how we ended up with Tessa, I'm not ashamed to admit it."

"You lucked out," Macy said, a little enviously.

"I did," Kate agreed. And then, "I guess your situation was a little different?"

"My situation was *very* different."

"The dad didn't want to have anything to do with his kids?"

"His involvement began and ended with the dona-tion of his sperm."

Of course, most people didn't take the words literally, so she wasn't surprised when Kate's follow-up question indicated that she hadn't, either.

"Any chance that he's going to change his mind about wanting to know his kids in the future?"

Macy shook her head. "Definitely not."

Kate opened her mouth, as if she wanted to say more, but she shoved a fry inside and closed it again.

Macy wished she could tell Liam's sister the truth about the father of her baby. She wasn't ashamed of the choice she'd made—how could she be when that choice had given her Ava, Max and Sam? But for all its recent growth and changes, Haven was still a small town where some old-fashioned beliefs were held dear. Proof of which was demonstrated by her own parents' shock and disapproval of her baby news.

She'd never meant for the paternity of her babies to be a big secret. But since coming back to Haven, she'd accepted that her actions were a reflection on her family. And though she was undeniably frustrated by their disapproval, she realized their attitudes were indicative of the larger community.

Maybe the residents would sympathize with and sup-port a couple with fertility issues who opted for IVF or adoption in their desire to have a family, but she sus-pected they'd be less likely to understand or approve of a single woman choosing the same path. As a result, whenever Beverly was asked about the father of her grandbabies—because yes, there were people in town bold enough to ask the question—she was uncharac-teristically cryptic.

"I don't know anything about Macy's relationship with him," she'd say. "She doesn't say much, and we never had the opportunity to meet him."

Of course, all those details were true—albeit deliberately misleading.

When Liam returned to the hotel following his lunch with Jenna, who was heading back to California later that day, he found Kyle Landry waiting in the library to see him.

"What can I do for you?" Liam asked, surprised by the unexpected visit of a man he knew only well enough to wave at in passing.

"Actually, I'm here because of what I can do for you."

Liam knew the beginning of a sales pitch when he heard one, and he was immediately wary. "Okay, what do you think you can do for me?"

"I can offer your guests a culinary experience that will be as unique and unforgettable as your inn," Kyle said.

"Thanks, but we already have a chef."

"You have someone who cooks breakfast," the young man acknowledged.

"That's all we need."

"You're doing your business a disservice by not offering dinner to your guests."

Liam's gaze narrowed suspiciously. "Have you been talking to Macy?"

"Not recently, but in the interest of full disclosure, we used to work together," Kyle said.

"Well, I'll tell you what I told her," Liam said. "There are other places in town where guests can get an evening meal."

"Diggers', Jo's Pizzeria or the Sunnyside Diner," Kyle said dismissively.

"I eat at those places frequently and have never had any complaints."

"But they hardly reflect the upscale image you're attempting to establish for your hotel."

"What do you know about what I'm trying to establish?" Liam challenged.

"The Dusty Boots Motel on the highway is never booked to capacity, so Haven didn't really need another hotel. Which suggests that you wanted to appeal to a different clientele. People who want to stay for a few days and not just sleep off their bachelor parties in Reno."

"How do you know about the hotel business?"

"Two years of restaurant and hotel management."

"Is that enough to get you a diploma?" Liam asked.

"No," Kyle admitted. "And then I went to England to get some practical experience."

The School of Artisan Food, he remembered Macy telling him. It didn't sound as fancy as Le Cordon Bleu in Paris, but Liam imagined the experience Kyle had gained there was still much more sophisticated than the palates of Haven's residents.

"And you think that qualifies you to run a hotel kitchen?"

"I think I'm more qualified than anyone else in this town," Kyle said. "I'd use locally sourced ingredients as much as possible—why truck ingredients in when we've got some of the finest dairy, beef and produce right here in Haven? The less we have to ship, the more we keep our food costs down. And I'd create hearty meals that would satisfy the hungry rancher and impress the sophisticated traveler."

Sure, the concept was appealing, but Liam still had reservations about venturing into the food service business—and especially about this particular chef. "Does your mom know you're here looking for a job?" he asked.

"No," Kyle said.

"Are you going to tell her?"

"When there's something to tell."

"I guess that's fair enough," Liam agreed.

"I could do a tasting menu for you," the chef suggested.

"What's that?" he asked, proving, no doubt, that he had no business in the restaurant business.

"Sample portions of appetizers, main courses and desserts," Kyle explained. "Do you have a girlfriend?"

Liam quirked a brow. "What does my relationship status have to do with your desire to work in my kitchen?"

"Nothing. I was only going to suggest that, if you do have a girlfriend—or any kind of significant other—I could do a formal meal presentation for both of you. A dinner for two slash job interview."

"You know what, Kyle? I think that sounds like a terrific idea."

"I was beginning to worry that you got lost on your way to the store," Macy's father commented when his wife came through the back door with the "few groceries" she'd gone out to get more than an hour earlier.

"You make me crazy sometimes, but I haven't completely lost my mind yet," Bev replied, setting her bags on the counter. "I guess I did lose track of time, though, chatting with Celeste Rousseau."

"What's the latest gossip from Miners' Pass?" Macy asked, referring to the name of the street where Ben and Margaret Channing had built the enormous home that Celeste took care of for them.

"The latest—and very exciting—*news*," her mother said, emphasizing the word because she did not approve of gossip, "is that the Channing family is going to grow by two."

Macy waved a hand dismissively. "That's old news. Deputy Neal told me weeks ago that Regan was expecting twins."

"Maybe I should have said *two more*," Bev clarified. "Because Jason's and Spencer's wives are both pregnant."

"That is exciting news," Macy agreed.

"I'd be more excited if I got to hear the news while I was enjoying the roast-beef-on-rye sandwich you promised would be my lunch," Norm said.

"Instead of just rummaging through the bags, you could actually put the groceries away," Bev remarked, gently lifting the carton of eggs that had been turned on its side by her husband's efforts.

"I just want the bread," he said. "Shouldn't bread be on top?" But he did as his wife had suggested—until he found the bread. Then he started pulling the other ingredients out of the fridge to make his sandwich.

Bev sighed. "Honest to goodness, you have the attention span of a gnat sometimes."

"My attention has been focused on a roast-beef-on-rye sandwich since you went out to get the bread."

"Sit." She pointed toward the table. "I'll make your sandwich."

"Horseradish and mustard," he reminded her.

"Because that's different than what I've been making for you for forty years," she muttered dryly.

Macy smiled at the familiar and affectionate bickering as she took over putting the groceries away.

When she was in high school—and helping a close friend deal with the fallout of her parents' divorce, she'd sometimes wondered what inspired one couple to weather the stormy seas of matrimony for a lifetime together while another might jump overboard when the first waves hit. She still didn't know the answer to that question, but she was grateful to her parents for providing her with an example of what a marriage could be. Bev and Norm's wasn't perfect, of course, but it was always a work in progress.

"When are the babies due?" Macy asked, when her father was happily chowing down on his coveted sandwich.

"Both in November, although Kenzie is due at the beginning of the month and Alyssa closer to the end."

"It's like there's suddenly a baby boom in this town," Norm chimed in, after gulping down half the glass of milk his wife had served with his sandwich.

Bev nodded. "And a sign that our young people are sticking around to help grow the community instead of running off to the cities, like they all used to do."

"You mean like I did?" Macy guessed.

"Like a lot of young people did," her mother said.

"And you're home now," her father pointed out. "Raising your babies where you were raised."

"And grateful to be here."

"Oh, don't start that again," Bev chided. "Tell me instead about your plans for tonight."

"My plans are to hang out with Ava, Max and Sam—reading stories, singing songs, rolling around on the floor and splashing in the tub." She grinned. "In other words, the usual."

"You should go out," her mother urged.

"Where would I go?" she asked, startled by the suggestion.

"To see a movie?"

"Or I could stay in and watch a movie," Macy suggested as an alternative. "There's got to be something new on Netflix."

Bev shook her head despairingly. "You really need to set the bar a little higher. Do something for yourself. Reconnect with old friends. Meet new people."

"Ahh. Now I see where you're going with this."

"What do you mean?" her mother asked, feigning innocence—albeit not very convincingly.

"You think if I put on some pretty clothes and high heels, I'll somehow manage to dazzle an unsuspecting cowboy who will then declare his undying love and desire to marry me and be a father to my three babies."

"A little lipstick wouldn't hurt, either," Bev said.

"While I appreciate your confidence in the power of painted lips, my days of dazzling anyone are long past. I don't have the time or the energy for any romantic entanglements right now."

"I don't want you to grow old alone," her mother admitted.

"I think I'm pretty much guaranteed not to be alone for the next eighteen years."

"And since you brought them into the conversation,

I'll say what I've been saying since they were born—those babies need a daddy."

"No," Macy denied, though perhaps not as vehemently as she had a few months earlier. "They need to grow up in a stable and loving environment, and I'm so grateful to both of you for helping to give them that."

"She gets that stubborn streak from you," Norm said to his wife.

"Whose side are you on here?" Bev asked him.

"Yours. Always yours," he placated her, rising from the table to put his plate and cup in the dishwasher. "But in this case, I think we all want the same thing—and that's what's best for Ava, Max and Sam."

"Of course, that's what we all want," Bev said.

"We just can't agree on what that is," Macy noted.

"I'm only suggesting that our daughter shouldn't close herself off to any possibilities," her mother said, refusing to let the issue drop.

"And I only wish—"

The ring of her cell phone cut off that thought.

Macy grabbed for the device, grateful for the interruption. But her finger hovered above the screen, hesitating to answer the call when she saw Liam Gilmore's name and number on the display.

"I'm going to hang out with my grandchildren," Norm announced, moving toward the living room.

"They're napping," Bev said.

"Then that's what I'm going to do, too."

His wife smiled as she shook her head.

"Are you going to answer that?" she asked Macy, when the second ring sounded.

"I probably should," she said.

Because while it wasn't often that her boss contacted

her when she was away from the inn, it wasn't out of the ordinary, either. He'd called her once because he couldn't remember the password for the computer—ST@G3_C0@CH_1NN—and another time to ask her where she'd hidden the laundry detergent—cleverly and deviously, in the cupboard beside the washing machine in the laundry room.

She didn't mind these harmless inquiries. What she minded was the way her heart inevitably skipped a beat when she saw his name on the display, and then another when she heard his voice. He'd made no more overtures since he'd kissed her in the barn the day of his niece's birthday party, but the memories of the kisses they'd shared continued to keep her awake at night—and tease her in explicit and erotic dreams when she finally did sleep.

Macy pushed those thoughts aside and connected the call.

Chapter 10

"Can you come in tonight?" Liam asked.

"Aside from the fact that today is one of my days off, I don't work nights," Macy reminded him.

"It's not work, really," he hedged. "More like a favor—with food."

"The last time you offered to feed me, I got pizza."

"Jo's pizza," he said, as if that somehow elevated the basic meal.

And, okay, Jo's pizza was the best she'd ever had. Vegas might have a lot more dining options, but she'd never found a pizzeria in Sin City to rival the local favorite.

"And tonight it will be Jo's son doing the cooking."

"You hired Kyle?" she asked, surprised and pleased to hear of this apparent change of heart.

"Not yet," he said. "I'm still not completely convinced that there's a market for upscale dining in Haven. But as part of his interview, he's preparing a tasting menu."

"That sounds tempting, but—"

"Great. I'll pick you up at six," he interjected.

"I didn't say—"

But he'd already disconnected.

She huffed out a breath and scowled at the now silent phone.

"Is something wrong?" her mom asked.

"Liam wants me to have dinner with him tonight."

"A date?" Bev asked hopefully.

"No," she responded immediately. Firmly. "A working dinner."

"Regardless of what you call it, sharing a romantic meal with a handsome man sounds like a date to me," her mother remarked.

"I didn't say I'd go," she pointed out.

"I didn't hear you say no."

"Because he hung up before I could get the words out. But I'm going to call him back now and say it," she announced.

"Why?"

"Because I don't like being manipulated. And because I want to have dinner with you and Dad, Ava, Max and Sam."

"Honey, you have dinner with us every night."

"And I rely on you to look after my babies too much."

"Who says it's too much?" her mother demanded.

"I do."

"Well, I disagree."

Macy sighed and tried again, "I know they're a handful—"

"Actually, they're three handfuls," Bev interjected. "But between your dad and me, we've got four hands and we love spending time with our grandbabies."

"Maybe you should check with Dad before you volunteer him for extra babysitting duties," Macy suggested.

Her mother immediately waved that suggestion away. "Now forget about making excuses not to have dinner with Liam and go downstairs to find something to wear."

"I really don't think this is a good idea," she hedged.

"Because you don't like Liam? Or because you do?" Bev wondered aloud.

"It doesn't matter whether I do or don't—I'm a single mother with three babies."

"But maybe you don't have to be a single mother forever."

She sighed. "Are we really back to this again?"

"I'm not telling you to marry the man," her mother said. Then she winked. "At least, not before you've had dinner with him."

It did take some time for Macy to figure out what she was going to wear. After a quick shower to ensure she didn't smell like baby spit—or worse—she stood in her undergarments in front of her open closet, surveying the contents.

She had work clothes: skirts and pants with matching jackets and an assortment of coordinating tops, and she had mom clothes: yoga pants and stretch leggings with oversized shirts and hoodies. She also had two pairs of pre-pregnancy jeans that she was able to squeeze into again, but she wouldn't count on the button holding through a meal. And tucked in the back of the closet were half a dozen dresses from her I'm-a-single-woman-in-Sin-City days, but as she rifled through them, she doubted there was even one that would accommodate the extra pounds she continued to carry, even eight and a half months after giving birth.

Although maybe…

She lifted the hanger holding a long-sleeved sheath-style dress off the rod. The fabric was a silky jersey knit in royal blue that had a fair amount of stretch and give and just might—if she crossed her fingers and held her breath—be suitable.

So she removed it from the hanger and wriggled into it. Smoothing down the skirt, she turned to check out her reflection in the mirror and decided that she didn't hate it. And if she put on a pair of Spanx—

No. She wasn't going to squeeze herself into Spanx for a dinner outing that wasn't even a date.

Then why the lacy underwear?

She ignored the taunting question from her subconscious. She'd selected her bra and matching underwear because they were comfortable, not because anyone else was going to see them—especially not her boss.

Although there wasn't a lot of snow on the ground, the frigid temperature had her opting for boots rather than shoes. Thankfully, she had a stylish knee-high pair with a chunky heel and silver buckles that worked with the short-skirted dress. She added silver earrings and a trio of bangle bracelets and decided she was good to go.

With her mother's earlier remarks still fresh in her mind, she almost ignored the makeup bag on the counter, but her vanity was apparently stronger than her obstinacy. And okay, even at her best she didn't look anything like a twenty-year-old Swedish model, but dinner with Liam wasn't anything like a real date, either.

"You look lovely," Bev said, when she came downstairs to check on her daughter's progress.

Macy glanced down. "I don't think my stomach is ever going to be flat again."

"You used to be too skinny—now you've got some curves."

"What I've got is ten pounds of baby fat."

"And it looks good on you," Bev insisted.

"Thanks, Mom. But it doesn't really matter how I look, because this isn't a date," she reminded her mother—and herself.

"I don't care what you call it—I just want you to relax and have a good time."

"I've got my phone," she said, tucking it into the outside pocket of her handbag. "Call me if you have any problems with the kids."

"You seem to forget that I raised three children of my own."

"I know you're more than capable of taking care of Ava, Max and Sam, but—"

"But you're looking for an excuse to weasel out of this da—dinner," Bev quickly amended.

The upstairs doorbell rang, and Macy sighed.

"And now it's too late," her mother pointed out unnecessarily.

Macy didn't stall any longer, because she knew that if she did, her father would answer the door, and she didn't want him to give Liam the same third-degree interrogation he'd given her boyfriends in high school.

But she was too late.

She reached the top of the stairs leading to the main

foyer just as her father's fingers closed around the handle of the door.

"It's okay, Dad, I'll get…"

She was too late again. Her words trailed off as Norm opened the door—and were completely forgotten when she caught a glimpse of her boss. He was wearing his usual jeans and cowboy boots, but with a dress shirt, tie and jacket. He hadn't bothered to shave, and she itched to reach up and stroke the stubble that darkened his jaw. Looking at him, she knew why sexy cowboys remained a popular fantasy for many of her friends, and when his eyes locked on hers and his lips curved, her blood heated in her veins and pooled low in her belly.

Obviously this was a bad idea.

A very bad idea. Because her hormones were clamoring for her to forget about dinner and feast on *him*.

And the blatant appreciation in his gaze as it boldly skimmed over her made her suspect that he wouldn't object if she proposed such a change of plans. Or maybe that was just her own hormonally charged imagination running away with her.

"Good evening, Mr. Clayton." Liam offered his hand.

Norm shook it firmly. "You take care of my girl tonight," he instructed the younger man.

"I will, sir."

Macy could tell that the "sir" scored points with both of her parents, compelling her to interject.

"Your girl is thirty-three years old," she reminded her father. "And this dinner is for business, not pleasure."

"Why can't it be both?" Liam wondered aloud.

"Now that's a good question," Bev said, her remark earning a conspiratorial grin from her daughter's boss.

"Because it's not," Macy said firmly, before she brushed her lips against her mother's cheek. "Good night, Mom." Then she stopped by the playpen and bent down to drop kisses on top of each of the babies' heads and instruct them to be good for Gramma and Grampa.

"They're in good hands," Norm promised.

"I know they are," she said, and bussed his cheek, too.

Liam turned his head, a silent invitation for her to touch her lips to his cheek.

Macy rolled her eyes and shook her head.

He shrugged and helped her on with her coat. "I figured it was worth a try."

"I won't be late," she told her parents, as she knotted the belt at her waist.

"It doesn't matter if you are or aren't," Bev said. "We're not waiting up." Then, in case her point wasn't clear enough, she winked at Liam.

"Good night," Macy said firmly.

"Have a good time," her mother said.

She shoved Liam ahead of her out the door and closed it firmly at her back.

"Can I say now what I didn't dare say when your father was staring me down?" Liam asked, after Macy was buckled into the passenger seat of his truck and he'd taken his place behind the wheel.

"What's that?"

He looked at her and, even in the dim light of his truck cab, she could see the heat in his gaze. "Wow. Just…wow."

She felt her cheeks flush. She didn't know how to respond. She'd told her parents—and herself—that this wasn't a date, but the way Liam was looking at her, the way the butterflies were winging around in her stomach, she kind of wished that it was.

Or maybe she was just hungry.

"So what's on the menu tonight?" she asked when he'd backed out of the driveway and turned toward the inn.

"I have no idea. I told Kyle to put together the menu...and I didn't even think to ask if you had any food allergies."

"No allergies," she assured him.

"That's a relief," he said. "And while the chef didn't tell me what he was cooking, he did suggest that I could feature Circle G beef on the menu and highlight the connection between the ranch and the inn."

"What a great idea," Macy said.

"I thought so," he agreed. "Of course, I might need my manager to negotiate the terms of any supply agreement with the ranch's owner."

"Your father's still not happy about your career change?"

He shrugged. "I shouldn't have expected anything different. After all, Gilmores are ranchers."

Macy had heard the same refrain spoken by various people countless times, and she could only imagine how difficult it had been for Liam to buck that trend—and how much more difficult his father continued to make it by refusing to respect his son's choices.

The subject was abandoned when they arrived at the inn.

"Do you have a timeline for opening the restaurant?" Macy asked.

"*If* I open the restaurant," he clarified. "And no."

"I don't think you would have let Kyle prepare this tasting menu tonight if you weren't leaning in that direction."

"Leaning isn't the same as committed. And it usually takes more than a single meal to get me to make a commitment."

"I'll keep that in mind," she said. "But right now, I'm hungry, so lead the way to dinner, cowboy."

Kyle had enlisted help with the setting up and serving. He introduced Erin as a friend of his sister's—and also a part-time waitress at Jo's. The chef then proceeded to give them a preview of the menu.

White wines would be sampled with the starters— sweet potato soup garnished with Greek yogurt and toasted pumpkin seeds, arugula and pear salad with Gorgonzola dressing, goat cheese crostini with fig and olive tapenade, bacon-wrapped dates stuffed with blue cheese, and caramelized onion tart with a balsamic reduction; and red wines would be served with the mains—prime rib au jus accompanied by roasted fingerling potatoes and glazed baby carrots, chicken breast stuffed with spinach and mushrooms served on a bed of creamy risotto, and grilled salmon with couscous and a steamed vegetable medley.

Every detail of the meal was perfect. The presentation of each plate was as exquisite as its flavor. And sitting at a candlelit table across from a man whose smile was enough to make her blood hum in her veins was dangerously intoxicating.

"I'm trying to pace myself," Macy said, as she nibbled on a bite of salmon. "But it's not easy. Everything tastes so good."

"And nothing like what you'd find on the menu at Diggers'," Liam remarked.

"I didn't realize your reluctance to venture into the restaurant business was based, at least in part, on an unwillingness to step on the toes of the other dining establishments in town."

"Haven's a small town, and it's important that we support local businesses if we want them to stay here."

"And that's exactly why you need to offer fine dining," she told him. "To give people a reason to stay in Haven rather than trekking to Elko or Battle Mountain."

"With every bite, I'm growing more convinced," he admitted, reaching across the table to scoop up a forkful of the risotto on the plate in front of her.

"And when word gets out that there's a fancy new restaurant in Haven, you'll start to get people from Elko and Battle Mountain coming here for a meal."

"You think so?" he asked, still sounding dubious.

She tapped her fork on the edge of the plate with the prime rib. "I'd travel more than fifty miles for a bite of that flavorful, melt-in-your-mouth beef. Pair it with a glass—or a bottle—of that California cabernet sauvignon, and suddenly your diners are not only happy they made the trip but realizing that they can linger over dessert and another glass of wine and then check into one of the luxurious suites upstairs.

"And, of course, you could put together special dinner and room packages as part of your usual offerings or a special-occasion thing."

"Or *you* could," he suggested.

She smiled. "I'd be happy to."

"Did you have any questions, comments or concerns about anything on the menu?" Kyle asked, coming out of the kitchen after they'd had a chance to sample each of his offerings.

"I have one," Macy said, glancing at Liam across the table. "Who gets the doggy bag?"

The young chef smiled. "I'll let the two of you figure that out."

"Arm wrestle for it?" Liam suggested.

"Yeah, that would be fair," Macy noted dryly.

Liam grinned. "Why don't we put the leftovers in the fridge here? Then we can both enjoy them again for lunch tomorrow."

"I guess that would work," she agreed. And then, to Kyle, she said, "You must have been cooking all day."

"It's what I love to do," he told her.

"And your passion for food is evident in every bite," she assured him.

"It's only long-ingrained table manners that held me back from licking my plate," Liam said.

Kyle's smile grew. "Should I send out dessert now, then?"

"I don't know that I could eat another bite, but if your desserts are even half as good as everything else, I have to try," Macy said.

"Desserts aren't my specialty," the chef confessed. "But I have mango sorbet with fresh raspberries, a pecan tart with caramel sauce, and white chocolate mousse dusted with cocoa powder and garnished with sprigs of mint."

As he spoke, Erin set each of the referenced desserts on the table.

"If you wanted fancier options on the menu, you could consider partnering with Sweet Caroline's Sweets," he suggested.

"Another great idea," Macy agreed. "It would expand the options for your diners and support another local business."

"Did anyone want coffee? Tea?" Erin asked.

"Not for me, thanks," Liam said.

Macy shook her head. "I'm going to finish my wine," she decided.

"Then we'll leave you to enjoy your dessert while we clean up the kitchen," Kyle said.

Macy lifted a spoon and waved it over the three dishes, as if she didn't know where to begin. She decided on the tart, breaking off a piece with the side of her spoon, then sliding it between her lips.

"Oh. My. God." Her eyes closed in blissful pleasure. "Oh, yes."

The unintentionally provocative words combined with the expression of pure bliss on her face made Liam wonder if Macy would respond with the same passionate enthusiasm to the experience of other pleasures. No, not just wonder. Made him want to know.

Made him want.

He shifted in his chair as his body immediately began to respond to the contemplation of that possibility. He shoved a spoonful of sorbet into his mouth, as if the flavored ice might cool the heat rushing through his veins.

He cleared his throat. "It's good?" he asked.

She shook her head. "Good doesn't begin to describe it. It's—" she took another bite of the tart, sighed "—better than sex."

"Now *I* have to try it," Liam said, reaching across the table with his spoon.

She curled her hand protectively around the plate. "I don't want to share."

He chuckled. "Well, if you won't let me try the tart, then I'm not going to share the mango sorbet with fresh raspberries."

"Fresh raspberries in March?" Her tone was dubious, but her expression was interested.

"They might not be local produce, but they're delicious," he said, and nudged the glass dish toward the center of the table.

She spooned up another bite of the tart before reluctantly sliding the plate closer to his.

"Mmm...that's good, too," she said, after she'd sampled the frozen treat. "*Really* good."

"But is it better than sex?" he wanted to know.

"It might be," she decided. "The truth is, my memories of the event are a little foggy while this sweet taste of heaven is right here, right now."

"Dessert definitely satisfies a sweet tooth, but sex—" Now *he* sighed. "Sex done right satisfies the body *and* the soul."

She snorted at that.

His brows lifted. "You don't agree?"

"I probably shouldn't even express an opinion," she admitted. "Because I haven't had sex in...well, let's just say it's been a long time."

"How long?" he wondered.

She waved her spoon at him. "That's an inappropriate question to ask an employee."

"You're the one who brought up the subject of sex," he pointed out.

"You're right." She nodded. "But it's your fault."

"How is it my fault?"

"Because before you kissed me, I never thought about how much I missed sex."

"*You* kissed *me*," he reminded her.

"The first time," she acknowledged.

"You kissed me back the second time."

"Has any woman ever not kissed you back?" she wondered.

"I'm not interested in any other woman right now," he said. "I'm only interested in you."

The intensity of his gaze made her belly flutter. "I've got three kids," she reminded him.

"That's not what's been holding me back."

"What's holding you back?"

"I'm trying to respect our working relationship."

"Yeah, that complicates things," she agreed. Then she finished the wine in her glass and pushed away from the table. "Will you excuse me for a minute? I want to give my mom a call to check on Ava, Max and Sam."

"Of course," he agreed. "But I can't promise the rest of that tart will be there when you get back."

She gave one last, lingering glance at the pastry before she said, "You can finish the tart."

He was tempted by the dessert, but he managed to resist. He didn't know how much longer he could hold out against his attraction to Macy—or if she wanted him to.

Had he crossed a line by flirting with her? She hadn't reacted in a way that suggested she was upset or offended, but she hadn't exactly flirted back, either.

"Is everything okay?" he asked, when she returned to the table several minutes later.

She nodded. "I got caught in the middle of an argument."

"With your mom?"

"With myself."

His brows lifted. "Did you win?"

"I hope so," she said.

Then she set an antique key on the table and slid it toward him.

Chapter 11

Liam immediately recognized it as the key to the luxury suite on the top floor.

"You do know that I have an apartment upstairs?" he asked.

"Yeah, but it seemed presumptuous to invite you up to your own place," she said. "Plus, I've been dreaming about sleeping in that bed since the day you gave me the tour." Then she smiled and shrugged. "Or maybe not sleeping in it."

He wrapped his fingers around the key, gripping it so tightly that the cold metal bit into his palm.

"Are you sure, Macy?" Then, without pausing long enough to give her a chance to respond, he said, "Please say you're sure."

"I'm sure."

He exhaled a grateful sigh of relief.

But still, he had to ask one more question. "Should I worry that your decision is being influenced by the wine?"

"I've only drunk enough to lessen my inhibitions about letting you see me naked," she told him.

He abruptly pushed back his chair and stood up. "Then let's go upstairs so I can see you naked," he suggested.

"Are *you* sure?" she asked him. "On my way back from the desk, I started to wonder if maybe I was jumping the gun."

He drew her into his arms, felt her tremble a little as he pulled her close. Nerves? Anticipation? He was admittedly experiencing some of each.

He'd wanted her for so long but had managed to convince himself it couldn't happen and that, eventually, his feelings for her would go away. He'd been wrong. And now that he knew Macy wanted him, too, he wasn't going to deny those feelings any longer.

Instead, he lowered his head and covered her mouth with his own. It seemed like an eternity had passed since he'd tasted the flavor of her lips. They were as sweet as he remembered, her response as passionate as he recalled.

He slid his hands up her back, tracing the line of her spine. Then down again, cupping the curve of her bottom. She arched into him, her breasts crushed against his chest, her hips aligned with his so there was no way she could be unaware of his arousal.

"Does that answer your question?"

Macy blinked. "What was the question?"

He chuckled softly and lifted her into his arms.

She gasped. "What are you doing?"

"What I've wanted to do for months—I'm taking you to bed."

"Do you know how many stairs you have to climb to the top floor from here?"

"I've never actually counted them, so no," he told her. "But I'm pretty sure it's the same number to get to my apartment."

"And too many for you to carry me the whole way," she protested.

"Is that a challenge?" he asked, starting up the first flight.

"Of course it's not a challenge. It's a reasonable statement and a legitimate concern for your physical well-being."

"I promise, I won't be too tired when we reach the bed to remember why we're there."

"I wasn't—" She huffed out a breath. "Never mind."

If he was determined to carry her, why should she object to the ride? And truthfully, she quite enjoyed being held in strong arms, cradled against the hard muscles of his hot body.

Despite her extensive dating history, she'd never known another man who made her insides quiver with just a look. Who made her knees weak with the flash of a smile.

It had been a purely physical attraction in the beginning—she hadn't known Liam well enough for it to be anything more. But working in close proximity with him over the past few weeks, she'd been pleased to discover that she also liked and respected the man who was her boss.

"Fifty-two," he announced, as he unlocked the door. The room was dark, but he was familiar enough with the layout to navigate it without turning on a light. He carried her through the sitting room and past the bathroom to the bedroom before setting her on her feet. He bypassed the lamps in favor of the fireplace, creating light, heat and ambiance with the press of a button. Then he located the box of long wooden matches and turned his attention to the fat pillar candles lined up in a row along the mantel. Candles he'd bought when he went with her to the antique and craft market.

She wouldn't have thought he was the type to waste time with such romantic trappings. She certainly didn't want or need romance. She didn't want or need to pretend this night was anything more than two people succumbing to their long-denied attraction.

While he finished lighting the candles, she lowered herself onto the edge of the mattress, her hands folded in her lap. She was admittedly a little nervous and uncertain. Not about making love with Liam. She had no doubt that was what she wanted, but it was the details that eluded her.

What to do next.

Apparently he didn't suffer from the same uncertainty. He knelt on the floor between her knees and lifted one of her booted feet into his hands. "All night, I've been wondering what you'd look like wearing these boots and nothing else."

"I can't imagine how I'd look—"

"Sexy," he interjected.

"—but I'd probably feel ridiculous."

"We'll take them off, then," he decided, tugging on the zipper pull.

She was wearing tights, of course, because it was early spring in northern Nevada and the nights were still frigidly cold. But the slow, sensual glide of his knuckle along the inside of her calf as he dragged the pull downward made her skin heat, burn.

He drew the first boot off her foot and set it aside, then repeated the same shockingly sensuous process with the second. Then he lifted both feet into his hands. His thumbs stroked the sensitive inside arches, then skimmed over the tops to her ankles.

"Do you have a foot fetish?" she asked, a little breathlessly.

He chuckled softly. "I have a Macy fetish. I want to touch and see and taste every inch of you tonight."

While he spoke, those clever hands continued their exploration, over her knees and under her skirt, along the insides of her thighs.

He eased down the waistband of her tights. She lifted up off the bed to assist him, though her muscles, already quivering from his touch, trembled with the effort.

"Maybe I should help with some of your clothes," she offered.

"Let's just focus on you right now."

"As I recall, this was *my* idea," she pointed out to him. "So I don't see why you get to call all the shots."

"This might have seemed like your idea tonight," he acknowledged. "But it's been my fantasy for weeks, months. Since the first time I saw you."

"Maybe I've been fantasizing about this, too."

"Have you?"

She realized she'd backed herself into a corner. If she confessed that she had, he'd no doubt want to hear about her fantasies in explicit detail. If she denied that she had, he'd take that as justification to control every step of their lovemaking.

So she only responded by kissing him—long and slow and deep. Teasing him with her lips and tongue and teeth.

"You make me crazy." He muttered the confession into her mouth as his hands traced the curves of her body over her dress. "I want you naked, now, and I can't find a zipper anywhere on this damn dress."

She laughed softly, though the sound was a little strained by her own desperation. "There is no zipper."

"Then how the hell did you get it on? And, far more important right now, how the hell am I supposed to get it off?"

She stood up, praying that her wobbly legs would support her, and reached for the hem of her skirt.

"I wish I'd thought to put on music," Liam said. "Because watching you wiggle is just about the sexiest thing I've ever seen."

She finished drawing the garment over her head and let it fall to the floor.

"Correction," he said, his eyes moving over her body in a slow visual caress. "The second sexiest thing."

She blushed at the implication that *she* was the sexiest, grateful that the muted light from the fire didn't spotlight her stretchmarks or scar.

He finally yanked off his own boots and jacket, then added his jeans and shirt to the growing pile of discarded clothing on the floor. As they tumbled onto the mattress together, their mouths met, mated. Their bodies arched, yearned.

His hands stroked her skin, stoked her desire. He cupped her breasts in his palms, his thumbs circling the aching peaks through the silky fabric of her bra. She'd wondered if nursing her babies would decrease the sensitivity of her nipples. It appeared the answer was a clear and resounding *no*. Because, when he finally brushed his thumbs over the peaks, sharp, shocking arrows of pleasure speared from the tips to her core.

When he lowered his head to replace his hand with his mouth, suckling her through the fabric barrier, she nearly came apart right then and there. When he pushed the strap of her bra off her shoulder and freed her breast from the constraint, the sensation of his mouth, hot and wet, on her bare skin, did make her come apart.

As she continued to shudder with the aftershocks of her release, he made his way down her body. Kissing and licking, nibbling and sucking. He paused at her navel, his fingertip tracing along the horizontal line a few inches below it.

"My C-section scar," she confided.

"Does it hurt?"

She shook her head. "No."

He pressed his lips to her belly button, then the scar, then continued his downward trajectory.

She felt anticipation building inside her again, and when his tongue brushed against the ultrasensitive nub, she found herself teetering on the brink of another climax. But she wanted him with her this time, so she reached between their bodies and wrapped her hand around him. His groan vibrated through her.

"I'm not finished down here yet," he protested.

"I want you inside me."

He started to rise up, over her, then paused. "I didn't plan for this to happen tonight, so please tell me the basket of amenities in the bathroom has been checked and restocked."

"Every day," she assured him.

"In that case—" he pressed a quick kiss to her lips "—I'll be right back."

He slipped away, and Macy knew that if she was going to change her mind, this was her best chance to do it.

But she didn't want to change her mind.

She wanted this.

Wanted *him*.

Sure, she had some reservations, because she knew that once they were intimate, everything would change. Or maybe everything had already changed. Already she knew that she'd never felt about anyone the way she felt about Liam.

Working side by side with him over the past few weeks, her feelings had continued to deepen and grow. She'd observed many of his different moods: happy, annoyed, frustrated, amused. She'd seen him with his family, noted the obvious bond he shared with each of his siblings, the easy affection that characterized his relationship with his grandparents, his evident adoration of his young niece. And though he tried to pretend otherwise, she could tell that he was deeply troubled by the tension that had grown between him and his father. He was a man of many facets and every single one of them appealed to her.

"Now...where was I?" he asked, returning to the bedroom with two foil packets in hand.

"You were going to open one of those, put it on you and then put you in me."

His lips curved in response to her concise instructions. "So you want me to climb on top and get right to it?"

"Did you hear what I said downstairs? It's been a really long time for me, so there's no need to waste any more time on foreplay."

"Do you feel as if I've been wasting your time?" he asked, sounding more amused than insulted as his hands continued to move over her, making her sigh with pleasure, squirm with need. "Are you suggesting that you're not enjoying this?"

"You know I am."

"Then relax and let yourself enjoy," he suggested, just before he captured her nipple in his mouth again, swirling his tongue around the peak, making her moan.

He took her to the precipice again, and left her teetering on the edge while he rose up over her, spreading her knees farther apart and positioning himself between them. He nudged at her opening, testing, teasing. She lifted her hips, a wordless plea that he answered by burying himself deep inside her.

She gasped with shock, with pleasure, as the glorious friction of his invasion created a storm of sensation, enormous waves of pleasure crashing down on her again…and again…and again.

Finally, when she was certain she couldn't survive the barrage any longer, he linked their hands together and let the waves carry him away with her.

It was a long time later before she became aware of the weight of his body sprawled over hers, pinning her against the luxurious mattress. She knew her body would probably feel stiff and achy in the morning, but she didn't care. Because every muscle twinge tomorrow would be a reminder of the incredible pleasure he'd given her tonight.

Liam finally gathered up the strength to roll off her,

though he didn't move away. After another minute, he broke the silence to ask, "Are there any guests below this room?"

"Not tonight," she told him.

"That's good. I wouldn't want my manager to have to field noise complaints about the wild guests in Wild Bill's Suite."

Heat rose up her neck and into her cheeks. "I'm not usually... I mean, I never...well, not never but...okay, I'm going to shut up now."

He chuckled softly and brushed his lips against hers. "No, don't. I want to hear what you were going to say."

"I'll bet you do."

"You never..." he prompted.

"I've never...been particularly vocal before," she confided. "I've never...really lost control—certainly not like that—before."

His smile was satisfied. "I liked watching you lose control," he told her. "Whoever would have imagined that the tidy, efficient and organized Macy Clayton would be so uninhibited in the throes of passion?"

"Not me," she admitted. "I wasn't sure I believed the throes of passion even existed."

"Are you a believer now?"

"I think I might need just a little more convincing."

"Well, we do have one condom left," he said.

She felt a spark of arousal flicker through her body. "That would be a good start."

Macy knew she'd never be able to walk through the doors of this suite again without a smile curving her lips and erotic memories flooding her mind and teasing her body. The hours she'd spent here with Liam had been a perfect fantasy in so many ways, but now it was time to get back to reality—and her reality wasn't a sexy man and a luxurious hotel room but a basement apartment where three babies waited for her.

This brief interlude from the reality of her life had been fun, but it was only an interlude.

She nudged her elbow into Liam's ribs.

He grunted in protest.

"You can't fall asleep," she told him.

"I'm pretty sure I can," he countered in a drowsy voice.

"Let me rephrase," she said. "I don't want you to fall asleep."

"I'm flattered, but I'm definitely going to need some time to recuperate before we go another round."

She elbowed him again, a little harder this time.

His eyes stayed closed, but his lips curved as he wrapped his arm around her and drew her back against his body, nuzzling her throat, making her shiver.

"I can't stay," she told him, sincerely regretful.

"I know."

"And since Uber hasn't yet found its way to Haven, I'm going to need a ride home."

"I know," he said again. "But I'm not ready to let go of you just yet."

Whether she cuddled with him for another minute or two or ten, this night was only a stolen moment out of her ordinary life, and it was already over.

She hadn't expected that getting naked with him would magically transform their relationship. They were at completely different stages in their lives, looking for different things. Except that tonight they'd wanted the same thing. And that want had proven stronger than everything else.

She wouldn't trade Ava, Max and Sam for anything in the world, but she couldn't deny that she'd enjoyed feeling like a woman instead of a mom for a brief while. But she'd told her parents that she wouldn't be late, and she'd already been gone a lot longer than she'd intended. Plus, Max would inevitably be up early, wanting some cuddle time with his mom before his siblings woke up to demand their breakfast and—

"You're thinking about your kids, aren't you?" he guessed.

"Sorry. Occupational hazard."

"There's no need to apologize," he said, but he released her now to climb out of bed and gather up his clothes.

She did the same, more than a little sorry that the night was already at an end.

"How are we going to explain the tangled sheets to housekeeping?" he wondered aloud.

"I'm housekeeping tomorrow," she reminded him. "And I'll change the bed first thing."

"Or I could do it when I get back," he offered.

"You could try," she acknowledged. "But the result wouldn't fool anybody."

"True enough," he agreed.

Macy took a quick look around to ensure they hadn't left anything while he blew out the candles and turned off the fire.

They were mostly silent as they made their way down the stairs to the main lobby, where they'd left their coats. He held hers while she slid her arms into the sleeves.

When she lifted her hair to pull it out of the collar of her coat, he touched a hand to the side of her throat.

"You've got marks from my beard," he told her.

She suspected the marks weren't only on her throat, though she didn't worry that those other places would be visible to anyone else. "Hopefully they'll fade before morning."

"I'm hoping they don't," he said, as he led her out to his truck. "Then, when you see them in the mirror, you'll remember tonight."

"I don't think I'm going to forget anytime soon," she assured him.

The journey back to her parents' house was short and silent.

"Thanks for dinner," she said when he pulled into the driveway. "And…everything."

"Thank *you* for everything," he said, as he killed the engine.

"You don't have to walk me to the door," she told him.

"How else am I going to steal a goodbye kiss?"

She knew that she should protest, that despite Bev's assertion that she wouldn't wait up, it was entirely possible that her mother wasn't just awake but watching through her bedroom window. But if Liam walked her to the side door, no one would be able to see him kiss her—and just the thought of one more kiss was enough to make her insides quiver.

The kiss itself liquified her bones and turned her brain to mush. Even after making love with him twice already tonight, her body ached for more, yearned for the fulfillment only he could give her.

"Do me a favor?" He whispered the words close to her ear.

She had to moisten her lips with her tongue before she could respond. "What's that?"

He brushed his thumb over her bottom lip, tracing the plump curve. "Think about me."

Then he stepped back and waited for her to open the door.

As she slipped inside, Macy knew that she would.

She could hardly do anything else.

Chapter 12

Macy's former supervisor in Las Vegas had often commented on her professionalism. Even when she was confronted by unruly and obnoxious guests, she never lost her cool or raised her voice. She was always a consummate professional.

Until last night—when she'd slept with her boss.

That had been an admittedly *un*professional move, but she wasn't going to compound it by letting anyone at work know she'd slept with the boss.

Liam gave her a brief nod of acknowledgment when he walked through the door. She hadn't expected anything more, and yet she found herself wondering what his impersonal greeting meant. Of course, it was possible that it didn't mean anything, especially as she was busy with Mrs. Hemingway and her daughter, helping to plan their local activities for the day.

When the guests from Boulder City had gone on their way, he poked his head out of the library, which he used as an office when she was occupying the front desk. "Can you come in here for a minute?" he asked.

"Sure," she agreed, pausing on her way to peek into the solarium and ensure that everybody was being looked after.

Of course, it was a Wednesday morning, and aside from the Hemingways, who had already gone on their way, "everybody" consisted of a young couple who had booked the Bonnie Room and two middle-aged women—lifelong friends nearing the completion of a cross-country road trip—who were staying in the Clyde Room. At the moment, they were all digging into their cooked-to-order breakfasts, ensuring that she wouldn't be missed if she was away from the desk for a few minutes.

"What can I do for you?" she asked, stepping through the doors and into the library. It wasn't an unusual question but considering the things she'd done for him—and vice versa—the night before, the ordinary words suddenly took on a whole other layer of meaning.

Liam's gaze locked onto hers, his sparkling with heat and humor, and she knew that his mind had gone in the same direction. Then his expression sobered, and he said, "You can tell me if I crossed any lines last night."

"None that I didn't want crossed," she assured him.

He seemed visibly relieved by her response. "Good. But I realized this morning that we didn't talk about what was going to happen next."

"I didn't know that there was going to be a next... but I was hoping."

He smiled at that. "Me, too." Then he lowered his

head and kissed her, slowly, deeply and very thoroughly. "Next... I want to take you upstairs and pick up where we left off last night."

"Me, too," she admitted. "But my boss isn't paying me to lie down on the job."

"Is that your way of suggesting we should try it standing up?" he asked, and followed the question with a lascivious grin.

She shook her head. "It's my way of telling you that any extracurricular activities will occur outside of my working hours."

"You drive a hard bargain," he lamented.

But somehow, over the next few weeks, they made it work.

It wasn't easy, especially when The Home Station opened to offer evening dining. At first, it was only guests of the inn who showed any interest in eating at "that fancy new restaurant," but when those guests were overheard at The Daily Grind or The Trading Post talking about the fabulous meals they'd enjoyed, a few daring locals decided to give it a try. Then a few more.

The only downside was that Liam was no longer enjoying Jo's pizza two or three times a week—but not for lack of trying. He'd placed several orders that were somehow either lost or missed or made wrong, such as when he'd ordered a five-meat pizza and been given a vegetarian instead. He knew Jo was upset that Kyle was working at the inn now, but he hoped she wouldn't hold a grudge forever.

After only a few weeks, the restaurant was booked to capacity every night. Of course, the success of the restaurant meant longer hours for Liam at the hotel—and fewer trips out to the Circle G. But Caleb was right—

they didn't really need him there, so he stayed where he *was* needed.

And since Macy was usually at the inn, it was also where he wanted to be.

It took some creative juggling of other responsibilities for them to steal time alone together, and it was still easier for him than her, because he didn't have three babies depending on him. As a result, he found himself planning outings that were suitable for Ava, Max and Sam, too—even if that simply meant going to places where the triplets could ride around in their stroller and watch the scenery or other people passing by. And the more time he spent with all of them, the more he realized he was in serious danger of losing his heart to the single mom and her three adorable kids.

Liam was yawning when he walked into the inn's kitchen Wednesday morning, desperate for a hit of caffeine. He'd gone to bed after midnight and been up since dawn, and he wasn't sure how he was going to get through the day.

He halted in the entranceway, as if to remember why he was there. Macy came to the rescue, putting a mug of steaming coffee into his hands.

"Thank you."

"You looked like you needed it."

He swallowed a mouthful, willed the caffeine to jumpstart his brain.

"Is everything okay?"

He blinked. "What?"

"You seem really distracted this morning."

"I've just got a lot on my mind."

"Anything more than usual?"

"I went out to the ranch yesterday morning, to show my grandmother the updated menus for The Home Station," he confided. "And, not unexpectedly, crossed paths with my dad while I was there."

"Did you argue?"

He shook his head. "No. In fact, he was almost civil."

"Now I know why you look so worried."

When he didn't respond to her teasing tone, she realized that he really *was* worried.

"Maybe it's just that I haven't been out to the ranch in a few days, but he didn't look right."

"What do you mean?"

"I'm not sure," he admitted. "But he seemed pale, tired."

"Did you ask him how he was feeling? No," she answered her own question before he could. "Of course, you didn't. You don't communicate with your father."

"No more than he communicates with me."

"Did you say anything to your brother?"

He nodded. "Caleb didn't think there was any cause for concern."

"Then there probably isn't."

"You're right," he acknowledged. "I'm probably just feeling guilty that, as everything has amped up around here, I've been spending less time there."

"Is it only guilt?" she wondered. "Or is there maybe a little bit of second-guessing going on?"

"What do you mean?"

"You could have emailed the new menus to your grandmother instead of taking the time to drive all the way out to the Circle G," she pointed out. "Which makes me suspect that you wanted to make the trip—either to ensure ranch operations were running smoothly or to touch base with your family."

He scowled. "You sound like you've been reading my sister's psych textbooks."

"Or maybe just talking to your sister," she said.

"Why?"

"Because she stopped by yesterday morning when you were out at the ranch."

"Why?" he asked again.

"Because she wanted to know if we offered a family discount."

"For Sky? Yeah, she can pay a hundred and fifty percent of the usual rate."

"Even if the room is for your grandparents? For their sixtieth wedding anniversary?"

"I'm one step ahead of her," he said. "Wild Bill's Suite is already booked."

Macy smiled. "You're a good man, Liam Gilmore."

"Come back here later tonight, and I'll show you how good," he suggested.

Of course, she did.

Because even after more than a month together, the physical attraction between them showed no signs of abating.

She didn't have enough experience with relationships to know if this was normal, but she did know that she was well on her way to losing her heart to the sexy cowboy.

"Can you do me a favor?" Liam asked, a few days later.

Macy finished logging a new reservation into the system and clicked save. "Sure—what do you need?"

"Lunch."

She looked up from the computer, her expression quizzical. "You want me to make lunch for you?"

"No. I just want you to order it for me. And pick it up."

"I'm pretty sure running your personal errands isn't part of my job description."

"Not even if I offer to share my pizza with you?"

"Jo's still refusing to serve you?" she guessed.

His concern about backlash from the owner of the pizzeria had not been unfounded. Jo was furious with him for giving Kyle free rein in his fancy kitchen—a surefire guarantee that her son wasn't going to be tossing pizza dough anytime soon.

Liam nodded. "And I'm going through pizza withdrawal."

"What am I ordering on this pizza?"

"Pepperoni, Italian sausage and bacon crumble."

She wrinkled her nose. "And after lunch I'll make an appointment at the medical clinic in Battle Mountain so you can have your arteries cleaned out."

"My arteries are fine—and my stomach is empty."

"Okay," she relented. "Pepperoni, Italian sausage and bacon crumble on one half, ham, pineapple and black olives on the other. I'll order it in my name, but you're going to pick it up."

"Last time I went in there, she threw a ball of dough at my head."

"Which is why you need to go back and talk to her."

He grumbled, because he was certain that Jo wouldn't listen to him, but in the end, he walked over to the pizzeria.

The reception he got when he entered the restaurant was no less than he expected.

In response to the tinkle of the bell, Jo glanced up from the pie she was making, a sauce-filled ladle in hand. "You." She narrowed her gaze and lifted her other hand to point a bony finger at the door. "Get out of my restaurant."

He held up his own hands in a gesture of surrender. "I'm here to pick up a pizza for Macy."

"If she really wants her pizza, she's going to have to come and get it herself, because I'm not giving it to you."

"Come on, Jo," he cajoled. "Don't you think you're being a little unreasonable?"

"I don't have to sell my pizza to anybody I don't want to," she said stubbornly.

"That's not really true. A public business can't randomly refuse service to someone."

"Oh, don't worry. This isn't random at all."

"I've been buying pizza here for as long as I've had money to buy pizza," he pointed out to her.

"It's the only place in town to get pizza," she said, obviously unimpressed by his claim of loyalty.

"Exactly," he said. "And I have no intention of competing with your business. In fact, I've always encouraged my guests to come over here."

"Are you waiting for me to thank you for that?"

"I didn't do it for thanks, but I didn't expect to be punished, either."

"You hired my kid," she reminded him.

"Duke hired him first," Liam noted.

She waved a hand dismissively. "I knew he wouldn't be happy at Diggers' for long—and then he'd come back here."

"He came to me looking for a job," he said in his defense.

"He had a job here."

"You wouldn't let him make anything but pizza."

"The sign over the door says Jo's Pizza."

"A lot of pizza places do other things," he remarked.

"We do calzones, too."

Which was essentially folded-up pizza. "I was thinking more along the lines of wings or pasta."

"Folks want wings or pasta, they go to Diggers'."

"They might appreciate having another option."

"You plan on serving pizza in your fancy restaurant?"

"No," he immediately replied.

"Why not?"

"Because everyone in Haven knows that nobody does pizza better than Jo's."

"And you're not going to get around me by stating what everyone knows is a fact," she told him.

"I'm not trying to get around you."

"Then what do you want?"

"I want my pizza."

Her brows lifted.

"I mean, Macy's pizza." And then, since he knew she'd already seen through the ruse, he opted for honesty. "I also want you to stop canceling my orders—or deliberately screwing up my orders. And I want you to come to the inn one night to enjoy a meal prepared by my new chef."

"Unless your fancy new restaurant is somehow in a different time zone, dinner time there is dinner time here, which means I'm working."

"You could try leaving your daughter in charge for

one night," he suggested. "Then maybe *she* won't be looking for a job somewhere else in a few years."

Jo's eyes narrowed dangerously, then she turned around and picked up a flat white box. An order slip with Macy's name on it was tucked into the end. "I think you should take your pizza and go now."

He didn't have to be told twice.

He picked up the box, dropped a twenty-dollar bill on the counter and left without waiting for his change.

"Do you think I've been spending too much time with Liam lately?"

"Why would you ask a question like that?" Bev wondered as she squeezed a rubber dolphin, squirting water onto Max's belly.

Her grandson giggled and kicked his feet in the water, splashing her back.

Macy shrugged as she rubbed a cloth gently over Sam's body. "Maybe because I'm feeling a little out of my element," she acknowledged. "I don't have a lot of experience with romantic relationships, and I can't remember ever feeling so much so soon."

Bev's sigh was both wistful and worried. "You're falling in love with him."

"Am I?" The panic that spurted inside of her at the thought must have been reflected in her tone, because her mother smiled and touched a hand to her arm.

"Love isn't anything to be afraid of," Bev assured her daughter.

Macy didn't think she was afraid of love—but she was afraid of offering Liam her heart and having it rejected.

"And if you had to fall, you could do a lot worse than Liam Gilmore," her mother continued.

"Why do you say that?"

"Because it's obvious the man is just as crazy about Ava, Max and Sam as he is about you."

"He's been great with them," Macy agreed, as she continued to wash her babies and her mother continued to distract them with play. "Of course, his sister has a little girl, so kids aren't a completely alien species to him." Despite his initial attempts to convince her otherwise.

"That's one child," her mother pointed out. "Three can be overwhelming for someone who doesn't have a lot of experience with kids."

"Believe me, I know."

"You caught on fast," Bev noted.

"As if I had a choice." She lifted Ava out of the bath and wrapped her in a thick, fluffy towel.

"The point is, he's caught on pretty fast, too. A lot of guys would have balked at the idea of dating a single mother with three kids."

Liam had, as well, Macy remembered. In fact, he'd taken a literal step back when he'd learned that she was a mom.

"Maybe I should take a step back," she mused.

"It's hard to make any progress when you're moving in reverse," her mother pointed out, with unerring logic, as she wrapped Sam in another towel.

"I thought I'd given up on having a traditional family," she admitted now. "But the more time I spend with Liam—especially with Liam and Ava, Max and Sam— the more I find those old dreams being resurrected."

"And what's wrong with that?"

"Maybe nothing—except that we haven't really talked about the future."

"So maybe you need to have this conversation with him," Bev suggested.

"You're right," Macy agreed, removing Max from the tub. "And I will. Tomorrow."

"Good. Because right now, we've got to get these munchkins into their jammies and into bed."

But their paths didn't cross until late the following morning, when Macy was on the phone with the wine merchant and Liam was on his way to a meeting with Kyle and a local organic wholesaler.

"Lunch?" he mouthed the request.

She nodded.

He glanced at his watch. "Twelve-thirty?"

She nodded again.

He returned to the inn at 12:25.

"You're early," she noted.

He leaned across the desk and kissed her. "I wanted to make sure I had time to do that."

She grabbed the collar of his jacket and brought his mouth back to hers. "You know, one-thirty is a pretty good time for lunch, too."

He drew away slowly, reluctantly. "It is—except when breakfast was a mere blueberry muffin more than five hours ago."

She pushed away from the desk and reached for her coat. "In that case, we better go get you fed."

"Over lunch, I thought we could review the website updates for the fall and winter—"

The ring of his cell phone cut through his words.

"Go ahead and take it," Macy encouraged.

"It's just my brother." He swiped the screen to send the call to voice mail. "Whatever he wants can wait."

But Macy had barely set the "Back at 2:00 p.m." sign on the desk when his phone rang again.

Liam frowned at the same name and number on the display.

"Obviously it can't wait," Macy said.

While he was talking to his brother, she tidied the brochures in the pockets of the wall display by the desk. The National Cowboy Poetry Gathering in Elko was long past, but she kept the flyers, in case they piqued the interest of anyone who might be planning a visit the following year.

She straightened the cards advertising the Basque Museum, replenished the Adventure Village brochures—and found a miniature Hulk action figure that she'd noticed a little boy playing with while his parents checked in the day before. Rick and Monica Wallace in the Clark Foss suite, she remembered now. They'd gone out to tour the town today, but she called up to their room and left a message that Harrison's action figure was at the front desk.

Though Liam was facing the front door, she read the tension in the line of his shoulders, heard it in his clipped tone. Obviously his brother had not called to share good news.

"What's wrong?" she asked, when he finally disconnected the call.

"I have to go. My dad—" He cleared his throat. "The ambulance is taking him to the hospital in Elko."

Chapter 13

"Give me your keys," Macy said.

Liam looked at her blankly. "What? Why?"

"So I can drive you to the hospital."

He immediately shook his head. "No, it's okay. I can drive."

Maybe he could, but she wasn't sure that he should. It was obvious that his brother's phone call had rocked him to the core. And understandable, considering that he'd already lost one parent and just learned that the other was in some kind of medical distress.

"Do you want me to go with you?" she suggested as an alternative.

"No," he said again.

"Okay." She understood that he was distracted and worried about his father, but she couldn't help feeling a little disappointed that he'd so quickly disregarded her offers to help. Maybe he didn't need her, but she thought that he'd appreciate having someone to lean on during a time of crisis.

"I need you here," he said now.

Which made sense and took a little bit of the sting out of his earlier rejection.

"Will you call me?" she asked, walking with him toward the door. "To tell me how he's doing. To let me know if there's anything I can do."

He looked at her, his gaze unfocused. "What? Oh. Yeah. Okay."

She gave him a quick hug. "He's going to be okay," she said, and fervently prayed that it was true.

While Liam was on his way to Elko, Macy called Rose to cover the desk at the inn. Then she went home to wait for Liam's call.

"You should go to the hospital," Bev urged, when Macy told her mother as much as she herself knew.

"He doesn't want me there," she reluctantly admitted.

"What are you talking about?" her mother demanded. "Why wouldn't he want you there?"

She shrugged. "Maybe because our relationship doesn't really mean anything to him?"

Beverly scowled. "That's ridiculous."

"Is it?" Macy wondered. Though she wouldn't put it in such blunt terms to her mother, she had to wonder if Liam preferred to keep her on the periphery of his world, as his inn manager and bed buddy, rather than let her be part of his life.

Thankfully her phone rang before her mother could question her further, and Macy immediately snatched it up.

"It was a heart attack," Liam said without preamble. "He had emergency bypass surgery and is in recovery now."

"So, he's going to be okay?" she prompted hesitantly.

"Apparently. We don't yet know how long he's going to be in the hospital, but the doctor made it clear that he's going to need time to rest and recuperate."

"Of course," she agreed.

"Which means that extra hands are going to be needed at the Circle G."

His hands, she realized.

"Well, you don't need to worry about the inn. Rose has already agreed to take additional and extended shifts, so the two of us can cover things for the short term. You might want to hire someone else for the longer term, but we can talk about that later."

"Yeah," he agreed. "My mind is spinning in circles right now."

"Understandable," she assured him. "You focus on your dad and let me know what you need."

"Thanks."

She'd hoped he might want to talk a little bit longer, and maybe open up about some of what he was feeling, but he told her that he had other calls to make, then said goodbye and disconnected.

The following night, she gave in to her mother's urging—and her own desire to see that Liam was holding up okay—and made a trip to the hospital. Anticipating that his grandparents and siblings would all be there, too, she took a couple of extra-large pizzas. Jo might still be mad at Liam, but when she realized who the pizzas were for, she refused to accept any payment for the pies.

Macy was greeted warmly by the family members

gathered in the waiting room, and she felt confident that she'd made the right decision in coming. But while she was in the middle of a conversation with Jack and Evelyn, Liam drew her away from his grandparents.

"Let's take a walk," he said.

It was more a command than a request, but understanding how worried he'd been about his father, she decided to cut him some slack.

He fell silent again as they made their way down the brightly lit corridor, so she ventured to ask, "Did you have enough pizza? Because I think there were a couple of slices left."

He turned to face her then. "What are you really doing here, Macy?"

She blinked, startled by not just the question but the coldness of his tone. "I know hospital food isn't the best, and I thought you'd appreciate something different."

His expression was dubious. "You came all this way to deliver pizza?"

"And to be here for you," she said, wondering if he was really so thickheaded that he didn't know how much she cared about him.

"I didn't ask you to come."

"No, you didn't," she said, silently acknowledging that maybe she was the obtuse one. She'd assumed he hadn't asked because he didn't want to seem weak and needy. Apparently she'd been wrong.

"Because I can't let myself be distracted right now," he told her. "I need to focus on what matters."

Which clearly meant that she did not.

"You're right," she said, fighting against the tears that burned her eyes. "I shouldn't have come. I'm sorry."

She turned toward the elevators, but she could hardly

see through the sheen of moisture that blurred her vision. As a result, she nearly walked into someone approaching from the other direction.

"Macy?" It was Skylar. "Are you okay?"

She nodded. "Yeah. Sorry. I was a little distracted—not really watching where I was going."

"*Why* are you going? You only just got here."

"It's been a long day, and my babies are at home," she said.

"I don't doubt both of those statements are true," Sky said. "But I'm guessing my brother also said or did something to upset you."

"It doesn't matter. What matters is your dad and his recovery."

"So stick around a little while. They only let two visitors in at a time, but we could slot you into the rotation. I know he'd be happy to see you."

"I really need to get back," Macy said. "But please give your dad my best."

"And my brother a smack upside the head?" Sky prompted.

She shook her head. "Not necessary."

"Even when it's not, it's fun."

Macy managed a small smile at that.

"Seriously, though," Liam's sister said. "He doesn't mean to be an idiot. He just can't help himself sometimes."

"He's got a lot on his mind right now."

"I'm not sure he does, considering that he dumped all of the inn responsibilities on you."

"I'm happy to help," Macy assured her.

"I know you are." Sky gave her a quick hug. "And in case my brother didn't say it, thanks for the pizza."

* * *

"Ow." Liam frowned at his younger sister and rubbed the back of his head. "What was that for?"

She stood in front of him, her hands fisted on her hips. "I'm not entirely sure," she admitted. "But I know you're an idiot, so that was for Macy."

"Macy told you to hit me?"

"Of course not. She's far too sweet and compassionate to express her feelings through physical violence. She's also far too good for you."

He didn't doubt that was true.

But before he could respond, he saw someone exit his father's room and turn quickly to walk in the opposite direction.

"Did you see—"

"What?" she asked.

But Sky was facing him, so she wouldn't have seen anything.

"Someone just walked out of Dad's room."

"A doctor? A nurse?" she prompted, clearly unimpressed by his observation.

"A woman. She looked like—" He shook his head. "But it couldn't have been."

"Couldn't have been who?" his sister pressed.

"Valerie Blake," he finally confided.

Sky snorted. "I didn't hear any reports that hell has frozen over, so no, it couldn't have been Valerie Blake."

"You're right," he agreed. "Stress and fatigue must be playing tricks on my eyes."

"Obviously something is," his sister agreed.

"Well, let's go find out if the doctors have a plan for when they're going to release him," he decided.

Sky held up a hand, holding him in place. "You know

that even when they do let him go home, he's not going to be able to step right back into working the ranch."

"You think?" Liam asked dryly.

His sister's gaze narrowed. "I'm just saying, I know Caleb would appreciate it if you stepped up to help out."

"Six weeks ago, Caleb made it clear that they didn't need my help at the Circle G."

"Six weeks ago, Dad wasn't in the hospital and Wade wasn't on his way to Billings for his son's wedding."

He nodded. "You know I'll do whatever I can to help."

"What about the inn?"

"Macy can handle the inn," he said, because it was undoubtedly true.

It was equally true that he hadn't done a very good job handling Macy—or his growing feelings for her.

Macy didn't go back to the hospital, and Liam didn't come to the inn, so the next three days passed with only a handful of brief text messages exchanged between them. David Gilmore was sent home from the hospital on Sunday, which she knew had to be a relief to his family, but she was a little disappointed that she heard the news from Frieda Zimmerman who had run into the Circle G housekeeper at The Trading Post earlier that morning.

Monday came and went, again with no communication from him. Obviously he trusted her to do whatever needed doing at the inn. It was just as obvious to Macy that he didn't trust her as someone with whom to share his thoughts and feelings about what was going on with his father and, as a result, his own future.

She tried to be patient and understanding. His father's heart attack had been a shock to all of them; it was natural that Liam would be reeling. But it worried her that he seemed to be withdrawing from her. And she suspected that he didn't see any purpose in talking to her about his future because he didn't see her as part of that future.

"That looks good," Macy said, when she got home from work Wednesday afternoon and tracked her mother down in the kitchen.

"It's a teriyaki chicken casserole. This one's for us, for dinner tonight, but there's another one in the fridge for David Gilmore."

It didn't matter that the man had a housekeeper to prepare his meals; sending food was what the residents of Haven did when someone was sick or injured. It was their way of showing that they cared.

"Can you drop it off at the Circle G on your way home after work tomorrow?" Bev asked.

"The Circle G is hardly on my way home," she pointed out.

"Thank you," her mother said.

Macy didn't object to making the detour, but she was a little apprehensive about crossing paths with Liam.

Maybe he hadn't meant anything when he sent her away from the hospital, but she wanted *to* mean something to him, and it was becoming more and more apparent that she didn't. At least not beyond the limited section of his life that he'd opted to share with her.

Martina took the glass dish that Macy offered, then ushered her into the living room, where the family patriarch was reclined in his La-Z-Boy and scrolling through channels on the enormous television.

He pressed the power button to blank the screen and

give his full attention to his visitor. "A pretty face beats repeats on the Game Show Network any day," he told her.

"Yours looks pretty good, too, considering your recent ordeal."

He waved a hand dismissively. "Much ado about nothing—and now I've got all the neighbors sending casseroles and stews and whatnot."

"My mom sent a teriyaki chicken casserole," she told him.

He smiled again. "Your folks are good people."

"I think so," she said.

His smile faded and his gaze moved past her, as if looking for something—or someone—else. "You come by yourself?"

"I did," she confirmed, wondering who he expected would have accompanied her.

His next question answered her unspoken query. "Where are those babies of yours?"

"At home with the good people."

He chuckled at that, then grimaced and pressed a hand to his chest.

"Are you okay?" Macy asked worriedly.

"Yeah. I just forget sometimes that they had to crack my chest open to get at my ornery heart."

She winced sympathetically. "I can't imagine that was much fun."

"Not much," he agreed. "And now the doctor wants me to cut down on red meat." He shook his head, as if baffled that someone with a medical degree could offer such outrageous advice. Especially to a cattle rancher.

"I think that's standard protocol after a cardiac event," she noted. "Less red meat, salt and sugar. More fruits and vegetables. And exercise." Of course, she knew that Liam's father—like most other ranchers—did not lead a sedentary lifestyle.

"That's exactly what he said," David grumbled.

"My dad had a heart attack—" she paused to do a quick mental calculation "—eighteen years ago."

"Norm would have been quite young then," Liam's father noted.

"He was young," she confirmed. "And a smoker. But he followed the doctor's advice. He gave up the cigarettes, made some dietary changes to control his blood pressure and cholesterol, and started to take a walk after dinner every night."

"Maybe the doctor isn't completely full of crap, then," he mused. "And there is one good thing that came out of all of this."

"You're still alive?" she suggested.

"Besides that," he said. "My eldest son is back on the ranch, where he belongs."

Macy bit her tongue. She wasn't going to pick a fight with a man who was recovering from major surgery, but she was worried that David might take advantage of his condition to manipulate his son. She understood why Liam had abandoned his responsibilities at the inn to help out at the ranch, but she couldn't help but worry that this temporary solution would turn into a permanent arrangement.

And if it did, what would that mean for her and her future?

She pushed that admittedly selfish thought aside. Whatever happened with Liam and the inn, she knew she had the support of her family. She wished Liam could trust that he'd receive the same unconditional support from her.

"He's out in the east paddock supervising the calving, but I can call him in, if you wanted to see him," David offered.

She did want to see him, but she was apprehensive, too. And she knew that pulling calves—if assistance was required—was hard and messy work, and the crew on-site had likely settled into a rhythm that she was loathe to disrupt. Not to mention that she wasn't sure of the reception she'd get if she did.

"No, I don't want to disturb him," she said. "And I should be getting home, anyway. My mom and dad have had the kids all day."

"Sky tells me that you've been putting in extra hours at the inn so that Liam can be here."

"Lucky for me, I love my job," she told him sincerely.

"And you don't think Liam feels the same way about the ranch?" he guessed.

"I honestly don't know anything about his feelings." She was responding to his question about the Circle G, but realized the answer was equally applicable to Liam's feelings for her.

And perhaps that came through in subtext, because David shook his head. "In that case, my son's a damn fool."

"Don't worry about your son," Macy said. "You just concentrate on your recovery."

"I promise I will if you promise to bring those babies of yours to visit me soon. There's nothing like the laughter of young ones to soothe an old and aching heart."

She kissed his pale, weathered cheek. "I'll do that."

* * *

She was almost at her car when Liam came out of the barn, heading toward the house. Her heart bumped against her ribs when he spotted her and, after lifting a hand to wave, abruptly changed direction.

"Why didn't you call or text to let me know you were coming?" he asked, as he drew nearer.

"Because I didn't come to see you."

"Your mom sent food, didn't she?" he guessed.

"It's what people do in this town."

"Apparently," he noted. "Did you see my dad?"

Macy nodded. "He seems to be in pretty good spirits, considering."

"Considering," he agreed.

But she could tell that he was still worried. Of course, less than ten days had passed since he'd almost lost his father, and that was the kind of potentially life-changing event that made a person take stock and reevaluate.

"He looks as if he's aged ten years in the past ten days," he said to her now.

"He had a heart attack," she reminded him gently. "It's going to take him some time to recuperate."

"I know, but...he always seemed so strong, so powerful. Invincible."

"He's going to be okay," she told him, this time much more confident that it was true.

He nodded again, then surprised her by asking, "What about us? Are we going to be okay?"

"What do you mean?"

"I know we haven't talked much over the past few days, but whenever we did, I got the impression that you were pulling back."

"Really? Because I got the impression that I was pushed."

He winced. "Sky took me to task for my behavior at the hospital. All I can say is that I was worried about my dad and—"

"And you needed to focus on what really mattered," she said, echoing the words he'd used.

"And you thought that didn't include you," he realized.

"It's okay," she said. "We didn't make any promises to one another."

"It's not okay," he said. "And you do matter to me, a lot more than you know. Maybe more than I wanted to admit."

She sighed. "Am I an idiot for wanting to believe that's true?"

"It *is* true." He dipped his head and brushed his lips lightly against hers. "I've missed you like crazy."

"I've missed you, too."

"I'm getting back into the routine here," he said. "Which means that I should be able to squeeze some time out for us—if you want."

"I want," she admitted.

He smiled, and she realized that he seemed genuinely happy.

She'd originally suspected that his return to the ranch was a form of penance—his effort to atone for the perceived sin of choosing a career and life away from the ranch. But though he was obviously sweaty and exhausted from the work he'd been doing, he also seemed entirely within his element in a way that he never had at the inn.

Oh, he did an admirable impression of an innkeeper,

but she was beginning to suspect that, in his heart, he was a rancher.

But she wasn't getting into the middle of that mess— that was something he would have to figure out for himself.

Chapter 14

Over the next week, Liam did manage to sneak away from the ranch for a few hours now and again. Including Friday afternoon, when he found Macy in the kitchen arranging cheese cubes and crackers on a platter.

"What would you say to a movie?" he asked.

She tipped her head, considering. "Probably nothing, because I don't think the movie would talk back."

He rolled his eyes and tried again. "Okay, what would you say if I asked you to go to a movie with me?"

"If you're asking for tonight, I can't."

"Got a date with someone else?" he teased.

"Actually, three someone elses."

"I should have guessed."

She nodded and continued to prep for the guests' wine and cheese, starting a second plate with soft cheeses and pâtés, little bowls of olives and pickled onions.

He snagged a pimento-stuffed olive from a bowl and popped it into his mouth, earning a disapproving look.

He grinned, unrepentant, and chewed.

"You know, this is the point in our conversation where you could invite me to hang out with you, Ava, Max and Sam," he said, as she replenished the supply of olives.

"Is it?" she mused.

He folded his arms across his chest, waiting.

A smile tugged at the corners of her mouth. "If you really have nothing better to do, you're welcome to hang out with me, Ava, Max and Sam," she finally offered. "It's not Mann's Theater but we do have Netflix *and* popcorn."

"An irresistible combination," he said. Then, after looking around to ensure they were alone, he slid his arms around her middle and drew her into his embrace. "Or maybe it's just you who's irresistible."

He lowered his head to nibble on her lips—intending to keep the contact light and playful. But she closed her eyes and hummed low in her throat, and the sound stoked the fire that burned in his belly. The tenor of the kiss quickly shifted from casual affection to serious arousal. He captured her mouth and deepened the kiss; she pressed closer and kissed him back.

It had been a long time since he'd had his hands all over her, and he was tempted to lift her up onto the counter and—

"I'll have what she's having."

The dry remark was followed by giggles, and then two different female voices echoed in stereo: "Me, too."

Macy immediately pulled out of his arms, and though Liam could tell she was embarrassed to have been caught in a compromising position by a trio of guests, she responded without missing a beat. "Sorry, ladies, but this prime specimen is currently off the market."

"Damn." The first speaker, with bold purple streaks in her short dark hair, lamented.

Elaine, Liam remembered her name now.

The three women had checked in late the previous afternoon and boldly flirted with him throughout the process. He'd quickly determined that they were shameless but also harmless, and learned they were from nearby Elko and grateful that there were quality accommodations closer than Reno so they could enjoy a girls' weekend away.

The shorter of the two blondes—Serena—sighed. "I guess we'll have to settle for the wine and cheese."

"The wine's already set out in the library—and the cheese is on its way," Macy said, lifting a tray in each hand.

"We can take those through for you," Kelly—the taller blonde—offered, plucking one of the trays from Macy's hand, as Elaine took the other. She winked at the inn's manager. "I think you've got more important things to do."

"Enjoy your wine, ladies," Liam said, as the trio exited the room. Then to Macy, when they'd gone, "I think I'm the 'more important thing' you have to do."

"With laundry that needs to be transferred from the washing machine to the dryer, fresh flowers to be delivered to Wild Bill and fruit to be cut up for breakfast, you don't even crack the top three," she told him.

"I bet I could convince you to rearrange your priorities."

She quickly stepped to the other side of the island, putting the butcher block slab between them. "I'm not taking that sucker's bet," she told him.

He grinned at this confirmation that he only had to put his hands on her and she'd forget about everything else.

"You deal with the flowers and the fruit," he said, because she was a lot better with things like that, "and I'll take care of the laundry and see you later tonight."

"Thanks," she said. "The kids should be—" she held up her crossed fingers "—settled down by eight, so we can start a movie around then."

"I'd offer to come earlier and bring pizza for dinner but…" He let the sentence trail off on a sigh.

"But Jo's still messing with you?" Macy guessed.

"Worse," he said. "She's messing with my pizza."

"Well, I took lasagna out of the freezer this morning, so if you want to join me for that—and if you don't get waylaid by your guests at the wine and cheese—dinner will be on the table at six."

"I'll be there," he promised.

Liam arrived at 5:45.

Ava, Max and Sam had already been fed, but they stayed in their high chairs at the table while their mom and her guest dined on lasagna, warm bread and green salad. After dinner, Macy invited Liam to relax in the living room while she bathed the triplets and got them ready for bed, but he—after an almost imperceptible hesitation—insisted on helping.

An extra set of hands allowed the task to be completed more quickly and easily, and Max and Sam were soon clean and dry and zipped into their sleepers, ready for bed.

"Hey, Big Guy—is that a new tooth you've got?"

Macy glanced over her shoulder to see which "big guy" Liam was talking to as she wrestled her stubborn little girl into her pj's.

"Two new teeth," she confirmed. "The top ones broke through his gums yesterday morning."

"Good job, Sam," he said, lifting the baby's hand for a high five.

Macy was startled by his remark. "Why'd you call him Sam?"

His gaze shifted between the two boys. "Was I wrong?"

"No. But most people struggle to tell them apart. Even my dad calls them by the wrong names half the time."

"They do look a lot alike, but Sam's eyes have a little more grey mixed with the green, and Max's chin is a little more square."

"Good eye," she noted.

"Plus Max is a more introspective and Sam more demanding."

She couldn't disagree with those distinctions, either, but they were hardly apparent to anyone looking at the babies. That he'd obviously been paying close enough attention during his interactions with the boys tugged at something inside her.

You're falling in love with him.

Her mother's words echoed in the back of her mind, and she realized that they were true.

Liam, oblivious to the direction of her thoughts,

turned his attention to Max. "How many have you got now?"

The baby smiled, revealing two pearly whites on the bottom.

"That's a good start, but you're going to need a few more than that to chomp on a Gilmore steak," he told the infant.

"Quite a few more," Macy agreed, pleased that her tone didn't give away anything of the emotions churning inside her. "Although Ava is well on her way to becoming a carnivore—she left six distinct tooth impressions in Gramma's finger yesterday."

"I'll bet that's the last time Gramma puts her finger in Ava's mouth," he remarked.

Macy's lips quirked. "That's what I said."

This is what it would be like to have a family, Liam thought, as he sat close to Macy on the sofa with her baby girl cuddled against his chest. The boys were both asleep in their cribs, but Ava had fought against gravity every time her eyelids started to close.

She'd eventually lost that fight, but she still looked ready to do battle, with her tiny hands curled into fists. Although her pose said warrior, her face was pure angel, with her little cupid's bow mouth slightly parted and her eyelashes—long and dark, like her mom's—fanned against the curve of her cheek. Beneath the now-closed lids, her eyes were blue like her mom's, too.

Of course, it was possible that her dad's eyes were also blue. Or maybe green, like Max's and Sam's. There were other features he noticed when he looked at the boys that he suspected had been inherited from the man who had contributed to their DNA. Of course, he didn't know for sure, because Macy remained frustratingly tight-lipped about the father of her children and her relationship with him.

Whenever he asked any questions, she just said that he wasn't part of their lives. The vague response was hardly reassuring. Did he still live in Las Vegas? She'd shrugged, claiming not to know. Was she still in love with him? She'd denied ever having been in love with him.

He wanted to believe her, but he couldn't shake the feeling that she was holding something back. And every time he tried to wrangle more details out of her, she sidestepped his queries. When he determinedly pressed for more information, she shut the subject down. And then she'd point out that she didn't ask him about his romantic history, the implication being that he shouldn't care about hers.

He wished she *would* ask about his past relationships, so that he could be open and honest and prove that he had nothing to hide. The fact that she didn't, that she was obviously wary of an expectation of reciprocity, made him wonder what she was hiding.

Or maybe she wasn't hiding anything.

Maybe he was making a whole lot of something out of nothing.

It was possible, he knew, that she didn't want to talk about her relationship with the babies' father because there really was nothing to talk about. It might have been a casual relationship that had run its course, or a short-term fling, or possibly even a one-night stand.

Certainly she'd given no indication that she was harboring any feelings for another man. And when they made love, she didn't hold anything back. But she had yet to give him a glimpse of what was in her heart and, as a result, his own remained wary.

"Do you want me to put her in her crib?" Macy asked now, her voice pitched low so as not to disturb the baby.

"Nah, she's okay where she is," he said.

"Let me rephrase," she suggested. "Why don't I put Ava in her crib so that we can make more effective use of the sofa?"

He immediately rose to his feet, careful not to jostle—and wake—the baby tucked close to his chest. "I know where her crib is."

"Then I'll wait for you here."

Later they moved to her bed.

She was sprawled half on top of him on the narrow mattress now, and sighed contentedly as he stroked a hand down the length of her naked back.

"I missed this," she said.

"I did, too," he told her. "But I didn't come over here tonight to get lucky—I figured I was lucky just to hang out with you and your kids."

"It was a good night, wasn't it?"

"It was," he agreed. "Although I have no idea how the movie ended."

"The way all good movies do," she assured him. "They fell in love and lived happily ever after."

"Good movies have bad guys chasing good guys and battles to the death," he said.

"And Rodents Of Unusual Size in the Fire Swamp?"

"Huh?"

"*The Princess Bride*. We'll watch that on our next movie night," she promised.

Then she fell asleep in his arms.

Our next movie night.

The words echoed in his mind, tempting him to believe that this could be a regular event for them. That they could be a real couple and do all the things that real couples did.

He liked to pretend he enjoyed his bachelor lifestyle, but the truth was, he wanted to find the right woman, get married, have a couple of kids. Or maybe three. Maybe even more.

That was when he realized he didn't just want *a* family, he wanted *this* family.

And the longing was so sharp and strong, it scared him.

Macy isn't Isabella.

He knew that, but the knowledge did little to alleviate his concerns.

Because what else did he really know?

Nothing about Ava, Max and Sam's father. Certainly not enough to be sure that the man wouldn't show up one day to lay claim to the children that were rightfully his and the woman who was their mother.

And then Liam would be shut out of their lives.

Alone.

Macy wasn't surprised when she woke up alone, but she was admittedly disappointed. She should have asked Liam to stay, so that she wouldn't now be missing the warmth and strength of his arms around her.

Still, she was sure that last night had marked a turning point in their relationship. And, in the interest of open and honest communication, she resolved that the next time they were together, she would share her feelings—she would tell him that she loved him.

The idea of saying the words aloud was a little daunting, but she felt confident they were the first step on the path of their future together.

Her conviction wavered a little when he didn't stop by the inn at all that day. And a little more when he failed to even call or text.

Late in the afternoon, she finally sent a brief message, just to check in.

Everything okay?

His response was equally brief: Fine.

It was late Sunday afternoon before he made another appearance at the hotel. Ordinarily she would have been gone by two, but she'd promised Rose that she could stay until four, so the other woman could attend her niece's bridal shower.

When Liam showed up, around 3:30, Macy couldn't help but wonder if he'd timed his arrival expecting that she would be gone. She wished she could dismiss the idea as paranoia, except that he looked so surprised to see her, she knew that was, in fact, what he'd done.

She continued to reply to email inquiries and, since she was working at the desk, he took the folder Kyle had left for him into the library.

After a few minutes of internal debate, she followed him. "Are you going to tell me what I did wrong?"

"You didn't do anything wrong."

"Really?" she challenged. "Because you didn't even look up from your file when you said that."

Liam lifted his head to meet her gaze. "You didn't do anything wrong," he said again.

"Okay, *now* I believe you," she said, though the sarcasm in her tone indicated otherwise.

But she turned back to the double doors, and he exhaled a silent sigh of relief.

A premature sigh, he realized, when she closed the doors instead of exiting through them.

"I'm busy here, Macy."

"I only want ten minutes of your time—and an explanation. I think you owe me that much."

She was right. He did owe her an explanation. But he didn't have one to give. Certainly not one that would satisfy her.

"What do you want me to say?" he asked wearily.

"I want you to tell me why, after a thoroughly enjoyable evening together, you disappeared in the middle of the night and have been incommunicado ever since."

"And what if you don't like the answer?"

"I want to hear it anyway."

"Fine," he relented. "The truth is that hanging out with you, Ava, Max and Sam the other night…it just got a little too real for me."

"I don't understand," she said. "It's not as if that's the first time we've hung out together. What changed all of a sudden?"

What changed was that he'd realized he was falling for her—and her kids. Why else would he have spent a Friday night sitting on an uncomfortable sofa in the basement apartment of her parents' house with her children sprawled around them? All the while basking in the feeling that he belonged there, with them.

And when Ava had climbed into his lap and laid her head against his chest, his heart had swelled so much that his ribs actually ached. It had been an exhilarating—and terrifying—feeling.

Because he knew that if he let himself get in any deeper, he might not survive losing them. It would be smarter, easier, he'd decided, to walk away now.

"Being with your kids simply reminded me that I'm not daddy material," he said.

"Disregarding the blatant inaccuracy of that statement for a moment—have I asked you to step into the father role for my kids?" she challenged.

"No," he admitted. "But if we keep seeing each other, isn't that what you're going to expect? If I keep spending time with your kids, isn't that what *they're* going to expect?"

"They're nine months old," she pointed out. "I don't think you need to worry about their expectations. You definitely don't need to worry about mine."

"I never meant to hurt you, Macy."

She shook her head, her eyes glittering with moisture. "And I never meant to fall in love. In fact, I'd given up believing it would ever happen," she confided. "I thought maybe I didn't have it in me to give my heart to someone else. And then you came along."

Was she saying that she loved him?

Was it possible?

No, he didn't—wouldn't let himself—believe it. He wouldn't be led down that garden path again where poisonous weeds could wrap around his heart.

"You don't love me, Macy."

She lifted those tear-filled eyes to his. "You don't have to feel the same way—and you've made it perfectly clear that you don't," she said. "But don't you dare presume to tell me how *I* feel."

Then she exited the library, grabbed her coat off the hook and slammed the intricately engraved wood door she'd once admired behind her.

Chapter 15

Macy knew better than to go straight home.

She needed some time to bury her heartache before facing her mother's inquisition—and if she arrived home early in the day, Macy knew there would be an inquisition.

She also needed ice cream. Because nothing soothed a wounded soul like ice cream.

She left The Trading Post with two bags of groceries and a fresh perspective.

"I saw Alyssa Channing this afternoon," Macy said, setting her grocery bags on the counter. "She was on her way home from the hospital."

Bev reached into one of the bags for a familiar-looking box. "Regan had her babies?" she guessed.

Macy nodded as she opened the freezer to tuck away her stash of ice cream.

"What did she have?" her mother immediately wanted to know. "And how are they all doing?"

"Two girls, each just over five pounds, and everyone's doing fine. Although both the new mom and dad are exhausted after twenty-two hours of labor."

Bev winced sympathetically as she opened the flap of the box and pulled out the cellophane package inside. "Bet you're glad your doctor finally opted to do a C-section."

"Yeah, the sixteen hours of labor that preceded it only felt like forever," Macy remarked dryly.

"But Ava, Max and Sam are worth every minute, aren't they?"

Her gaze shifted from one to the next and the next, and her heart overflowed with so much love it almost filled the cracks caused by Liam's rejection. "They are," she agreed.

Bev distributed teething biscuits to her grandbabies as Macy continued to unpack the groceries.

"You should go see Regan and her twins," her mom suggested. "I don't mean now, but when she's home from the hospital. I'm sure she'd appreciate talking to someone who has experience with multiples."

"I will," she promised.

"Good. And now, you should scoop up two bowls of that ice cream and tell me why you're home in the middle of the day."

"I haven't seen you around here in a while," Sky remarked, when her brother settled onto a stool at the bar.

"I've been busy," Liam told her.

"And suddenly you're not?"

"I just needed a break."

She set his beer on a paper coaster in front of him. "Is that what you told Macy?"

He scowled at the amber liquid in his glass.

"Alyssa came by earlier and mentioned that she saw Macy at The Trading Post—and that she looked upset."

"Why would you immediately assume that has anything to do with me?"

"Because I know you," she said simply.

He lifted the glass to his mouth.

Sky picked up a towel and began wiping and shelving the rack of glasses the dishwasher had brought out to her. "Successful relationships require honesty and communication."

"Did I ask for any advice?" he challenged.

"No," she acknowledged. "But you're here."

"Only for the beer," he assured her.

"Did you tell her about Simon?"

Her gentle tone failed to soften the blow of the question. "There's nothing to tell."

"And maybe she'd say the same thing about the father of her babies."

"Except she doesn't say anything about him at all," he remarked.

"And that's what worries you."

"I'm not worried," he denied. "I just decided that I wasn't interested in taking our relationship any further."

"Really? Because if I had to guess, I'd say you're hurting just as much as she is right now."

Maybe he was, but he figured it was better than continuing along and hurting even more later.

"How'd the calving go today?" David asked his sons, as he poked at the grilled salmon on his plate.

Liam could tell by the disinterest on his face that his father was wishing he could be cutting into a juicy hunk of sirloin instead of heart-healthy fish.

"No major snags," Caleb said.

He nodded, confirming his brother's assessment. There had been a few scary moments when they'd had to turn a breech calf—a situation that could quickly turn fatal for both the mom and baby—but in the end, they'd got the job done and there was no reason to worry their father with the details now.

Of course, Caleb's response exhausted that topic of conversation, and with not much else to talk about, the rest of the meal passed in relative silence.

When he was finished eating, Caleb folded his napkin on the table and pushed his chair back. "We're starting early again tomorrow, so I'm heading up to bed now."

Liam should do the same, but there was a question that had been niggling at the back of his mind for some time now, and he knew that it wasn't going to go away. So he stayed where he was while Martina cleared the table.

"Can I ask you something?" he said, when the housekeeper had finished.

"Can I stop you?" his father grumbled.

It wasn't exactly an invitation, but Liam forged ahead anyway. "When you were in the hospital, did Valerie Blake stop by to see you?"

His father's gaze shifted away. "Where would you get a crazy idea like that?"

"At the hospital," he said. "When I saw a woman who looked a lot like Valerie Blake leaving your room."

David was quiet for a long minute, as if uncertain

how to answer his son's question. "Yeah, she stopped by," he finally said.

Which, of course, led to Liam wanting to know: "Why?"

"She's a Blake. She probably wanted to know if I was going to kick the bucket."

"That's sounds like a credible explanation—except that she was wiping her eyes, as if she was crying, as she walked out."

"Mourning the fact I wasn't dead, I guess."

"I don't think that's why," Liam said.

"It doesn't matter what you think. Her visit didn't mean anything," his father insisted.

He should let it go. Everything about his father's body language and tone warned Liam to let it go—and that's why he couldn't. "Did you and Valerie Blake… were you ever…involved?"

"No," David denied, not looking at him. "We were never involved."

"But you slept with her," Liam guessed.

His father sighed wearily. "Once. A long time ago."

The reluctant admission made him feel both vindicated and sick. "You cheated on Mom?"

"No! Never." David scrubbed his hands over his face. "How could you possibly think…?" He shook his head. "Your mother was the love of my life," he said. "From the minute I set eyes on her, I didn't even see anyone else. She was it for me."

"Then it was after she died," he realized.

His father exhaled and slowly nodded. "Five years after. Five years to the day, in fact." And although he'd been reluctant to start talking, now he couldn't seem to stop. "Five years and I still missed your mom just as much as I had every single day since her passing. So I went into town and had a few too many drinks at Diggers'.

"Valerie was a waitress there at the time. Being a Monday, the bar was practically empty, so she sat with me and we talked. We talked until the bar closed—and then we went back to her place.

"She moved away to Washington shortly after that, and only returned to Haven three or four years ago. I've crossed paths with her in town a handful of times since then, rarely exchanging more than a nod of acknowledgment."

"She never stopped by the ranch?"

David shook his head. "Never."

"And yet, when she heard that you were in the hospital, she went all the way to Elko to see you?"

This time his dad nodded.

"Why?"

He sighed again. "Because she wanted to tell me that her daughter, Ashley, is my daughter, too."

Two weeks, Macy realized, noting the date on the computer screen.

Two weeks had passed since the last time she'd made love with Liam. Two weeks since she'd accepted that she was all the way in love with him. And twelve days since he'd made it clear he was never going to feel the same way.

But her heart, battered and bruised as it was, continued to beat inside her chest. And she continued to enjoy her job at the inn, even if she wasn't particularly fond of her boss right now.

"Jensen." The male voice broke through her reverie. "Gord and Isabella."

Macy offered a welcoming smile. She noted the couple's linked hands and the easy affection in the look they exchanged. She keyed in the name and quickly found the reservation—for Wild Bill's Getaway Suite.

"And Simon," a young boy piped up. "That's me."

"Hello, Simon." She smiled at him as she took the platinum credit card his father slid across the desk. "I'm Macy, and if you have any questions or need anything at all, you come to me and I'll see what I can do to help you."

"I'm thirsty," he announced.

"There are complimentary hot and cold beverages, and some light snacks, available in the solarium—" She pointed across the hall. "That's also where you'll have your breakfast in the morning."

"Can I have pancakes?"

"I'd guess that's up to your mom and dad," she said, looking to them for direction. "But there are pancakes on the menu."

The boy's mom smiled indulgently as she brushed a lock of hair away from his forehead. "You might want to try something else for a change," she suggested.

"Nuh-uh," Simon said. "I want pancakes."

"Then you can have pancakes," his dad confirmed.

"Yay!" He punched his fist in the air. "I'm gonna have pancakes."

"Are you in town for business or pleasure?" Macy asked the couple.

The wife spoke first. "Pleasure."

"Definitely pleasure," her husband agreed.

"Nuh-uh, Dad," Simon protested. "You said we're goin' to Adventure Village to ride the go-karts."

His dad chuckled. "And we will," he promised.

Macy handed over the key to the room and gave a brief summary of the inn's features. "And please, let me know if there's anything you need to enhance your enjoyment," she said again.

"Thank you," the husband said, reaching for his wife's hand again. "But I think we've got everything we need."

Liam's head was still reeling over the revelation that his father might have another child—and that he might have a twelve-year-old half sister he didn't know anything about—but he pushed that information to the back of his mind and focused on the ranch. Apparently his grandparents thought that focus translated into neglect of the inn. Although they trusted that Macy had everything running as smoothly and precisely as the gears of a Swiss watch, they reminded Liam that the inn was his investment and his responsibility.

And that was why, after breakfast Saturday morning, he found himself behind the wheel of his truck, driving into town.

He had mixed feelings as he walked through the doors of the inn. He was proud of the success the hotel had already achieved and grateful to Macy for all of her work. But he missed her—so damn much. And not just the warmth of her naked body tangled with his—though he definitely missed that, too—but working alongside her, talking to her, laughing with her.

But he still believed he'd done the right thing in ending their relationship before they got in too deep. Sure, he missed her sometimes—maybe even all the time—but he'd get over her. He just needed a little more time.

And he needed to live his own life separate from hers and her kids so that he didn't start to think of them as a family. He wasn't going to go through with her what he'd gone through with Isabella. He wasn't going to risk his heart that way again.

Maybe it was because he was thinking about her that he almost wasn't surprised when he walked into the solarium and saw Izzy there. Or maybe he was *so* surprised that it took him a moment to realize that she wasn't simply a figment of his imagination.

But she was obviously startled to see him, because her fork slipped from her fingers and clattered against her plate when her gaze locked with his. The man seated across from her—Gord, he guessed, though he'd never met her husband—said something, and she forced a smile in response as she picked up her fork again.

As if of their own volition, Liam's feet propelled him closer to their table, his gaze fixed on the boy seated between the adults.

"I had pancakes for breakfast," Simon announced, and his lightning-quick smile was like a sucker punch in Liam's gut. "And *four* strips of bacon."

"That's a lot of bacon," he remarked, pleased the even tenor of his response gave away nothing of the emotions churning inside him.

Simon's head bobbed as he nodded. "I like bacon."

"Extra crispy?"

The boy's eyes went wide, as if he couldn't imagine how Liam might possibly have guessed such a thing, and he nodded again.

Liam forced his attention to shift to the boy's parents. "And was your meal satisfactory this morning?"

"It was," Gord agreed, as he dumped a packet of sugar into his coffee.

"Delicious," Izzy said, a tentative smile playing around the corners of her mouth.

"That's good." He didn't smile back. "If you need anything at all during your stay, please don't hesitate to contact the front desk."

He started across the room, in the direction of a smaller table where a young couple was just being served. But his heart was heavy and his smile was stiff, and he knew he couldn't go through the motions. Not right now.

Instead, he turned and exited the solarium.

Of all the days to come into town, why had he chosen this day? And how soon could he make his escape without appearing to be doing exactly that? He decided that until then, he would take refuge in the library. He only wanted a moment alone to gather his thoughts and his composure. Of course, Isabella had never given him what he wanted.

"Please, Liam," she called out to him. "Don't walk away from me."

He turned to face her, his voice low and tightly controlled. "You're the one who walked—no, ran—back to your supposedly ex-husband."

She lifted her chin. "Because I owed it to him, and to Simon, to give our marriage another chance."

He hadn't been distressed by the sight of his ex-girlfriend with her husband, because he had no lingering romantic feelings for her. But seeing the little boy who'd once asked Liam if he could call him Daddy had cut to the quick.

"He doesn't even remember me," Liam said now.

"He's eight," Izzy pointed out, her stance and her tone noticeably softer. "And he hasn't seen you in more than four years."

He nodded. Four years was almost half of Simon's lifetime, but the blink of an eye to the man who'd once thought he'd be part of the boy's life forever. Liam cleared his throat. "He's gotten so big."

She smiled at that. "Don't I know it? He outgrows new clothes almost as soon as I take the tags off them."

"I can imagine."

Her expression grew serious again. "I'm sorry, Liam. I didn't know... Gord booked the room. The weekend away was a surprise for me and Simon," she explained. "But if this is too weird, we can—"

"No, it's not too weird," he told her.

"Are you sure? Because it feels pretty weird to me."

"It's fine," he said. "I'm not going to be here most of the weekend, anyway, so you probably won't see me again."

"Well, I'm glad I saw you now," she said. "And I'm glad you finally got away from the ranch."

He just nodded and said, "You should get back to your breakfast—and your family."

After she'd done so, Liam remained where he was, a dull ache in the center of his chest. But that pain wasn't anything he couldn't handle. It sure as hell didn't compare to the gaping wound he'd been left with when Izzy took her son and walked out on him four years earlier.

Or the gut-wrenching emptiness that had nearly consumed him when he shut Macy out of his life.

Except that she was there now—and looking at him
with sadness and sympathy in her beautiful blue eyes.

Chapter 16

"I didn't mean to eavesdrop," Macy said apologetically. "I came in to reshelve the books that housekeeping had retrieved from various rooms and King—" she pointed to the lowest shelf in the bookcase behind the sofa "—goes between Kellerman and Koontz."

"Or anywhere on the shelf, for those of us who don't have OCD," he noted dryly.

"Are you okay?" she asked, ignoring his remark.

"Of course."

"I checked them in yesterday," she said, and almost felt guilty for having done so.

She remembered thinking they were a beautiful family: Gord and Isabella Jensen, and their inquisitive son, Simon.

"Is the boy...is he...yours?"

Liam immediately shook his head. "I would never have let him go if he was mine."

Macy nodded, his words confirming everything she believed about the man she loved.

"But I dated his mom for eleven months," he confided now.

"Almost a year," she murmured.

A long time in the life of a child. She could only imagine how close the little boy and the man had grown in that time—and how hard it had been for both of them when the relationship between Liam and Isabella ended.

"I thought we were going to get married," he admitted.

"You were in love with her." Though Liam had never claimed to love Macy, the realization that he'd loved the other woman still hurt.

But he shook his head again. "No, but I was crazy about her kid. Not the best reason to get married, I know," he acknowledged. "But Simon really wanted a dad and I wanted to be his dad."

She hugged the books against her chest. "Why didn't you ever tell me about her? About him?"

He shrugged. "It was four years ago. Ancient history."

But she knew it wasn't. And she understood now why he'd tried so hard not to let himself get close to Ava, Max and Sam. It wasn't because he was incapable of letting them in, but because he didn't know how to keep them out. Because he was trying to protect his heart, which had been bruised and battered already by the loss of a child who wasn't his own.

She started toward him, then remembered the books

in her hand. Setting them on the edge of the closest shelf, she moved around the sofa.

He watched her progress, a little warily at first, but as she drew nearer, his expression changed. Heated.

Then she was in his arms and their mouths were fused together, their bodies straining to get closer as awareness gave way to want, want to need. Need to hunger—a desperate, aching hunger.

"Macy, I can't find—" The housekeeper's words halted as abruptly as her steps in the doorway of the library. "Oh."

Macy gave a vague thought to pulling out of Liam's arms, but they tightened around her, as if he wasn't going to let her go. And it felt so good—so right—to be in his embrace, that she didn't bother to pretend otherwise.

"What is it you can't find, Camille?" she asked.

"Nothing," the housekeeper decided. "I mean, it's nothing that can't wait."

And she turned on her heel and disappeared again.

"Now the staff are going to talk," Liam warned.

"I think *we* need to talk," she said. "Because there's something I've been holding back, too, about Ava, Max and Sam's father."

"You never wanted to talk about him," he noted.

"Because I didn't know what to say—how to explain."

He waited, silently, for her to find the words.

"Do you remember the first night we were together?"

"In clear and vivid detail," he assured her.

She smiled at that. "Then you must remember my blurted and awkward admission that it had been a long time since I was intimate with anyone?"

"It had been a long time for me, too."

"More than two years long?" she asked.

"Not quite."

Then his brow furrowed, and she knew he was realizing that the length of a standard pregnancy—nine months—added to the age of her kids—nine months again—came up well short of her two-year claim.

"How is that possible?" he wondered.

"It's possible because I never had sex with Ava, Max and Sam's father," she confided.

"You're not going to claim it was immaculate conception?"

She shook her head. "No. It was intrauterine insemination—or IUI."

His brows drew together. "They were test tube babies?"

"No, that's intro vitro fertilization—or IVF," she clarified. "IUI is what my friend Stacia refers to as the turkey baster method."

"So who is Ava, Max and Sam's father?" he wondered.

"He's a college professor of English and German heritage, six feet tall and 190 pounds with curly brown hair, green eyes and a dimple in his left cheek. He volunteers as a dog walker at his local SPCA, plays guitar, enjoys classic literature and contemporary art, and he likes to read and cook in his spare time."

"That's a pretty detailed description," he noted.

"But I don't know his name," she said. "I only know him as Donor 6243."

"Well, that clarifies some of your earlier and always abrupt responses to my inquiries," he decided. "But it doesn't tell me why."

"Because I wanted a family and my efforts to make that happen via more traditional routes were unsuccessful," she told him.

"So why didn't you just tell me that when I asked about their father?"

"I should have," she said. "But when I told my parents, they were so vocal…and harsh…in expressing their disapproval that I worried other people might react the same way. And I didn't want my parents—or my children—to be the subjects of gossip and ridicule because of the choices I'd made.

"But when I told you that Ava, Max and Sam didn't have a father, it was the truth. The man who contributed half of their DNA was literally nothing more to me than a sperm donor. And while I will admit to feelings of deep and sincere gratitude for that contribution, I'm not, and never have been, in love with him."

She lifted her hands to Liam's face, so that she could look him in the eye, so that he could see the truth in her own. "But I am in love with you. And at the risk of freaking you out again, I happen to think you'd make a pretty great dad to Ava, Max and Sam someday…if that idea appeals to you at all."

The idea appealed to him—a lot more than Liam was willing to admit. Even more appealing was the prospect of spending his life with Macy and her children.

But love?

That was more than he was capable of giving.

Nope. No, thank you. No way.

He drew back, and her hands dropped to her sides.

She tucked them into her pockets and worried her bottom lip. "You're not saying anything," she remarked quietly.

"It's a lot to take in."

She nodded.

He'd envisioned various scenarios to explain Macy's reluctance to share any information about the man who'd fathered Ava, Max and Sam, but none of them had included a sperm donor.

On the one hand, he no longer had to worry about Macy reconciling with the guy, because she'd never been with him. On the other, he had to wonder if she was really in love with him, as she claimed, or if she was looking for a father for her children who didn't have one. To give them a normal family and spare them from becoming the focus of small-town gossip as they grew up.

"I should probably get back to the desk," she said lightly. "I don't want my boss to catch me slacking off."

She was offering him an out, and he was only too eager to take it. "And I need to get back to the ranch."

She nodded again. "I didn't mean to put you on the spot or make you uncomfortable. I just wanted to clear up any miscommunication."

"I know," he said. "And you didn't. I just need some time…to process everything."

"Well, you know where to find me, if you want to talk."

"I do," he confirmed.

And then he fled, pretending he didn't see the tears that shimmered in her eyes.

When Liam returned to the Circle G, his jumbled thoughts and feelings were forced to refocus when he discovered his father in the barn, measuring out grain and feed.

"What are you doing?" he demanded.

"The doctor said I could do with some fresh air and exercise."

"And lots of rest."

"If I was any more rested, I'd be dead."

"A few weeks ago, you almost were," Liam felt compelled to remind his father.

"It'll take more than a heart attack to put me in the ground," David promised.

He didn't doubt it was true, but he didn't want to talk—or even think—about his father's mortality. Instead, he said, "Well, it's good to see you back on your feet."

"And now that I am, you can wash your hands of your responsibilities here?" his father guessed.

"I never washed my hands of anything," he pointed out. "Even when I was spending twelve and fifteen hours a day at the inn, I was here every morning to help with chores."

"We would have got along just fine without your help."

"I know you would have," he acknowledged. "But maybe I didn't want you to."

"You're not making a heckuva lot of sense," David said.

"It didn't make a lot of sense to me, either," Liam said. "Especially considering that, for so many years, I felt trapped here."

"You made that clear enough."

"When I bought the inn, I thought I was freeing myself of the responsibilities and expectations that weighed on me here."

"You didn't think running a hotel would come with

responsibilities and expectations?" his father challenged.

"Of course I did, but those were completely my own."

"You think I demanded too much of you?"

"Maybe I did," he allowed. "But I knew it wasn't any more than you demanded of anyone else—including yourself. And when Caleb called to tell me that you'd collapsed—"

"I staggered a little," David interjected. "It's not like I was lying in a boneless heap on the ground."

"You had a heart attack," Liam said again. "And it was scary as hell for all of us."

His father didn't dispute that.

"So I came back."

"We needed you here, Liam," David grudgingly admitted.

"Maybe. But more than that, I *wanted* to be here. Because Gilmores are ranchers."

"They have been for more than a hundred and fifty years," his father noted. "Because that was the choice Everett made when he bought this parcel of land. And then he built a modest home on that land and, with the help of his sons, they turned a small herd of cattle into one of the most successful ranches in the whole state."

"I know the history of the Circle G, Dad."

His father nodded. "But maybe you don't know that I'm trying to offer you an apology."

Liam was intrigued by this grudging admission. "I'm listening."

"Over the past few months, I've realized that I might've been wrong in trying to force you into a life you didn't want. Every time you tried to tell me that you wanted something different, I shut you down. I refused to consider the possibility that you might actually leave the Circle G because—" His gaze shifted away and he cleared his throat. "Because then I'd lose you, just like I lost your mom.

"It was your grandmother who helped me see that I was holding on too tight—to you and your brother and sisters—trying to hold on to the only part of Theresa that I had left."

Liam was stunned by this admission. He'd been working through his own demons over the loss of his mother, and though he knew how deeply his father had been affected by the tragic death of his wife, he hadn't considered how that loss might have impacted his subsequent actions.

"She also pointed out that your mom would be disappointed in me for driving you away—not from the ranch, but from the family. She had such grand dreams for all her children. She didn't care if any of you wanted to be doctors or lawyers or ranchers—she only wanted you to be happy. To find someone to love as we loved one another, to raise a family...

"So, with that thought in mind, I've decided to support you—and your siblings—in whatever you want to do with your lives. Because maybe Gilmores can be anything they want to be."

"For a man of few words, that was a helluva speech," Liam remarked.

"It was a long time in the making," his father said.

"Well, I've been doing a lot of thinking, too," he confided. "And it turns out that *this* Gilmore wants to be a rancher."

David was understandably taken aback by his eldest son's confession. "You really mean that?"

"I mean it," he confirmed. "Maybe I needed to take some time away from the ranch to appreciate what it means to me. To realize how much I enjoy working with you and Caleb and Wade and Uncle Chuck and Michael and Mitchell."

"You can't know how happy that makes me," his father said. "But...what about the hotel?"

"It's already proven to be a sound investment, and I'm confident that it will be in very capable hands under Macy's management."

"And since you mentioned her name," David prompted.

"I've still got some things to figure out there," he admitted.

"Well, don't take too long to figure them out," his father cautioned. "Because those babies of hers shouldn't have to grow up without a daddy."

He shook his head. "You're already looking for the next generation of ranchers, aren't you?"

"The next generation of Gilmores," David clarified.

Though he was pleased to know that his father would accept Macy, Ava, Max and Sam as part of the Gilmore family, Liam knew that wouldn't happen unless he found the courage to put his heart on the line again.

She thought about turning around.

As Macy drove toward the Circle G, her fingers wrapped tightly around the steering wheel, she couldn't help but wonder if she was making another mistake and worry that she was setting herself up for more heartache.

She'd told Liam to find her when he wanted to talk. Instead, he'd sent a text inviting her to come out to the

Circle G to see Mystery's new foal. She didn't know if that was the real purpose of his message or merely a pretext to get her out to the ranch, but, remembering the promise she'd made to Liam's father the last time she saw him, she went home first so that she could take Ava, Max and Sam with her.

And maybe she was counting on the presence of her precious babies to help her hold it together if Liam told her that he had no interest in a future with her and her family.

She didn't regret the things she'd said to him earlier. He deserved to know the truth of her feelings and everything else. If, when he'd had his say, it turned out that he didn't want what she was offering, at least she'd know that she'd given it her best shot and not held anything back.

She strapped her little ones into their triple tandem stroller and was making her way toward the house when Caleb came out of the barn.

"Liam's in there," he said, jerking his thumb toward the building he'd just exited.

"Actually, I thought we'd say 'hi' to your dad first," she said, because she didn't know that she'd want to stick around after she'd talked to her boss.

He pointed a forefinger toward the house.

She took Ava, Max and Sam into the house. David was genuinely pleased by their surprise visit and unhappy when she tried to cut it short. He insisted that she could leave the babies with him while she went out to the barn, and her protests were silenced by the housekeeper's assurance that she would keep an eye on Ava, Max and Sam—and the recovering rancher.

Macy found Liam watching over the dappled mare

she recognized as Mystery, along with a chestnut foal she was nursing.

"Sky named him Enigma," Liam told her.

"Fitting," she remarked.

He fell silent again for a moment before confiding, "I've been waiting for you."

She knew he meant today, but she felt as if she'd been waiting for him forever—and she hoped that, after today, they could move toward a forever together.

"Have you had time…to process everything?" she asked him.

"I didn't really need time," he said, his voice raw with emotion. "I only needed to think about everything I could have with you, Ava, Max and Sam, and how empty my life would be without you in it." Finally, he drew her into his arms. "I don't know if there are any words to express how much I've missed you."

"I think I know," she said. "Because I've missed you just as much."

He kissed her then, with a hunger that bordered on desperation.

And she kissed him back the same way, expressing without words the truth and depth of her feelings.

And then, when the kiss finally ended and she managed to catch her breath again, with words: "I love you, Liam."

"You said that earlier," he reminded her.

"And you didn't trust my feelings."

"I didn't trust my own," he said. "And I didn't know if I was capable of being what you needed."

"You *are* everything that I need," she told him. "Everything that I want."

"I hope you mean that," he said. "Because I love you

and Ava, Max and Sam, too. When you asked me earlier if the idea of being their dad appealed to me at all, I didn't say anything because I was afraid to admit how much I wanted what you were offering. But I'm admitting it now. I'm putting my heart on the line—for you and our future together. Our family."

Tears filled her eyes and overflowed along with the joy in her heart.

"Please don't cry," he said. "You know I can't handle tears."

"You're going to have to get used to them," she warned. "Because I sometimes cry when I'm really happy, and I know we're going to be really happy together."

He lifted his hands to frame her face and gently brushed her tears away. "Happily ever after," he promised.

Epilogue

August 13th

"Okay, we've practiced and practiced, but this time it's for real, so I need you to stick to the script. Do you understand?"

His tone must have conveyed the seriousness of the situation, because Ava, Max and Sam—officially toddlers now—nodded solemnly.

They were dressed in coordinated outfits that their grandmother had picked out: Max and Sam in denim overalls and red T-shirts, Ava in a denim skirt and white shirt with a glittery red heart on it. They all wore cowboy boots and hats and held oversized cue cards in their hands. One by one, he lifted them up to sit on the hay bales he'd arranged for this moment.

It wouldn't be Valentine's Day again for another six

months, but that was exactly how long it had been since Liam and Macy had shared their first kiss, and he figured that was enough time to convince her he knew what he wanted.

"No, Ava, you're in the middle," he reminded her, pointing to the spot between Max and Sam.

She stubbornly stayed where she was, her legs stretched out in front of her, booted feet crossed at the ankles. He picked her up and settled her on the hay between her brothers. She gave him a mutinous look that he recognized all too well as a precursor to trouble.

"And if we get this right, we can go for ice cream later."

His promise seemed to placate the little girl—at least for the moment.

"You ready, Max?"

Max responded by extending both of his arms, proudly displaying the blank side of the card he held.

"That's good," Liam said. "But when Mommy comes out, you're going to turn the card over."

He turned the card, so the word was visible—albeit upside down.

Liam rotated the cardboard. "Just like that."

While he was getting Max organized, Sam dropped his card. Naturally, he leaned over to pick it up—and nearly toppled off the hay bale. He lost his hat in the process and cried out in distress.

"It's okay," Liam soothed, settling the hat back on top of the boy's head and placing the card back in his hands—and beginning to question the wisdom of his own plan.

He recognized the sound of Macy's SUV pulling up outside and breathed a sigh of relief that she was on time. Checking the kids again to ensure they were in position and ready, he pulled out his cell phone to send a quick text message asking Macy to meet them behind the barn.

Half a minute later, she came around the corner, a smile lighting her face when she saw them. "What are you guys doing out here?"

"We have an important question to ask you," Liam said, then turned to her children and prompted, "Max?"

The little boy turned over his card, his sister did the same with hers, his brother followed and then Liam showed his own.

Each card held a single word that, when put together, should have spelled out: WILL-YOU-MARRY-ME?

But when Sam dropped his card, Liam had mistakenly given the boy his, and Ava had turned hers over upside down so that what Macy saw was: ⌐TIIW YOU-ME?-MARRY

Thankfully, she was savvy enough to figure out what he was really trying to ask. Of course, the princess-cut diamond he pulled out of his pocket might have helped, too.

She laughed through her tears. "You once said a man would have to be crazy to want to marry a single mom with three babies," she said, reminding him of the words he'd spoken months ago.

"I am crazy," he confessed. "About you and about them. And there's nothing I want more than to make our crazy family official."

"In that case, yes," she said, then responded to his question the way he'd asked it: "I will you marry."

He slid the ring on the third finger of her left hand, then drew her into his arms for a long lingering kiss as Ava, Max and Sam clapped their hands in approval.

Then the clapping stopped and Ava demanded, "I-cweam!"

Liam broke the kiss on a sigh.

"You bribed them with ice cream, didn't you?" Macy asked, amusement in her tone.

"I wouldn't call it a bribe…it was offered as more of a performance bonus."

"And did they perform according to your expectations?"

"Well, my expectations were pretty low," he acknowledged. "But I'd say my mini cupids did their job."

"I love that you made them a part of this," she said.

"They are part of this—part of us. *Our family.*"

Fresh tears shimmered in her eyes. "And that's only one of the reasons I love you."

"And I love you right back."

"I-cweam!" Ava said again, stamping her booted foot for emphasis this time.

A stern look from her mother had her reconsidering her strategy.

She shuffled closer and looked at Liam with big blue eyes. "P'ease, Da."

She'd picked up the word from hanging out with Tessa, and though he doubted Ava understood the significance of it, she'd quickly discovered that using it often got her what she wanted. Because every time she uttered that single syllable, Liam's heart melted just like her ice cream would do in the summer heat.

He looked at Macy now. "What do you think?"

She smiled. "I think we're going for ice cream, Da."

And that's what they did.

* * * * *

**WE HOPE YOU ENJOYED
THIS BOOK FROM**

Believe in love. Overcome obstacles. Find happiness.

Relate to finding comfort and strength in the
support of loved ones and enjoy the journey
no matter what life throws your way.

6 NEW BOOKS AVAILABLE EVERY MONTH!

HSEHALO2020

SPECIAL EXCERPT FROM

H HARLEQUIN
SPECIAL EDITION

*Oak Hollow, Texas, was supposed to be a temporary
stop between Tess's old life in Boston and the new one
in Houston, which includes her daughter's lifesaving
heart surgery. But when Hannah wraps handsome
police chief Anson Curry—who also happens to be
their landlord—around her little finger, Tess is tempted
for the first time in a long time.*

Read on for a sneak peek at
A Sheriff's Star
by debut author Makenna Lee,
the first book in her Home to Oak Hollow series!

"Sweet dreams, little one," he said and stepped out of
the room.

She took off Hannah's shoes and jeans, then tucked
her in for the night. With a bolstering breath, she braced
herself for being alone with her fantasy man.

He stood in the center of the living room, looking
around like he'd never seen his own house. She
followed Anson's gaze to the built-in shelves she'd
filled with precious and painful memories. Things she
wasn't ready to share with him. Before he could ask any
questions, she opened the front door.

"Even though we were coerced, thank you for carrying her home. And for the house tour." Their "moment" in his bedroom flashed before her. *Damn, why'd I bring that up?*

"Anytime." Anson's blue-eyed gaze danced with amusement before he ducked his head and stepped outside. "Sleep well, Tess."

Fat chance of that.

She closed the door to prevent herself from watching him walk away. Tonight, Anson hadn't treated her indifferently like before and, in fact, seemed to be fighting his own temptations. Sometimes shutters would fall over his eyes as he distanced himself, then she'd blink and he'd wear his devil's grin, drawing her in with flirtation. Maybe he wasn't as immune to their attraction as she'd thought.

"I can't figure you out, Chief Anson Curry. But why am I even bothering?"

Don't miss
A Sheriff's Star *by Makenna Lee,*
available November 2020 wherever
Harlequin Special Edition books and ebooks are sold.

Harlequin.com

Copyright © 2020 by Margaret Culver

HSEEXP1020

IF YOU ENJOYED THIS BOOK
WE THINK YOU WILL ALSO LOVE

LOVE INSPIRED
INSPIRATIONAL ROMANCE

Uplifting stories of faith, forgiveness and hope.

Fall in love with stories where faith helps
guide you through life's challenges, and discover
the promise of a new beginning.

6 NEW BOOKS AVAILABLE EVERY MONTH!

LIXSERIES2020

SPECIAL EXCERPT FROM

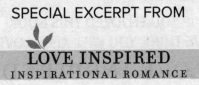

LOVE INSPIRED
INSPIRATIONAL ROMANCE

*When Mennonite midwife Beth Ann Overholt went to
Evergreen Corners to help rebuild after a flood, she
never expected to take in three abandoned children—
especially with an Amish bachelor by her side. But this
temporary family with Robert Yoder might just turn out
to be the perfect Christmas gift...*

Read on for a sneak preview of
An Amish Holiday Family
by Jo Ann Brown,
available November 2020 from Love Inspired!

"You don't ever complain. You take care of someone
else's *kinder* without hesitation, and you're giving them a
home they haven't had in who knows how long."

"Trust me. There was plenty of hesitation on my part."

"I do trust you."

Beth Ann's breath caught at the undercurrent of
emotion in his simple answer. "I'm glad to hear that. I got
a message from their social worker this afternoon. She
was supposed to come tomorrow, which is why I stayed
home today to make sure everything was as perfect as
possible before her visit."

"I wondered why you didn't come to the project house
today."

"That's why, but now her visit is going to be the day after tomorrow. What if she decides to take the children and place them in other homes? What if they can't be together?"

Robert paused and faced her. "Why are you looking for trouble? God brought you to the *kinder*. He knows what lies before them and before you. Trust *Him*."

"I try to." She gave him a wry grin. "It's just…just…"

"They've become important to you?"

She nodded, not trusting her voice to speak. The idea of the three youngsters being separated in the foster care system frightened her, because she wasn't sure what they might do to get back together.

"Don't forget," Robert murmured, "as important as they are to you, they're even more important to God." His smile returned. "How about getting some Christmas pie before we have to fish three *kinder* out of the brook?"

With a yelp, she rushed forward to keep Crystal from hoisting Tommy to see over the rail. Robert was right. She needed to enjoy the children while she could.

Don't miss
An Amish Holiday Family *by Jo Ann Brown,*
available November 2020 wherever
Love Inspired books and ebooks are sold.

LoveInspired.com

Copyright © 2020 by Jo Ann Ferguson

LIEXP102O